CW01082603

Time to Visit a Lady

About the author

Colin J Reed was born in Southampton, Hampshire, towards the end of 1943 when WWII was finally taking a turn for the better.

His first taste of adventure came when he joined the Junior Civil Defence in 1956, and one activity was to recover life sized dummies from under the remains of the roof of a four story bombed-out building opposite the main railway station. When that closed, he joined the Southampton Sea Scouts, and learned to sail, and row, a 27ft Montague Whaler, the standard ship's sea boat of the day.

He served in the Royal Navy from 1960-70, and his first ship, *HMS Albion,* was the cornerstone of the Borneo War in 1963. During time onshore, he developed a passion for racing dinghies of various classes. After he left the RN he spent 40 years in the upstream oil and gas industry in various categories, and was one of the first crew members on BP's most successful offshore production platform in 1974.

A keen sailor he gained two sailing championships in dinghy racing in the 1980s, and in 1990 orchestrated the historic visit of the Royal Findhorn Yacht Club to Russia, the only UK yacht club to visit and race in the USSR.

He met his second wife in Rio de Janeiro in 1983, two years after losing his Scottish wife after a long illness, in only her mid-30s. He has two daughters from his first marriage. He is now semi-retired, living in the UK and Rio de Janeiro.

Time to Visit a Lady

Colin Reed

Also by Colin Reed

Dangerous Voyage
Danish Gold
Memories and Forgetfulness
The Third Reason

First published 2017 by Tell Tale Books
Copyright 2017, 2023 © Colin Reed.
All rights reserved.

ISBN-13:978-1544662824
ISBN-10:1544662823

www.telltalebooks.uk

Chapter 1

NICOLA SLOWLY regained consciousness on the deck in a main saloon in what appeared to be a large luxurious yacht buffeted by violent waves. Dazed and confused she struggled to remember where she was; and where the hell were her jeans and knickers?

She restored her Victoria Secrets bra from around her neck to its usual place of duty and buttoned up her McDowell tartan shirt.

She shook her head, trying to gather her thoughts. What had happened? Gradually, her head cleared as it started to come back to her.

She had been enjoying a girl's weekend with best friend Victoria. Nicola had been the head scientist of a prestigious forensic department in one of Oxford University's more famous colleges. A turf war developed between the competent and the incompetent, exacerbated by the never-ending competition between the sexes.

Nicola specialised in research and development of new techniques, highly valued by the British security services. Special Branch were always interested in new advances in technology and her department had solved hitherto unfathomable criminal cases.

Being devoted to her work, Nicola had no time for political infighting, eventually leading to her downfall and resignation. A generous termination package had been negotiated, but Nicola remained deeply bitter about the whole experience.

Still, she learnt to have her catharsis, take a deep breath, and move on.

To make matters worse, her friend Victoria had suffered the same experience as a department head in a high technology company.

RATHER THAN VISIT the Isle of Wight for a sailing regatta, the two girls decided on a girl's weekend in South Wales. Vicky had a thing about famous Welsh actresses, their famous looks, longing to see the areas or homes where they had either been born or brought up.

No way was she going sailing so soon after her usual expensive visit to her hairdresser. She was jealous of Nicola's hair. No matter what hurricane recently passed it by it only took a quick brush and comb to restore Nicky's lustrous brunette locks.

The weekend had gone well. The seaside hotel had an excellent restaurant, and to their surprise a lively bar. A few handsome men had chatted them up and it felt just like the happy days during their years of study at their respective universities.

Still, they were both still single. Nicola in her mid-thirties with Vicky only a few years younger. This evening they preferred to enjoy taking the fresh air walking down the seaside promenade. Making an inventory of eligible Welsh manhood could keep for later.

The evening weather was pleasant for the time of year and the promenade blessed with buskers and artists selling the usual offerings of amateur bric-a-brac.

Suddenly, Nicola saw a Ford Transit van approaching at a speed driven by a strange woman receiving frantic directions from an even stranger and disreputable man. As it reached them the van screeched to a halt, two heavies threw open the sliding door, grabbed Victoria and Nicola, and dragged them into the van.

The van sped away, with the man yelling profane instructions to the woman driving on how to find the exit road from the city. The van headed west along the fractured Welsh coast.

Inside the van, the two girls were violently bound, gagged, and thrown on top of a large number of sacks bearing bank markings.

What happened next was a violent succession of physical and sexual assaults on both girls.

The van arrived at a deserted small harbour and the two victims, and the large number of sacks, were dragged aboard a large yacht, which sailed immediately. The yacht, a large modern cutter, seventy feet on the waterline, capable of travelling over the oceans of the world in style, covering great distances quickly and easily no matter the weather. She came complete with the power systems to handle her powerful rig, making crewing such a large yacht relatively easy.

The assaults on the two girls continued aboard the yacht. The leader of the gang, clearly out of his mind with drugs and alcohol, dragged Victoria to the main after cabin. Terrible sounds of screaming and sobbing soon followed for what seemed a very long time.

The other two crooks took it in turn to rape Nicola using less excessive physical violence. She could do nothing but submit and try her best to reduce any further physical abuse on top of the sexual abuse.

There came a lull in the assaults, then a second round. Nicola passed out, and whatever happened, happened. Then, there was another lull. Nicola had no idea of timescale or where the yacht was headed. What she did know was the yacht had entered severe weather, as a full gale emerged from the deep Atlantic looking for victims attempting to cross her stormy waters.

As Nicola gathered herself, she found her two attackers in a comatose state. One lying on a berth of the other side of the yacht, the other one huddled on the floor, having been sick. The yacht was under the command of the third kidnapper, a sadist who would be one of those crazy's all too common in the criminal world.

Knowing worse was to come, Nicola gathered herself together. If she could incapacitate the two inside the cabin, she might stand a chance against the brute in the cockpit. She carefully considered the kill, or be killed, situation she found herself in.

FEAR MADE HER hesitate, but from the sounds of distress coming from Victoria, she knew she could not survive another assault. Nicola struggled to keep her feet as the yacht pitched violently through the heavy seas.

She raked around in the galley for a kitchen knife, strong enough to finish off these two vile men. She found a large, razor sharp, chef's knife and moved back to the kidnapper lying face down on the deck. She grabbed his clothing and wrenched him onto his back. A small handgun fell out of a pocket and she bent down to pick it up.

'Ah, a much better idea,' she thought, 'Less mess.'

She picked it up and examined it. As a forensic scientist, she had examined many different types of firearms but this gun looked different. It was small, fitting easily into her hand. With the palm of her hand facing downwards, the gun would be almost completely hidden.

It was also beautifully made, with a quality coming only from a bespoke gunsmith, most likely in Prague. She broke the gun open and removed a bullet, a short cartridge .32 calibre round. The gun frame was small, a modified .22 calibre revolver based on the North American 'noisy cricket' design. The barrel looked standard, but the cylinder had only four rounds to allow for the larger size of the more powerful bullets.

This was a top of the range assassin's gun, for professionals only. She gathered herself. She had never shot or harmed anyone in her life before, but the dreadful sounds of distress from the main owner's cabin gave no other way forward.

Nicky rolled the other prone body over, rifled his clothing to find a similar weapon. As the yacht dropped off each passing wave, the sounds of loose pots crashing in the galley's twin sink gave an ideal opportunity to deal with these two first.

She checked both guns were fully loaded. Surely eight rounds would be sufficient to dispatch all three of the kidnappers to an early watery grave. She needed to take care. Steeling herself she bent over the first comatose body, put the gun under his chin, placed a cushion on top, and as the yacht fell heavily off a passing wave, she fired, and didn't feel a thing.

The .32 calibre round passed into the skull of the victim, bringing certain instant death.

She rose from the lifeless body with a rising level of purpose and confidence. She lifted the first body on to the settee, rolled him onto his side and put a pillow under his head. Little blood seeped from the entry wound as she placed a towel to catch the still warm blood seeping from his neck. Nicola finished off the other kidnapper where he lay, lying in a pool his own blood and vomit.

The yacht fell off large wave and lay pinned on its side until, after an agonising wait, shook itself free. Nicola knew the yacht was close to floundering. She struggled into a waterproof jacket, put a handgun into both side pockets, and went on deck. All she saw was dark confusion.

She dropped back into the cabin, found the electrical panel to activated the deck flood lights under the lower set of mast spreaders.

She returned topside to take stock. The yacht carried full sail and looking aft she could see the fear in the face of the third kidnapper, the man called Rufus Stone, the monster who had so violently desecrated her best friend.

The full width of the mainsheet track split the cockpit into two areas. Stone had wedged himself behind the lee steering binnacle, flying spray lashing his body. He should be wearing goggles but the lack of them was but a minor bonus as far as she was concerned.

Nicola found the control lines to furl both foresails, but it took a few moments to work out what control line did what. She wrapped the line for the outer foresail around an electric winch jamming the tail-end into the self-tailing jaws and switched on the winch. She dropped down to the outer foresail sheet winch and surged the heavy rope around the drum. The reefing winch slowly furled the outer foresail flapping violently in the wind, the noise ripped away by the increasing wind. Nicola clawed her way back to the furling winch and hauled secured the now fully furled outer sail.

Nicola repeated the process of furling the inner foresail, leaving just a tiny vestige of sail set to keep a semblance of order of balance in the sail plan.

The yacht slowly regained a little composure, as Nicola eased the mainsail track down to leeward. The top half of the huge mainsail feathered itself losing much of its power, but the noise of its flogging was more than sufficient to bring fear to both her and the kidnapper at the helm.

Nicola looked at the man at the helm with such hatred she surprised herself at its intensity. The yacht remained in great danger as another heavy gust of wind pinned the yacht on its side once more. Nicola motioned to the man at the helm to come up on the wind to let more power out of the sail.

'Now what to do?' thought Nicola. 'Can't go aft, say hi, and shoot him in the neck.'

The answer came in the form of violent language, hurled abuse and a demand for food as soon as possible. Nicola thought, 'Thank Christ he doesn't know how to engage the auto-pilot.'

Nicola waved and went below safe in the knowledge he couldn't chase after her. She found all she needed in the yacht's large and comprehensive galley in a large locker containing a good assortment of tinned food.

She wedged a deep pan on the gimballed stove and emptied tins of meat and vegetables into it. Five minutes later steam began to rise as the stew bubbled, giving off an aroma which made Nicola even hungrier. She took a taste. The stew tasted very bland. Ideal she thought.

The kidnapper sounded as though he came from the rough side of Manchester, that giant middle England industrial city with its many different communities. A man used to fish and chips with too much salt and vinegar or other salt laden sauces.

She planned to hand the food to him in a deep bowl and prayed her attacker would demand salt or other accoutrements. Her hand would naturally dig deep into her waterproof jacket, with a handgun in each side pocket. Her intended victim, with his penetrating eyes, was bound to recognise what would happen, but she prayed a delay in his recognition would give the edge she so badly needed.

She would just have to blast away with whatever hand was free, as she held on to anything to stop the motion of the yacht throwing her overboard. As the food became ready Nicola rifled the pockets of the kidnapper lying on the settee and found additional bullets to reload the gun she had just used.

Nicola filled a deep metal bowl with the stew, placed a crust of bread and a spoon on top. Taking a deep breath, she paused to gather herself. This would be a kill or be killed moment, for both herself and her badly abused companion.

Nicola struggled back on deck; hanging on to whatever handhold presented itself and made her way aft. She reached the windward steering binnacle opposite to her intended victim. Rufus Stone demanded in the most profane language for her to hurry up. He looked exhausted but his inner strength burned like a fire. He was still a very dangerous man.

Nicola looked at the binnacle control panel, saw the maker's name, a system she knew well, pressed the button to select auto-pilot, and set the course to steer, 'as is.'

She handed the food over to Rufus Stone. He tasted it, swearing loudly, where the hell was the salt. Nicola shouted she had it in her pocket. Reaching into her right-hand pocket she grabbed the gun securely and with one swift movement made to shoot.

Even in the poor light from the mast floodlights, and the confusion of sea water spray flying in his face, Stone recognised his fate at the ultimate moment.

Nicola fired four times. The first bullet caught Stone in the right eye; the second bullet smashed into the left side of his forehead but caught the edge of his headgear and did not enter his skull. One round missed altogether, and the last round entered his cheek and came out behind his left ear.

Stone screamed in pain, lurched at lightning speed towards Nicola, the wind whipping the blood streaming from his eye across his face. He tripped as the yacht rolled violently and he fell at her feet. Her heart was thumping with fear. She saw Stone looked incapacitated but still breathing, his chest pulsing with the effort to breathe and combat the terrible pain quickly taking over his bodily functions.

Nicola shuddered. Just what would it take to kill this man? What force could possibly resist three shots to the head? She grabbed a handhold with her other hand, reached for the other gun and emptied it into the back of his neck. At last, the life left his body as the corpse lay limp and lifeless on the cockpit sole.

'Thank Christ that's over,' thought Nicola. 'He certainly wasn't going to become an equal opportunity employer, that's for sure.'

Her next thoughts were rudely interrupted as the yacht, became pinned on its side by the rising wind.

'Must get this mainsail down,' said Nicola to herself. 'The yacht can't take much more of this.'

Getting the mainsail down with the wind coming full on the starboard beam would be difficult. She fired up the main engine. With the engine running at full speed, she spun the wheel to head directly into the wind.

She reset the autopilot to head into the wind and slipped and slid her way back to where the control lines were gathered.

Next, she had to find which one of the three larger control lines was the halyard for yacht's mainsail. She chose the left-hand one, wrapped the tail around the winch drum and applied sufficient tension to release the rope clutch. She surged three feet of control line from the drum and was more than grateful when she saw the luff of the mainsail start to sag. Taking care not to lose control of the halyard she lowered the mainsail into the lazy jacks, that strange arrangement of ropes leading from both sides of the boom up to the midpoint of the mast forming a virtual basket for the mainsail to fall into.

Judging the moment carefully, Nicola spun the yacht around and quickly set a course downwind heading south to gain distance from the storm as it passed to the northeast. With the noise of the flogging mainsail thankfully gone, she set a little more sail area on the inner foresail and relaxed a little in the corner of the cockpit to regain her strength.

The yacht, freed from the overpowering force of the wind, surged quickly downwind bringing a measure of confidence she could leave the yacht to its own devices.

Nicola went below to check-up on Victoria and eat some badly needed hot food to recover her strength. The 'all-day' slow cooking pot was half empty, but it took little time to empty more tins of meat and vegetables into it.

Now, she could attend to Victoria. Nicola was shocked at what she found but set down to do what she could. Victoria lay face down, with blood seeping from her bodily orifices. She saw in the half-light of the cabin her terrible injuries. She rolled her over and placed a pillow under her head and additional pillows on either side to provide support as the yacht rolled in the heavy seas.

First, she fashioned a nappy from a large towel placing it between her crutch to soak up the seeping blood. Next, she fastened a blanket over her, leaving her arms free, using the fasteners around the double berth to firmly secure the blanket to stop Victoria being flung onto the deck of the cabin. Nicola found a well-stocked medical cabinet and began the treatment to save her best friends life. Victoria's blood pressure was dangerously low and she quickly fixed an intravenous drip to her bare left arm. Next, she injected morphine and a dose of antibiotics into her other arm.

Nicola rechecked Victoria's pulse to see if anything else could be done. Her pulse remained weak but stable for the moment. She cleaned her face as best she could, but Victoria had been badly beaten. There was little else she could do; it was time to look after herself. Nicola felt afraid for her friend's life. She needed to be strong to bring her to safety.

Nicola took a large bowl of stew, sat down at the navigating table to eat and to try get a fix on the yacht's GPS position. She felt very tired; the numbers hard to read. She jotted them down as best she could and marked the position on the chart.

Nicola realised her vision was poor and she desperately needed rest. She lashed herself into the pilot berth next to the navigation desk hoping she would not fall fast asleep. The rest brought some relief from the many pains in her body. Her medication started to wear off, so she just lay still staring at the roof of the cabin. The motion of the yacht became as restful as it was reassuring as it sailed effortlessly downwind.

She looked at her watch. Forty minutes had passed, time to get up. She ate more of the stew. A strong hot coffee followed and Nicola returned to her comfortable pilot berth. She allowed herself to fall into a badly needed sleep, despite the many matters needing attention. She awoke an hour later stepped over the prone bodies in the main saloon on her way to the heads and thought, 'You guys still here? It's about time you went home.'

She finished her toilet in the heads urgently feeling the need for a hot shower. She couldn't describe how dirty she felt with all that had befallen her. She raked around in the yacht's storeroom and found a pair of white overalls, a thermal vest and under trousers.

As she looked around the storeroom, she saw two different types of coloured sacks with bank markings. A quick look revealed the white sacks contained used bank notes; the grey sacks with new and unissued bank notes.

There was no time for further investigation. Time to get clean and there was plenty of hot water available in the main owner's cabin and its luxury bathroom. Victoria continued to sleep with just a slight increase in the colour of her face. There was no immediate need to attend to her which allowed Nicola little bit of optimism in her ability to hang on until help could be found. Nicola filled the shower compartment with steam as she cleansed her body inside and out. She took stock of the many bruises on her body, a massive black eye, cut lip, and her internal hurt. She still found it hard to believe what had happened.

Nicola dried herself, dressed and returned to the main cabin. The sight of Victoria lying on the bed continued to fill her with a rage; a rage she could diminish only by taking positive action. She spoke harshly to herself, take stock Nicola, take control Nicola, and overcome.

As she cooled off, Nicola looked around to take stock of this luxurious yacht. The cherry wood interior looked classy, expensive, and quite old school. The galley was huge with every possible appliance, with a substantial amount of storage and a deep freezer for food stores. Up forward she could see a long passageway containing doors to double guest cabins and crew cabins on either side.

Forward of the mast would be the usual sail locker and she guessed a large workshop with extensive storage. Just aft of the main saloon, the navigation station was the most comprehensively equipped a competent mariner could wish for. The passageway to the main owner's cabin had two pilot berths, one above the other. She discovered similar pilot berths on the other side of the yacht behind the galley.

Nicola sat down in the comfort of the main saloon, kicked the nearest dead body in the head, and poured herself a large brandy, thinking about how she would go about disposing of the trash.

The yacht, replete with its comprehensive powered systems, could haul and pull on any size of cordage. She donned a waterproof jacket and trousers, made her way forward to the main storeroom and found a quantity of diver's lead weights. She placed six off two kilo weights into a sack, went on deck, raked around in one of the cockpit seat lockers and found a long length of nylon rope, pulley blocks, a seaman's pouch with a marlin spike and a wicked looking, very sharp, seaman's knife.

It took but a few moments to hang one of the pulley blocks under the boom, attached another to a ring fitting on the deck, and run the nylon rope from one of the unused foresail winch drums, though the pulley blocks and across to Mr Stone.

'Looks like a nice day for him to go for a swim,' she said to herself with a grim smile. Dealing with dead bodies was almost like being back at work in her laboratory. Knowing a naked dead body gave a great deal less information than a clothed one, she quickly used the seaman's knife to remove all clothing until he was as naked as the day he was born only wearing an attractive necklace of two lead weights, and the nylon rope wrapped around his feet.

Nicola paused for a moment. As a scientist she wondered what drugs these lunatics had taken to give the enhanced physical strength and the mental alteration to whatever civilisation and culture they possessed, enabling them to do such terrible things without any thoughts of remorse.

During her long years at her university, she had conducted research on the new designer narcotics that continually flooded onto the market.

Nicola didn't have the time or the inclination to do anything other than to take DNA samples of hair hoping this evidence could be worked upon by others who remained on the front line of helping the police and security forces in the never-ending battle against evil.

Nicola looked out to sea, ensured the coast was clear, moved to the nearest winch, and slowly hauled the corpse up into the air. As she swung the boom over the side of the yacht she plunged the razor-sharp seaman's knife deep into the stomach of the corpse and cut the rope as corpse number one vanished forever into the cold, deep and restless sea.

Nicola took stock, looking nervously around her out over the sea. The next two potential bathers would take longer to heave overboard. She stripped both corpses for their voyage into the land of Jules Verne. Still, Nicola need not have worried, and just thirty minutes later the yacht was a male-free zone.

Extreme tiredness struck once more as Nicola slumped down on the quarter berth next to the navigation station. From here she could regain her strength and watch the overhead repeaters of the yacht's instruments giving course, speed, and wind strength.

She took to wondering, rather late in the day, why not sail directly to the Spanish port of Vigo, the closest point of call. She had dealt with the Spanish police before, remembering the experience to be very mixed.

Clearly, the demise of the three kidnappers could be classed as self-defence, but looking at it from their perspective, the Spanish police could easily consider her a murderer, which technically she was.

However, the yacht had achieved fast progress toward Oporto. This northern Portuguese port had just entered in its sleepy post summer season stupor. Her uncle, Dr Adam Duncan, lived and practiced in a convent hospital somewhere overlooking the city from high up on the south bank of the River Douro.

For sure, he would be the best doctor to save Victoria's life. But there was also the matter of the loot stored up forward, hidden under a mess of nautical junk and old sails. No, she would continue to Oporto and hope for the best. Her luck had to change soon, even if she had to change it herself.

She went to the navigation station to check her position and transferred the numbers from the GPS onto the chart.

'Hell,' she said to herself, 'We're only fifteen miles offshore.'

She checked her notes from the earlier GPS reading, seeing in her tiredness she had misread the numbers. Now, it was only a short run to the entrance of Oporto harbour.

The yacht had a firm pace about her, even with only two foresails set, and with the main engine running at half speed, arrival at the outer channel marker to the harbour would be achieved just after six a.m. in the morning.

Nicola knew from previous visits; Oporto was not a city where officialdom engaged in excessive early morning activity. She worried about customs and immigration checks on arrival, hoping that during her early arrival at Oporto, only the offices at Oporto's main commercial harbour at Leixões would be manned.

With any luck, the harbour master based at the marina could complete any arrival formalities and telephone the details to the appropriate authorities. No matter what, she just had to get urgently needed help for Victoria.

Chapter 2

Oporto, Portugal

NICOLA CAREFULLY examined the pilot book, trying to match what she could see. Daylight arrived but slowly and the sun had yet to show itself over the dark hinterland. The pilot book advised entering Oporto Harbour in anything other than calm conditions, required great care, with the entrance giving danger in any swell. Local fishing boats were mentioned as being a secondary hazard mooring up to channel buoys and obscuring marks.

Care would be needed if the river current was strong due to an ebb tide or excessive rainfall along the length of the Douro valley. Still, just inside the harbour entrance there existed a reasonable marina with its harbour office close to its entrance.

So this was the good news. How would she manage to arrive in a foreign country without documents except for her UK driving license? What story would she use? Now that was a good question.

As she prepared the yacht for entering the Duro River, it occurred the best she could achieve would be to create a panic, shout for urgent medical assistance, add some female helplessness to add to the scene, hopefully with good effects.

She wrote down the name of her family relative, Dr Adam Duncan, hoping upon hope he actually existed at the convent, or perhaps it used to be a monastery, maybe the 'Hospital de Santa Maria de Douro de Avintes,' shown on the chart.

Nicola knew Oporto quite well, but she had never heard of the hospital or its neighbourhood. She didn't like hospitals and a hospital run by nuns didn't seem like it was going to be any fun.

Quite how long Uncle Adam had been practising there would another minor detail she didn't know, although something in the back of her aching mind said he was probably teaching there. She doubted the last part; Uncle Adam always pandered to private patients, with great discretion usually being a major part of his usually high fees.

Anyway, there was a patient in need of urgent medical attention. Keeping

16

the police unaware of their current predicament was another pressing matter.

The Oporto's main commercial harbour at Leixões and its hideous petrochemical works came into view. Two kilometres from the harbour entrance Nicola prepared for her unannounced arrival in Oporto. With the main engine running hard, she quickly reefed the two foresails. So far so good. As the daylight gradually improved, Nicola felt more comfortable with her approach to the harbour.

As the yacht reached the harbour entrance Nicola was relieved to find a flood tide under her. She steered the yacht close to the north bank to keep away from the southern sand bar and the protective breakwater forming a major part of the harbour entrance.

The Marina do Douro lay just one kilometre upstream. Nicola steered the yacht past its upstream facing entrance to then turn to bring the yacht inside the marina breakwater. Surprisingly, the berth for new arrivals was empty, enabling Nicola to bring the yacht slowly alongside.

Choosing her moment carefully, she killed the main engine and jumped out onto the quayside with a mooring line, quickly making fast with other lines. She returned to the cockpit to await developments. No one stirred at this early hour. She went below to make breakfast and to check-up on Victoria, still sleeping peacefully but with little colour in her face. The intravenous drip in her arm had run out, so there could be no delay in getting medical treatment.

As Nicola was finishing a large mug of tea and a ham sandwich, an elderly voice shouted down from outside. She arrived on deck with her breakfast in both hands and saw a rather scruffy uniformed official.

'Bom dia, como voce esta,' called the scruffy individual, as he lowered himself into the cockpit, his piggy eyes darting around taking in all detail. His show of officialdom was brief. Nicola saw a kindly face belonging to a man engaged in the well-worn practice of doing as little as possible while waiting for his retirement to make its long-awaited arrival.

Nicola used her rusty Portuguêse, 'Bom dia, senhor, bem-vindo a bordo. Eu preciso de alguma informação urgente. Eu tenho um amigo lá embaixo que esteja gravemente enfermo e eu posso perguntar se você conhece um Dr. Adam Duncan É muito urgente.'

'I am Sr. Carlos Gilberto de Souza Santos, the assistant harbour master,' the individual replied in surprisingly good English. 'How do you know Dr Duncan?'

'He is my uncle, meu tio. He must come very quickly. Do you know how to contact him?' 'All too well as I am waiting for a date for him to operate on my lovely Vivianna, my wife; she is not well these last two months.'

Nicola pleaded, 'Please call him urgently. I know it's early, but matters cannot wait.'

Carlos Gilberto pulled out a battered cell phone quickly pushing a fast dial button. The call answered almost immediately, the voice trying to reassure the caller his needs would soon be answered. Carlos Gilberto, with urgency in his voice, told the voice on the other end of the line he had an urgent call from an English lady.

The voice asked for the person's name. Carlos Gilberto handed the cell phone over. 'Uncle Adam, it's Nicky Stranraer, I'm on a yacht in the marina. I have my best friend Victoria down below. She is very badly injured, very close to death in fact.'

'Is that the marina under Sao Pedro da Afurada,' he asked.

'Yes, come quickly with an ambulance with emergency life support systems and a paramedic,' Nicola shouted, almost in a panic.

Uncle Adam thought to question her emotional outburst. He told Nicola to calm down and he would be with her very quickly. He didn't have an ambulance, but he did have his ageing Citroën estate car, used many times as an ambulance in an emergency. He rushed from his office in time to collide with Sra Maria Camargo, his long-term nurse and confidant.

'Maria, get your coat, the emergency medical bag and meet me in the courtyard,' Adam ordered.

They hurried into the hospital courtyard. Thankfully, his ageing car started at the first turn of the key. He quickly navigated his way through the decorative convent archway onto the narrow streets. Fortunately, traffic was light at this early hour, as Adam tried to remember the quickest route through the chaotic streets in this old part of the City of Oporto.

The journey down the narrow streets to the marina took longer than hoped but his estate car was never made for the narrow streets and its badly parked cars. However, he made it in one piece and searched for the visitor's berth. Adam saw a rather grand yacht, its mast towering over the other more modest yachts. Although it flew the Portuguese flag, for sure it was a foreign visitor. He parked his car as close as possible, tooted his horn and jumped out onto the quayside.

He caught the sorry sight of his favourite niece waving with honest urgency. He put away his thoughts things were not as bad as expected. He rushed up to Nicola, shocked to see the state of her face.

'What on earth has happened to you, he asked?'

'Never mind me. Bring yourself and your nurse below, there is not a second to lose,' she cried

Adam followed Nicola into the main saloon and then aft into the main owner's cabin. He stopped dead in his tracks, shocked to the core to see the body of a young lady wrapped up in sheets, with blood seeping from her pelvic area, clearly brutally injured. The death-white colour of her face said it all.

With Nurse Maria helping him, he commenced his examination. Undressing the body revealed a bloody mess. The young lady lay naked, her body covered in hideous injuries to her back and between her thighs. Blood continued to seeped from her body.

He stood up shocked, looked at Nicola demanding an explanation. Nicola was close to tears.

'We were kidnapped and forced onto this yacht in South Wales. We were brutally attacked. Victoria had the worst of it, raped, buggered, and tortured all by the one lunatic. By chance, the yacht had a well-stocked medical cabinet, so I did what I could. The intravenous drip and the morphine have probably helped; I didn't know what else to do. I cleaned her up as best I could, but it's taken all my strength to bring us to safety.'

Adam seeing the full urgency of the situation moved into action. From his medical bag he fixed a butterfly injection point to a vein on her left arm removed two doses of drugs from his medical bag and quickly injected them.

'Nicky, whilst Nurse Maria gets Victoria ready to move to the hospital, go to my car, bring two bags of intravenous drip from a box at the back. You will find a collapsible stretcher. Bring them to the cockpit,' he ordered.

Seeing the look of concern on her uncle's face caused Nicola to feel a deepening worry, this situation could go from bad to worse. She rushed on deck and out onto the quayside, found the bags of intravenous drip, the collapsible stretcher rushing back on board and down into the main cabin.

'How is Vicky?' she asked.

Adam replied, 'She's not too good, it will be touch and go.'

Between them, they lifted the prone body of Victoria onto the stretcher and strapped her in. It took a lot of manoeuvring to get the stretcher down the yacht's narrow passageway into the main saloon, and up into the cockpit of the yacht. Nurse Maria held the stretcher steady whilst Adam and Nicola stepped over onto the quay wall.

Carlos Gilberto lent a hand to man-handle the stretcher into the back of the estate car with Nurse Maria holding onto the intravenous drip bottle and keeping a steady hand on the patient's head.

'If you've got any cash you'd best bring what you can,' said Adam, 'And lock-up the yacht as well.'

Nicola went below and threw five bundles of used bank notes into a spare sail bag. Hurriedly, she locked-up the main hatchway, waved at the harbour master and told him she would be back as soon as possible if it was OK with him. Seeing his chance to use Nicola to get influence with Dr Duncan, the assistant harbour master waved her away saying he would be glad to look after everything.

Nicola jumped into the front passenger seat as her uncle gunned the Citroen's motor and set-off. The journey to the convent hospital mercifully encountered little traffic as the ambulance wound its way through the narrow back streets.

They arrived at the hospital to find the convent sisters waiting with an operating theatre trolley. Adam was greatly relieved to see his good friend Dra Antonia, his anaesthetist, who had dropped everything in a rush to prepare for what she understood to be an emergency operation.

Within moments, Victoria was transferred to the theatre trolley, rushed into the operating theatre and connected to its vital monitoring equipment. Her pulse remained very low. With little or no time for a full a pre-med, the intravenous drip hung from a support close to her side and an oxygen mask pressed to her face.

Nicola went to Victoria's side, smoothed her hair, and bent over to speak into her left ear, 'Nicky, can you hear me?' You are in hospital now and Uncle Adam will do his very best for you. Just hang on for a little while longer. When you wake up you will be alive and well.'

Nicola kissed her best friend on the forehead and thought she saw a momentary flicker of Victoria's eyelids.

Adam cleaned-up and donned his scrubs in record time, as did Dra Antonia, Nurse Maria and the other Sisters who formed the surgery operating team. Adam paused for a moment to think. Was the patient sufficiently strong for a long and difficult operation?

He consulted with Dra Antonia, now busy performing a vital pre-med procedure. She had the same worry and suggested a small delay to conduct further treatment. Victoria's pulse was not strong, varying between feeble and inconsistent. Further work would be vital to bring the patient to a stronger level.

'Would you recommend a blood transfusion?' asked Adam. 'She must have lost a great deal.'

'Yes, yes Dr Adam, good idea,' replied Dra Antonia. 'I too wish a blood test. The local lab can offer an express service if you have the funds. I think we should establish the true situation, as I am not getting much response from the treatments I'm carrying out at the moment.'

'Is she stable?' asked Adam

'More or less,' replied Dra Antonia. 'She should be better after a blood transfusion.'

Dra Antonia left the operating theatre, went next door to the office, and quickly returned. 'They are sending someone right now, and they wish to remind you about outstanding accounts.'

Adam looked over at Nicola, 'Can you help, did you bring any cash with you?' he asked. 'If they will take UK Stirling, I have five thousand with me,' she whispered.

'Excellent, this will be a big help. OK Nicola; let me spend some time with you. Go to the examination room next door, strip off and take a shower where you will find bars of pre-med soap. When you are ready, don one of the patient gowns hanging up in the closet and sit on the bed.'

At that moment, the Mother Superior barged in, surprised to see so much activity. 'Dr. Duncan,' she demanded roughly. 'Just what is going on?'

'Good morning Mother Superior,' he replied. 'It's an emergency, and it's bad. What is worse it involves my sister's daughter, Nicola, and her best friend Victoria. Their yacht limped into the Marina do Douro at first light. Both are badly injured from an unbelievable sexual and physical attack by three armed and dangerous men. Nicola will survive, but the other lass is very close to death. Now if you will excuse me, I have a lot to do.'

'What about payment for all this activity doctor?' the Mother Superior demanded. 'Mother Superior, the Lord will provide, I have no doubt.'

Adam disappeared into the adjacent treatment room to find Nurse Maria busy helping Nicola with her preparations.

'Good morning Doctor, once again, I thought you would need some additional assistance.' Adam was very pleased to see her. The convent sisters and nurses had rallied to the call, fully understanding the gravity of the situation. Nurse Maria was one of his favourites. She had studied hard to pass her exams as a trauma recovery nurse, achieving a high level of skill.

Nicola stepped out of the shower, dried herself, dressed in a white hospital gown tentatively asking what was next. She looked and felt worried, feeling very much out of place. A medical examination from a close relative seemed, well, unusual, and she didn't know how she would react. Adam saw her concern and realised the importance of maintaining his calm and professional appearance.

'It's OK my dear, this is what we are going to do. It is necessary to conduct a full body examination and check for symptoms needing treatment. You have a lot of bruises externally. Internally it will be most important to give you a thorough check-up. You were raped; is this correct? Nothing on the other side, shall we say?'

Nicola confirmed his assessment, 'Now what?' she asked in a hesitant voice.

'OK Nicky, lie down on your front. Nurse Maria will make the examination as I take notes. Please try to relax. Don't worry about Victoria she will respond to treatment, of that, I have no doubt.'

Nicola laid down on the examination table, trying hard to settle herself from the deep fear about Victoria. Nurse Maria slipped a shaped pillow under her forehead, commencing her examination starting at Nicola's head with a gentle massage and manipulation of the neck area and shoulders, followed by each arm in turn. The examination continued until she reached Nicola's feet. Bruising was common along almost all her back. Nicola had received a lot of punishment fortunately most of it superficial.

Adam bid to turn her over. Nurse Maria replaced the pillow under her head and continued her examination while Adam continued taking notes. Her face showed bad bruising. The area around her left eye badly swollen and her lower lip exhibited a cut that had started to heal leaving an ugly red mark.

Adam handed his notepad to Nurse Maria to commence the inspection of Nicola's abdominal area. Fortunately, he could find nothing serious to worry about at the moment.

It took many soothing words to prepare Nicola for the examination inside her two passageways, but much to Adam's relief he found little real damage before starting the procedure for internal cleansing.

As he finished Adam said, 'OK Nicola,' he said, 'I have cleaned you internally and the good news is you are clear from any problems. Once you have rested up and recovered your monthly cycle should return with no long-term damage. However, you must get as much rest as you can.'

Nurse Maria helped a much-relieved Nicola to dress then guided her to the convent dining hall. As they ate, Nurse Maria gave as much comfort as she could to this poor girl. Nicola leant on her shoulder, choking back her emotions, trying hard not to let the tears flow.

Adam hurried back to his operating theatre anti-room and scrubbed up again, bidding Nurse Maria do the same. With the transfusion of new blood completed Victoria's vital signs showed welcomed improvement.

Dra Antonia felt more relieved as the patient became more stable.

The first task was the treatment for the terrible wounds to Victoria's back. It looked as though it would require the deep cleansing of each laceration, a long and delicate task.

Dra Antonia asked the theatre team if anybody had any previous experience of performing this treatment on such a scale. The risk of infection would be high and could quickly spread with disaster not far away.

Nurse Maria suggested the Mother Superior, who in her previous life had worked in A & E in a major hospital in her hometown.

'And just where was this?' asked Adam.

'She'll never tell you, but I know she did just by the way she runs this place. I heard her muttering under her breath once about the subject, but I paid no attention at the time.'

A timid Sister Isabella spoke up, 'Excuse me, Adam, the Mother Superior has been giving me training so the convent could offer this service, especially to children who have had an accident.

With that, the lady herself returned to the operating theatre. 'Your ears are burning?' asked Adam.

'Pardon,' replied a testy Mother Superior.

'I understand you can give guidance on the treatment of the patient's back injuries,' asked Adam.

Dra Antonia guided the Mother Superior around the operating table and showed her the extent of the problem. Mother Superior stifled what could have been a very ungodly remark; the look on her face said it all.

'Just who did this disgraceful and disgusting act?' she demanded. 'Never mind. Just what would you recommend?'

The Mother Superior looked around the theatre team. Someone had been casting assertions about her past, and she was definitely not pleased. Her past always a very private matter but she would deal with the matter later.

Adam saw her discomfort and moved to act.

'Mother Superior I understand you have been training Sister Isabella. Getting this treatment wrong would be the end, so can you help?'

Slightly mollified by Dr Adam's earnest request, the Mother Superior shrugged her shoulders with a muttered, 'OK, let me see. It happens I recently purchased a number of new products for the convent, so let us see how they work. Do we know the patient's tetanus status, as it will be most important to avoiding infection?'

The Mother Superior went over to a storage cabinet and removed several items.

'First things first,' she instructed, 'Total cleanliness, nothing else will do. Everyone must keep their face masks on. Nurse Maria, can you give the patient a tetanus shot?'

'Sister Isabella have you scrubbed up? I need you to assist me in this long and difficult procedure.'

Mother Superior entered the theatre preparation room, scrubbed up and donned her surgical scrubs, cap and surgical gloves. She returned to the theatre, moved to one side of the patient, and looked down at the horrible damage to Victoria's back.

Mother Superior bent over Victoria's back and began to gently work with Sister Isabella at her side. Clearly, the training of Sister Isabella was not a new event, as the pair of them showed their ability to work closely as a team.

The other members of the theatre team stood back and watched, as though a new era had been born in the convent. Dra Antonia watched her monitoring equipment closely and felt relieved this treatment appeared to cause no additional stress.

Victoria's pulse remained stable, albeit very low, and her shallow breathing of the oxygen mixture remained stable.

Adam became intrigued with this activity. He felt the added bonus was the theatre team paying great attention to the procedure rather than feeling sick at the dreadful sight of the poor patient.

After a long ninety minutes, the Mother Superior stood up, thanked Sister Isabella; congratulating her on her help and skilled attention, and looked over at Adam.

'Take care when the time comes to put the patient onto her back,' she told him. 'If you can keep most of her weight on her shoulders and bottom, it will help to reduce any disturbance to the foam dressing.'

Adam nodded his agreement. He collected his team around him and explained the procedure he wished to conduct. The surgery team took the opportunity for a ten-minute break. The atmosphere in the operating theatre had become heavy and sombre.

Nurse Maria and a few of the sisters were clearly suffering from the trauma of being this close to the patient. Sister Andreia called them all together, said a quick prayer, telling them to be strong, restoring their calm and purpose to make the operation a success.

Adam looked at Dra Antonia with raised eyebrows. Dra Antonia checked her instruments, made some notes, and looked back at Adam. 'She's holding up, I think we can go ahead as soon as you are ready.'

Nurse Maria looked around the operating room and thought she didn't see sufficient surgical implements ready at the operating table.

'Doctor, this will be a long operation, do we have the right number of sterilised items?' Adam asked for Sister Heidi, the sterilisation technician. 'Heidi is all we need, ready?'

Sister Heidi consulted the list she received from Dr. Adam, checked the instruments on their trays in the steriliser confirming they were good to go.

'Sister Heidi,' asked Adam, 'Where did you learn and train to be a sterilisation technician?'

Sister Bibianna piped-up from the back of the operating theatre, 'In a vasectomy clinic at the local hospital in Baden-Baden, West Germany. Under her surgical scrubs and behind her face mask Sister Heidi is five foot ten inches of German blonde shot-put athlete, with enough muscles to wield an axe all day in the Black Forest. Which is why she is known as the 'Mad Axe Girl,' and what she doesn't know about male sterilisation isn't worth knowing.'

The other sisters giggled, as Adam thought for a moment and said, 'Err, Sister Heidi if you have any other qualifications, see me sometime tomorrow. OK sisters; let us concentrate.'

In truth, he was glad the heavy atmosphere in the operating theatre had been relieved by this brief interlude.

Adam explained the procedure for treating Victoria's private areas. The team around the operating table nodded their understanding. The very thought of the damage he found filled him with anger and disgust, momentarily causing him to pause to recollect his focus.

The final phase of restoring the damage to Victoria was long and technically difficult with the need for a considerable amount of micro-surgery. Exhausted, Adam asked Dra Antonia how the patient had held-up?'

She replied, 'So far so good, thank goodness,' she replied, 'Everything has remained stable and her pulse has improved just a little.'

Mother Superior came to ask how things had gone, stating God had stood next to him and success would be assured. Adam smiled thanking her for the kind words.

He felt drained as he completed his work. The experience of the day slowly got to him. He looked over at his beloved niece, Nicola, her bruised and battered face now improved with the treatment she received at the hands of the sisters. She would need to become presentable to visit a shopping centre to purchase clothing and lady's articles to replace all their items lost during the kidnapping.

Adam needed a drink, waved at Nicola to follow him to his office and closed the door behind him.

'Mother Superior doesn't approve of alcohol, but there are times nothing else will do,' he said pulling a half bottle of scotch from the back of his desk drawer.

'Water?' he asked, as he poured two Christian size drams into two China cups. 'Not too much,' she replied.

Adam replied, 'Fraid it will need to be a little weaker than you normally like. You have taken quite a range of medication. I, on the other hand, will need something quite strong,'

'Today has been very stressful for you,' Nicola replied, 'But you have done a marvellous for both of us. I feel a hundred percent better.,

Sister Anna, the silent one, is very good at this remedial massaging. Best to have one every day. The more treatment you receive, the quicker your recovery,' he counselled. 'Which reminds me, can we change some of the stash you have on your ship.'

Nicola had little problem with his suggestion and readied herself to return to the yacht.

Chapter 3

NICOLA AND ADAM finished their drinks and headed towards his ageing Citroen. Nicola was intrigued, obviously an ideal dual-purpose car due to its enormous length, becoming most impressed by its ride quality and comfort on Oporto's badly maintained roads.

Traffic was light as Oporto's morning rush hour had long passed its peak. As they arrived at the marina, Carlos Gilberto wandered over in a rather deliberate manner. Nicola smiled and made him welcome. This was a man she definitely needed to keep on-side.

Adam asked about Carlos Gilberto's wife, hoping she was still OK; promising to take care of her soon and carefully brought the pleasantries to an end. Nicola asked if the Immigration and Customs officials needed to be satisfied. Carlos Gilberto confirmed he had contacted both offices and completed the necessary formalities. They might call later, but then again, they might not.

'Great, our man is on-side,' thought Nicola.

Then followed a discrete but intense conversation about what was in it for Carlos Gilberto. Both sides fenced with each other until both parties became comfortable with what was on offer. The conversation stopped, awkwardly, with everyone stood looking at each other for what seemed like a long time.

Nicola saw she needed to break the impasse. 'Carlos Gilberto, let me give you a thousand Euro's tomorrow, for mooring fees. In addition, I can pay for the operation for your wife. I will lodge the money with the Mother Superior. Perhaps it will be possible to hire someone to come to your home to do the housework while your wife fully recovers. Can't say fairer than that, concordar, combinado?'

Carlos Gilberto looked relieved. He had achieved what he had set out to achieve but tried hard not to show it. Adam saw she had reached a deal and smiled at Nicola.

Carlos Gilberto said, 'Senhora if I do not register your yacht's arrival, how can you pay mooring fees. No registration means I cannot connect the electrical shore-supply, but water supply will be no problem.'

Nicola smiled, told him the money for the mooring fee could stay in his deep pockets until they departed. Then, it would be up to him what he did with it. Carlos Gilberto smiled, took her hand, shook it very warmly and said, 'Senorita you are a saint sent from God. Muito obrigado,' and with that, he left.

'Well done Nicky,' said Adam. 'A smooth performance. What's next?'

The two of them went aboard closing the main hatch behind them. Adam looked around, taking a few moments to appreciate what a fine ship this yacht was. With quality American craftsmanship everywhere, very special, and clearly cost a great deal of money.

Nicola led her uncle into the dark interior of the forward sail locker, pulled away the spare sails she used to cover the money sacks stolen during the violent robbery in Manchester.

She stopped her uncle from moving the bags, telling him he must leave no trace of his being there. Nicola uncovered eight sacks, discovering an equal number of dark grey and light grey sacks, complete with the bank name printed in bold letters in the centre.

Taking a pair of plastic gloves from the workbench, she opened a dark grey sack and found bundles of unissued fifty-pound notes in their clear wrappers. She knew from experience the sack would hold about a hundred and twenty-five thousand British pounds and four dark grey sacks added up to half a million quid.

The light grey sacks contained bundles of used bank notes, and the bundles would hold a similar amount.

She looked up at her uncle and said, 'Adam, this looks like a million pounds but I remember the kidnapper's van had many more bags than this.'

Her uncle replied, 'I remember the TV news reported over four million pounds were stolen, so where is the rest?'

'My guess, still in England; delivered to the authors of the crime. The sister may have kept some, who knows. Anyway, what do we do with this lot?'

'Well,' he replied, 'I have a contact looking to purchase UK bank notes. He's always ringing me up to see if I have any to sell.'

'How much is he looking for?' asked Nicola.

'No idea, but it sounds to be quite a lot. My contact is connected with somebody trying to buy machinery in the UK for cash, destined for a construction project down the coast. The principles are a shady load of buggers that's for sure, always looking for things on the cheap.' 'Right,' said Nicola. 'Help me. We need to remove the wrappers from the used notes, it won't take long.'

Adam gave Nicola a queer looked but she insisted.

'Just replace the wrappers with a rubber band and put them in this waste bin.'

The pair quickly got to work. They finished forty minutes later and the sacks of bank notes shoved back under a pile of old sails.

Nicola emptied the waste bin into the yacht's cast iron dual fuelled stove, switched it on and soon reduced the bank note wrappers to ash.

'OK Adam, let's go, I'll empty the stove later,' said Nicola. 'I've taken fifty grand from one of the sacks, so let's get out of here. Go aft and see if you can find a bag or holdall. One that doesn't have swag written on the outside.'

Adam smiled at his niece's attempt at humour and found an old sailor's grip in one of the under-bunk lockers in the crew's quarters.

'This grip will do nicely,' she said. 'Now let us go eat while you call your man.'

Nicola locked-up the sail locker, looked out of the elegant main saloon cabin windows to see if the coast was clear, then went on-deck, locked up the yacht behind her and followed her uncle over to his car.

'Where will we dine? I'm famished,' she said.

'Oh, just up the hill to my favourite Portuguese Restaurant, 'Adega Flor de Coimbra' and it serves excellent 'bacalhau,' made from Norwegian dried cod fish. The duck is very nice, or just ask for something you like and they can make it if they have the ingredients. Be careful with your choice, your system is still recovering from a great deal of stress.'

As they arrived at the restaurant, Adam warmly embraced the owner who led him to a table in a quiet corner. The restaurant had few customers this early in the evening. Adam ordered two Sovina's and hors d'oeuvres of olives and sardines with tasty home-made sour biscuits

'What beer is this Adam?' asked Nicola.

'It's a 'cerveja artisanal.' It's different and quite delicious,' he replied, as he pulled out his cell phone.

'Excuse me for two minutes,' he said, as he pushed a fast dial button and waited for an answer. Nicola waited as her uncle held a very fast, low-key, conversation with the person at the other end of the line.

The call ended. Adam looked up at his niece and simply said, 'His courier is bringing Euros to the value of thirty thousand pounds, OK?'

'I guess so. That was quick,' she replied.

'The courier is a lady. Be prepared, she will not wish to be kept waiting,' said her uncle.

Nicola turned her back to the customers in the restaurant, opened the grip, taking out six packets of notes. She flicked through them just to check, before wrapping them in a napkin.

The hors d'oeuvres of olives and sardines arrived at the table as the garçon took their order. Adam requested the 'bacalhau da casa.' Nicola chose the pork loin with boiled potato and a side salad. Adam requested his usual bottle of Vinho Verde and two bottles of ice-cold water.

They were halfway through their main course when a very attractive lady arrived wearing the bright vivid colours peculiar to the Portuguese national dress of bouffant long skirts made of striped fabrics known as saia, with a vivid multi-coloured kerchief, completed by black headgear decorated with coloured ribbons. She carried a large wicker-work basket filled with flowers in her arm and started selling them to the other customers. She received few takers before making her way over to Adam and Nicola.

The flower girl commenced the usual, quite loud, sales pitch for the flowers in her basket. With her back to the other customers, she unexpectedly pulled out a large packet dropping it on Adam's lap. Nicola pointed to the napkin lying on top of the table and smiled, taking two of the flowers and placing them in front of her.

'How much?' asked Nicola. The flower girl whispered, 'Free with every transaction of trinta e oito e setenta' mil Euro.'

Adam thanked her in the Latin manner, kissing her strongly on both cheeks whilst holding her tightly around her waist and patted her derrière as a goodbye.

As the flower girl departed Nicola looked at her uncle, smiled, commenting, 'That was efficient, a friend of yours?'

'You could say,' he smiled back. 'Finish your dinner. We have time for a quick coffee and a visit to the local shops. I'm sure you will need a few things, change of clothes, ladies' stuff, make-up, et al.'

'Good idea,' she said. 'Nice food, quite tasty.'

THE PAIR LEFT the restaurant to head to the other side of the River Douro, eventually finding a parking space at El Corte Ingles. Nicola made a beeline for the cosmetics counter, followed by a long rake around in the pharmacy department. Adam gamely hung on as his niece conducted a whirlwind shopping spree.

Finally, Nicola landed in the ladies clothing department, as her uncle slumped into a waiting chair thoughtfully provided for bored husbands. He cringed as he saw hundred Euro notes being spent at pace. Adam did not do shopping, in fact, he constantly sought a cure but with little success. He told Nicola he had to attend to a small errand and would meet her in the coffee bar just outside the entrance to the store.

A happy Nicola eventually decided she had finished, for now, headed to the coffee bar, meeting her uncle just as he arrived. She had finished shopping, her uncle silently gave thanks to the Lord above, as they headed fully loaded in the direction of the car park pay machine.

Twenty minutes later he slumped wearily into his comfortable padded armchair in his comfortable office, in time to intercept a welcome cup of strong coffee from Sister Anna.

'You sleeping here tonight?,' he asked his niece. 'Or are you going back to your ship?' 'I need to sleep aboard. I don't wish to leave the yacht unattended,' she replied.

'In this case, take Sister Anna with you,' he replied. 'The marina area is not too unsafe, but occasionally some rowdy yobs get active at chucking out time from the local taverna.'

Coffee finished, the two girls, complete with Nicola's shopping, went outside to a waiting taxi, taking a strong wooden staff which Sister Anna always carried. The taxi dropped down past the many port wine warehouses to the road along the River Douro and headed towards the marina.

The area where the yacht was moored remained quiet, but the local bar seemed full of obviously drunk customers shouting at the top of their voices in the Latin manner.

Nicola unlocked the hatchway, entering the main saloon, only to find the internal lighting very dim. She cursed herself for allowing the main batteries to go flat. Not a serious problem as the small electrical generator would be easy to turn over.

Nicola wiggled her way into the small compartment but found difficulty in turning the engine over. She called Sister Anna to help by swinging the starting handle while she stood behind the engine holding up the stiff cylinder head lifters.

With one mighty swing, Sister Anna swung the start handle, Nicola dropped the lifters, and the engine thankfully started to complete a rapid charge of the yachts' main batteries.

Nicola felt tired out. The last two hectic days and the medical treatment had drained her strength. She slumped down on the comfortable settee in the main saloon reaching out for a bottle of VSOP Brandy. Sister Anna intercepted the brandy bottle to pour a small measure into a glass with a great deal more water than Nicola would have wished. Sister Anna looked down at Nicola, waving her index figure in disapproval. Nicola surrendered, she knew the score, but she sure felt like a stiff drink.

As the two girls relaxed, a commotion started outside on the jetty. Drunken yobbos were shouting, inviting the two girls to come and get it. Nicola looked at Sister Anna. She just was not feeling up to fending off any marauding men looking for sex. She flicked open her newly acquired cell phone, dialled her uncle, asking to send assistance.

One of the men jumped into the cockpit of the yacht holding a weapon looking like an old rifle bayonet. Sister Anna grabbed her wooden staff and made for the companionway ladder. The man took shock at seeing a sister of the cloth entering the yacht's cockpit and made the mistake of attempting something new.

Little did he know Sister Anna possessed a strong physique and an expert in the Japanese martial art of Bōjutsu or fighting with a wooden staff. She leapt with one bound onto the deck of the yacht, swung the staff around in the air, fended off a feeble blow from the bayonet and delivered a massive blow to the man's neck area breaking his collar bone like a dry twig. He howled in pain, as the weapon fell from his hand.

His associates came to his rescue, only to be bemused by the speed of Sister Anna and the accuracy of two further blows, producing the same result.

Sister Anna stood there, silent waiting and watching. An impasse resulted until the sounds of a police car siren was heard in the distance. The police patrol, ever ready for the usual Saturday night trouble, considered all participants guilty. The more problematic revellers were generally taken to the nearby police station and treated to the well-known 'police event' called 'falling up the stairs', before being thrown into police cells and left until Sunday morning when matters could be dealt with by the day shift.

The sight of injured and drunken hooligans lying around in great pain, being looked down upon by a sister-of-the-cloth holding nothing more than a stout wooden staff, was a new experience. The sergeant-in-charge of the police patrol bent down to examine the injured.

The one remaining uninjured hooligan suddenly took off in retreat, but he didn't get far. In his drunken state, he mistimed a leap over a stone barrier crashed to the ground face first and broke his collar bone, badly scraping his face in the process.

The sergeant strode over to Sister Anna and started haranguing her with many questions in generally obscene Portuguese. She just stood there unable to answer, which the sergeant took to be dumb insolence. He tried to take away her staff, but she prevented him by spinning away and jumping back aboard the yacht.

The sergeant, his patience exhausted, and with his anger rising, was about to go into violent action when Nicola cried out for him to stop.

32

'An English woman,' he thought. 'What the hell?'

As the sergeant became even angrier, a second police car screeched to a halt alongside the yacht, a police inspector emerged and ordered everyone to remain as they were.

He came to the side of the jetty and bid Nicola Stranraer good evening in perfect English. 'Do I know you Inspector?' she asked.

'You gave a lecture in London last April, I believe, to the Inter-European Committee on 'The law, forensic research, and the need for progress in modernising legislation. I remember you well, most impressive.'

Nicola was surprised but recognised a good opportunity when she saw one. 'Thank you, Inspector, I remember you, but sorry, your name escapes me.'

'Inspector Ricardo de Luis Fonse, at your service.' he replied.

Nicola recounted the unpleasant events following the intrusion of the drunken hooligans. 'This one with the broken collar bone attempted to attack Sister Anna with the bayonet lying at my feet. The sister defended herself, with her staff. See it is almost cut through. And, if I am not mistaken, this bayonet is a pre-war 1910 example made from the finest embossed Krupp steel, a real antique from the German Kaiser's Honour Guard and possibly quite rare. It could be part of the robbery from the Hungarian Court Armoury Exhibition in Madrid some weeks ago. It will not take long to verify.'

The police inspector went to recover the bayonet, but Nicola stopped him whilst she found a plastic bin bag so he could pick it up without contaminating any evidence. Inspector Ricardo de Luis Fonse turned around to his police sergeant, ordering him to arrest the four drunken men, get them to the military hospital for treatment and then securely locked them up for the night.

He asked Sister Anna if she felt OK. She indicated a yes. 'Inspector, she is a deaf-mute, so she cannot answer,' said Nicola.

Inspector Ricardo de Luis Fonse' took out his notebook to start recording details of all those present. Nicola thought for a moment, she didn't want her name to end up in any police report.

'Inspector,' she said, 'The owner of the taverna can give you the details you need. Is it possible to leave our details out of your report? Mother Superior will be most annoyed if one of her sisters has been involved in this unfortunate incident.

I have just been discharged from her hospital only two hours ago, which is why this sister is with me, to help me to bed and take care of anything during the night.'

Adam arrived looking worried. 'Nicky are you OK?' he asked.

Nicola replied an affirmative. Adam went over to Inspector Ricardo. 'Good evening inspector, everything OK?' he said.

The Inspector returned his greeting, told him everything had been taken care off, as he put his notebook away.

'I have all I need,' he answered. 'I will let your patient return to her recovery. She looks very tired and unwell.'

And, with that, he was gone.

'That was lucky,' thought Nicola, 'Very lucky indeed.'

Sister Anna assisted Nicola into the main saloon, sweeping away the alcoholic drink Nicola had left on the saloon table. Adam dropped lightly down into the saloon, helped himself to a stiff brandy and sat down.

'Anything to eat,' he asked hopefully. 'Or do I need to call over to the taverna?'

Sister Anna put her hand out for some cash and disappeared to bring something to eat for everybody. She smiled to herself. She had enjoyed the action with her antique staff, but the damaged caused by the bayonet looked bad.

Could it be repaired? She knew little about the wood used to fashion the staff. She had inherited it from her father. He'd told her the staff had been made from a dense tropical rain forest wood called 'peltogyne,' more commonly known as 'purple heart.'

The staff had been in the family for generations, but she did not know its exact age. She only knew her great-grandfather had spent many years exploring the tropical rainforests of Central and South America.

Sister Anna returned to find Nicola showered, dressed ready for bed, relaxing, lying on the comfortable settee in the main saloon, and Adam busy making up the beds in three cabins.

Sister Anna unwrapped the food consisting of Portuguese snacks of cod puffs, mini meat pies and other pastries and laid them out on the main saloon table. Nicola rose, put the kettle on to make a large pot of tea and found a can of beer for her uncle.

Adam asked who would sleep where?

Nicola chose the double guest suite forward. She chose not to remind her uncle or Sister Anna, the main owner's cabin at the stern of the yacht was where Victoria had been so savagely assaulted, although Adam knew full well after stripping away the soiled bedding.

Nicola suggested Sister Anna use the prepared pilot berth in the corner behind the galley; it formed a nice cosy comfortable corner. Nicola set the skylights for the best ventilation, closed the hatch and its companionway to the main cockpit, and set the locks. As an extra precaution, she set the alarm system to warn of any further intrusions to what she hoped would be a peaceful night's rest.

'Here, drink this,' said Adam to his favourite niece. 'It's a sleeping draft to help you get to sleep.'

Nicola drank it without comment and bid everyone goodnight. Soon the yacht sank into peaceful darkness. Nicola slipped into her comfortable bed for a welcomed sleep in the knowledge she was safe at last. Her uncle, seeing she could have difficulties sleeping thoughtfully provided a night-light to give a warm glow on the deck close to the bottom of her berth.

She woke only once to answer the call of nature in her cabin's en-suite heads. She opened the cabin door and looked down the companionway into the main saloon just to satisfy herself all was well.

She felt a slight rocking movement on her feet, could something or someone be moving at the stern of the yacht. Perhaps the wash from passing fishing vessels on their way to distant fishing grounds. The movement ceased and feeling very sleepy she decided she must have dreamt it. She climbed back into bed falling sound asleep as her head hit the comfortable down filled pillow.

The next thing Nicola became aware of when Sister Anna gently woke her up with a hot mug of steaming hot tea and a chocolate biscuit.

'This is more like it,' she thought, drank the tea, rolled over and fell asleep once more.

Much later, she woke with a start, as a cargo ship made its presence known as it docked in the adjacent commercial port, its siren making one hell of a din. A loud crashing sound accompanied the wailing siren so she guessed the captain of the cargo ship was not having a quiet Sunday.

'Come on Stranraer, time to get up.'

It was Uncle Adam calling an end to the best night's sleep she had enjoyed for many a long day.

'How're things?' she called back.

'Things to do. Mother Superior will be here in a few moments to check-up on where the hell I spent last night,' he replied. 'Best tell her Sister Anna shared your bed in case you felt ill during the night. She did sleep in the pilot berth, but Mother Superior is a suspicious old witch at the best of times.'

Nicola dressed and wandered into the main saloon, just in time to intercept a toasted ham and cheese sandwich and a cup of coffee. She plonked herself down at the settee next to the table and looked around. Outside of the yacht, the harbour had regained its tranquillity now the cargo ship had ceased its unwelcome excursions.

She thanked Sister Anna her for breakfast and saw an enigmatic smile which would not have been out of place on a certain painting hanging in a well-known Parisian museum. Her uncle also looked remarkably relaxed; strange considering how stressed he'd been the night before.

'Hum,' she thought. 'I wonder.'

She could see the pilot berth had been slept in, or it looked as though it had, which proved nothing.

Mother Superior barged into the main saloon, accompanied by Sister Isabella, complaining at length about all manner of things she considered incorrect.

'Good morning Mother Superior, how are we today? Dispensing the love of Christ to us miserable sinners,' greeted Adam.

'Have you committed any sins?' she asked pointedly.

'Sorry, I don't do confessions,' replied Adam. 'I'm a doctor who has had one hell of a day yesterday. Can't a man get a good night's sleep in peace?'

Mother Superior looked around at Sister Anna, who just sat stock still at the navigation desk nursing a hot coffee, with the best poker face Nicola had ever seen.

Mother Superior was not convinced, but in her dark mood, she never would be.

'And what about all this fuss last night,' she asked. 'I had Inspector Fonse, who I know well, asking did I have a Sister Anna in my charge.'

Nicola butted in to give the Mother Superior a shorter version of last night's unfortunate events. Sister Anna demonstrated the damage to her favourite staff, with a tear in her eye.

Nicola took the staff and examined it. The wood was very hard, containing natural oils to make gluing the damaged area quite difficult. The staff was very old, its beautiful colour being a good indication of its age. The damage consisted of a clean split which had almost severed the shaft. She seized the chance to change the subject and the atmosphere in the main saloon of the yacht.

'Sister Anna,' started Nicola. 'This can be repaired. A solvent will remove the oils from the wood where it is split, then I will use some epoxy glue to make it good as new. In fact, this yacht is constructed from long wooden strips, held together by this type of glue. It's very strong.'

Sister Anna did not look convinced but nodded the repair should go ahead as soon as possible.

'Uncle,' said Nicola. 'Make Mother Superior and Sister Isabella a cup of coffee, we won't be long,' as the pair of them disappeared to the yacht's workshop.

By the time, the repair had been completed, Mother Superior and Sister Isabella had returned to the convent, and Nicola found Adam resting on the settee in the main saloon.

'Well done Nicola,' he said. 'That got kind of tense for a moment. Any plans for today?' 'Nope,' said Nicola, 'And you?'

'I best make my way back to the convent, check-up on Victoria, and catch-up on my paperwork.'

Nicola replied 'OK, we'll hang out here, maybe get some supplies from the local shops. I have some maintenance to do to and maybe get some of this rest you keep going on about.'

As Adam departed Nicola dressed to go out. The yacht had ample supplies of basic stores, but everyday items, milk, bread, biscuits, and fruit were almost finished. Mother Superior rarely allowed her convent sisters to visit the city unless they were in a group, dressed in full regalia.

Sister Anna prepared herself for a day out, dressed in a simple black skirt which came below the knees, a simple top with her nuns' smock, and a simple blue and white habit.

Nicola secured and locked the yacht, saw it was a nice day for a walk, looked at Sister Anna, asking which way. Sister Anna pointed the way towards a local housing district. After a short walk, they came upon a traditional Sunday street market where the stallholders took advantage of the city shops being closed on the Sabbath.

The stalls were laden with almost everything one could wish for in an ordinary street market, from fresh food and vegetables, poultry and other meats, jams, eggs, et al. Nicola marched quickly to the far end. Sister Anna struggled to keep up wondering why Nicola seemed so uninterested in the street market.

Nicola reached the far end of the market, turned around, smiled and said, 'OK, Sister Anna, let's go shopping.'

Sister Anna was delighted. They slowly cruised along the stalls, picking up and putting down items of interest. Nicola bargained with skill, never too pushy, always leaving the stallholder with a smile whether she bought anything or not.

As they reached half-way, their shopping bags were full and heavy. Nicola bid Sister Anna to buy any items she needed, refusing all offers of compensation. She assumed her friend from the convent had little or no money.

What seemed strange was the way the stallholders and the general public took to the sight of a nun walking amongst them. A few of the older ladies touched her clothing uttering a quick 'Hail Mary', others just smiled and crossed themselves. The men folk just stared, wondering whether to say anything or just admire her womanly charms, despite the formal religious clothing she wore.

Nicola came across a large stall selling many of the local Oporto's specialities, all the best examples of comida caseira, or Portuguese home cooking.

The food stall enjoyed a roaring business. Fortunately, it didn't take too long to get served. She looked at the strange foods, but the stallholder, a large and rather vocal lady with barely understandable Portuguese, explained the foods on offer.

The first dish on offer, tripas à modo do Porto, tripe cooked with dried beans, vegetables, pigs' trotters, and offal served with rice. Nicola smiled and wrinkled her nose, not for her. Sister Anna didn't seem too interested either.

Next on offer, francesinhas, bread topped with steak, sausage with cheese and a beer-flavoured sauce. Sister Anna waved her finger in rejection of a beer flavoured sauce.

The seafood looked wonderfully fresh, local sardinhas with boiled potatoes and grilled red peppers. The other types of fish came mostly grilled, but Nicola looked at a thick fish and potato stew, caldeirada de peixe, served as a kind of risotto. She looked at Sister Anna smiled a big smile and asked for two big portions.

The stall owner produced a small table and two plastic chairs. Nicola thanked her in her appreciatively. She had to admit she had not returned to full strength and the day had become quite warm. Nicola ordered two bottles of mineral water and drank heavily.

Their food arrived with an accompaniment of home-made multi-pepper sauce in a small, decorated porcelain bowl with the consistency of nitro-glycerine and a fiery taste which would last for a week.

As they ate, Nicola noticed a large scruffy man slumped in a corner of the building behind the stalls, fast asleep. Occasionally the swirling breeze distributed his doubtful body odour for the benefit of all.

Nicola asked who he was. The stall owner raised her eyes towards the heavens. This was Magote do Magno or Magote for short, a former prize fighter well past his best, with a hungry wife and child looking down upon them from a first-floor balcony. She doubted if the family had eaten that day, in fact for the last few days.

Nicky looked up at the family, shocked to see an emaciated woman of Romanian gipsy origin, with matted dark hair, badly dressed, with a small child hanging on to her pleated skirt. The child cried with hunger, that much was obvious. It was also apparent the local population had long given up on any worry about their welfare. Sister Anna clearly had the same opinion. Nicola engaged with the stall owner in a gentle conversation about the situation. Sr. Magote had fallen into depression, without work or income, and had almost abandoned his family.

Nicola gave the stall owner ten Euros for a large plate of food for the family on the balcony. She waved at the gipsy lady on the balcony to come, but the gipsy lady froze not understanding what was going on. The stall owner told her the gipsy lady, shunned by her neighbours, rarely spoke to anyone.

Sister Anna picked up the plate of food, helped herself to bread rolls, a large bottle of mineral water and headed inside the building. She returned with tears in her eyes, so bad did she find the conditions this family were living in.

Nicola struggled in her conversation with the stall owner, until her daughter, Anna Rita, a university student, arrived. She spoke good English, and Nicola quickly got down to brass tacks regarding the family, asking why the wife and daughter looked so poor and hungry.

The daughter gave a long sorry explanation. The husband, Magote, had been, in his day, a good boxer, but as his era passed, he started to lose more fights than he won. His prize money dwindled to nothing and the repeated blows to his head and body took their toll.

MAGOTE HAD MET his wife in Romania during an unsuccessful trip to regain his fortunes. He returned to his hometown of Oporto, practically penniless, homeless, and hungry. Magote did not look hungry; his large belly announced his arrival sometime before the rest of him. He needed charity but was too proud to accept it.

Anna Rita asked if Nicola could offer any help. She saw her concern, and Sister Anna's face set in a grim and disgusted expression of what would happen next. Anna Rita said her mother would like to help but it would become a commitment that wouldn't go away anytime soon, and she just didn't have money to spare. To be fair, she said, the community struggled to stay together, so bad was the economic situation in this part of the city.

Nicola decided something must be done. Quite what was another matter? She asked Anna Rita to volunteer to help the family of Sr. Magote if she provided the funds for the next few months. Anna Rita explained handing money directly to the family would be a waste of time. It wouldn't last five minutes. Nicola agreed.

'OK, let's do this,' said Nicola. 'I will employ Magote for seven days at fifty Euros a day. I will give you forty and give ten Euros to Magote just to keep things straight. I won't tell him about the forty Euros. Your mum's food is what, ten Euros a plate, so your mum can provide at least one decent meal a day. My guess is by the end of the week, the situation will turn around.'

'OK,' said Anna Rita, 'Can do. I can also scrounge stuff from the local stall holders and this can be a project for my studies.'

'Oh,' said Nicola, 'And what are you studying, social services?' 'Exactly,' replied Anna Rita. 'And what use do you have for him today?'

'Well for a start, I have a lot of shopping that needs carrying down to the marina. Scrounge some clothing whilst I get him fed, then at the marina, I'll throw him in the shower and his clothes into one of the commercial washing machines.'

Anna Rita spoke to her mother, who was glad someone had the gumption to do something positive. Having Magote fast asleep on the ground outside of his home did not go down well with her customers and moving Magote anywhere else had always been a difficult task.

Nicola woke him, putting a plate of food in his hand. He rubbed his eyes and looked up very suspiciously, saw a female stranger looking down at him, grunted and ate his food without comment.

Anna Rita went to Magote side with the good news. He looked at the ground in sorrow nodding his head in acceptance of this small turn of good fortune. Nicola saw a proud man suffering from the lowest of fortunes he had ever experienced.

Nicola and Sister Anna waited until Magote was ready. He struggled to his feet. Nicola wondered if he wasn't ill. Eventually, he readied himself looking at Nicola for what to do next.

Nicola pointed at the shopping and the direction down the street towards the marina. Sister Anna elected to carry the lighter of the shopping many bags. Nicola, by this time, was feeling well past her best and very glad of any assistance.

The three of them walked slowly down the street to the amusement of the local population, a female tourist and a sister of the cloth followed by a heavily laden Magote.

As they were passing by one of the local bars, an attacker launched himself at Sister Anna from a side gully with a wooden club. Sister Anna, dropped her bags, spun around, deflected the first blow but took a second blow on her back just below her waist.

What the attacker had not banked on was the lumbering dirty

downtrodden giant behind her. Magote dropped the shopping, shouted a curse to get the attacker's attention, rose gracefully onto the balls of his feet and pole-axed the attacker with the fastest left jab Nicola had ever seen. A second attacker came from the other side. Nicola screamed a warning. Magote ducked the swinging scaffold pole, grabbed it, and with a low swinging blow broke the attacker's shins.

Nicola caught sight of an almost familiar face, a man with his shoulder and left arm heavily bandaged across his chest, sitting in a wheelchair.

'Ah,' she thought, 'One of the Saturday night mob who ruined such a promising evening.' She urgently called her uncle asking for the police inspector to come as soon as possible.

Within minutes a police car arrived. The Inspector jumped out to find the very untidy local giant holding onto a wheelchair, complete with a worried occupant, and two prone bodies spread out on the ground.

The police inspector walked over to Nicola, told her the local public hospital was full and now she was making things worse. Nicola smiled, shrugged her shoulders, and explained what had happened. A stout lady started hurling abuse at the police complaining about the lack of peace in this otherwise quiet neighbourhood.

Having ascertained Nicola would not press any charges, the police inspector bid Nicola good day, and waved her party on its way. Nicola smiled at Magote and said a big thank-you.

THEY REACHED THE yacht and dumped their shopping in the cockpit. Nicola and Anna Rita led Magote over to the marina washrooms. Magote, with a look of horror, was forcibly bundled inside the washroom. Anna Rita told him to strip handing him a towel to hide his modesty. Nicola removed his clothing and headed into the DIY laundry room.

When she returned, they pushed Magote into a shower cubicle armed with a sponge and a large bottle of shampoo. Anna Rita stood guard shouting a myriad of instructions of what to wash and what not to miss. Several times Magote tried to terminate this torture only to be propelled back into the steaming cubicle.

Nicola returned to the washroom and asked how it was going.

'Well,' said Anna Rita, 'He keeps trying to escape, but I just shove him back in.'

To their surprise, they heard Magote trying to sing under the steaming flow of hot water.

Anna Rita shouted back at him 'Not to give up the day job, and to get a move on.'

Eventually, a clean Magote emerged from the shower cubical a changed man. More was to come. Nicola pulled him over to a bench seat, wrapped an old sheet around his neck and produced a pair of hair clippers. Fifteen minutes later Nicola had finished. Not the best haircut in the world, but what a transformation.

She dragged Magote over to a full-length wall mirror. He didn't recognise himself. Nicola gave him a bag full of clothes telling Magote to get dressed whilst they went to see if his washing was ready.

Ten minutes later a sheepish Magote joined the two girls outside busy nursing a cold drink from the vending machine.

Time to get a move on. They returned to the yacht, unlocked the hatch, and made their way below. With the shopping passed below into the main saloon, Nicola set about storing what she could and left everything else piled-up in the twin sinks of the galley.

Nicola asked Sister Anna to make ham salad sandwiches and a large pot of coffee. Relaxing in the spacious main saloon the conversation turned to the subject of the future for Magote, relaxing along the comfortable side bench seat of the forward cockpit.

Nicola thought long a hard and came up with an idea.

'Anna Rita, Magote could be an answer to the problem of security in the street market. The police are short of resources. If the street formed an association they could manage their own affairs and keep things cool.'

'That's a good idea,' replied Anna Rita. 'The subject has been discussed before and mother is the one to get the other stall holders to form an association. The market is expanding with its low prices and access to goods from far and wide.'

'And goods that fall from the back of trucks to order?' suggested Nicola.

'Who knows, but local suppliers who can't be bothered with EU rules and bullshit paperwork are always looking for an outlet,' said Anna Rita.

'Well let's find out,' said Nicola, 'The street holders will be impressed with the new Magote. He even refused a beer and when was the last time this happened?'

And so, Sr. Magote joined the newly formed association of traders in what became known locally as the Rua das Compras.

Chapter 4

Vicky is reawakened in Oporto

WITH VICTORIA kept under sedation at the convent, Nicola had little to do. Mother Superior relented in allowing Sister Anna to keep Nicola company aboard the yacht during the night.

During the day, Nicola completed maintenance tasks and cut a deal with Carlos Gilberto whose cousin had a job delivering diesel fuel in and around the City of Oporto.

The yacht would need about a thousand litres to fill its substantial tanks. On a long-distance voyage, the water tanks were topped up by the water maker, the water maker ran on electricity, and electricity was generated by either the auxiliary diesel generator or the diesel-powered main engine.

He assured her the fuel would be half price, but it took a little time to wheedle out of Carlos Gilberto the details of just how this welcome situation came about. Clearly a well-established 'business on the side.'

The yacht's fuel tanks had a sight glass, providing an easy to read and accurate reading of the delivered quantity and then slip the cash to Carlos Gilberto. In all; a very cosy arrangement.

When there was little else to do Nicola would go up forward to the storeroom and the hidden cash. She slowly but surely removed the wrappers from the new unissued bank notes, repackaging them into cardboard boxes.

During this boringly repetitive task, Nicola allowed herself the luxury of still resenting the loss of her elevated position in the scientific community, her influence, her contacts, her friends, her colleagues, and more importantly her comfortable salary and pension contributions. All because her results were about to become a serious embarrassment to unnamed persons in the present government.

In the evening she enjoyed the company of Sister Anna, sitting in the comfortable cockpit, sipping cocktails, feasting on locally made foods and snacks from a grateful street community.

Tuesday evening, Nicola's was asked to return to the convent first thing the next morning. The time had come to bring Victoria back into the land of the living. When she arrived, Victoria had been partially re-awaken so the 'dressing' covering her back could be replaced after her skin had been examined.

The transformation of what had been little more than a bloody mess was quite remarkable.

A new dressing was applied and Victoria returned her comfortable bed in her private ward.

Nicola found the ward decorated with a lavish display of cut autumn flowers, with the early morning sun streaming through the side window, so everything looked bright and cheerful.

'Uncle Adam,' she whispered, 'When Vicky wakes-up she'll think she's in heaven.' 'Schh,' he replied. 'Mother Superior knows what she's doing.'

Sister Teresa slowly injected the recovery medication into Victoria's arm, as everyone sat down to await the moment of full awakening. They didn't have long to wait.

Victoria opened her eyes, and in a strange voice whispered, 'Is anybody there?'

'I'm here Victoria, its Uncle Adam.'

'You don't look like Uncle Adam,' said Victoria in a sad ghostly halting voice, 'You must be…the Arch…Angel…Gabriel. And look, there is another 'saintly angel,' pointing at the Mother Superior.'

'No, it's the Mother Superior,' replied Uncle Adam.

'She looks like a saint,' she whispered in her ghostly voice. 'So… good….and…forgiving of all sins committed by everyone here.'

'I haven't committed any sins,' said Uncle Adam.

'That'll be bleedin' right Guv,' said Victoria loudly, in her best Eliza Doolittle voice, 'I've a bin a lying 'ere with nutin' to do since last night, just bleedin' lyin 'ere just thinkin.'

Nicola laughed out loud. Victoria had not been as unconscious as they thought. Now she had seemingly returned in full fighting trim, trying making fun of the situation.

'Oh, hello Doctor Adam,' said Victoria, in her high-pitched regal voice. 'I'm so pleased to meet. And what do you do?'

Smiling, Adam said, 'I'm the local undertaker, welcome to heaven.'

'Huh,' said Victoria, in her normal voice, 'Explains where all these bleedin' flowers have come from.'

'Have' you done Victoria Stanwick,' asked Nicola, 'Enjoyed your re-awakening have you.'

'I guess, 'ave I bin out long?'

'A few days I'm afraid, it took a while to bring you back from the dead,' said Adam. 'When you two have finished this comedy show,' spluttered Mother Superior, 'Can we get on?'

'Yes of course,' said Adam. 'Just need to check you over Victoria, just follow my finger as I move it from far left to far right.'

Mother Superior waved the other sisters away to let Dr Duncan return to his doctoring. She smiled to herself. She had never seen, in all her years in A&E, a patient returning from the dead, with such style, if you could call it that.

Adam wasn't so sure. These two girls had been through hell, and he needed to address the physiological problems which surely should exist. First, he interviewed Nicola.

Nicola told her uncle she was still coming to terms with the assault. Being a criminal forensic scientist had brought a level of mental toughness. Dispatching the three attackers and saving the life of herself and Victoria had brought a large measure of closure. As the physical hurt went away, the memory would fade. She was having private moments of stress, but she would deal with them in her own way.

Adam knew she could always talk to Great Aunt Violet for counselling. Nicola confided in Adam her real concerns about Victoria. Her awakening, funny though it was, did not ring true. Adam said he was deeply concerned for Vicky's mental health, but he did not have the experience of being as close to her as she did.

Nicola felt glad to talk about her concerns regarding Vicky. Vicky had a Jekyll and Hyde personality. She was highly intelligent, sometimes too much so. A member of Mensa; with two engineering doctorates to her name, all at just over thirty years of age. On the one hand, she was sweet innocent giggly little Victoria, her default position with strangers. On the other hand, she could be the complete opposite.

Nicola knew Vicky was trying to reach the middle ground, which she would one day. 'Adam, do you have any experience in this? I will tell you why. I think at the height of the

assault Victoria would have passed out or just switched her mind off. She can do this when she wants to you know.

Now, when conscious, she will completely suppress any memory of what happened. For her, it never happened, which is why the subject must never be mentioned in her hearing. But when she is sleeping, her sub-conscious is going to get to work.

I fear she will have terrible nightmares and Great Aunt Violet thinks so too. She must not be allowed to sleep on her own. There must be someone she knows and trusts when it happens. Someone to snap her back into consciousness and give her the comfort she will desperately need. The convent must surely have sisters who can do this.'

'Yes Nicola, I believe we can do something whilst she is here. But when you two are alone, sleep together in the same bed. Keep her close. It will give her the courage to put this dreadful event behind her. You never know, it may help the pair of you. I will seek advice and see what medication can help.'

'Thank you very much, Adam, it has been very comforting to speak to you,' replied Nicola.

Chapter 5

A Day Out in the Vale do Douro, Portugal

LATE WEDNESDAY afternoon Adam completed another thorough examination of his favourite patient to allow Victoria to get up and get dressed. Time for Victoria to take a little gentle exercise and fresh air. She moved slowly, unsteady on her feet, supported by Adam and Nicola. After a slow circuit of the inner courtyard, she managed another lap on her own using a walking stick.

'This is better,' said Victoria. 'Just a lying-in bed like a cripple was doin' me 'ead in.' Please at her rapid progress, Adam let her continue with Nicola at her side. He had warned Nicola not to speak of the past events which had caused her so much distress.

Satisfied, Adam bid them sit with him at the wrought iron garden furniture and wait for tea and cakes to arrive. Adam served the refreshments asking if the girls would like to take a trip up the Douro Valley. The time had come to call on an existing patient, the daughter of an English widow, who needed a final check-up to give her a clean bill of health.

Afterwards, a traditional country lunch had been promised, with some local wine, which would be very good and some interesting conversation.'

'And just how far up this valley of yours do we have to go,' asked Nicola.

'About three hours by ferry to Pinhão. Then, we get picked-up by the lady's driver, across the bridge, along the river on the south bank, finally up a hill to the big colonial house. It's a vineyard, quite famous in its day and still hanging on to a reasonable amount of market share. It will be a very pleasant journey by ferry, very scenic. We can take our overnight things, just in case, OK?'

'Sounds interesting. Will Vicky be able to cope?' asked Nicola.

'I recommend a wheelchair, so she can rest if she needs to,' he replied. 'You make me feel like an old lady,' complained Victoria, 'But OK.'

'The area is very beautiful, and tranquil. Somewhere to escape and recharge one's batteries, just the job for you two, don't you think,' commented Uncle Adam.

'So, no disco, no booze and no boys to chase,' said Victoria glumly. 'I've just had three days, or is it four, lying in bed, sore as hell and unable to go anywhere.'

'Let's do things my way for a change. You can ruin your health later, in your own time and elsewhere.'

Victoria looked at Nicola and said, 'So that's me told off, what do think?'

'Sounds like a nice day out. You can terrorise the natives when you get back to full strength, which I might add, you don't have at the moment.'

'OK,' said Adam. 'The area is called Alijó, in the district of Vila Real. The railway to Pinhão opened in the late nineteenth century which we won't be using. It takes forever and it is not very comfortable.

The area has UNESCO's world heritage designation, including its many vineyards. The industry of the vineyards is called 'viticulture,' the science, and production of grapes, and how to deal with the differing events which occur each year. The 'viticulturists' are the specialists who look after the vines and are intimately involved with the winemakers.

Adam was about to continue when Nicola asked was there a point to all this detail, interesting as it maybe. Victoria giggled and Nicola kicked her foot.

'Pray continue,' said Nicola. 'What is the lady's name you obviously have a great interest in; and the daughter's for that matter?'

The mother's name is Pamela,' said Adam, trying not to give too much away, 'And the daughter's name is Rosemary, in her early twenties.'

'And the husband died two years ago, is this right?' asked Nicola.

'Yes, heart attack, very sudden and no previous indications of any problems. The Lady Pamela has had a long hard time of it, what with grief for her husband and multiple problems with the vineyard. We'll find out more tomorrow when we get there.'

By the way, where are you sleeping tonight?' asked Adam. 'Not sure. Why do you ask?'

'The ferry terminal is past the two bridges, so sleeping here will save time in the morning. Why don't you wander back to the marina? Take Sister Anna with you and do what you need to. Get something to eat and come back here for say 7 p.m. and keep Victoria company until bedtime. Bring your posh togs it would be nice to see you two looking your best.'

'Ah,' another clue thought Nicola. 'OK can do,' she said, and with that, she disappeared into the convent to collect Sister Anna.

Early next morning, Adam was relieved to see his two charges had risen on time, busy tucking into a substantial continental breakfast. He expected Victoria to be slow off the mark, but he did not know Nicola had convinced Victoria the day would turn out to be very special.

With her interest aroused and glad to be escaping from another day confined to the boring routine of being bedbound in a convent full of nuns, Victoria was looking forward to the journey.

Adam bid them an energetic 'bom dia,' sat down to his breakfast, pleased to see his two girls, dressed in the chic fashion of white slacks, open-neck silk blouses in autumn colours, loose fitting silk scarves, matching designer label high fashion loafers, and all accessories to match.

Clearly, Nicola had used the remainder of yesterday afternoon to execute an in-depth shopping spree, bringing a small measure of commercial joy to a city that had succumbed under the cosh of EU-imposed austerity as dictated by the German master race.

The European Union was not popular in this part of the world. Portugal maybe on the edge of the great European economic federal experiment, but the feeling prevailed Portugal would one day be dropped into the Atlantic Ocean.

The 'Povo do Portugal,' on joining the EU, had a popular expression when their currency, the 'Escudo,' had changed for the mighty and greatly overvalued Euro, "Agora eles roubarem o nosso Escudo, ao lado eles vão roubara a nossa bandeira" (now they have stolen our Escudo, next they will steal our flag).

OK, the EU had funded many fine new roads and people had borrowed to the hilt to drive new cars upon them. But 'cheap money' had long gone. The banks were almost bust and 'no money' had become the new norm. The continuing depression had led to widespread unemployment, and the more educated of their young were going abroad in search of a future, leaving behind a brooding and dissatisfied ageing population.

As they finished their breakfast, Sister Teresa told them their taxi had arrived. Time to be going. Adam carried their bags, as Nicola took Victoria's wheelchair to the taxi. It took less than ten minutes for the taxi to drop down to the road along the river and pass under the two magnificent iron bridges, the Ponte Dom Luis 1 and Ponte Maria Pia, their design originating from the offices of one Alexandre Gustave Eiffel. They arrived at the jetty just past the modern São João Bridge where the steam ferry would pick up its passengers.

The steam ferry, built in the early 1940's, a converted commercial vessel restored by a band of steam enthusiasts, who had formed a registered charity to save the ship for its original British made reciprocating steam engines. The ferry made a twice-weekly round-trip voyage from Oporto to the City of Pinhão. For some years now, it had proved very popular with local businesses, the local population at large, and of course, tourists.

The ferry business ran as an all-cash operation, giving great flexibility to the way the ferry service conducted its business, especially when purchasing services from the many maritime engineering specialists 'working on the nod,' and the provision of the mandated annual accountancy reports to the local fiscal's office who was more than prepared to accept them on the basis he enjoyed a good novel when he saw one. Cash in the community benefited the community and the ferry operation was not making any one person rich.

They arrived at the ferry terminal to find a long queue for the time of year. Nicola nodded at Victoria to sit in the opened wheelchair. The ferry loading supervisor waved them forward. Without further ado, they boarded the ferry and shown to a favoured position on the upper deck, with a fine, wind free, all-around view and overhead canopy to keep the rain off in the unlikely event of a shower.

'Works every time,' said Adam. 'Easy boarding every time with a small child or someone in a wheelchair.'

Victoria was not amused, but smiled anyway, her teeth clamped tightly together, vowing revenge.

'Don't bother sweet one,' chided Adam. 'Just be on your best behaviour.'

They settled down in comfortable reclining deck chairs. The ferry captain passed by on his way to the bridge to say good morning hoping they would enjoy a comfortable journey. The weather was going to be just fine, the river was running slower than usual due to the lack of rain, and their arrival time would be a little ahead of schedule.

'See,' said Uncle Adam, 'I told you the service was going to be good. The steward will bring coffee and snacks soon. So just get comfortable and relax.'

Victoria wriggled in her reclining chair and Adam asked what was causing her obvious discomfort.

'My back could be better. Any chance of some additional padding?'

Adam went to look for the steward and returned with three plastic covered mattresses and blankets. Victoria settled down and had a little doze. She'd got up far too early this morning and felt a little stressed. She wasn't going to complain as it would only result in a fussing Uncle Adam who still worried this journey would be too much for her.

The ferry cast off at the appointed time, picked up speed with black smoke pouring from her funnel. The City of Oporto soon slipped behind them. The summer was coming to a close and the autumn colours were bringing its usual 'end of season' beauty. The promised snacks and coffee arrived and Victoria fell asleep once more.

Adam looked over at Nicola, who was staring into space, rather than the passing scenery. 'A penny for your thoughts Nicky?' he asked. 'What's bothering you?'

'I'm having a quiet moment, trying to come to terms with all that's happened. A classic case of being in the wrong place at the wrong time. Now we must get out from under. We will succeed, but we need some good luck. By the way, a million thanks for everything, I can't believe how much you've achieved.'

'Well, there are some positives to balance the obvious negatives. The staff at the hospital performed very well. Mother Superior is now keener than ever to set-up shop on a more formal basis and we both expect to make a success of the adventure. Lots to do though, it's a tricky market setting up a high-class expensive clinic in this day and age.'

'I do have one favour to ask,' he continued. 'Unfortunately, I have some outstanding debts, and please don't start about my gambling habits, which I might add are long past. I need twenty thousand Euros and my time to pay is running out fast.' 'Have we reached the 'hate mail' in the post stage?' asked Nicola.

'No, we have reached the 'pay up in less than two weeks or else its 'broken legs time' stage. Mother Superior knows nothing about this, and she mustn't. God knows what she would do. I know so little of her past. She's not as saintly as you might think.'

'The funds you have to find will go where 'Costa del Crime' in southern Spain?' 'Correct. One of a chain in three adjacent cities, you know the ones.'

'I'm sure we can do something, give me a few moments to think it over,' whispered Nicola who saw Victoria trying to turn over in her chair.

'Best get her settled. I don't want 'big ears' listening to our conversation.'

Adam rose, adjusted Victoria's position in her reclining chair, made sure she was comfortable, placing his hand on her forehead to see if everything was OK.

'Tell me about the three men who kidnapped you two.'

'I prefer not to tell, as don't know, can't tell. You know how it is,' replied Nicola. 'But if the police ever catch up with you, do you have a believable story to tell them?'

'This's what I am working on. I have something that may work,' she replied, realising the moment had come, 'So what I'm about to tell you, you must forget and never repeat.'

'The three men, one called Rufus Stone and his two heavies were buried at sea with four kilos of divers lead weights wrapped around their necks, stripped naked and punctured stomachs.'

Nicola paused for a moment. Clearly, she did not sound as matter of fact as she tried to make out. She related the story about the dreadful events which had caused such harm to Victoria and herself.

'So now you have it. They will not be missed, except by Special Branch who want to know where the hell they are.'

'That is some story,' said Adam, 'Poor you. Any nightmares since I asked earlier?' 'Actually, and surprisingly, no,' said Nicola. 'I must be a chip off Great Aunt Violet's particular block. You must know some of her wartime exploits in WW2?'

'I met with her French companion, Jus William, just the once,' said Adam, 'And asked him about her wartime story. He told me the French Resistance use to call her 'Violent,' which for me was sufficient information. I know the Gestapo had a huge reward for her capture, but it only motivated her to kill even more of them.'

'Anyway, this is all you need to know,' said Nicola, 'And if anybody asks, I shall just tell them the yacht reached the south of Spain on the Atlantic side where Mr Stone and his friends were recovering from the storm and all the drugs and alcohol they had taken.

I dressed Victoria, launched the yacht's tender, loaded her into it as carefully as possible, grabbed some food, and a sack of cash. Before I setting off to the beach. I opened the seacocks in two of the yacht's heads, unfurled both foresails, cut the anchor line, and watched the yacht sail gently offshore, slowly sinking as it went.'

'And how did you get back to the UK,' asked Adam.

'Well, I'm working on the detail, but something along the lines we found a long-distance lorry from Scotland, bribed the driver to take us near Paris, and disappeared into the care of Great Aunt Violet's French Resistance chums. You know President Charles de Gaul gave her France's highest honour, twice, the 'Ordre National de la Légion d'honneur,' the Legion of Honour. The useless UK government still has her exploits listed as a state secret.'

'So, Uncle,' continued Nicola. 'This is what you can do to help me. I will give you twenty thousand pounds of the new unissued notes. No sequential numbers and if you rough them up a bit this would be helpful. Then, after we leave Oporto, slip down to the 'Costa del Crime' by road.

Public transport is best, with minimum checking of ID documents.

Check-in to a local B&B, then at night, dress up like the dandy you are today. By the way, why are you all poshed-up? Going a-wooing with what's her name.'

The lady's name is 'Donna Pamela de Souza Henrique,' answered Uncle Adam, 'And since you asked, no. She is still in mourning and grappling with a myriad of problems. I used to dress up like this at medical university. I was well noted for my appearance, thank you very much.'

'Anyway, go to another casino, change say four grand into Euros. Buy a few chips and play the tables being careful only to lose the difference between the two currencies. Take a pause, go eat something, call it a day, cash in the chips and take the cash to the pay desk of the casino you must placate. Then, go back to the B&B.

Now be careful, everybody knows casinos are a great way to launder money. Make it look like you're a punter on a winning streak. Take it carefully and in no time at all, you will have created the illusion of repaying the outstanding debt by a run of good luck.

Then, slip home back to Oporto with as little fuss as possible and all will be well' 'And this does what exactly?' asked Adam.

'It creates the illusion the yacht has somehow managed to slip unnoticed into the Mediterranean and the bad guys are starting to launder their ill-gotten gains in the 'Costa del Crime. If nothing else it will cause confusion and I will gain time to do whatever we need to do. The question is do you feel this is something you can do for me and Vicky?'

Adam answered, 'Of course, sounds like fun. A little bit of intrigue won't do any harm.' 'Remember Adam. Just don't get caught with these new British banknotes. Just drop them in a fire or whatever. You have sufficient Euros to back you up, OK,' cautioned Nicola.

The ferry made good progress, time to order more snacks and coffee. The steward served Adam and his two girls compliments of the captain. A nice touch thought Adam.

Victoria awoke to ask where they were and how much longer before they arrived. She took the last of the coffee, still hot in the vacuum flask, and a sweet pastry.

Adam looked at the familiar scenery and decided to go walk-about to see who he knew among the passengers. Drawing a blank, he returned to Nicola and Victoria, told them the ferry had reached the district of Vila Real and the journey would soon be over. Victoria asked Nicola to accompany her to the ladies' room, and the pair of them disappeared to return laden with a large bunch of flowers and trinkets, as gifts for the hostess they had become anxious to meet.

As they relaxed, the City of Pinhâo slowly came into view. The ferry reduced its speed, barely making way against the river current. Soon the ferry would moor at the municipal landing and an interesting lunch awaited them.

Chapter 6

An Interesting Lunch in the Vale do Douro

ADAM LOOKED down at the riverside dock as the steam ferry completed mooring. With docking quickly completed, the dockside workers pulled the gangway onto the ferry, making it secure for disembarkation.

The passengers rushed to disembark, for whatever reason thought Adam. He bid his party wait a few minutes to let the hubbub die down. The steward came to help with getting Victoria ashore and making her settled in her wheelchair. Adam and Nicola came behind with their overnight luggage and the presents for their host.

Adam stepped ashore and waved to a Sr. Antonio, an elderly gentleman leaning on the bonnet of a rather old, first edition, short wheelbase Land Rover, in remarkably good condition. As he waved the Land Rover made its way to the waiting passengers.

Pleasantries completed, Adam and Sr. Antonio looked to see how best to load the Land Rover.

'Sr. Antonio, por favor bring the wheelchair with the senorita to the tailgate. Together we can lift her in,' said Adam. The pair of them lifted Victoria in her wheelchair into the back of the Land Rover and found straps to secure it.

'I'll sit in the back with Victoria. Nicola best you sit up front Sr. Antonio,' suggested Adam.

Sr. Antonio set off for the vineyard driving to make the ride as smooth as possible. Not an easy task on roads long abandoned by the local authority. It was not far to the vineyard. Across the bridge, then along the south bank, and up a narrow-unmade farm road, over the hill to the southern facing flank of a long ridge.

Victoria hung on grimly as the journey started to take its toll, but she tried hard not to show her discomfort. The entrance to the vineyard was formed by an elegant wrought iron framework, overgrown with flowering creepers. A sign announced their arrival at the 'Quinta de Souza Henrique do Douro.' They passed a small copse of broadleaf trees surrounding a small chapel at the far side.

Victoria was grateful to see a large colonial style farmhouse, or Quinta, come into view. She saw an extensive two-storied building with a deep veranda enclosing all four sides of the property. Traditional heavy clay tiles covered the roof and the veranda overhang. The building displayed signs of needing maintenance.

Waiting on the veranda, Nicola saw a very attractive lady in her early forties, medium height, dressed in a very stylish outfit consisting of walking shoes, pleated skirt, and a soft fluffy white blouse. Her chestnut hair fell in cascades around her shoulders. She wore very expensive accessories and a wedding band on her right hand.

'Another clue,' thought Nicola.

By her side stood Rosemary, her daughter, quite tall, in her early twenties. She wore more modern clothing of designer jeans, trainers, bobby socks, and an Italian silk top. Her hair was tinted in the modern fashion and cropped short. She looked thin compared to her mother, no doubt the result of the recent illness Uncle Adam would not elucidate upon.

Two dogs lying on the veranda showed a brief and momentary interest in the new arrivals before returning the task of the day, sleeping. One, a large black Labrador, with a collie's head and an Alsatian tail. Clearly an unplanned conception. The other dog was a pedigree Shih Tzu, mostly white with brown and cream colourings.

As the Land Rover pulled up at the front of the Quinta, Adam turned around, warning his two girls not to say anything concerning the past. Rumours in this valley spread faster than the speed of light and considering their impending weekend departure, it would be best to keep a very low profile.

Adam helped Victoria to alight, handing her the flowers and other presents. Nicola jumped from the passenger seat waiting for Uncle Adam to complete the introductions.

Adam made his way to the veranda, greeting his hostess in a slightly formal manner.

Nicola thought this strange, given the information she had assumed.

Pamela smiled and stepped forward to Nicola.

'I'm Pamela, you must be Nicky and this must be Vicky. Very pleased to meet you, come on in the pair of you.'

Sra Margareta, Pamela's loyal housemaid, placed wickerwork armchairs around a similar bidding everyone to make them themselves comfortable.

Victoria handed the flowers to Pamela, who thanked her for her thoughtfulness. Rosemary received a gift of a small package containing the latest fragrance from the teenage fashion counter at El Corte Ingles.

'My lucky day for flowers, Adam,' Pamela announced. 'A huge bunch of cut autumn flowers arrived this morning with a card from 'a known admirer.' Adam smiled saying nothing.

Sra Margareta returned with a tray laden with homemade lemonade, a large pot of tea, and delicate delicious cakes. As everyone relaxed, conversations quickly started up. The ladies quickly engaged in some serious girl-on-girl talk, as Adam sat back, silent, enjoying himself.

Nicola looked at her uncle deciding here was a man trying to remember his lines. She could see his lips move almost imperceptibly, wondering what would come next.

After twenty minutes, Pamela suggested Rosemary should take the girls upstairs, take their bags to her bedroom suite and to refresh themselves in her spacious bathroom. Adam felt relieved to be alone with Pamela. He moved his chair to sit alongside hers.

Adam took her left hand noticing her wedding band had moved to her other hand. 'Gosh, better get the next bit right,' he thought.

'Pamela,' he began nervously, 'Let's talk about us. You see when I first started to come here to attend to Rosemary, and her unfortunate condition, I once saw you sitting on this very veranda looking wistfully at this beautiful view of the river below. I thought to myself this is the Lady I would like to grow old with. You looked so calm and serene, but somehow sad, wondering about the future for yourself, your daughter and this vineyard.'

Plucking up courage at her receptive and beautiful face, he continued, 'The fact is I wish to ask you to be my wife, to have and to hold, forsaking all others, in sickness and health, for better or poorer, until the fateful day when nature takes its final course.'

Pamela stared at Adam in amazement. She knew her answer but needed an extra few moments to gather herself. She'd guessed this visit would be more than an ordinary house call and had prepared, accordingly.

And here was her favourite man, a wonderful friend and doctor, who had brought her daughter through an unfortunate failed pregnancy, caused in part by the death, two years ago, of her dear and beloved husband.

What a wonderful proposal, honest, sincere, and straight from the heart. He was unlike all the other carpetbaggers who had plagued her life all these months after her husband's death. Men with only sex and her assets on their mind. Divorced men whose wives had found good lawyers, and the usual incriminating evidence. Bastards all of them.

'There is an answer?' Adam asked gently. 'Crikey,' she replied.

'That's different,' said Adam, vaguely realising the noise from the upstairs bedroom of Donna Pamela de Souza Henrique's daughter had ceased.

Pamela replied, 'So you want me to be your wife,' 'Correct,' he replied.

'To have and to hold, forsaking all others.' 'Correct,' he replied.

'Tell me about the having and holding.' 'Up to you, of course,'

'In sickness and health, for better or poorer.' 'Correct,' he replied.

'Until the fateful day when nature takes its final course.' 'Absolutely,' Adam whispered.

'In this case, having answered all questions correctly, you are today's lucky Scotsman,' and flung her arms around him to give him the best kiss ever.

'I'll take this as a yes then,' Adam said, in a very relieved tone of voice. 'Correct.'

Pamela thought for a second, 'Crikey, what have I said. So, when do you think we should get married?'

'End of the year sounds about right, lots to do between now and then.'

'This means we should be engaged, don't tell me you've a come a wooing fully prepared,' said Pamela.

Adam smiled, reaching into his pocket to retrieve a bright red jewellery box, which he very slowly opened to reveal a fine engagement ring. It consisted of a three stone ring with equal settings, three centre settings with two deep blue stones and one white diamond, just over one carat each, and small settings on either side consisting of single diamonds about a quarter of a carat each, all set in the body of the ring.

'Crikey,' exclaimed Pamela, 'I've never seen topaz and diamonds together, what a beautiful combination.'

'Oh,' said Adam, 'Err, actually the blue stones are aquamarine. At this colour depth extremely rare, as they are the darkest blue with the strongest intensity.'

'Never seen aquamarine before. The colour is very deep, just like a swimming pool. Guess they are expensive,' she said.

'Only if you have to buy them. These stones are part of a much larger stone my grandfather brought back from Brazil many years ago. My father gave it to me before he died six years ago.' Pamela did know about his father's death, a very sad chapter in a man's life.

'The Rock,' as it was called, had a flaw detracting from its value, but I eventually found someone I could trust to make a smaller flawless stone, carefully leaving the leftover pieces to use in smaller settings. Which is what you see here.'

Adam reached into his other pocket and revealed a much bigger jewellery box from which he took out a magnificent high setting ring, in a halo design, comprising of a ten carat aquamarine stone, with a cluster of yellow diamonds surrounding the base. It glistened in the sunlight, and Pamela thought it looked just gorgeous.

'This will be for special occasions when we are together and you need to be a bit flash.

Otherwise best to keep it locked up very securely,' he said. 'What's it worth?' asked Pamela.

'In terms of sentimental value, it's priceless. Fiscal value, not sure. Probably buy something like a four-bed cottage and a couple of acres in the Cotswold's with stables, I should think,' replied Adam.

'Crikey, lucky me, big kiss coming,' she cried.

As the big kiss commenced, a large hubbub commenced from behind the open window into the main living room.

Siblings arrived on the veranda, happy, jolly, and shouting 'oh's, and ah's, and parabens. Pamela looked up, 'Crikey, we've been spied on.'

Rosemary rushed out, flung herself around her mother and started joyously crying, hugging, and kissing her.

'That was wonderful mummy,' she cried, 'I can't say how happy I am.'

Nicola emerged, gave her uncle a huge hug and a kiss congratulating him for the best proposal of marriage ever. Victoria came last. Adam went to give her a big hug, but remembering nor to touch her back, his embrace became rather personal.

Pamela gave him a look, 'A bit low that one,' she said. 'You can save this for me much later.'

'Comment accepted,' Adam replied. 'It's her back, it's still in recovery.' 'Can't be that bad,' said Pamela.

'You have no idea, but let's keep the subject until much later,' replied Adam.

Sra Margareta arrived with a tray laden with glasses and one very cold magnum of Champagne.

Sr. Antonio accompanied by Pamela's viticulturist, Sr. Vincente, arrived to join in the celebrations. Clearly, someone had been leaking confidential information to Sra Margareta, who saw it as her duty to have everyone around Pamela, her wonderful mistress, at this joyous moment of ending the past and the beginning of a very promising future.

Adam looked across at his nice niece and raised his glass.

'This hasn't been the surprise to you as I thought it would be,' he said.

'An inspired guess,' Nicola replied, 'So many clues. So little time to organise.'

With the champagne nearly finished, Pamela rose to thank everyone for their kind wishes and welcomed them to what had become an engagement party.

She continued, 'I must say I am overwhelmed; the future has arrived. Let us give a toast to the past and raise our glasses to say thank you for the wonderful past.'

Everyone stood and gave the toast, 'To the wonderful past.'

'And now for the future, well the champagne is finished, so now a little homework. Sr.

Vincente, if you would be so kind as to bring the wine which is to be our future.'

Sr. Vincente brought a tray with fresh glasses and two bottles of red wine. The bottles were hand-made by the local glassblower from recycled glass in many colours. The bottle had a distinctive art deco shape, with a slight twist and indentations where a finger and thumb might grip the bottle whilst pouring.

He explained this bottle came from the safra three seasons past, a year that proved to be, in his opinion, an exceptional year. He'd held back a number of barrels from that safra for long-term ageing of the wine. His hunch had proved correct, and now this wine had reached the exalted standard of 'vin de garage' or 'vinho de garage,' in Portuguese.

This was a full-bodied red wine, which should be bottled in the vineyard's bottling plant before it passes its best. This particular bottle had been laid down some six months past and he was convinced it had improved even more.

Victoria spoke up, 'What is a 'garage wine?' That's a new one on me.'

Sr. Vincente replied, 'Senhorita, a 'vin de garage' is an exceptional wine, sought by serious collectors, generally produced by little-known vineyards with low production, which fetched seriously high prices.'

'And how many barrels this wine do we have?' asked Pamela, 'And where are they stored?'

'Fifty barrels, in the south warehouse,' he replied.

'I thought the south warehouse stored only empty barrels. Anyway, when did this project start?'

'Donna Pamela, your late husband started this project four years ago,' replied Sr. Vincente, 'Thinking back, I guess he knew he had an illness he was determined to keep from us all. He had developed a new vine on the south slope extension where it showed remarkable promise. I guess this is his legacy for you and Sra Rosemary.'

Sr. Vincente wiped a tear from his eye and continued, 'This wine was above our normal average when it went to the barrel. I received detailed instructions on how to best manage this safra, and I added my own experience of many years. Now I serve and let you all be the judge.'

The wine was served and tasted in the traditional manner. 'Damn,' said Adam. 'This is good; exceptional in fact.'

'Patron, you must wait a few moments, then rinse your mouth and take another sip to get the full flavour,' cautioned Sr. Vicente, 'You see, a new wine has no expectations, so you cannot taste it before you sip. Normally you know the taste of a wine you have previously enjoyed, and this clouds judgement. Is the wine served correctly, at the right temperature, had it been treated correctly before serving, all these things are important to the connoisseur.'

Adam took the second sip, and yes, the taste had improved. Smoother, with more intriguing flavours he didn't recognise. The wine was strong increasing his hunger for lunch.

He had to agree with Sr. Vincente, he had indeed produced an exceptional wine. Time to make the next move. He fished around in his jacket pocket, pulled out his cell phone and pushed a fast dial button. The phone was answered almost immediately.

'That you?' said the husky voice on the phone. 'Marmaduke, you old fraud, how are you?' said Adam

'Never mind the platitudes. I need good news,' said the husky voice on the phone.

'My dear Marmaduke, I think we have a new wine for you. I'm sure it is what you are looking for your exhibition next month,' said Adam.

'OK, we are on our way,' said the husky voice.

'And just who is 'we,' your girlfriend?' asked Adam.

'I shall bring Mr Prince Eugen, a valuable addition to my own expertise,' said the husky voice. 'He has a new 'classic rocket ship' to test drive. We will arrive at nine a.m. in the morning.'

'OK, see you tomorrow, and thanks.' And with that Adam hung up. 'And just who is coming tomorrow, Darling?' asked Pamela pensively.

'My good friend Duke Marmaduke and his partner Mr 'Prince' Eugen Esq.,' replied Adam.

'I've heard of them; the 'East London' mafia. Isn't Mr 'Prince' the well-known motor trader?' she asked.

Adam replied, 'Prince' Eugen is a purveyor of exclusive antique and classic motor carriages to the upper gentry, a wide range of experienced specialist collectors, the 'hoi palloi,' and mug punters, of whom he takes great advantage, as he should.

Marmaduke tells everyone he originates from deepest Surry and received his education at Britain's finest establishments.'

Pamela replied, 'His schools were 'approved' no doubt; not Eton and Oxford surely?' 'No no no,' answered Adam, 'Winchester and Cambridge, or so he says.'

Pamela laughed out loud, 'Oh my, how posh, and how bloody unlikely.'

The others around the veranda looked on with interest, seeing the happy couple enjoying themselves.

'If Mr Prince is a classic motor person, perhaps he could have look at my late husband's collection of exclusive antique and classic motor carriages,' asked Pamela.

'I've never seen them,' replied Adam, 'How many are there.'

Pamela pointed at Sr. Antonio, who said, 'Patron, there are fifteen in total, ten with title, a mixture of right and left-hand drive, and five pre-war large luxury limousines, all with Spanish plates, unfortunately with no documentation.'

'Intriguing,' said Adam, 'There must be an interesting story?'

'Indeed patron,' replied Sr. Antonio, 'As the end of the Spanish civil war slowly came into view, five upper-class Republican families, not known for their love of Franco, loaded their

expensive vehicles with as many goods, valuables, and cash they could carry, then made their way into Portugal over a little-known mountain track that ends at the top of this valley.

Where they crossed the border is unknown, believed to be an old smuggler's route the forces of General Franco knew nothing or very little about. The track would have been very poor and considered impassable. That they made it into Portugal, past the Portuguese guards, became a result of either very good luck or high expense, if you know what I mean.

They made it to this Quinta and Sr. Henrique's father stored their vehicles at the back of the north warehouse. Quite what the arrangement was nobody knows. The families, their baggage, and impedimenta, were taken down to a tugboat which appeared from nowhere. It took them overnight to Oporto, where they shipped aboard a freighter bound for Central America, loaded with a local cargo of wine, olives, olive oil and other produce. What became of them has never been discovered. Sr. Henrique did make some very discrete enquiries but to no avail.'

'Interesting story.'

'Sr. Henrique always told me, he had acquired his collection, bit by bit, by diverting spare funds, or spare wine, from the business and the tax man. His intention? To build a nest egg for his family if their finances were ravaged by bad weather or misfortune. He did not intend the collection became sacred.'

'So, Pamela has a nice tax-free income just when she needs it,' commented Nicola, 'And by the sounds of it, your bank man is becoming more strident each day. Did I hear you correctly Pamela?'

'Yes, the little shit is becoming most trying, trying to get his grubby, pudgy little hands on my assets at ten cents on the dollar, or Euro in this case, trying to make himself look good with head office in Oporto. To gain the promotion he always seeks. Useless little git that he is.'

Pamela spat out these words. This horrible insignificant man had pestered her all the way through her bereavement. She sought in vain for the method to drop him in it. Now if Mr Prince is worth his salt, that day might just be on the horizon.

Sra Margareta entered the dining room with a flourish declaring lunch was more than ready and they should make a start. The extensive meal laid out before them consisted of a seafood cocktail on a bed of crisp salad and herbs, a clear consume soup from local onions, white fish from the river cooked in white wine and more herbs, and the 'piece de résistance,' local pork baked in the Portuguese style with English vegetables, crisp roast potatoes, a tasty thick gravy, and a homemade mustard sauce.

Pamela bid everyone take their places at the table alternating gentlemen and ladies so the gentlemen could move one place to the right after each course. As it became time for the delicious main course, Adam found himself sitting opposite his wife to be. He marvelled at his luck. She had accepted his proposal with little hesitation and saw a great weight had fallen from her shoulders. Now she was getting back to her best, smiling and laughing with everyone, and looking just drop dead gorgeous.

Pamela sensed she was being stared at, looked across at Adam, gave him a big smile, and winked. The next two courses, the dessert course, then cheese and biscuits would bring him back to her side.

The moment of reunion arrived, 'Hello stranger, come this way often?' 'Always,' replied Adam.

Chapter 7

The Future Arrives at the Quinta

THE SUMPTUOUS lunch slowly came to an end. The diners made their way to the comfortable armchairs on the veranda in which to doze for the remainder of the afternoon. Adam saw Victoria was comfortable. She had eaten her first big meal sensibly throughout. She looked much better, but tired, which he considered normal. Victoria dozed off as Nicola and Rosemary disappeared upstairs for some extended girl talk.

Adam found himself alone with Pamela sitting on the comfortable double rattan sofa. They cuddled and found themselves dozing off. After an hour Pamela decided she wanted to go for an after-dinner walk.

'Get up lazy bones,' she whispered in his ear, 'walkies,' at which both dogs woke up presenting themselves ready for a much-needed run about.

'No rest for the wicked,' muttered Adam, slowly rising to his feet. 'Where are we off to, anywhere exciting?' he asked.

'No. Just a slow perambulation around the estate. I thought we could look at this car collection I know so little about. Sr. Antonio will be there. He knows the cars are in play, I suspect he has an offer of a bonus from my dearly departed husband, it's the sort of thing he used to do.'

The happy couple set-off arm-in-arm. Pamela couldn't be happier. The two dogs raced ahead such was the level of joy in the 'Quinta da Souza Henrique.' Pamela asked if Adam thought it an idea to change the name of the vineyard.

Adam gave her a definite no. The vineyard should stay in the family name. Rosemary would eventually inherit, and he hoped the family name would continue. Rosemary could be what, sixth generation or perhaps seventh. Pamela wasn't sure, but the vineyard had certainly been in operation a long time in the same family.

Now Rosemary had put the unhappy past behind her she had thrown herself into understanding every aspect of the business, making Pamela feel more at ease with her daughter's future.

They discussed who would live where. Adam had his clinic in Oporto, and by the sounds of it, could achieve a rapid rise in business. Here in the Upper Douro Valley, the vineyard was also poised for good advancement, so what would be the best way to stay together.

'Good question?' thought Adam, but he assured Pamela they would spend their happy days and nights together. The clinic would need an additional partner by the middle of next year, so there would be a good option for them to travel together when the need arose.

He also expected to get out from under the suspension of his UK licence by the British Medical Association. The BMA had acted in error. Great Aunt Violet had influence and discovered the truth of the matter. He had his EU Licence, recently confirmed, courtesy of friendship with certain female patients with influential husbands. Adam continued to slowly build his reputation the correct way, never hurrying, just letting things fall into place in their own time.

As the happy couple breasted a rise in the landscape, Adam saw the industrial area of the vineyard. He saw four large warehouses, laid out in a diamond shape, giving rise to their obvious names, north, east, south, and west.

Hidden in a small dead-end valley, Adam could see a number of buildings which he took to be the modest bottling plant, a similarly sized distillery, and a large building for the making of the wine itself.

'Very self-contained. Well organised,' he thought.

The large doors on the north warehouse were wide open. Adam saw Sr. Antonio waiting for them with the cars at the far end. The rest of the warehouse was full of empty wine barrels ready for this year's harvest.

Sr. Antonio removed the protective covers from each vehicle. Adam stared at the quality and diversity of the collection. The front row consisted of the cars which Sr. Antonio confirmed had the correct titles and were available for sale. Adam didn't see a single car he wouldn't gladly buy. .

The first; an early first edition 3.8 litre Jaguar E-Type. Next, a 1952 XK120 and a 64' Mini Cooper S convertible with a factory competition engine, and one of the last of the big three litres Rover Coupes. Behind, stood a parade consisting of a two door Mercedes sports car, a '61 Bentley coupe, Fiat Spider coupe with a Ferrari engine, and an Austin Healy 3000.

'Oh my God. I'm in heaven,' thought Adam.

At the far side, he saw a competition Lancia Delta. Last but not least, surely not a Maserati, in a stunning metallic red.

Adam pointed at the Maserati, as Sr. Antonio broke into a very broad grim. 'Senhor, you do not recognise this car?' he said.

Adam shrugged and said, 'Err no, unfortunately.' 'Patron, this

Maserati, could be close to priceless.'

Pamela stood in awe, with no idea what she was looking at, but the best day in her life was getting better.

'Adam. I vaguely remember Henrique talking about this car, but the details never registered. Antonio, how valuable is this car?'

'I have no idea of value without ringing the specialists. The last thing you need is someone getting all excited and making himself unwanted. This is one of the last genuine Maserati Mille Miglia's which could be worth millions of Euros. My father told me how it came to be here, all legal but in very unusual circumstances.'

'Maybe a tax thing,' suggested Pamela. 'I think we should go for a spin.'

'It's never been registered,' said Sr. Antonio, 'It arrived in a horse box and has very few kilometres. In fact, most of these cars have never been registered. All the cars are in excellent condition. Send any of these cars for detailing, they will return as new. They all have matching numbers, are original in every respect, and have provenance. Let me show you the vehicles at the back.'

The three of them made their way to the back of the warehouse, and Adam's jaw dropped open. Stood in a row, with the rear of each car against the back wall, he saw a parade of wealth from the 1920's and 1930's he couldn't imagine, the best in luxury motoring of the era. He was speechless.

'Here we have Donna Pamela,' began Sr. Antonio, 'The vehicles abandoned in the late 1930's by their escaping owners, as General Franco's forces closed in around those he wished to, err, 'interview,' in his usual vigorous manner. We have two Rolls-Royce's, a Mercedes, a Hispano-Suiza, and a Maybach.

There are no papers with these cars, but all are fully functioning. Three years ago, Sr. Henrique made a visit to Madrid to try to obtain their records, only to be told the office holding such records had been bombed during the civil war, so there is no providencc. Perhaps Mr Prince Eugen could assist in this matter.'

Adam thought for a moment and said, 'It is possible, this can't be a totally unique case. Perhaps collectors are more interested in the cars; perhaps the factories would have records.'

'Sr. Henrique also had these thoughts, but with so many records lost during WW2, especially in Germany,' said Sr. Antonio. 'Donna Pamela do you have any idea of what cars you would like to sell; and which ones to keep?'

'Well, we need the money, so the right-hand drive cars can be sold first. I guess I had better sleep on it. By the way, can you prepare my Citroen for tomorrow? We will go to Oporto to see Sr. de Oliveira.'

It was time to return to the Qunita to see what mischief the other ladies were up to. Pamela's two dogs had long vanished to the comfort of their dog baskets and their canine senses had detected food was ready on the veranda.

Pamela found Victoria fast asleep upstairs. Rosemary and Nicola were in deep conversation about matters that looked a little suspicious.

'You two are getting on well, penny for your thoughts?' asked Pamela. She received no reply.

'Well, that's nice,' thought Pamela, as she headed to the kitchen to ask about the evening meal. Sra Margareta had prepared a cold table on the dining room sideboard for everyone to help themselves. A Russian silver and enamelled samovar gently issued steam; next to it a range of different teas in a Harrod's gift set box.

AS THE SUN surrendered to the onset of nightfall the happy couple helped themselves, then repaired to the veranda to wish goodbye to a very successful day for the pair of them. Adam felt very relaxed. He couldn't believe his luck.

Pamela considered going to the small chapel buried in the small wood near the main entrance to the vineyard. It was her late husband's favourite place. Much good all this praying did for his health. She reluctantly decided to remain by the side of this wonderful man who had come to save her day.

Adam turned to Pamela to ask about sleeping arrangements, being careful to accept any edict. Pamela smiled inwardly, telling him the three girls, as she called them, would use Rosemary's extensive on-suite apartment. The guest bedrooms dividing Rosemary's quarters from her own were unfortunately, unavailable as they were undergoing restoration in preparation for a new line of business, taking in paying house guests.

Pamela offered him the choice of the sofa in the office next to her bedroom suite, or the more comfortable sofa downstairs in the main parlour. It would be necessary for him to use her on-suite bathroom and did he need a bathrobe?

As night fell, the family gathered for the evening meal. Sra Margareta left them all to it, as both Sr. Antonio and Sr. Vincente said their goodnights to return home. As the meal came to an end, the three girls did the honours clearing everything away into the kitchen.

With little to watch on television, Adam and Pamela retired upstairs to continue talking about the many matters coming into focus now they were soon to become man and wife.

Adam suggested a more romantic evening. Pamela felt relieved at the suggestion, leaving more serious matters to discussed later. The only thing he wanted to discuss, business wise was the upcoming visit to Sr. Augusto de Oliveira, the owner of Oporto's leading high-end port manufacturer, the following day.

There had been a big falling out between Pamela and de Oliviera just under a year ago. Pamela had been to see de Oliveira about the sale of the next Safra and de Oliviera had been in a bad mood for whatever reason. He was under pressure with his finances, but who wasn't in the Douro Valley.

Pamela had reached an exceptionally low depth with the second anniversary of her husband's death remaining a very recent memory. Her daughter was in the middle of a major rebellion, her usual was two months late, and the local bank manager more than unusually difficult.

Having been good friends for many years she relied on de Oliveira's support and here he attempted to play her off against a rival vineyard. She had snapped letting de Oliveira have it, both barrels, 'sans repetition' and no holds barred.

De Oliveira had been shocked to the core, his English wife Charlotte saying nothing. When she had finished her rant, Pamela stormed out, little expecting de Oliveira would indeed buy that season's Safra from the other vineyard.

Now she had been stuck with two hundred barrels of wine she saw no market for, other than bottling it herself and selling it cheap to a cold-hearted UK supermarket chain.

Pamela looked at Adam and simply asked, 'Why are we visiting de Oliveira, what's the big occasion?'

Adam lay back in the comfortable bedroom sofa, pulled her towards him and gave her a big cuddle. She moulded her body into his, relaxed and thought, 'What's next. What conjuring trick had this heaven-sent man brought to ease my worried mind?'

'Well Darling,' he started, 'de Oliveira misses your friendship terribly. Too proud to say so of course. Charlotte, his wife, had been chipping away at his ego for some time and now the message is loud and clear. 'Get it sorted, and soon.'

So, I end up as piggy in the middle, so what to do? Now then, very recent events have worked in your favour. The wine de Oliveira bought from a.n.other had not responded to his tender loving care and the next batch of his high class and expensive product was well below par.

Then, two days ago, the large Ageing Vat 'Number #7' was badly damaged by fire when a carelessly parked vehicle caught fire ruining the wines from the other vineyard.

Pamela purred deliciously, 'Oh, what a shame.'

Adam continued, 'Now de Oliveira is in a mad panic to get his 'Number #7' Vat repaired and he's desperately looking for a supply of aged wine to get his production back on track. He knows about the two hundred barrels you have, but not from me.'

'There's nothing in this damn valley de Oliveira doesn't know about,' snapped Pamela. 'So tomorrow will be the tearful reunion. Charlotte will be conducting affairs. She is a good friend and calls me quite often when 'he' is out.'

'So Pamala,' said Adam, 'You are we feeling a lot happier and relaxed?'

'Yes, thank you. Time for bed. You can use my bathroom first. Have a shower and I'll make your bed up in the office.'

Adam took a long hot shower to remove the exertions of the day. What a wonderful day it had been. Now he needed a good night's sleep. He dried himself, found a small bottle of men's body spray in his wash bag, cleaned his teeth, donned his bathrobe, and headed for the office sofa.

Pamela by this time had changed into her silk nightdress. She asked Adam to bring up two glasses with a jug of water for the night. He heard her upstairs taking a shower, so he sat down for a few minutes. The sounds upstairs ceased, time to kiss his beloved good night and head to bed.

As he entered her bedroom Pamela asked him to lock the bedroom door. This done Adam wandered into the adjacent office. His sofa bed had been made up and it didn't look too uncomfortable.

'Goodnight kiss time, Adam,' her voice whispered through the doorway. He returned to find Pamela already under the sheets, in the middle of a large ornate king-sized double bed.

A low-level bedside light bathed a warm glow to the bedroom and didn't she just look like the most beautiful woman in the world. Adam bent down to give Pamela her goodnight kiss. As he finished, an arm appeared around his neck, holding him down to her.

'And just where do you think you're going to mister? Sit with me and be comfortable,' she said, nibbling his ear

The arm wrapped itself tightly around his neck, as he fell onto his side, lying next to her. 'This is more comfortable, eh!' she said, 'Better get under the sheets before you catch a cold, which you will do when you divest yourself of your bathrobe.' He laid down next to her in a tight embrace.

'Is this heaven,' he thought, as he rolled on top of her and felt her starting to move under him in a most sensuous manner. They kissed and kissed again. Hands wandered invitingly bringing even more feelings of pleasure to both.

After a while, Adam raised himself up to look down on her beauty. Pamela wore the flimsiest baby doll night dress he ever had the pleasure of looking at. She wore similar baby doll knickers, with one side tied together with a thin bow of material, where one tug would cause the garment too, well, reveal all.

No words were said, none were needed, as the natural course of two lovers got down to catching up on what comes naturally. As he lay still, deep inside her, she pulled him down repeatedly, ever hungry for his kisses.

Her face was a picture of passion and contentment, he lay still for a moment, and then, she started to whisper instructions into the ear she had been licking for the last ten minutes.

'Now, slow, nice and slow. It's been a long time,' she said.

Slow felt good, slightly faster became better, then faster still, and with Pamela groaning with pleasure under him, they both climaxed together. Adam rolled onto his side, his mind a whirl of pleasure and achievement. If this was going to be married life, just where was the nearest church, and a waiting priest?

'To have and to hold,' she whispered in his other ear, 'I love those words when you proposed. Fair make a girl's heart all of a flutter.'

'Is your heart fluttering?' he said, 'I should check, as he lowered his lips to her fulsome breasts and started to drive her crazy by kissing her erect nipples.'

'I'll give two hours to stop,' she said.

'Message received and understood,' came the reply. Later, much later, matters came to a gentle stop. 'Crikey,' she said. 'That felt good, whew what a day.' 'Happy?' he asked.

'Wine please. It's open, under the bedside table.'

Adam realised Pamela had prepared for a long night of passion. He served the wine which tasted even better than at lunch time. Tonight would be a night to remember.

He drank his glass dry, and lay on his back, resting. A fair pair of breasts, the fairest in the land, landed on his lips. Pamela had moved on top of him, her hand searching for signs of life. He responded and soon she started giving him the 'magic fingers' treatment. He responded in kind; this was his area of specialisation. A mini contest ensued, but not for long. The lady could not wait any longer as she lowered herself on him.

This was heaven; as he slowly arched his back, his lady pressed down upon him. He relaxed, and then repeated the motion. The motions increased, and soon she was in full song with pleasure and sensuous movement.

Her climax came quickly with more intensity. Exhausted she lay upon him, still content, her face a picture of happiness.

'Crikey, I really do love you, Adam. We shall live happily ever after,' she said, Adam replied. 'No doubt about it.'

They lay in the stillness of the night, then Pamela's back stiffened. She heard something, and that something was outside her bedroom door.

'The little bitch,' she muttered to herself. 'Listening at my door, goddamn it.'

Pamela rose, donned the high heel ankle strap shoes she'd flung into the corner of her room a few nights ago and had failed to tidy up the following day.

She stood up in all her magnificent glory. Adam could only look in wonder, 'What a girl,' he thought.

'Like the view doctor?' she said. Adam spluttered, barely able to speak.

'Let's show this young upstart of mine what sex is really all about.'

Pamela carefully unlocked the door without a sound, flung the door open to confront two giggling ladies kneeling at her door, with a startled Nicola half sitting on a chest of drawers in the hallway.

'Well, you two, learn anything?' Pamela snarled at them.

She was angry at the interruption. Rosemary and Victoria looked up in shock and awe at the sight of Pamela, standing there, in her altogether, proud, and angry.

'Shouldn't you be wearing a vest under your outfit, Mummy?' spluttered Rosemary, only to receive a sharp slap around her ears. Victoria retreated. Nicola sought to gain distance too. Should they leave Rosemary to her fate, or rescue her, but they saw Pamela had broken into a big smile.

'If you've bugged my room Miss Rosemary, you'll be homeless tomorrow morning.'

A shocked Rosemary could only splutter the video bug had stopped working, but she thought the sound recording would be OK. Victoria burst into loud laughter,

Nicola stood calmly by. The high spirits of her two companions in crime had caused a fuss, but the fuss would not last long. This was a happy household. She saw her uncle propped up in bed, enjoying the view, remaining calm with his enigmatic smile.

Pamela sensed her lover enjoying the spectacle of her derrière just peeping below her baby doll night dress. She wondered if the vision would lead her lover to find additional energy, now there's a thought?

Pamela marched the three younger members of the female household back to Rosemary's bedroom, returned, locked the door halfway down the interconnecting hall, locked her bedroom door behind her and knelt beside him. Adam looked up at her, admiring the view and wondering if he could rise to the occasion.

'More wine vicar?' he requested, 'It's thirsty work, this 'changing of the guard.'

She laughed as she served the last of the wine. As his glass emptied, she fell upon him, but to no avail. Half-post was of little use to this lady, and try as she might, time had come for kisses, cuddles and sleep, so operations could resume as the cock crowed its strident message at five-thirty in the morning.

The kissing and the cuddling lasted sufficiently long enough for the happy couple to fall into a deep blissful sleep, or as Adam would ask the next morning, 'What was best, the sleep of the just, or the sleep of the just after.'

No contest, she thought, as for the first time in a long time, she would have the very best of sweet dreams.

Five-thirty a.m. arrived bang on time with the infernal noise made by a very strident cockerel. Many times Pamela had thought to ring its neck and confine it to the large cauldron on the wood fuelled stove in the main kitchen. There was little point, Sra Margareta was a farmer's daughter and would only replace it with another.

Pamela looked over at her sleeping fiancé. He looked sound asleep, past the promised hour of early morning sex, for which Pamela was more than ready.

'Let's see what we can conjure up,' she thought.

She lifted the sheets, admiring Adam's fully erect manhood.

'That's a good start,' she thought. 'Handy in the shower room. Somewhere to hang a large bathroom towel.'

She nibbled his ear. He seemed to like it, but he didn't waken. She slid on top of him and helped herself. With Adam deep inside her she slowly nibbled at his other ear, but his face remained calm and static. She wriggled her pelvis a little bit but received no response. She wriggled a bit more for the same result. Pamela was in no hurry, as she rested upon him, enjoying the peace of the morning.

'Bom dia Amor,' whispered a wide-awake Adam. 'Is this to your satisfaction?'

Pamela reached the moment of climax, 'You cheeky sod,' she told him. 'Now get busy.' 'Plenty of time for that,' he said. 'You started and I shall finish.'

Pamela climaxed, but Adam kept going and going, and soon she entered a different world she didn't want to leave. Adam tried to prolong the magic moment.

He kissed her nipples as hard as he could dare. She writhed under him and in a moment, it was all over.

She lay on top of him panting, both arms around his neck, smothering him with deep kisses. What a way to start the day. Eventually, she rolled onto her side and cuddled him as tightly as she could. Adam responded and gently fell once more into a deep sleep.

Pamela followed suit, this wonderful man had fulfilled all her longings and desires.

Chapter 8

Another Interesting Day in the Vale do Douro

THE BEDROOM alarm clock announced the half of the hour of eight a.m. 'Oops, guests are due in thirty minutes' thought Pamela; guests with a promise of getting her business back on track. Time for a hot shower and beautification.

When she had finished, she slipped downstairs wearing smart cotton slacks, a colourful silk top, and her favourite and extravagant house slippers. She had put her hair up in a bun, fixed with a bejewelled clasp and adorned her neck with an expensive multi-coloured necklace of semi-precious stones.

Pamela found Sra Margareta busy putting out breakfast, laying nine places with cutlery, napkins, and fruit juice. In the centre of the large dining room table lay a selection of various fruits, cereals, and large jugs of farm fresh milk. The sideboard was covered with ornate wooden panels under electrical hotplates so the various dishes of a full English cooked breakfast could be laid out.

Pamela picked at the dried fruit bowl and went to the samovar to make her first coffee of the day. Sounds of movement from either end of upstairs were absent, so Pamela rang the fire bell to make everyone get a move on.

With only five minutes to go before the appointed hour, she could hear no signs of her impending guests arriving. Sra Margareta heard something and opened the kitchen windows.

The sounds of a powerful engine screaming for mercy became apparent. The sound came and went as the vehicle quickly made its way up the winding road that followed the contours of the hills and valleys on the north side of the river.

The engine dropped a note as gears changed to the lower end of the gearbox, the engine screamed once more, then a split-second respite, followed by the engine bring thrashed to within an inch of its life.

'It's just crossed the bridge, now it's coming along the south side of the river, and now up the hill to the main entrance to the Quinta,' said Sra Margareta, 'And it is 08.58. Good timing.'

Two minutes later, a Lamborghini 400 GT slid to a halt in front of the veranda and two gentlemen got out. Pamela used the word 'gentlemen,' but she sure as hell didn't know what she was looking at. They both wore white racing overalls and crash hats, quickly removed, and flung into the rear their car.

The taller of the two wore an extravagant outfit of outrageous coloured clothing which screamed 'fag,' and the other, a shorter slim person, dressed uniformly in black.

Pamela moved to greet them. She looked at the taller of the two and said, 'Mr Duke Marmaduke I assume, and this must be Mr Prince Eugen?'

Duke Marmaduke extravagantly kissed her out-stretched hand and replied, 'It's my immense pleasure to meet you my dear, and this is indeed my partner, Prince Eugen.'

'Come inside,' Pamela invited. 'The others are struggling into the day and won't be long.

Can I serve you some tea or coffee?'

The two visitors gratefully accepted a mug of tea. It had been an exciting drive from Oporto, between excessive speed and waking up half the population of the Douro Valley.

The 'Lambo,' as they insisted on calling it, had undergone a full restoration. Its Bizzarrini V12 engine had undergone full upgrading, transmitting more power than the chassis could usefully use. Still, the new owner, who lived at the head of the Douro Valley had given Prince Eugen 'carte blanch' to meet his exacting specification.

As they drank their tea, Pamela asked how long it had taken to drive from Oporto. The standard time for ordinary mortals was usually just under three hours, depending upon the traffic and the number of farmers who drove at the same speed as their crops grew.

'Yes ducks. Took it kind of steady, kind of running it in as you might say, just under two hours.'

His Cockney accent washed over her like a wave, a real 'hello guv, awright' accent. It would never change, even for royalty which, apparently, was quite often.

'So, you avoided the speed cameras then,' said Pamela, 'And you have knocked an hour off my best time.'

'Well love,' Prince replied. 'There's a cover over the back of the car, it ain't registered anyway, so the law can fill its boots. I've got an 'orse box comin' to collect and deliver to the new owner, a recluse apparently, wants to put the damn car in 'is new garden conservatory extension, just to look at.'

Obviously, the early morning jaunt had done him the world of good, man versus the law, bloody law. Duke said nothing, as though it had all been as expected, and anyway, he was just the passenger. He enjoyed going fast and did not have the skill to match his partner.

Time for breakfast. Adam arrived all spruced up, looking trim and incredibly pleased with himself. It was cravat day. He sported a particularly colourful example in dark shades of red, purple, and yellow. Quite symbolic of what. Who knows?

'Morning everyone,' Adam greeted, 'Hi Duke, glad your chauffeur got you here in one piece. Another warp speed experience I trust?'

Duke returned the greeting. He considered his journey had been quite restful and sedate, so much so he almost fell asleep, having risen at such a hideously early hour.

The three girls from Rosemary's bedroom clattered down the stairs, looking all prim and proper, said a general hi to everyone, and plonked themselves down at the table.

The magnificent breakfast took an hour. By ten a.m. everyone had eaten their fill, and the day's programme had started to slip away. Pamela knew the discussion on the wine would take some time. She also needed Prince to look at her late husband's car collection.

As breakfast slowly came to a close, Pamela stood up asking if everyone had had sufficient. Time was limited, suggesting that Prince, Rosemary and Sr. Antonio go to the North warehouse to examine the car collection, whilst she, Duke and Adam concentrated on the wine he had an interest in.

'Wot car collection, and 'ow many cars and where from?' exclaimed Prince excitedly. Pamela handed him the list without prices.

'You gotta' be kidding me.' 'Interested, or not?' asked Pamela. 'Is the Pope a Catholic?' said Prince.

Prince looked across at Rosemary, 'Come on darlin,' we've work to do,' and with that, they disappeared out the door to what Prince hoped would be Aladdin's Cave.

Sr. Vincente arrived and announced he was ready to receive everyone in the library.

Pamela, Adam, Duke and the two girls trouped into the library.

Duke delighted in the sight of two large wooden trays carrying wine bottles, still water in glass decanters and wine glasses, all sitting on top of a large antique sideboard.

One tray was mysteriously covered over, which Duke paid little heed to. The uncovered tray was brought to the table, and Sr. Vincente bid everyone sit down and get comfortable.

He served everyone a glass of water to refresh their taste buds. Next, he commenced with a quick review on how to taste the wine he was going to present, making his apologies to Duke, a recognised master of the art.

Sr. Vincente commenced his brief class. 'First, to Look; to experience the wine's breadth, start by drinking in its appearance, its clarity and colour.

Next, to Smell; the nose connects directly to your mouth, stimulating the palate. Inhale deeply and identify the first scent you detect.

Then, it is time to Taste; Take a small sip and hold it in your mouth. Different areas of the tongue detect salt, bitterness, and sweetness

A wine,' he said, 'Is considered 'balanced' when its components work in harmony. Tannins should have an agreeable astringency, the acidity should be pleasant, but not overwhelming.'

To finish, assess the wine's 'Finish,' the taste in your mouth after swallowing. What is it like and how long does it last? Ripe, balanced flavours and a lingering finish are the signs of a quality wine.'

Duke started to get restless. He was an anxious man and this preamble not what he had expected.

Sr. Vincente handed Duke the first glass, commenting that around the table was a wide forum of different drinkers and a non-expert opinion, which in his view, could be just as helpful as an expert view.

Duke followed the established and well-trod procedure, looked at the glass in his hand, wondering what his opinion would be.

The wine did not meet his expectation, but he sipped some more water and repeated the process. Duke could see Adam was with him on this one. Pamela kept a blank face, as the two girls swigged the wine down asking for more.

'Pamela,' started Duke, 'This is not a 'garage wine' by any respects. Explain. I 'ave not come all this way for this.'

'Keep calm Duke, I just need your opinion. This is not the wine you have come to taste.'

Slightly mollified, Duke sat back to think what his honest opinion would be. He thought for a moment and then said, 'Well it's not a bad table wine. The upper range of what a supermarket would sell. But then another table wine the market doesn't need.'

'So, what would be its best use, given we are in the Douro Valley,' asked Pamela. The penny dropped, 'Is this the wine you want to sell to de Oliveira?' Duke asked. Pamela nodded an affirmative.

'Well now, there's a thing,' mused Duke. 'If de Oliveira could work his magic, he should be able to make a very decent 'Colheita Port,' in which case yours truly would be extremely interested indeed in bringing it to market.'

'Excellent judgement, my thoughts entirely,' commented Sr. Vincente.

'And how much of this wine do you have Pamela and is the quality even?' asked Duke. 'Sr. Vincente has forty thousand litres minimum before losses due to ageing. Can you handle this quantity?' asked Pamela.

'Of course, here in the vineyard I could distil the necessary volume of wine to produce the 'aqua quente,' the alcohol needed for blending. this should bump up the quality, don't you think? Should give over twenty-five hundred cases, what do you think?'

Duke asked for the test sheet he saw on the sideboard. Sr. Vincente handed him a copy. Duke looked hard at the figures, smiled, and said, 'Well, jolly good show chaps, now what about the real wine.'

Sr. Vincente replaced the first tray on the table and with a flourish removed the covering from the second tray. Duke stared at two art deco bottles, clearly hand crafted.

'Nice touch,' he thought. 'Should be good for product identity.'

Pamela's viticulturist moved smoothly into action, now came his moment after years of hard work. He poured a glass of wine for everyone, put them down in front of each expectant person and stood back.

Duke looked at his glass. He needed this tasting to be a success. He needed one new wine to present at his upcoming show in his favourite castle. His guests and his potential customers had to be satisfied in their expectations.

Step One, hold the glass and look. The wine seemed to grin back at him, the colour deep, clear, and different. The wine assaulted his nose, wow, this was different, new sensations flooded his senses.

He hesitated, everyone in the room stared at him. Step Two, now to the taste, he took a sip, rolled it around his mouth and spat it into the waiting spittoon.

He took another deeper sip, waited for the sensations to come, and then swallowed the wine in one go. The tension in the room was palpable. Duke bid everyone complete their evaluation.

Pamela could not wait any longer, 'Well?' she asked.

'Is there anymore, please?' asked Duke. 'That was absolutely wonderful.'

Pamela let out a big sigh of relief.

Adam agreed the wine did have very special qualities. Victoria drank the whole glass and started to giggle. Adam told her off and drink more water. The wine had strength she did not have.

Nicola said she liked the wine, agreed it tasted special, but she was no expert.

Sr. Vincente handed the test sheet for Duke to examine. 'This wine is still strong. A slightly higher alcohol content than usual, both a plus and a minus point,' he thought.

Duke asked, 'And you have fifty barrels; quantity per barrel?'

Sr. Vincente was sure each barrel had a minimum of two hundred litres. 'We can supply ten thousand bottles or about eight hundred cases; we can also supply the art deco bottles in a range of assorted colours, or any other colour he wanted.'

Duke was impressed, the wine met his expectations. The added ideas to bring a different identity to the product a definite bonus and he thought he knew all the marketing ploys for the wine industry.

'OK. An excellent wine. Well up to my expectations. The art deco bottles are a nice touch should have thought of it myself. So how about price?'

'Now there is a very good question,' replied Pamela, 'I have discussed this at length with Sr. Vincente, and the answer is sixty-six Euros a bottle, or eight hundred Euros a case. This is a net gate price, everything else is up to you. We need to start bottling very soon to keep the maximum quality, which means I need to place an order for bottles, for which I shall need funding.'

She saw Duke in deep contemplation. Pamela continued, 'This is not a one-off. Last year's crop comes from the same special area in our vineyard. It is just as good if not slightly better, and about the same quantity.

'A bit steep,' replied Duke. 'Don't know if I can go this high. I have collection and shipping costs; plus any fiscal duties I cannot avoid. Is there a better offer?'

Pamela looked at him dead-eyed and said nothing. She was not going to get into any discussion. Sr. Vincente had assessed the market with great care. His research suggested a price of over one hundred British pounds per bottle, with the expectation this rare wine would be snapped up by collectors. This assumed Mr Duke was the master of his craft.

Sr. Vincente added, 'Senhor, you could lay down half of what you buy and sell the remainder to meet your costs. This wine will improve in the bottle for sure, the price could go anywhere.'

Duke could see 'Team Pamela' had done their homework. For him, his basic price would be a thousand quid a case, end of subject. If he could not sell this wine, if Prince couldn't sell this wine, it would be time to retire.

Victoria broke into the conversation. She had been busy scribbling on a sheet of paper, showed it to Adam who agreed he could do that.

'My suggestion,' said Victoria, 'Duke forks out thirty Euros a bottle for the ten thousand bottles. The wine is moved to Oporto and laid down in the Convent underground cells. The cells are secure, and the environment is ideal, cool, with little change in yearly temperature. Then, on collection, the balance can be paid by whatever means. You could have your clients come and collect if you wish. Anyway, it's all on this sheet of paper. Here you are.'

Duke sat back and thought a moment, but his thoughts were destroyed by the arrival of a hyperactive Mr Prince, with Rosemary and Sr. Antonio trailing behind.

'Bleedin' 'ell Guv,' he started, 'Just bin' to Aladdin's bleedin' cave. What a collection.' 'Language, if you please Mr Prince, we 'ave ladies present,' chided Duke, 'Sit down, calm down, shut up, and taste this wine.

Prince did as he was bid. His version of the wine tasting procedure was shorter than his partner, but he went through the motions.

'Not bad, like the art deco bottle. Do the deal; then we can talk cars.'

Duke handed him Victoria's sheet of paper. 'Blimey, that's fair old number, give me two seconds.'

Prince studied the sheet of paper, looked at Duke, 'It's a steal, is this agreed?'

'I haven't said yes, but then I haven't said no,' intoned Duke, 'I need your honest considered opinion. With a value well over a quarter of a big one, this is a step that needs a firm understanding of the issues.'

Prince asked for a refill of his glass and held it out until full to the top.

'Any cheese and biscuits,' he asked, as he sipped carefully taking his time. The cheese and biscuits arrived; he sipped and munched his way through a plate of blue cheese and plain biscuits.

'Ah, the reception test,' thought Pamela, 'I have never seen this before.'

Prince looked around. He didn't like being stared at. He liked the look of Nicola, 'I could fancy 'er,' he thought. Too late Mr Prince had a loving wife at home, who could read his thoughts the second he walked into the house.

'Looks good to me,' he said, 'Trim up the details later but give the Lady the bank draft, we can sure make money on this deal,' he concluded smiling like a contented Cheshire cat.

Pamela's heart leapt with joy, trying hard not to show it. The future continued to build.

Adam looked very happy, as was everyone else.

Prince turned to Pamela, 'Darlin,' can I get an exclusive to shift these cars for you, please.' 'I'll think about it,' she kidded.

A large horse box arrived at the front of the veranda and backed up to the waiting Lamborghini.

'Good timing,' said Prince, 'Let me complete this car deal first.'

Prince and Duke went outside. An impeccably dressed man came up to them, asked various questions, handed over a very thick packet to Prince, bidding his two assistances load his master's new pride and joy into the horse box. Then, he was gone.

'Now where was I,' asked Prince, 'Oh yes, 'ow much for the Mini Cooper, I'll offer forty grand in Euros, cash this minute. You got the papers, right.'

Pamela looked astounded. She did need the money urgently. Her staff were behind in their wages and there were bills to pay. Where was the list of cars with the prices? Sr. Antonio gave her his copy. The money was bang on, a good deal it certainly was.

'Prince, are you going to, as you say, flip this car, or what?' she asked.

'Nah, it's for me, 'bin lookin' for a good one 'ver ages, scarce as rockin' 'orse dung they are,' he replied.

'OK, deal,' as Pamela shook his hand.

Prince could hardly wait to extract the cash from the packet he had just received. Prince finished his wine and asked for a refill, the last of the bottle. Celebrating with the contents of a hundred quid a bottle wine seemed a good idea to him.

'Duke, me old son,' started Prince, 'I'm a goin' to buy you a present; there's a car that's just you. A nice big flashy Rover, a three-litre, in Admiralty Blue and Light Grey, the last of the big coupes. It will match your most extravagant togs and you can give your favourite punters a smooth ride whilst hit them with your even smoother patter.

'Ow' much Mrs P, another forty?'

Pamela knew the price of this car. She had considered keeping it, a gift from her late husband, but the future had arrived, and she was very comfortable with her Citroën DS 23 Cabriolet d'Usine, with its soft top.

'Put another six in the pot, and it's a deal,' she said.

Prince looked hard at Pamela. Did this family know everything about anything he wanted to talk about?

'OK, love, it's a deal, well done, you deserve it,' he said, as he handed over the money.

'I'll take the Mini today and collect the Rover later. I need my man to come and check your other cars if that's OK.'

By the time the Mr Prince 'floor show' was over, Duke had made a few amendments to Vicky's sheet of paper and handed it to Pamela. No real changes, so she initialled, passed it to Rosemary to put her mark and handed it back.

Duke signed it, asked Prince to make his mark, and returned it to Pamela. 'Can you make some copies, please,' he asked.

Duke handed over a banker's draft for the wine he had just bought. Pamela looked at the draft. Her financial worries fell away. Time for coffee, it had been a busy morning and the grandfather clock in the hall chimed the middle of the day.

Sra Margareta served coffee with sandwiches and pastries, with a water jug and glasses for those who wished.

Pamela told Duke they could not delay much longer as they had to get to the bank in Pinhâo and then to visit with Sr. Augusto de Oliveira.

Adam had a quiet word with Pamela, nodding in agreement at what he told her.

'Duke, an idea for you and Prince,' he started, 'I think an arrangement between ourselves and de Oliveira could work to the advantage of us all.'

Duke asked a few questions, but it boiled down to the basics. Pamela Ltda would make high-grade wine; de Oliveira would transform it into high-grade port and Duke with Prince would market the products to their exclusive clients.

Duke and Prince both agreed they would let Pamela bring this idea to the table and take it from there.

Coffee finished, Pamela told Duke and Prince they had to be off. Sr. Antonio disappeared to extract the Mini Cooper from the warehouse to get it ready for their return journey to Oporto, meanwhile, they could help or relax as best suited themselves.

Prince had a word in Rosemary's ear. He told her de Oliveira's son, Marcos, had returned to work with his father, and she should dress to impress, something simple and classic. He pointed at her mother wearing an expensive white pleated skirt, silk top just showing off her classic bra underneath, hair up and the correct accessories.

Rosemary looked at Mr Prince in a new light. This man's rough act was just that. Underneath was a calm and cunning man, no wonder he made a lot of money. She asked him a question about Marmaduke and his outrageous clothes.

Nicky and Vicky hadn't turned a hair when they met him. Prince replied, 'Oh, that's just Duke, he always dresses outrageously in public. It's like being in show business, just a style to show he's different and interesting. You have to be really smart to get away with it. At home with his wife and kids, he just wears a simple dress.'

Rosemary smiled at this introduction to the outside world and dashed upstairs to change. Eventually, with Team Pamela sat her wonderful Citroen, they bid farewell to Duke and Prince, wishing them a safe journey home.

IT TOOK LITTLE time to reach the bank in Pinhâo. Pamela looked serious, asking Adam to come with her and for the others to sit still or hang out in the next-door café.

The bank had few customers. She waved over to the chief counter clerk to serve her. They exchanged pleasantries, as she reached into her handbag and pulled out a large bundle of Euros.

'Please can you deposit forty thousand into my personal current account, and forty thousand into my savings account,' she requested, 'Then, transfer four thousand Euros into my Rosemary's current account.'

The clerk dropped the money into the banknote counting machine and handed her the receipt for the transactions.

'Do you wish the balances in each of your accounts,' he asked and wrote them down on a sheet of bank embossed notepaper. Pamela looked at the numbers. Much better, all her accounts were in the black, for a change and she could now catch-up with her finances.

'Anything else?'

Pamela handed him the bank draft for the wine; asking for the funds to be deposited in her 'safra' account,' which had been seriously overdrawn. Now her 'safra' account was firmly in the black and free of the objectionable little bank manager. She was in the process of counting the remainder of her euros when the man himself arrived.

'How dare you withdraw addition funds without my authorisation,' he shouted.

The bank manager grabbed her arm and told her to return the money immediately. Adam stepped in disengaging the bank manager from his fiancé.

'Bank managers assaulting his customers. Whatever next, how dare you even touch Sra Pamela,' he said.

The clerk hastened to advise his manager Sra Pamela had been making deposits to all her accounts which were all now positive.

The manager's face dropped, asked for the source of the funds, only to be told it was none of his damn business. The clerk showed him the bank draft for the large sum of over three hundred thousand Euros, payment for one of madam's 'safra' accounts the bank was holding as collateral.

'You will be hearing from my lawyer for your assault on my person. My good friend, the area manager in Oporto will certainly be hearing about this too,' Pamela said with all the force of a person revenged.

'I shall be moving my accounts elsewhere. I will leave you to explain to head office in Oporto.'

Pamela stormed out of the bank, followed by an impressed Adam.

They headed to the café to find the three girls each nursing a large cappuccino. 'How was Mr Bank manager today?' asked Rosemary.

'He's just had his goose cooked.'

'Or rather overcooked,' added Adam, as he relished the task of telling them what had happened. 'Let's all drink up and get a move on. Want me to drive Darling?'

'Negative,' Pamela replied, 'A slow gentle drive will do me the world of good.'

'That's code to make sure your seat belts are fast and tight, Mummy means business,' suggested Rosemary.

What followed was a master class of how to drive a DS Citroen fast, and with style, whilst managing to avoid the law and the many speed cameras littering the countryside.

In no time at all, the party arrived at the main entrance to the de Oliveira port factory. Pamela beeped the horn impatiently and the great gates opened. Inside, the workplace had frantic activity, as the workers concentrated on repairing the damage caused by the unfortunate fire.

Charlotte de Oliveira rushed out to meet them all, welcomed them to the chaos, and suggested they go straight up to the 'big' house, a large colonial building and main residence.

'Darling Pamela,' Charlotte said, 'So good you could make it. The jungle drums have been busy, so this is your fiancé. Welcome Adam, yet again. Please introduce your family.'

Adam introduced Nicola, his niece, and Victoria. Compliments exchanged, the party were invited up the grand staircase into the library, to find refreshments waiting for them. Victoria slumped into a comfortable leather chair to allow Adam to take her blood pressure and check she had survived the car journey without problems. Victoria quietly told him her back had become a bit sore, but the wine had helped and now she needed a strong cup of tea.

'Tea, everyone,' announced Charlotte, as her maid brought in a large ornate China teapot, 'Adam you can be Mum, teas all round? Help yourselves everyone to the cakes and pastries.'

'Where is the master of the house,' asked Pamela, wondering how their reunion would turn out.

'He's just changing from his work clothes and trying to remember his lines. Don't worry Pamela it will all be OK.'

With that, the man himself arrived with a flourish, introduced himself to Nicola and Victoria, and turned around to look at Pamela.

'Darling,' he cried, 'It's so good to see you and with good news. I hear congratulations are in order.'

'Thank you, Augusto,' said Pamela. 'Yes, Adam gave a wonderful proposal of marriage and I accepted. We are officially engaged.'

'There must be a ring,' said de Oliveira. Charlotte intercepted his move to be the first to examine the ring.

'Why that's just wonderful,' said Charlotte, 'What a wonderful combination.'

Victoria sat back concentrating on the delicious pastries, wondering when all this coo-cooing over an engagement ring was going to end. Nice stones, nice colours, looks expensive, blah de bloody blah. Nicola smiled; she was with her all the way on this one. Still, the tea was hot and strong, and the cakes were wonderful. Nicola found herself sitting with Rosemary, who had also heard enough about engagement rings.

Victoria started a giggling fit, taking Nicola and Rosemary with her. They moved to the other side of the room to let the grown-ups get on with the preliminaries.

Charlotte looked around to discover the split in the assembly and joined with the girls to give her husband the space to complete the repair job on his relationship with Pamela.

'Soon be over, girls,' she said. 'He can't keep this 'I'm so sorry' routine going for long. He has more important matters to talk about.'

'We know,' they all replied in unison.

Nicola bid Charlotte sit close whilst she updated her on the last twenty-four hours. 'Really,' said Charlotte. 'Lucky lady, no wonder Adam looks like he needs a good night

sleep. He must have kept his end up very well.'

Victoria burst out laughing and whispered, 'And Rosemary has a sound recording, on a pin drive, just ten Euros each.'

The girls all burst out laughing so loud de Oliveira stopped in mid-track of his conversation with Pamela and asked what was so funny.'

Victoria giggled, 'We're discussing Adam's exploits on the 'bouncy castle.'

Nicola told Vicky to stop being naughty, but everyone had big smiles. Pamela could hardly be unaware of the subject of the conversation, but she let it go.

De Oliveira turned around to Pamela, and said, 'I must ask about the wine you have in store. A wee birdy, namely madam over there, said you could help.'

'It is possible,' said Pamela, 'I have, as I'm sure you already know, two hundred barrels.

What you don't know is Mr Duke Marmaduke's opinion of this much-improved wine.'

'Well, I knew he had come to town. A friend of my son went drinking with him and his partner Prince Eugen. So, he came to visit?'

Adam explained the Duke was an old friend, looking for a new wine for his yearly exhibition in two months' time. Pamela's viticulturist had developed a new wine, the original project started by Pamela's late husband.

He, Adam, had tasted it yesterday afternoon and called Duke to come check it out. 'And his visit was successful?' asked de Oliveira with great interest.

'Oh yes. Duke confirmed Sr. Vincente's opinion his new wine could be graded 'vin de garage' and bought the entire safra for the year.'

De Oliveira almost choked on the drink he was sipping, declaring, 'I don't believe.'

'Yes,' mused Pamela, 'Yesterday became much more than a wonderful day. It had been the end to her financial worries too.'

'Um,' thought de Oliveira, 'She is in a much stronger position to negotiate; pity.'

'Let me serve you something stronger Adam, this is my latest port. I'm sure you will find most agreeable.'

The maid handed out glasses of de Oliveira's latest port wine, a delicious late bottled port, with good body and flavour.

'So, what was Duke's opinion on this wine Pamela has for sale?' said de Oliveira. Adam took out a bottle of the wine in question and asked the maid to open and pour.

De Oliveira took the offered sample and sat down to collect his thoughts. 'Not bad,' he thought, 'not bad at all. Now what?'

'Duke's opinion,' started Adam, 'Is if you could work your magic, you could produce a very passable 'Colheita Port,' in which case Mr Duke would be extremely interested in combining with you to sell your new product to his exalted clients in his upper-class marketplace. He knows as well as you do, new products are the way forward.'

'Pamela darling, how much did you receive for this 'vin de garage', can you tell me?' asked de Oliveira.

'Sorry no, but he did give me a large cheque in part payment. We will deliver the wine to Duke in our new artisan bottles, bottled on site.

My guess he will sell this 'vin de garage' for about a thousand pounds a case. Good profit for everyone. Now you've tasted the wine in your hand, I can let you have two hundred barrels, or I can distil fifty barrels on site, to supply the alcohol you need to turn this wine into a very good 'Colheita Port.'

De Oliveira was dumbfounded. He was surrounded by clever ladies. Rosemary looked firmly on her mother's side and his wife was about to say something that could force his hand. Then, de Oliveira's son arrived, 'Oi Marcos, tudo bem. Let me introduce you to everyone.'

Rosemary looked at Marcos, a fine-looking gentleman. His time in California had been good for him.

De Oliveira explained the proceedings, asked him to taste the offered wine requesting his opinion. Marcos performed the look, smell, taste test, and told his father it was well above average. Perhaps, he could make a new product for the port market.

De Oliveira repeated the suggestion from Adam, 'Any thoughts,' he asked.

Marcos replied, 'It could be a promising idea. I only know about wines, you're the port expert. Let us do something different, you haven't made a Colheita port for years. Now is your chance. Sounds as if you have a buyer if you succeed.'

De Oliveira accepted the advice from his son, looked at Pamela and asked, 'How much.'

Pamela gave de Oliveira a sheet of paper with a price for the wine, and the alcohol if he wished, with the terms and conditions to be observed. He saw a carefully crafted document in a handwriting he did not recognise.

Victoria smiled at him, all knowing.

'Pamela has brought in hired guns,' he thought. 'There's not a lot of room for manoeuvre.'

The insurance company had assessed his losses with a generous figure. Something to do with the fact a certain layabout and close relative of his was the insurance agent for his company and de Oliveira had made it plain his continuing business should be included in his calculations.

Time for dinner he thought, 'OK Pamela, I can accept this, I will write a cheque after dinner.'

The party repaired to the adjacent dining room laid out in a classical colonial style with an expensive chandelier hanging over the oval shaped deep mahogany dining room table.

Charlotte organised the seating arrangement with her husband at the head of the table, herself with Adam sitting next to her, followed by Pamela and Rosemary, Marcos, and Victoria, and then Nicola.

Dinner was a simple three-course affair, which pleased the party from the vineyard after the blowout lunch of yesterday. The conversation remained light and uninvolved with current affairs of the port wine industry.

De Oliveira was itching to know more of Pamela's details regarding marriage, business, and her relationship with Duke Marmaduke. Mr Duke, always a potent force in the upper echelons of the wine trade. The suggested deal to align Pamela, himself and Mr Duke grew strongly upon him.

Adam had been correct. The port wine market had become static and the question of how much product de Oliveira could produce and then try to sell to keep his bank manager happy had become a long-term concern. His employees relied upon him.

On the other side of the room, Charlotte was pleased to see her son getting on well with Rosemary, with Victoria being very much a part of the process.

Nicola struck up a lively conversation with de Oliveira. She found he was more than just a bluff owner of a large port wine operation. Clearly, he was slightly jealous of Adam. He had always admired Pamela, even during her previous marriage. He had never strayed from the nest, but this didn't stop him dreaming.

As dinner ended, Adam looked across at Victoria, and saw she needed an early night. It was time remove the dressing on her back and let her skin breath naturally. Adam thanked his hosts for a genuinely nice dinner, apologised, but he had to take Victoria back to the convent hospital for her treatment.

He blew a kiss across to Pamela promising to return 'tout de suite, collected Nicola and after the interminable hugs and kisses in the Latin manner, they made their way down to Pamela's car.

It was but a short drive to the convent. Adam quickly put Victoria back to bed whilst Nurse Maria removed the dressing. Victoria back was clear with no further bleeding. The cuts had healed nicely although her back still showed all the signs of the horrible torture.

Mother Superior arrived to supervise. She too was anxious to see what progress this new wonder treatment had made. She was relieved to see the treatment had fulfilled its promise. Mother Superior dusted Victoria's back with an anti-inflammatory powder and suggested it would be best if she slept on her side.

Duty done, Adam bid Nicola and everyone goodnight, leaving Nicola to fill-in the details of what had proved to be a wonderful couple of days.

Chapter 9

The Departure from Oporto

SATURDAY MORNING arrived on time. Nicola rose early to shower, took breakfast, and return to the yacht to complete preparations for her planned departure late the following day.

The assistant harbour master had her work list, and she was more than pleased to see the work had been completed.

The yacht's diesel and water tanks were full and there was plenty of food for the journey to Scotland. She hoped upon hope the departure of the yacht would remain as unrecorded as its arrival.

The first caller of the day came when Carlos Gilberto arrived. He became more than pleased to know his wife should present herself at the convent hospital late on Sunday afternoon, to enable her to rest and prepare for her operation on the Monday morning.

Carlos Gilberto confirmed the riggers would arrive shortly to carry out the modification to the yacht's headsails. Nicola figured if anybody were looking for a black cutter, a yacht with two headsails, the removal of the existing inner headsail and repositioning of the larger outer foresail at the bow would convert the yacht to a sloop. Nicola had examined the mast carefully and discovered this would be easy to achieve.

Also, with only one headsail, it would be easier to sail the yacht single handed. Victoria, she hoped, would be able to act as a lookout during the voyage.

The weather forecast looked favourable, in as much the usual northerly wind would be along the Portuguese coast without any forecast of harsh weather. Nicola planned to head out in a north-westerly direction into the deep Atlantic Ocean. Then, the yacht would encounter a low-pressure system forecasted to arrive from the west, bringing favourable winds to drive the yacht up to the southern coast of Ireland.

From there, she could either keep going or hole-up somewhere if the weather became too rough. She worried about Victoria's real capability to help, but with so many powered systems on this fine yacht all should be well.

The yacht had a full set of electronics to assist with a good radar set, radar detectors, radio receivers for weather information, twin GPS systems, marine communications, and the all-important twin channel self-steering system. As long as everything kept working the yacht would sail itself, and if the weather got up, an alarm would sound, so the yacht's needs could be attended to. All very well in theory. Practice usually proved the ability of any expensive equipment to fail at the wrong time.

Whilst the riggers got to work Nicola busied herself fitting white self-adhesive plastic panels to the main saloon cabin roof. Every little bit of disguise could only help, who knows.

The riggers finished their work inviting Nicola to examine and then pay the agreed fee. Now the yacht had been transformed from a masthead cutter into a fractionally rigged sloop.

Magote arrived at lunch time looking all prim and proper in his new clothes provided by the street traders. He felt most comfortable looking like a guard in his new employment to bring a much-needed security in the street. He prided himself on his cleanliness and Nicola was delighted to see his self-esteem and confidence had returned. Nicola asked him to run a few errands to give extra time to finish the last-minute items.

Work completed she relaxed in the cockpit with a cup of coffee and biscuits. A scruffy unshaven individual arrived to spoil her rest period in a broad Irish accent asked to talk to the lady in the cockpit.

The individual asked if the yacht could be leaving soon and was there any chance it would be heading north. Nicola asked why. He said he had been abandoned two weeks ago in a port up the coast. His story came along the lines he had been acting as second mate on a converted

North Sea trawler heading south. The trawler had docked to load supplies and refuel. The voyage had been fractious and he had fallen out with the skipper.

During the refuelling, he had gone ashore, got drunk in a shady bar, and fallen asleep. When he woke up, the trawler had left him behind taking all his belongings with him, including his ID and passport.

'Name,' asked Nicola, 'Let us start with the basics.' 'Patrick,' he replied.

'And there's a surname?' she asked.

'Oh, sorry, McManus, I'm a merchant seaman in between contracts,' he added. 'I need to get back to Ireland to look for more work.'

His voice seemed pleasant enough, with not too much of the Irish blarney, and he seemed a likeable enough guy. She thought his story kind of thin, with no way to check it. She asked who had been looking after him, considering he said he was destitute. The Irishman offered a story about a local padre with Irish connections who had given him food and shelter in exchange for some manpower in tasks around his parish he couldn't do himself.

On being asked why he had not contacted the local consular office; Patrick became quite evasive. Nicola told him she could not help him without references, and as he didn't wish anyone to inquire too closely into exactly who he was, what could she do?

Nicola told Patrick she was the member of a delivery crew; taking the yacht to West Scotland to meet up with the new owner. She added there was no plan to land in Ireland, and in fact, there was every chance she would be short of time to meet the given delivery dates.

Nicola was in two minds; she really didn't want to have to helm the yacht for the most part on her own. Victoria would not be fit enough to stand watches. Also, she had little experience of life at sea, and if anything happened to her, Victoria would find herself in a tough situation. Nicola re-examined her planned journey, setting sail at Sunday midnight to head out into the Atlantic Ocean on starboard tack to clear the main shipping channels. The forecasted incoming weather front looked to be on-track, enabling a switch to port tack, and with the auto-pilot set for southern Ireland, she could sail with a fair wind for Ireland. When she cleared the southern tip of Cape Clear Island the yacht would be sailing in the lee of the Irish mainland, and if the weather did turn nasty, shelter should not be far away. So far; so good.

Easy really, which if all went well, which would depend on the co-operation of 'mother nature,' assuming the cooperation would be forthcoming. A big ask indeed.

She thought this could be sufficient. She had been unable to find any experienced sailors in the area. She felt most uncomfortable offering passage to anyone she didn't know. It was nearly evening when Uncle Adam arrived and asked how thing were going.

'OK,' she replied, 'But I wish I could find a reliable crew member, but there's just no one around.'

Adam told her Victoria had checked out OK, the skin on her back had healed nicely, but the scars would take time to disappear. Nicola told him about the encounter with the Irishman. Adam agreed she had been correct not to offer passage. With that, the Irishman returned with the Padre he had mentioned. The Padre began an extended plea to take the poor lad to his home country; to enable him to renew his somewhat fractured life.

For a change, Nicola wavered, unable to make up her mind. Adam was only half-convinced by the Padre. The Padre had plausible excuses why he hadn't done this or that, so they arrived at an impasse. As they got to know the Irishman better, he seemed to be reasonable, a touch of the Irish charm no doubt.

Nicola still worried about sailing almost single-handed. This was a big yacht to manage, and powered systems or no powered systems, the yacht could easily get out-of-hand very quickly.

'OK,' she said, looking hard at the Irishman, 'Be here at eight o'clock tomorrow evening.

You'll need warm clothes, but I have spare waterproofs and safety clothing on board.' The Irishman looked happy at the good news and the Padre most relieved.

'Could I sleep on the yacht tonight?' he asked.

'Eight p.m. tomorrow evening, otherwise no deal,' Nicola told him sternly. 'We will dine at nine p.m. and sail at midnight on the tide, OK?'

The Irishman nodded his acceptance. He thought about arguing the toss but backed away when Magote returned with the shopping. Nicola asked him to stay and guard the yacht during the night one more time. Magote told Nicola he would be deeply sorry to see her leave. He had a great deal to be grateful for.

Nicola returned to the convent with Adam. Victoria was up and about, being very chirpy now her back had the ghastly dressing removed. It felt a bit itchy at first, but another covering of baby power soon solved the problem.

Pamela arrived to take them out for an evening meal. She said Rosemary sent her apologies but Marcos had asked her out to dinner and Pamela did not see the force of interfering with what she hoped would be a step in the right direction for her daughter.

They were taken to a discrete colonial house in the old quarter of Oporto. Generally, one had to be known to get a reservation. The menu consisted of the old style, traditional Portuguese fare, with a strong emphasis on seafood. The bacalhau crepe looked especially delicious.

Dinner turned out to be a quiet affair. Adam said how sorry he would be to see his niece and Victoria depart. Their visit had been brief, starting with the bad trauma, but leading to a multitude of good memories. Adam had been extremely glad to have family with him when he proposed to Pamela. Nicola's presence had been a steadying influence and it was good to share the magic moment. At the end of dinner, they all elected to save their goodbyes for tomorrow evening.

Adam did not elaborate too many details to Pamela on the necessity of the voyage. Adam dropped Nicky and Vicky off at the convent, on his way to share another night of bliss with Pamela at the Casa de Oliveira.

The next day dawned bright, slightly overcast with little wind. The end of summer was coming, and an early morning mist hung over the River Douro, soon dispersed by the rising sun.

Adam arrived at the convent late morning to take Nicky and Vicky down to the yacht. He stood by whilst tearful farewells took place with Mother Superior and all her staff of the convent and its fast-growing hospital.

It was quiet when they arrived at the marina. Nicola busied herself finishing few last-minute preparations. Little had changed in the weather forecast, so that was a relief.

Just after lunch, Anna Rita and her mother came down from the now famous food stall to say thank you and give their farewells. They could not stay long; Sunday's had become a busy day for all the traders in the Rua das Compras.

ADAM AND PAMELA arrived at 4 p.m. Pamela remained more than interested in what she perceived as an interesting story regarding the yacht. Nicola could see she would have to diminish the inquisitive nature of this highly intelligent lady. Whilst Victoria made another large pot of coffee and snacks in the galley, Nicola took Pamela to the main owner's cabin to explain a few things.

'It's like this Pamela, the whole story you must not know until many things, and some will be terrible, have passed. There is no timetable, that's it. Technically, this yacht is not here. Its arrival has not been recorded at the Harbour Office and a deal done with the assistant harbour master. We sail at midnight as his boss will arrive in Oporto late this evening and return to his office in the marina first thing tomorrow morning.

'What happened to Victoria and I was unbelievably bad. We were truly fortunate to have Uncle Adam save Vicky's life. I know which master criminal is behind all that happened and until the matter is sorted out, we must disappear. This means arriving in the UK unannounced, collecting papers and passports to then vanish to somewhere safe until it's all over. Please don't ask what 'it' is.

All being well, so far, I see no problem, Adam will be clear of all these matters, but much care is needed at all times.'

Pamela looked confused, as well she might, but she did not want any more unhappy experiences to cloud her new future. So, she nodded her acceptance of what little she had been told, promising to forget everything.

With hugs and kisses all-round Adam was anxious to be clear of the yacht before the Irishman arrived. He remained doubtful of Nicola taking him on the voyage but could see her predicament. He knew Victoria's experience was limited and although she could be useful as a crew member, she needed guidance most of the time.

Nicola would just have to make the best of it and hope for the best. Secretly he understood both she and Victoria were armed and hoped there would be no need to use them.

Twenty minutes after they had left, the Irishman and the Padre appeared on the scene. The usual pleasantries took place, but before the Padre left them to it, Victoria had a quiet word with him as he clambered out of the cockpit onto the dockside. Victoria had a lot of doubts about this Irishman, his story of how he ended up in Oporto seemed far too short on facts, and she just didn't plain trust him, but couldn't say why

The Padre repeated the story about the Irishman being abandoned in a port up the coast. Yes, he had got drunk in some downtown bar and the story had some truth about it. A ship had indeed arrived and the Padre had asked a fellow priest in the district to check this out. The ship did leave before schedule, there had been some altercation on the dockside, but that's all there was.

All he knew was this son of Ireland was off his hands and he felt more than pleased to be clear of the unknowns surrounding the whole affair. Anyway, he had done his Christian duty and first thing tomorrow he would transfer a new post in the interior of Spain leaving Oporto with few regrets.

During the next two hours, Nicola spent time with Patrick, showing him the ropes, so to speak. How to make sail, reef sail, and get the sails down in a bloody hurry should the need arise. She felt pleased he showed a strong interest. Next, the initiation on all things mechanical, the main engine, the small diesel generator, and the electrical switchboard.

Later, the three of them sat down to a hearty dinner, with a single glass of wine. Nicola would not tolerate drinking alcohol at sea, it was just too damn dangerous. After clearing away the galley, and making sure all cabins were ready for sea, Nicola handed out waterproof safety clothing, life vests and safety harnesses to her crew.

The clock crept towards eleven p.m. Patrick suggested they may as well sail early. Nicola shrugged her shoulders and agreed they may as well.

Patrick cast-off and pushed the bow towards the sea. Nicola took the helm and motored slowly out of the marina into the Douro River. High tide was still an hour away, but there would be little current over on the north side of mid-stream. She manoeuvred to a position just under the northern breakwater to enable the sails to be set in comfort. The northerly wind outside was holding just under twenty knots.

With Victoria at the helm holding the yacht steady, Nicola and Patrick raised the mainsail with one slab reef and then fully unfurled the foresail. The electric winches hauled in the sheets as the yacht quickly entered the cold Atlantic Ocean, close-hauled on the starboard tack.

Nicola showed Patrick how to set the auto-pilot to maintain the wind at a constant angle on the bow. The wind would vary about a mean wind direction, but it mattered little as it would all average out.

She took Patrick down to the navigating station, marked their position on the chart, and showed him the approximate position where the yacht should pick up the cold front coming in from the Atlantic. When this position had been reached, the yacht would tack onto port, and all being well, have a fast easy run to the south coast of Ireland. The voyage would be round about one thousand miles, so she expected to reach Ireland in just over one hundred hours

Patrick thought they should tack up the Portuguese coast, but Nicola told him she wanted to get out in the deep ocean, away from the continental shelf into the longer swell of the deeper water. Their voyage would be well outside the Bay of Biscay and its busy shipping lanes, making watch keeping much easier with no interference from commercial shipping.

As the yacht ploughed on at a steady nine knots, Nicola took a long hard look at the radar display, saw there was no shipping to be aware, and shut it down. She also shut down the yacht's communication systems, leaving only the radar detector on high up on the mast operational. Patrick said he thought it best to have these systems operational and went to reactivate them.

'Patrick,' said Nicola sharply, 'Do you wish to arrive in Ireland, flags waving, bands playing, searchlights in the sky, or do you wish to sneak ashore unannounced and in safety?'

'Why's that?' he retorted.

Nicola replied, 'Because Patrick, military air forces patrol the sky, monitoring any frequency, with the ability to give every 'splash' its own signature ID. Even radio receivers transmit a small signal. Therefore, we shall sail 'dead-ship,' as I call it, and avoid any unwanted interference.'

Patrick said arriving unannounced in Ireland would be a good and mentioned a small harbour where he could find former friends to get some desperately needed help. He was only half-convinced by what Nicola told him, but he accepted the advice. He reluctantly accepted the need to fill the yacht's logbook every half-hour.

The yacht powered ever deeper into the Atlantic. Patrick took the first watch of three hours. He had spent most of the day in bed at the vicarage's refuge, so he was well rested. With nothing to look at except an empty sea, Patrick studied the sky, trying to remember the stars, but with the weather on the turn, clouds arrived to hide nature's glory.

He spent his time, dozing, and making coffee to keep himself awake. Watchkeeping was boring when there was nothing to do. He would have taken turns helming the yacht, but he didn't remember how to reset the auto-pilot, so he kept a look-out when he felt like it, but Nicola was correct, once the yacht had crossed the shipping lanes, they were out on their own in the vast expanse of the ocean.

Patrick woke Nicola just after four a.m. She was glad of the extra hour in bed and took the offered hot drink of cocoa and biscuits. She had slept fully dressed in the pilot berth next to the navigation station; secure, comfortable, and well located if the helm on watch needed assistance.

Patrick turned in for some much-needed sleep. Nicola checked the log and brought it up to date and made breakfast for herself. As dawn crept over the horizon an hour later, Nicola found herself sitting comfortably on the lee bench seat in the cockpit watching the world go by. The seabirds had yet to start the morning shift, so all remained in tranquillity.

The only real worry was Patrick. He had a fractious temperament and sweet-talking him might not be such a clever idea. Better to be just sensible and matter of fact. She didn't speculate on his past. The Irish were one of her favourite people, but that unhappy land had created many bad persons who were as violent as any in this sad but beautiful world.

As the sun rose above the horizon, so did Victoria. She had slept well and overcame the slight feeling of 'mal de mare' when the yacht sailed. She took breakfast with Nicola and asked how things were with the Irishman. Nicola confided her thoughts and took no surprise when she saw Victoria had her 'little gun' carefully hidden in her overall pocket, wrapped up in a handkerchief.

'Nicky,' she said, 'You must do the same. Keep yours close to hand. Hide it somewhere on you at all times, and do not let him see you have it. This guy is bad news, but I understand the predicament. If anything happens to you, then what?' Nicola nodded her head in approval. Sound advice indeed.

They let Patrick sleep until he woke naturally. Nicola catnapped, as Victoria kept a lookout. There was little to see but ocean, and there was a lot of it, everywhere in fact. A few contrails could be seen in the sky, international flights heading to the other side of the 'pond.' It occurred to

Victoria there didn't seem to be a plan when they reached the UK.

Nicola had been musing a few ideas, but nothing concrete came to mind. Victoria suggested they keep the yacht, collect their passports and other documentation, and then they too could head to the other side of the Atlantic, only via the Canary Islands, and up past the islands of the Caribbean to the USA.

Nicola thought there a might be a possibility. The next 'Trans-Atlantic Rally for Cruisers' would start in two months' time. She would investigate the matter and then they could talk about it later. She was certain the yacht had been built in the USA, perhaps in the Boston area. Chances are the yacht had been 'borrowed' by the organisation who had conducted the robbery in Manchester, a wild theory, but one that could not be fully discounted.

Keeping the yacht long term in the UK would never work. It could not be registered, the VAT man would be chasing them once its presence became known, and Nicola had no idea who the real owner was. The whole thing would become a one-way ticket to severe aggravation with people she really did not want to get involved with.

By now there would be every chance the authorities were looking for a black yacht. She had spoken to Great Aunt Violet, who had made very discreet enquiries. So far nothing, but this could change at any time.

The routine on the voyage settled down quite well. Nicola and Patrick split the night hours between them, with Victoria looking after the domestics and keeping a lookout during the day. The strength of the wind oscillated either side of twenty knots. The sail configuration of the yacht, as a sloop, would allow furling or unfurling the foresail to keep the yacht in perfect balance. Its long lean hull curved the waves aside making little fuss of them.

During their time on watch, Nicola and Patrick shared time helming the yacht. Patrick appeared to be more relaxed and whatever worries he had seemed to have greatly reduced.

Nicola felt relieved the voyage was going well. The estimate of reaching Ireland in a hundred hours of sailing looked achievable. It just required the forecasted low-pressure weather system to establish itself in time to give a fast reach downwind to the designated 'waypoint' off the Irish coast.

Monday became Tuesday, and Tuesday became Wednesday. Late Wednesday, the new weather arrived from the forecasted southerly direction which would become south-west as the low-pressure system moved to cross through Ulster into southern Scotland.

The new weather brought clouds heavy with rain. Standing watches on deck became a miserable affair, but fortunately the visibility remained sufficiently clear not to require the use of the radar. During the previous day, the radar detector intermittently picked up fast moving signals which could only come from distant patrolling aircraft.

With the wind now coming over the port quarter, the yacht picked up the pace and showed this lady could devour miles at an impressive rate. The twelve-hour average speed crept up by a useful margin, with progress gained every time the yacht surfed down a following wave. With luck, Ireland would be reached sometime midday Friday.

The glass started its slow and expectant fall as the cold front approached, but then it unexpectedly started to hold steady. The cold front collided into a high-pressure system established over northern France, delaying its progress.

Nicola considered this carefully because the cold front would eventually prevail but in a much stronger way. The cold front could easily build into a strong storm and closing the Irish coast in a strong gale held great dangers for a short-handed yacht.

Patrick suggested they raise full sail, but Nicola told him they didn't have enough manpower to handle such a big yacht with so few crew. The yacht would have to be hand steered in the building seas, the auto-pilot could easily be taken past its limits and if things went wrong, they would go wrong very very quickly.

For the meantime, the yacht remained balanced under her sail plan and sailing very nicely under auto-pilot. And so, Thursday morning arrived bright, clear but windy. The established routine continued during the day, through the night into dawn on the Friday morning. A lull in the weather made life aboard a bit more restful, Patrick took the watch until 10 a.m.

Victoria was fast asleep in the main owner's cabin. Nicola thought it was time for a hot shower and a change of clothes before taking a snap-nap before her next spell of watch-keeping.

Nicola finished her shower and returned to her cabin, the double guest cabin just forward of the main saloon. She lay down on the double berth, with a towel around her head, wearing just a simple slip.

Next thing she knew, Patrick stormed in smelling strongly of brandy, wearing only his tee shirt and boxer shorts. He threw Nicola onto her back, clearly intent on having his wicked way with her. Nicola attempted to fight, but both her arms were pinned on either side of her. Her 'little gun' lay at hand under the other pillow but this Irishman was far too strong for her.

'Oh, not again,' she screamed. 'Get off me you Irish bastard.'

Patrick slapped her hard across the face, 'Time for a little fun, you stuck-up bitch. You've been ordering me around for the last few days and that's it. A girl with such nice tits deserves a good rogering, and I'm needin' a woman very badly.'

Nicola screamed again, but Patrick told her it would be no use. Victoria was fast asleep in the main owner's cabin and would not hear anything over the noise of the yacht as it sailed ever faster in the rising wind.

As Patrick prepared to rape Nicola, he felt a cold hard object being rammed in the back of his neck.

'Just hold it there Paddy,' said Victoria in a cold hard voice. 'I've been waiting for you to try something. Make one move and I'll blast you to hell.'

'Jeepers,' replied Patrick. 'Three in a bed, now this's more like it.'

'Last chance Paddy,' Victoria's voice was hard and determined.

Patrick stopped for a moment, released Nicola's left arm for a moment, whilst he weighed up what to do next. In a flash, Nicola grabbed her gun from under her pillow, pointing it at his drunken face.

'The object in the back of your neck, sunshine, is the same as this, and we know how to use them,' snarled Nicola.

'Well girls,' said Patrick, playing for time. He knew he possessed fast reactions but being faster than two guns would be a challenge.

'Keep very still, Paddy,' said Victoria.

How he hated being called Paddy. They would pay dearly for this insult.

'Very slowly lift your ugly body off my best friend and be very careful,' ordered Victoria.

As Patrick rose from Nicola on his hand and knees. Nicola moved from under him, the gun in her hand never wavering. Patrick looked at her gun, a small frame, but the nose of the bullets showed they were much larger than the normal .22 round.

At that moment, the yacht fell off an overtaking wave. Patrick started to move at lightning speed. 'Bang, bang,' as Victoria fired two rounds into the back of his neck. Patrick fell limp onto the double bunk, as Nicola rose to her feet, ready to shoot at the side of his head.

Victoria took a deep breath and asked if Patrick was dead. Nicola rolled him onto his back. His eyes were moving, but his body lifeless. Nicola stood up straight looking hard at Patrick's limp body. She spoke to him, calling him all the names she could think off. His eyes rolled in rage, but no other part of him moved.

Nicola jabbed a sharp knife into his side, but there with no reaction. She took the towel from around her head and wrapped it around his neck to catch the blood starting to flow from the wound.

'Thanks, Vicky,' said Nicola, 'This I didn't need; well done indeed. How do you feel, you've never shot someone before?'

'I feel fuckin' great,' she said. 'Irish bastard. Brings closure if you know what I mean,' 'He's paralysed from the neck down, he won't last long,' said Nicola.

'How can you tell?' asked Victoria

'Because we are going to dump his sorry arse over the side of this ship with the obligatory lead necklace, same as the other bastards.'

The yacht suddenly rolled as it was hit by a huge gust of wind. 'Shit,' shouted Nicola. 'Let's get topside.'

The two girls dressed quickly, went on deck, clipped on their safety harness, closing the saloon's main hatch behind them. The yacht had too much sail up, as it surged downwind too fast for safety.

Nicola climbed over the main sheet track and secured herself at the steering binnacle. What to do? Must get the mainsail down. It wouldn't fall on its own in this press of the wind.

She motioned Victoria to come to her and shouted to go to the winch on top of the cabin at the front of the cockpit and prepare to drop the mainsail. Victoria went to the winch, re-clipped her safety harness, wound the mainsail halyard around the winch, applied tension to the halyard and released the halyard rope clutch.

She looked back at Nicola, hanging on for dear life. Nicola brought the yacht onto the wind, as the mainsail started to flog itself into destruction. Victoria let go of the mainsail halyard, and phew, she was greatly relieved to see the sail drop into the 'lazy jacks.'

She turned to Nicola, thumbs up. The foresail flogging badly in the wind, Nicola made a spinning motion with a free hand, as Victoria made to bring the foresail reefing line to the winch and quickly wound-on four rolls in the sail.

She looked behind; the seas were building fast, the only thing in her favour was the length of the swell between the crest of the waves. Heart pounding, she chose her moment with care. The yacht spun around in the trough of the wave and started to surf down the next oncoming wave.

Order restored, but only for the moment. The real storm was now more than visible in the distance, its great menace obvious from the dark towering thunderclouds and impenetrable rain front.

Nicola carefully brought the yacht back on course to reach safety in the lee of the land. She re-engaged the autopilot, pleased it seemed to be coping. The yacht surged hard down the long period swell, fortunately remaining stable for now. Nicola brought the yacht a touch closer to the wind to prevent the chance of rolling hard to windward.

Before she left the steering binnacle, Nicola energised the main engine to recharge the batteries to power to the autopilot. She shouted to Victoria to open the main hatch so they could go below and take a breather.

Nicola sat down at the navigation table and was furious to see the errant Irishman had activated the radar. She took a quick look at the screen, saw nothing ahead for thirty miles and shut it down. Next thing, the VHF radio burst into life on Channel 16. It was a coastguard aerial patrol calling for details of the yacht.

Nicola answered the call in her reasonable east-coast American male accent. The voice on the radio repeated the request for details of the yacht. Nicola answered they had come from the south of Spain, and were experiencing severe electrical problems, preparing for the oncoming storm and could they be very brief.

The coastguard advised the main storm was building quickly, now just three hours away, travelling at ten knots, on a heading of zero nineteen degrees.

Nicola thanked the coastguard and rang off. As she shut down the radio, she heard a 'Mayday' call from a vessel in distress, forty miles behind.

'That's handy,' she thought. 'Now he's gone, we can get rid of our unwanted baggage and try to outrun this damn storm.'

Nicola saw the yacht's course was zero thirty-one degrees, so if they could hang on, the storm would pass slowly away to the north.

She looked up the instruments, saw the yacht possessed the same speed as the oncoming storm and gave thanks. Time to be busy! Nicola told Victoria to tie the Irishman's feet together, whilst she went on deck to rig-up the same line she had used before. Next she brought one end of the line through the main saloon and tied it around the ankles of the Irishman.

She asked Victoria to go topside and very slowly haul in on the rope using the windward foresail winch. The prone body departed from the double berth, crashed to the deck as it made its one-way journey through the cabin door, along the passageway and into the main saloon.

Progress was slow but steady. Where necessary she lifted the victim's head over various obstacles to prevent too much skin or hair being left behind on the yacht's deck. At the foot of the companionway up to the cockpit, Nicola asked Victoria to pause for a moment whilst she took a sample of hair before the body ascended into the cockpit and ended up hanging under the boom. Nicola attached two diver's lead weights around the neck of the soon to be discharged deck hand, removed the upper guardrail line to facilitate the discharging of Mr Patrick, or whatever his name was, overboard. Nicola swung the boom to the lee side of the yacht, and with a hurried slash of the seaman's knife, she cut the line and the limp body fell into the cold Atlantic forever.

Chapter 10

THE TWO GIRLS hurried below to recuperate from their fraught ordeal and plan what to do next. The GPS showed the yacht making fourteen knots over the ground. Nicola thought there must be lot of tide under them to add to the violent surfing down the face of the building waves.

After a little work on the chart, Nicola concluded they would pass under the lee of the Irish mainland just in time to get shelter from the oncoming melee. There existed the possibilities the weather would become a full-blown mega-storm. For sure it would be best to hole up in a small harbour somewhere along the fractured Irish coast.

Victoria suggested ducking into Cork, a harbour possessing the full range of those government organisations Nicola remained so very keen to avoid. The small harbour their departed crew member mentioned was called 'Goughal.' She searched the chart, locating it north of Cork harbour.

It wasn't listed in the marine almanack, and it looked like a basin harbour, one used centuries before by local commerce, but the weather had more than likely washed out the river connecting it to the sea which had only partial recovered.

The yacht drew just under two metres, with the chart showing an entrance into the estuary connecting to the harbour basin. It looked like the estuary did offer sufficient depth if used with care. She calculated they could reach safety if she hand steered the yacht to make the most of the surging waves from behind. Victoria dashed to the galley to serve a hot meal for them both from the three-day stew ever slowly bubbling in the deep stew pot.

Meal over, Nicola went on deck to unfurl the foresail by two rolls to gain the power needed to get the yacht up to her maximum speed. She settled down at the steering position, fully cocooned in her foul weather clothing.

She actually started to enjoy herself hand steering the yacht down and across the face of the oncoming waves. The yacht would accelerate from the following seas in a long surfing action, gaining hundreds of metres to demonstrate the yacht's great appetite for eating the miles.

As her watch progressed, Nicola became happy to see the outline of the Irish coast looming out of the murky weather with its frequent rain squalls. Victoria passed hot drinks up from a small skylight in the ceiling of the main owner's cabin. The seas started to moderate, as the sailing became much easier.

Later, Victoria took the helm to let Nicola take a break to get more food inside her and check their progress. It started to look like Goughal would be just in reach, but with little time to spare. Fortunately, the way ahead remained clear, the local fishing fleets and other craft having long since dashed for shelter.

Nicola switched on the marine radio to listen to the weather forecast, which only confirmed Ireland was about to experience a severe battering. Slates would fly from roofs, trees would transcend to the horizontal, and the usual chaos to fences and gardens would be everywhere.

As they approached the entrance to Goughal, the two girls were straining their eyes trying to see the estuary entrance. Nicola asked Victoria to fully reef the foresail, as she energised the main engine and selected half ahead. The wind was getting fierce, the only good thing was the wind veered to the west, which would be more or less head-on as they attempted to enter the estuary.

THE RAIN RETURNED in brief driving showers making navigation exceedingly difficult. Nicola brought the yacht to the correct GPS coordinates, but the low-lying land did not yield up its secrets. Nothing for it, use the radar. Nicola slowly brought the yacht closer to the land, keeping a wary eye on the depth sounder.

Victoria cried out as she saw a fishing dory, about twenty feet long, making its way towards where they guessed the entrance should be. Its engine smoking badly and the helm seemed to be looking down at his engine, either uttering encouragement or curses. Could've been both; hard to be sure.

Nicola gunned the main engine to catch-up with the dory, which was losing speed fast. She gave the helm to Victoria, telling her to slow down and come alongside. Nicola opened a cockpit bench seat locker, took out a strong length of tow rope, and took it to the bow.

As the yacht came alongside the dory, Nicola shouted out, 'We'll swap giving you a tow for directions into the harbour, as she expertly heaved the line to the fisherman on the dory.

He smiled a big thank you, secured the line to his craft. He quickly heaved a stern line to the yacht. With both lines made fast, he shouted it would be best to get a bloody move before the full force of the tempest drove them offshore.

With the yacht's main engine at maximum power, and the fisherman shouting frantic instructions, they entered the channel marked by withies planted in the riverbed. Victoria kept as close as she dared to the north side of the channel. The water depth became very shallow for such a large yacht.

The fisherman yelled at Nicola, 'What depth do you draw.' 'Just under two metres,' she yelled back.

He waved his arm forward, indicating all should be OK. 'If you touch bottom, just keep straight ahead on full power; should be OK,' he yelled back.

As the harbour pool approached, the fisherman indicated a hard left turn into deeper water. As the yacht turned the tempest struck with great force. Victoria slowed the yacht as it passed a floating dock and headed towards the only place to berth. The fisherman jumped aboard guiding Victoria past the mooring berth, yelling at Nicola to get ready to drop anchor.

'The berth is not strong enough to secure a yacht this big in this wind,' he shouted.

As the yacht reached the far end of the pool, the fisherman ordered full astern and shouted at Nicola to drop anchor. With way checked, the yacht went astern as the anchor chain rattled out of the spurling pipe.

As the yacht slipped back past the mooring berth, he ordered half ahead to hold the yacht into the wind. The yacht slowly crept forward until it became level with the mooring berth. The fisherman rushed to the bow, hauled on the chain with great force, and locked it down in the bits, satisfied the anchor had buried itself into the harbour mud.

The fisherman returned to Victoria instructing her to let the yacht pull hard on the anchor chain, then to put the helm down with a sharp surge of power to come alongside the mooring berth. Two dripping wet young men arrived at the berth to take the mooring ropes and make them fast.

The fisherman checked this novel way of mooring and declared himself satisfied. Nicola looked at the three Irishmen; they looked very thin and obviously hadn't eaten too regularly in the past.

'Get down below out of this damn weather,' invited Nicola. They needed no second bidding.

'Well then. I'm Nicky, and this is Vicky. And you are?'

The fisherman introduced himself as Liam, and his two boys, Liam Jr. 18 years, and Peter 16 years. His wife Miriam and young daughter Rosie lived in the cottage on the other side of the harbour.

The two boys were sopping wet, their waterproof jackets had lost the battle to keep their upper half dry, and their jeans were wringing wet. They shivered with cold, so much so Victoria became concerned. She went forward to the yacht's storeroom and found two pairs of dry overalls for them to change into. She wrapped small towels around their heads, and gave them other towels, telling them to dry themselves and get changed.

The interior of the yacht was not much warmer than outside. Nicola lit the dual fired stove in the main saloon and checked the hot water geyser was up to temperature.

'Cup of tea Liam,' she asked, and set about making hot drinks for all.

Outside, the tempest arrived with the full force of nature's fury. The yacht heaved hard on its anchor chain and the mooring ropes holding it to the berth. She thought about lowering the furled foresail to the deck but considered it too risky and she sure didn't want another soaking.

The three Irishmen sat shivering around the dining table in the main saloon. Victoria looked at Nicola as if to ask, 'Have you ever seen anyone so thin and hungry.'

She raked around in the locker over the galley sink, found some high energy sports bars, and handed them out as she served the hot teas with a large helping of sugar.

'When was the last time you three had a decent square meal?' she asked.

'Can't remember,' said Liam, 'I hoped to catch some fish, but the weather drove them deep, and in the process, I nearly lost the dory. Thanks for the rescue; I would have been miles out to sea by now. I think we all know what this means.'

'In this case, I shall make you all a grand meal, we haven't eaten today either.'

Liam Jr. spoke up, 'Me Mam will be waitin' for us in the cottage. Can she eat here too?' 'Is she just as hungry as you lot,' Victoria asked.

Liam Jr. nodded his head.

'OK, finish your tea, I will give you some decent waterproofs to keep you dry, then you can fetch her over, and bring the bairn too.'

Ten minutes later a pensive Mrs O'Brady arrived with her daughter. She climbed down the companionway into the main saloon to see her family huddled around a large table nursing hot drinks. Nicola introduced herself and Vicky and bid make herself comfortable. The new arrival gave her name as Myriam and introduced Rosie; her daughter of eight years old.

As the main saloon of the yacht warmed up, the Irish family started removing their top clothes. Victoria gathered up what quickly became a large pile of sopping wet clothing taking them to the drying locker up forward. Nicola started making the dinner, diving deep into the dark recesses of the yacht's large freezer to remove frozen meats that should have been used a long ago.

Myriam asked what was going on, accusing her husband of forcing himself on others kindness.

Nicola saw where this outburst would go; seeking to assure her they were all invited to dinner. The tempest outside the yacht started to reach its peak, as the mast began to shake the hull of the yacht.

Myriam was not impressed, demanding they should all go home. Liam told her he didn't catch any fish that day and what did they have for an evening meal? Myriam looked down at the floor, thoroughly depressed. She hated charity and had never accepted it under any conditions. But her family were not only hungry, but starving, and this was the truth of the matter.

Myriam was not a woman to see others do her work, demanding she should help with the cooking. Nicola did not have a problem and beckoned her to the galley to prepare the vegetables. She told Myriam they would just throw all the ingredients into a big cauldron and make a big stew.

Nicola became concerned if the family started gorging itself on large plates of food. They could make themselves quite ill. There was plenty of packet soup and the water geyser had plenty of hot water. Five minutes later she was handing out hot mugs of soup with dry savoury biscuits and attempted to slow down the speed of consumption.

'Liam,' Nicola spoke sharply, 'Get your tribe to slow down. Good job I only gave them half a mug.'

Liam swigged his soup down before attempting to slow his children down, but with marginal result. Little Rosie asked for more. Nicola explained to her and the two sons, they needed to eat small, but often, otherwise their tummies would overload, and they would become quite unwell. Liam Jr. wasn't interested and wanted all he could get now.

Nicola left the galley, leant over him, and whispered in his ear, 'Listen sonny, do as you're told or else, understand.'

She spoke with determination, leaving Liam Jr. in no doubt not to mess with her.

A violent gust of wind shook the yacht. Liam became concerned the anchor would drag resulting in the mooring ropes overloading the unfinished mooring berth. Nicola took him forward to the bow of the yacht telling him to open the skylight and get access to the mooring chain winch. She would go aft to use the main engine to drive the yacht forward so he could take-up any slack in the mooring chain.

Ten minutes later, and with Nicola and Liam getting another good soaking, the task quickly completed. Fortunately, the anchor buried itself even deeper in the thick clay laying under the mud in the basin. With the yacht secured for the third time, Nicola settled down to a stiff drink in the main saloon of the yacht.

By now, the main saloon was warm and cosy. The O'Grady family settled down, and with the prospect of a decent meal forthcoming, they sat talking with each other, waiting with little impatience. Myriam enjoyed herself in the galley. How she longed to be able to feed her family properly each day.

The last few months had been a trial. Her husband Liam had worked extremely hard to get his shipyard business up and running. He spent almost the last of his working capital, secure in the knowledge the MOU in his back pocket would lead to the confirmation of the contract he prepared for. At the last moment, a much larger shipyard up the coast had bought the contract out from under him, which for sure would lead to a big loss, just to keep newcomers out of the marketplace.

Liam told her, both client and contractor deserved each other. The course of this project would be hell, as the contractor began to realise the true costs, and would start to press every way possible to introduce extras for which they could invoice. The contract stated lump sum, with the scope of work reading very strongly in favour of the client.

Still, none of this mattered to Myriam O'Grady. Her family was in trouble and slowly starving without much hope. Now, this yacht had arrived out of the blue, saved her husband from being washed out to sea, or more likely miles up the coast, either option being as bad as each other, and she was cooking the biggest meal of the year for everyone aboard. Outside, the tempest raged, but Myriam couldn't be sure they were safe aboard this magnificent yacht, but what did she know?

As the stew became ready, deep aromas flooded the cabin. The O'Grady's looked on as Nicola calmly laid out small soup bowls in front of them. Liam Jr. looked at this a bit queer; he wanted the biggest bowl possible. Nicola ladled the stew into the bowls, half filling them before passing to the waiting diners.

The bowls were emptied in record time, as cries for more rang around the main saloon of the yacht. Victoria gave each person a glass of water, bidding them drink slowly. Nicola told everyone to wait and explained the dangers of eating too quickly.

The diners relaxed as they were presented with the second course. Nicola repeated the process once more, carefully watching little Rosie. She saw Rosie, having got halfway through a third bowl starting to look a little bloated.

'Rosie,' she said, 'I think you have had enough, so now you must rest.'

Rosie just nodded, but looked up at Nicola and asked, 'Is there any ice cream, please Miss,'

'Drink a little more water and we will see,' replied Nicola, 'Do you want to help me find the ice cream in the freezer. It's a very big freezer, so don't fall inside.'

Nicola took the little girl's hand to take her to the storeroom. Nicola played a game of hide and seek which delighted the little girl. Together they found the large chest freezer, as Nicola pretended to make a magic trick open the lid.

Nicola lifted the little girl and gave her a small torch to seek for the magic ice cream. Rosie shone the torch inside of the freezer, as Nicola moved things aside. They found the tub of ice cream at the bottom, which Nicola carefully lifted out, giving it to Rosie to carry proudly back to the main saloon.

The little girl plonked the tub of ice cream in front of mummy and with wide open eyes asked if she could have a little before bedtime. Myriam smiled at her daughter. It had been a while since she had been treated to her favourite desert. Victoria handed out desert bowls and spoons to all. Fortunately, the ice cream tub's label had fallen off in the freezer, hiding its origin from the ever-inquisitive Irish.

With the meal completed with coffees and green teas, Liam suggested to his family it was time to go home to their cold cottage. He thanked the two girls most profusely, they had been over generous, and he was most grateful.

Nicola opened the main hatch from the main saloon to show Liam the weather now getting worse. It could be dangerous to venture outside. The wind was strong, with debris flying everywhere as the rainfall got into its stride in keeping Ireland as green as possible.

Nicola would hear no refusals. The yacht had plenty of accommodation for all, the main saloon stove had warmed the interior of the yacht's many compartments and little Rosie was almost fast asleep in her mother's arms.

'Come Myriam,' she said, 'Follow me,' taking her aft to the main owner's cabin. She found a small sleeping bag and pillow and made a bed for Rosie on the bench berth alongside the large double berth.

'You and Liam can sleep here,' said Nicola. 'Get yourselves a quick wash and I will find some disposable toothbrushes. You will find everything you need in one of the lockers under the berth, and the heads, or bathroom as you would call it, is just through the side door.

Nicola marched back into the main saloon, 'Right boys, you two can sleep in crew cabin where you will find pillows and sleeping bags. Get yourselves washed and use the toilet. Now off you go.'

Liam looked up at Nicola, and simply said many thanks for looking after his family. The day started with no hope. Now it finished with hope all around.

Victoria told him, 'It's OK Liam. Just get a good night's sleep and tomorrow we can get busy.'

Nicola set the main saloon stove to its minimum and extinguished the lights. The yacht had plenty of hot water, the batteries were fully charged. She collected Victoria on her way to the double guest suite forward.

Happy at such a successful day, the two friends looked forward to a very restful night's sleep, tempest, or no tempest.

Chapter 11

Transformation in Goughal Harbour

NEXT MORNING, the tempest reluctantly commenced its relocation to somewhere else and although the wind continued blustery the rain squalls had not given up hope of making everybody wet in Goughal Harbour.

Liam was the first to rise, doing the decent thing by putting on the kettle. He looked in the refrigerator, found some long-life milk, and the only other food suitable to go with a cuppa, a few shortcake biscuits. He had eaten worse breakfasts.

Nicola swanned into the main saloon full of the joys of spring, in crisp clean white overalls and gym shoes. To keep out the chill in the air, she quickly increased the heating from the main saloon stove.

By the time Liam and Nicola finished their tea, the others had risen to join them, including a sleepy Victoria, looking for breakfast. A general discussion ensued as to the day's activities, which resulted in the agreement of two main requirements.

First, the need to get supplies to feed everyone for what would a busy week. And what was there for breakfast? The last of the bread had been eaten last night.

There was some porridge, but little milk to make a nice creamy meal. Liam suggested the local grocery shop com post office, just a few minutes' walk up the lane. Victoria offered to go if Liam Jr. would accompany her.

Liam suggested, while Victoria and Liam Jr. went shopping, the yacht could be moved into the floating dock as the precursor for lift-out to determine the scope of work Nicola wanted.

Teas finished, Victoria and Liam Jr. dressed for the weather, disembarked, and started up the lane.

Liam Jr. became quite chatty, which did not go down too well with Victoria who wondered why on earth she'd volunteered for food shopping. She detested food shopping and would have preferred a long lie in her very warm and comfortable berth.

The shop was owned and run by a Mr Jock Walker, an elderly Scottish gentleman from Aberdeen. He had let his Irish wife talk him into buying the local business as a means to retire from the oil industry, which was in the throes of another major downturn. His wife managed to sell their house in Aberdeen at a decent price, well before the downturn became fully identified in the industry.

'He's not one of these Aberdonian skinflints?' asked Victoria.

'No; not really. He gave Dad a lot of credit, but now we can't repay what we owe,' replied Liam Jr. 'There are a lot of people around here in the same boat. So, Jock is hurting as much as everyone else. It makes him awfully bad tempered. I'm not allowed in the shop unless I have cash to help repay him.'

'Any idea of the debt?' enquired Victoria.

'No, but it's quite a lot. We will need to humour him and that ain't easy.'

'Oh great,' thought Victoria. 'Now I have to humour a grumpy Scotsman. Perhaps he'll be happy it could rain this morning.'

When they arrived at the shop, Victoria was at least pleased to see it was open. The owner was outside, clearing away debris from last night's storm.

'A-mornin to you Jock,' shouted Liam Jr.

'Mr Walker to you, young man,' came a gruff voice.

'I've brought you a customer, a lady. 'er name's Nicky,' replied Liam Jr.

'I see the on-line elocution lessons have a long way to go Master Liam Jr.' replied Mr Walker, with as much cynicism as he could muster.

Victoria went inside to see what was on offer, closely followed by Mr Walker, whose shortage of paying customers was not helped by the current weather. Victoria mentioned the lights in the shop were kind of dim, making it difficult to see.

'It's because the electric's out and I'm usin' the temporary generator. My deep freezers are not so deep this mornin,' what can I get you? 'ave to be cash as the phone lines are down and there's no connection to the card centre.'

Victoria smiled sweetly, made a little giggle, pulling out five crisp 100 Euro notes. Mr Walker became very attentive at the sight of Europe's favourite greenback. Victoria handed him a list.

'I've got fresh milk from yesterday, a box of twelve, an' two boxes from the day afore,' said Mr Walker. 'Should still be OK, and there's a box three days old you can hav' for half price. There are four bread loaf's from yesterday, an' ten from the day before; should be OK for toast and such like.'

Victoria saw other things she wanted asking if he had a cart they could borrow.

Mr Walker showed the one he would like to sell, but Victoria just smiled at him sweetly telling him she would need a test drive before spending five hundred Euros.

Victoria told Liam Jr. to start loading the cart with sacks of potatoes and onions. She continued down her list of shopping, including more vegetables, breakfast foods, flour, spices, and other items until the cart became full to overflowing.

'OK, Mr Walker. And this comes to?'

Mr Walker, calculator in hand, told her it came to five hundred and thirty Euros. 'Excellent,' cooed Victoria wickedly, 'Here is five hundred, for cash, and the fact you'll be glad to get rid of most of this old stock.'

Mr Walker looked at Victoria. She was not the blonde bimbo he had first assumed. He waved her away and hoped she would come again.

'Mr Walker,' asked Victoria in her matter-of-fact voice, 'Do you trade?' 'What?' came the answer.

'Four boxes of VSOP brandy. Cheap at five hundred and fifty Euros, against Mr O'Brady's bill. Your brother owns a hotel I believe, nice little VAT free purchase, twenty shots a bottle, think about it. Your brother pays you for the brandy; you deducted it from Mr O'Brady's bill. I will return to spend more later on, Deal?'

A wizened hand was offered, but the handshake felt firm enough. Victoria promised to return the cart as soon as possible.

On the way back to the harbour, Liam Jr. congratulated Victoria on the way she had handled the reluctant Scotsman. Victoria told him it was easy and now they had an ally for future business. When clients brought their yachts to Goughal, his father could point them in the right direction and Mr Walker would always be a man they could do business with.

They arrived back at the yacht to find it moored inside the floating dock ready to be raised for a thorough examination of the hull. As the yacht left the water, two workers placed strong timbers to keep the yacht truly vertical and support the hull where needed.

Myriam had the wood stove lit in the cottage kitchen ready to start cooking breakfast. It was not long before everyone sat down to a much-needed repast of porridge with sugar and cream, followed by a cooked English breakfast. Nicola handed Liam a list of the work she thought necessary and what items required a thorough check-up.

As their meal finished, two very scruffy individuals entered the cottage looking for their promised breakfast. These were the brothers Grunt, #1 and #2. Their real names were not known, their current 'handle' had evolved over a number of years by the complete lack of any discernible vocabulary.

What vocabulary that did exist was apparently their version of Gallic, which had probably died out when the Romans retreated back to Rome.

Still, they worked hard, never complained, and possessed strength well beyond the capabilities of any Olympic weightlifter.

With the yacht now fully secured, Victoria purposefully headed towards her bunk. The morning exercise had been bracing, almost enjoyable in fact, but now came the time for a well-earned snooze. Nicola thought it a wise move. Victoria had fallen well behind her rest schedule mandated by Uncle Adam.

After a large mug of coffee, Liam and Nicola went into the dry dock to examine the condition of the yacht's hull. A strong power wash would soon complete the cleaning, and patches of exposed fibreglass were found needing attention and repair.

Liam asked if she wanted a fresh coat of anti-fouling, mentioning he had sufficient TBT anti-fouling paint, currently banned in Europe, he was keen to use up. If Nicola planned to cross the Atlantic to the Caribbean, and then up to the USA, she shouldn't have too much aggravation from the authorities and it was by far the best anti-fouling for warm waters.

Nicola nodded her consent. It would take too much time to go into the city to find fresh supplies of up-to-date anti-fouling, and there was the question of suitable transport.

She looked at the paint above the waterline on the hull. It appeared to be in a reasonable condition and a strong machine rub down followed by a different colour would certainly be a big help in bringing the change needed to divert the attention of those seeking a missing black yacht.

Liam took Nicola to an adjacent storehouse, to find it piled high with all sorts. Nicola thought it no wonder he was skint, too much stock and no clients, a sure-fire way to become bankrupt. He showed her tins of excellent two-pack yellow paint, but it looked far too yellow for her tastes. The only other colour of which he had a sufficient quantity was bright white, or as Nicola preferred, 'bathtub white.'

'Liam,' she said. 'What shade of yellow do we get if we mix these two colours together?'

Liam opened a tin he prepared earlier; well aware the yellow paint did indeed look very yellow.

'It looks like this colour,' he said, showing Nicola the pale-yellow paint he hoped would bring her approval. He really needed to recoup the money he had spent on the large amount of stock he'd bought very much on the cheap.

Nicola looked at the colour; then looked at Liam. Liam had taken a big chance. She looked again at the colour deciding it would be as good as any other colour. A newly painted yacht in this colour could be seen from outer space, a truly brilliant disguise.

'OK. Let's complete the grand tour to see what else needs to be done.'

An hour later, Liam completed a list of work; pleased it offered a chance to make a good profit. He scratched the numbers down on a piece of paper. Nicola looked at him strangely.

'What's this?' she asked. 'It's my estimate,' he said.

'Liam, is a guesstimate. This is not how to do business,' replied Nicola. 'Victoria is the expert. She will teach you how to present a scope of work and associated costs. If you want to build a successful business, you will need to become conversant with standard business practice; otherwise, you will never succeed in this day and age.'

Victoria appeared. 'My ears are burning. What gives?'

Nicola showed Vicky the scrap of paper Liam proffered, saying now was the time for her favourite master class.

'Best ask Liam Jr. to join in,' said Victoria as she prepared her computer to show how a professional spreadsheet should be used to itemise each work activity, assign it a number, to agree an estimate of man-hours, list of consumables to complete that item, and a cost figure for the overhead used to complete the work.

Liam remained doubtful such a flood of paperwork would help him actually do the work. Victoria explained the contractual side of the exercise. It would identify the extras which could be invoiced. The main point of the exercise was to give the client the information he needed to agree a contract with strong a measure of confidence.

Master class over; Victoria retired for a much-needed snooze. Nicola wanted to go for a good walk. She needed the exercise.

If Liam owned the land around the harbour then there existed the opportunity for investment in holiday homes, or even a guesthouse. It could be the sort of investment Great Aunt Violet might be interested in.

Great Aunt Violet had made, and still made, a pile of cash based on her unbelievable knowledge of horse racing and the turf accountancy business which supported it. Her favourite wager was the three or four race accumulator. She had many to her name or rather different names. The bookies would look at the selection and laugh; then ended up laughing on the other side of their face.

Great Aunt Violet delighted in bringing down the cheats who preyed on punters at the racetrack. There wasn't a trick she didn't have first-hand knowledge off and she used them all to very good effect. She had a group of oldies with time on their hands. They would attend the race meeting, dressed in a variety of disguises, old, young, poor, rich, discrete, and outrageous, and all combinations in between.

Many were the racecourse bookies, who would rue the day Great Aunt Violet saw something that really was not how their business should be conducted, and heaven help anyone she caught laundering illegal money.

Great Aunt Violet also possessed many contacts in the security services, concerned at the ever-increasing presence of eastern European gangs encroaching into the UK betting market. Gangs linked to other illegal enterprises coming to the attention of MI-5.

Nicola set off, pulling the laden cart behind her to drop off four boxes of VSOP at the local shop. By the time she arrived at the village shop the electrical power supply had been restored. Her time speaking to Mr Walker was brief, to the point, and highly productive.

She wandered off down another lane which looked like the back route to Liam's cottage on the other side of the harbour. As she crested a small rise, she came upon a long low wooden building with a two-story extension built on one end.

The twin doors halfway along the building showed a faded sign, almost illegible, the words sail maker just discernible. She knocked on the door, heard someone moving inside and waited patiently.

A tall lean man in his late thirties, dressed in jeans, an open sports shirt and soft slippers opened the door. Nicola introduced herself asking if he was Liam's brother. He nodded an affirmative. Nicola told him Liam suggested she called to see if he could spend the time to run his eye over the sails on her yacht, get them cleaned and make any necessary repairs. The tall man nodded again, saying he had been expecting a call.

He was busy finishing off a client's order, so he invited Nicola to come in and wait. Nicola was in no hurry and made herself comfortable in an old but comfy leather sofa at the far end of the sail loft. She saw the usual paraphernalia to be found in any sail maker's loft. Bits and pieces of sail cloth in rolls, boat covers waiting for repair, and more worryingly, what looked like finished orders yet to be collected.

Stacked high in the far corner she saw a large number of thick rolls of material, which looked like virgin Kevlar cloth, recognising the light-yellow cloth. She also noticed rolls of a much finer and lighter synthetic material in red and yellow; cloth that could easily make a mid-range asymmetrical spinnaker.

The sail loft floor looked straight and even, good surface quality, with the usual pits for the sewing machines. There existed a large rack with an assortment of sail battens plus a large sign with Celtic hieroglyphs, perhaps the sailmaker's logo.

Nicola knew the sailmaker's name was Kerrigan, although he hadn't introduced himself. He finished his work, wrapped the sail he had finished working on, and attached a label. He shouted out, and a female, who Nicola took to be his seamstress, appeared. The mobile phone in his pocket rang. The call was short, stressed and Kerrigan muttered to himself as the caller hung-up.

He looked around, without seemingly addressing anybody in particular, asked, 'Has anybody got a spare spinnaker for a sixty-five-foot ocean racing yacht by Friday lunchtime. Fat chance.'

Nicola thought for a moment. There was an unused full-sized spinnaker on her yacht. There was little chance she would ever use it. She would need at least four strong crew who knew exactly what to do with such a large sail.

'If the spinnaker bag looked like new, I wonder,' she thought. 'There's a spinnaker on my yacht if you're interested,' she said out loud.

The sailmaker came over to Nicola, smiled, asking if he could check out this lead. The client was a famous local sailor, engaged in a round of offshore and inshore round-the-buoy races. He had good results to date, but this coming weekend would be vital if he was going to win a prestigious cup, one he had always wanted to win.

'Ready when you are,' he said.

THE TWO OF them made short work of the journey back to Liam's cottage. They walked around the harbour to the floating dock, where Nicola saw substantial progress had been achieved. With the hull pressure wash completed the two Grunts were busy removing flaking anti-fouling to allow the surface underneath to dry before applying a red primer.

Kerrigan looked at the yacht, saw it had the spars and rigging to fly a full-sized spinnaker, and began to take a keen interest in what might just become a profitable afternoon. God knows he needed one. There were bills to pay and clients were not rushing to clear their invoices.

Liam appeared from one of the guest cottages, where Myriam was busy turning stale bread into delicious bread pudding. Liam offered Nicola a slice; it tasted exceptionally good indeed. Nicola told Liam his brother had a client with an urgent need for a large spinnaker.

The three of them clambered aboard the yacht. Liam went below to the sail locker. Nicola opened the foredeck hatch and stood back to let the men wrestle a large spinnaker bag on deck. Kerrigan wanted to hoist it up the mast admitting it would be kind of tricky with the wind still quite boisterous.

Nicola suggested it would be best to repair to the adjacent field, with its tall trees and bushes lining the windward side, where the spinnaker could be laid out on the ground. The men agreed, took the sail out of its bag, and laid it down with all three of them holding onto one corner. The sail looked new showing no signs of ever having been used.

Kerrigan could judge, more or less, its size, and reckoned it would be big enough for his client. Liam Jr. arrived to see what was going on, only to be told to fetch a large measuring tape. He soon returned and the sail was duly measured.

Kerrigan flipped open his mobile phone, pushed a redial button, passed the details of the sail and smiled when the receiver of his call told him it was a deal done. Kerrigan turned his back on the others to conduct an interesting negotiation regarding price.

Still smiling, he revealed the client had agreed to pay close to list price if they could forget about VAT.

Nicola started having additional thoughts. A repainted yacht would be useful to escape from Europe until the fuss died down and new sails would complete the process. Imagine, a pale-yellow yacht with pale yellow sails.

'Kerrigan let's think about a deal for new sails for my yacht. You have plenty of Kevlar cloth in your sail loft. I need three sails, mainsail, foresail, plus an asymmetrical spinnaker, which can be flown from the halyard point just above the foresail halyard point. You could factor in the value of the existing sails to adjust the price.'

Kerrigan feared he was about to be overtaken by some female cunning. He'd hoped to get this spinnaker cheap, flip it and make a quick and tidy profit. Liam warned his brother Nicola was an experienced sailor, able to talk her way past most things.

Still, he'd received an intriguing idea. Big yacht sails always had a good second-hand market, so just what did Nicola have to offer?

Nicola told him there were two foresails, the mainsail, of course, and two spare foresails stored somewhere down below. Also, she could throw in the large spinnaker pole and its rigging, as it would be no longer needed.

Kerrigan saw profit all around, but he needed to be careful. He thought for a moment and said, 'OK Nicky, I will make you a new mainsail and foresail for trade, and I'll only charge you two grand for the asymmetrical spinnaker.'

'How long to make three sails?' she asked. 'When do you want to sail,' asked Kerrigan

'Monday, on the tide, gives you the best part of a week,' replied Nicola.

'It's a tough call, but times are hard, and I can make good money. Just need to work flat out until Monday morning. Can I take the spinnaker now and collect the pole and the other sails on Monday? The client is waiting and he needs time to fit it to his yacht. He will pay me, then I can pay for the extra help I need.'

'OK Kerrigan best get on with it and thanks,' said Nicola.

They shook hands on the deal, Kerrigan packed the sail into its bag, and with that, he was gone.

Nicola, feeling more than pleased with herself marched around the harbour to Liam's cottage to find Myriam in the kitchen and her daughter playing in the garden at the back of the building. Nicola accepted a cup of tea with thanks and sat down. The usual girl talk ensued. Nicola felt very pleased to see the whole tenor of the O'Grady household had changed markedly for the better. No one was hungry after the big breakfast, and for a change, Myriam had taken the opportunity to catch up on house tasks long denied due to the lack of funds.

Nicola left her to it and wandered back to the yacht. She was impressed with the progress so far. Victoria was up and about, trying to chat up Grunt #1, but to no avail. The brothers were busy making money, getting fed, and would only focus on their work.

Liam Jr. was down below, raking around in the engine room, with a list of smaller tasks concerning the main engine, and its accessories. Apart from changing the oil, fuel and air filters, the engine required little attention.

Victoria made coffee, raided the biscuit box, and headed towards the cockpit to sit in the sun to get some colour on her face and relax. Having been pestered by one and all to take things easy, she was busy getting used to life in the slow lane.

Nicola told her about the deal regarding the sails. Victoria knew little about sails, but new sails, like a new lady's dress, sounded like a promising idea. She felt intrigued with Nicola's thinking. If the authorities were busting a gut looking for a black yacht, a yacht in bright pale yellow, with new yellow sails, easily seen by the blind, then the subtlety of the situation became obvious.

Nicola told her, she was expecting Jus William, Great Aunt Violet's partner, to arrive tomorrow morning, bringing their passports, replaced bank cards, and other documents. Victoria asked what time she expected him. Then, the man himself appeared out of nowhere.

'Bonjour Mesdames, allez vous bien,' enquired Jus.'

'Très bien merci. Vooulez-vous un café?' replied Nicola and went below to bring him a large coffee.

Victoria had never met Jus before. She saw an elegant and very fit elder statesman, with a ready smile and piercing eyes full of experiences of a full life through troubled times. His hair was grey, but he could be any age over sixty years. He was dressed in day clothes, buttoned-up shirt with no collar, and a smart Italian leather jacket which didn't come from eBay.

Everything about him was understated, one of those rare persons you would never notice if he stood stock still in the middle of a large car park.

Nicola returned with his coffee to receive a package of passports in return. She took a quick peek inside and said thank you. She asked how her Aunt was to be told Aunty hoped to meet them very soon.

'Mon chère,' Jus began, 'We are alone?'

'There's a mechanic below checking the engine systems; he's just about finished,' replied Nicola.

Liam Jr. appeared looking forward to a late lunch. He disappeared in the direction of the adjacent cookhouse.

'We must go below,' said Jus, 'I have vital information for you both.'

The three friends went below. Nicola locked the hatch behind her and closed the blinds in the main saloon windows. Sitting in comfort around the main saloon dining table, Jus started by bringing them up to date with recent events.

He told the two girls the police had identified the leader of the violent Manchester robbery gang as one Rufus Stone, a gentleman well known to them and one close to arch gang super boss Mr Harry Hackett, known as 'Hatchet Harry,' to all who had the misfortune to know him.

The police had arrived at this decision regarding Rufus Stone, based on the fact he was the most likely suspect to carry out a contract crime organised by others and now he had completely disappeared. Victoria muttered, 'What a shame,' but fell silent at Juss look of annoyance.

The Police also came to the conclusion a yacht had been used as a get-away, but any robbery organised by Hackett, would not entail all the funds disappearing abroad.

Thus, there had to be a van driver. The original van used in the robbery had been discovered dumped in mid-Wales. An in-depth forensic investigation led to the conclusion the driver had been a female.

Suspicion fell upon Stone's sister, a female with certain charms and a total lack of morals. They knew Hackett was a predatory sexual person and that Stone and his sister, a Miss Silva Stone, were the closest of friends, especially in the bedroom or more often than not, in his private dungeon. Mr Hackett and these two suspects regularly engaged in activities in Mr Hackett's dungeon in the underground labyrinths of his fortress castle, where no perversions were omitted.

Jus told them this information came from very secret intelligence, never to be divulged.

Jus continued, 'At 4 a.m. this morning, police from the Manchester's serious crime squad, accompanied by members of other security agencies, raided the home of Miss Stone to find a treasure trove of incriminating evidence, including some of the cash from the robbery, both used and new unissued notes.

'During intensive questioning, she started screaming about two women who'd 'volunteered' to accompany Mr Stone and his two accomplices, for the purposes of sexual exploitation.

These two girls had killed her brother and his two companions at sea during a large storm, and escaped, presumed to reach the intended destination, Spain.

When asked how she could possibly know, this, she started screaming she had psychic powers and was completely connected to her brother. She said she could tell, from a great distance, whatever he was up to. The interrogator asked if this included when he suffered from flatulence, and she had screamed 'Yes' very loudly.'

None of the police conducting this enquiry believed this nonsense, but when they examined the time scales, and the fact the escaping yacht would have passed through severe weather, something she could not have known about, they thought again.

What Jus couldn't tell them was whether the police authorities believed this outrageous story. However, 'Hatchet' Harry did. He had more contacts in the underworld than anybody becoming convinced his favourite male bed partner and two cohorts were missing without trace.

If he couldn't find them, no one could, and he was absolutely furious. A simple robbery gone pear shaped. A disaster of the highest magnitude and now the man's sister had started screaming blue murder at everyone.

Jus doubted if the police authorities were treating her drug addiction. They would just let her go 'cold turkey', so she would continue to rant and rave all the more. The endless rantings would have some truth included. Then, all they needed to do was a bit of gentle sifting.

To cap it all, they now knew this idiot female had kept some of the stash delivered to a Hackett intermediary, and now the police had real hard evidence that pointed only one way.

Jus continued, 'This case, Nicola, has top priority. Six million pounds stolen, two dead policemen, two dead security staff, six others injured, a classic robbery gone astray.

Now Stone has vanished, the police have come to one of two conclusions. Both he and his gang have escaped to somewhere new, unlikely given their profile, or they were indeed at the bottom of the sea.

And now some of the stolen money has turned up in Spain, so confusion reigns. The authorities are continuing their search for a black yacht and two females with a taste for maritime adventure.'

Nicola looked blankly at Jus, asking, 'So, what's the status now ?'

Jus replied he wasn't sure, implying Aunt Vee wasn't sure either. That confusion reigned was not a bad thing in itself. The authorities were concentrating on the most tangible, but unlikely scenario, of the Manchester gang having reached southern Spain, but without being seen or reported.

Jus asked Nicola if she had a story ready of how they had extricated themselves from the clutches of Rufus Stone and his friends, to return unnoticed to the UK. Their departure from the UK would not have been recorded, so returning, in the same manner, would be fundamental. Nicola said she had concocted a story, but still needed to work on the fine detail. Jus suggested her story might include making their way to Paris and using his contacts to provide safe passage back to Ireland or Scotland as required. Nicola nodded telling him this could well be a part of her thinking. Jus could not tell Nicola and Victoria the news 'Hatchet'

Harry was on the rampage and using all his resources to try and find them.

Great Aunt Violet Stranraer, Jus William, and others, were part of a secret group, dedicated to the downfall of 'Hatchet' Harry, whose organisation had, over the years, corrupted many persons at every level of society, including high officers in the UK government and the judiciary, with a complex range of wealth, favours and sexual perversion of every kind, cruelty, and murder. 'Caligula' himself would have been classified as a caring, equal opportunity employer, compared to 'Hatchet' Harry.

But now the tide was turning. A top-secret group of politicians, security personnel, and serving military officers joined in the fight back. The law would be used where judged appropriate; and more direct action would be carried out by 'others.'

Secrecy was fundamental. They even had a 'mole' inside 'Hatchet' Harry's empire, a person of considerable skill and bravery.

But, to more immediate matters. Jus told the two girls Liam was in deep trouble with a 'Mr John the Baptist,' who ran a large betting operation for Hackett, based in London.

Just over a month ago, there had been a famous race meeting at a course on the west side of middle England. They could guess where if they wished. The 4 p.m. race was the main event of the meeting and the heavily fancied favourite had been nobbled. Strangely, the mandated forensic examination did not reveal how, but the fact it left the stalls like a bolt of lightning, reached the first bend six lengths in front of the field, and then accelerated to the back of the field, seemed highly suspicious.

The race meeting had been a favourite with punters countrywide. East European gangs had infiltrated the event to make some serious money to fund activities in their own countries.

The syndicates and individual punters had arrived at the course to attend the meeting in fine style. Some of the syndicates were skilled, serious punters, using either three-or four-fold accumulator systems to make huge returns.

A few syndicates had lost a great deal of money, none more so than a cell of active members of the Irish Republican movement in Dublin. Liam was not, per se, a part of this movement, but he did share their aims and following the loss of his contract, he had placed the remainder of his resources into a treble. Experience told him the odds were good.

Now Liam desperately needed ten thousand British pounds. Jus knew he would ask the girls for a loan. Quite how Jus knew all this would never be revealed, and Nicola was never going to ask. Victoria made to ask a couple of questions, only to receive a sharp kick under the table.

The man himself arrived. Liam knocked on the hatchway and was invited into the yacht. He found himself nursing a welcome cup of coffee, looking at three people who seemed to know all. He was not mistaken.

Liam got straight down to asking the question, the one he had been afraid to ask during the last few days. Jus introduced himself as the partner of Great Aunt Violet, telling him he understood he knew his famous lady and Liam had been her link between UK and Republican interests, in a confidential, highly secret nature.

Now Liam recognised exactly who Nicola was. He had his suspicions simply by watching the lass, the way she looked, talked and the way she went about her business in a simple matter of fact manner.

Jus told him what he already knew asking did he need any assistance in this delicate and dangerous matter, because 'John the Baptist' had a very efficient way of dealing with non-payers of outstanding debts.

His favourite method was the interview with a large barrel full of water. The debtor would be immersed, head down, until the funds were promised.

Liam looked worried, and so he should be. He was not totally unaware of the issues but mistakenly relied on his republican friends for assistance.

Jus sat silently as Liam plucked up the courage to say he must arrive in London, between nine and twelve o'clock on the Friday morning, the very last day when matters could be resolved in the normal commercial manner. This was the day after tomorrow. He'd arranged to travel with a delivery driver friend of his, as he made his twice-weekly trip to London, via the ferry to Wales.

Liam offered this opportunity to the three other Irish republicans involved in this affair, which they accepted, as it was known that 'minders' for Mr Baptist would intercept punters on their way to pay their dues and relieve them of their funds in the usual brutal manner.

This had happened before to the same three Irish Republicans members. Revenge had been planned, and inside information from London suggested two of 'John the Baptist' minders would travel on the ferry to Ireland, holed-up in an unused cabin. On arrival at the Irish port, two crew members in the pay of 'John the Baptist' would disembark using the ID of the first two.

When the ferry commenced its return to Wales, the two minders in the unused cabin would venture forth, commit the robbery during the night and then sit out the remainder of the journey as stand-by crew in the ferry's crew quarters until their arrival in Wales.

The four republicans would travel together. The plan, in its simplistic form, was to find the 'minders,' lure them into an empty part of the ship, render them unconscious and gently drop them overboard.

On arrival in the UK, the lorry would take them overnight to London depositing its four passengers in a quiet street, where they could quickly merge into the great crush that was the early morning commute.

'Liam,' Jus started. 'Your plan I like. I can provide some assistance if you need.'

Jus had at his beck and call, a range of French 'tourists' who were always available to his personal secret organisation. These worthy Frenchmen were the sons of his former WWII French Resistant colleagues, dedicated to profitable enterprise, and always a noble cause.

Liam waved his hand as if to say, 'whatever.' The poor man was very confused and a long way from his comfort zone. He knew he'd gambled badly, a stupid gamble at that. Now he had become embroiled in activities bringing feelings of great concern.

Nicola looked at Jus and nodded as if to say, 'Just keep him safe.'

The meeting ended, as Liam rushed out to get back to work. Back to his world where he felt secure in the knowledge he was in-charge and working for his family.

Jus told Nicola it was time for him to go. Nicola asked if he needed anything. Jus requested a contribution of fifty thousand pounds of the unused notes, to be employed as the poisoned pill to be injected into the heart of 'John the Baptist's' business empire, and the start of a secret plan to dismember the vast empire of the 'Hatchet' Harry.

'And just how are you going to get this amount of cash through airport security?' asked Nicola.

Jus smiled a knowing smile, parted from his two female friends with the usual kisses on both cheeks, and with that, he was gone.

Victoria looked up at Nicola bemused by what she had just witnessed. Nicola sat down with her, took her hand, and calmly said, 'Victoria, none of this happened, OK?'

'Works for me,' said Victoria, and went to her cabin for a lie-down.

Chapter 12

Nicola finds Love in Goughal Harbour

THE TRANSFORMATION of the yacht progressed quickly, aided by calm and pleasant weather following the massive storm. The work below the yacht's waterline had been completed and two coats of anti-fouling applied. The propeller had been cleaned and polished by Liam Jr. who had also replaced the zinc anodes, checked the rudder pintles were OK and declared no more work was required.

Above the hull's waterline, the black paint had been sanded down, and two coats of white undercoat applied, and rubbed down to give an immaculate smooth finish. The two-pack topcoats would be sprayed onto the hull the next day and by Saturday morning the yacht would be ready to be re-floated.

Jock Walker, from the local shop, paid a visit to Nicola to ask if he could replenish the stores aboard the yacht before she sailed on Monday's high tide. Nicola agreed, one less task to carry out, and now she intended to enjoy a period of relaxation.

Nicola's only real worry centred on the delivery of the new sails. Her worry greatly reduced when the new foresail arrived. With the old foresail removed and put aside, the new fitted perfectly into the foresail foil. Kerrigan arrived soon after to check and admire his work.

Nicola congratulated him on a fine-looking sail, saying she had never seen better.

Kerrigan told her the new mainsail was well underway and all being well it would be ready Saturday afternoon. The asymmetrical spinnaker would be ready sometime Sunday.

Nicola asked if she could come and see the mainsail being completed.

'Come any time after teatime,' he said. 'About six p.m. when his seamstress ladies would be away, and he would be resting before continuing long into the night.'

Nicola thanked him for the invitation saying she would bring a bottle of wine they could share. Nicola wandered round to Myriam's cottage.

Liam had vanished on his mission to London. Nicola passed the message to a worried wife; Jus would pass the money Liam needed in London and not to worry.

Myriam did worry, she knew most of what was going on and felt deeply unhappy. Nicola told her to be calm, as she could be sure Jus would have his men keeping a careful eye on the proceedings. If anything, not quite legal was going to occur, it would be his men who would do the dirty deed.

Myriam felt better at the reassurance, but who knows what could go wrong. She reminded Nicola that Mr Fuck-up always lurked around the corner.

Victoria returned with little Rosie, after a long walk in the forest picking mushrooms, flowers, and berries.

'This is very 'mummsy' of you Vicky, getting in practice for motherhood,' chided Nicola. 'Very funny,' said Victoria. 'Rosie is my best friend, eh pet. She is well behaved, not like some people I know.'

The little girl smiled and handed her mother the flowers from the forest. 'Will Daddy be gone long?' she asked.

'No pet, he'll be back late Friday or early Saturday morning,' Myriam replied.

'Vicky,' Myriam asked, 'Could you bath Rosie, feed her and put her to bed. She'll ask you for a bedtime story.'

'Sure thing. You going to help Nicky?'

'Nope, I'm going up to the sail loft to see our new mainsail. Shan't be long,' said Nicola. 'Be you careful with Kerrigan; he has a way with the ladies,' cautioned Myriam.

'Is he the gentle caring type, or like an Australian,' she asked. 'And just what does 'dat' mean?' asked Myriam.

Nicola replied, 'Australian foreplay. "OK Sheila, brace yourself", one of the oldest jokes in the book.'

Myriam laughed out loud. It did her the world of good. Victoria yawned and suggested Nicky update her jokes book. Nicola smiled and left them to their domestics. She strolled purposely up the back lane to the sail loft, nursing a bottle of red wine.

She arrived at the sail loft and let herself in. A voice from above invited her to lock the door behind her, turn the loft lights off, and come upstairs.

She found Kerrigan drying himself off and donning his bathrobe. He looked relaxed and bid she make herself comfortable on the leather sofa. Snacks had been laid out on an ornate wooden Moroccan coffee table.

'Wine?' she asked.

'Sure,' Kerrigan replied. 'Good of you to come. Your mainsail is coming along very nicely. Tonight is fitting cringles night. Tomorrow, my boys will remove your mainsail from the mast, remove all the track cars to bring them and the sail battens for fitting.'

Nicola served the wine and relaxed. She felt comfortable with this man. None of the predatory male about him. A man who would let matters take their own course. They chatted for a while, watching the level of the wine descend to the bottom of the bottle. Kerrigan served a range of snacks made from traditional recipes, included Irish whisky cake, Irish chocolate potato cake and delicious bread and butter pudding with Irish whisky.

She noticed the common thread in the recipes. Nicola rather liked Irish whisky. She wondered if Kerrigan would bother to get dressed, as he clearly had little clothing under his bathrobe. In fact, he had nothing on under his bathrobe, as when he moved to and from the coffee table to serve snacks, all was momentarily revealed.

Kerrigan looked a fine fellow of a man, fit, lean from years of hard work and hard sailing. It hadn't passed his notice she'd noticed his brief display. He also noticed the top two buttons on her blouse were losing the battle to stay where she constantly returned them.

Kerrigan admired this girl. He didn't know the full extent of what she'd been through, but she had succeeded, saved the life of her best friend, and now she looked far better than when she first arrived.

He sat down beside her on the sofa, as she moved to his side. Kerrigan started to become aroused and she looked him in the eye as her hands moved slowly toward his arousal. He put his arm around her as she moulded into him. His arousal complete, his bathrobe could no longer hide his modesty. They kissed and fondled, as Kerrigan made a slow job of releasing her other buttons.

The kissing and the fondling continued until Nicola whispered, 'There's a double bed somewhere?'

He took her hand and led her into the bedroom. The comfortable double bed had fresh sheets on it, as it always did on a Friday. They lay down together and continued. Nicola slowly became without clothes and Kerrigan's bathrobe found its way to the floor.

Now she teased him and Kerrigan didn't know how long he could hold back. She rolled on top of him and gently eased his arousal deep into her.

'Damn, that felt good,' she thought. 'Now I'm back to normal.'

They lay and wriggled gently together, allowing Kerrigan to admire the view, and what a view it was. She teased him some more until the moment had come, as they both arrived at the ultimate moment at the same time.

Nicola rolled off him and lay hard against his side. Kerrigan had never been sexually seduced, but there was always a first time for everything and did he enjoy it.

He whispered in her ear, 'You must come again,' and then realised what he said.

Nicola returned his invitation and said, 'Give me half an hour and we'll see what we can do.'

Later, with Round Two successfully completed, time had come to let Kerrigan get some much-needed sleep. God knows he had little of it in the last few days. But he was relaxed and she was grateful. Nicola slipped back into her clothes, kissed him farewell and let herself out of the sail loft, mission accomplished.

She went straight back to the guest cottage adjacent to the yacht, took a long hot shower and dressed in a change of clothes. Nicola returned to the yacht, only to be intercepted by Vicky, who had by this time cottoned on to what had happened.

'Putting yourself in harm's way are we?' she asked, with a good long giggle. It was good to hear Victoria giggling again; it had been rather absent of late.

'Yes dear,' Nicola replied. 'To satisfy your extraordinary curiosity. It was 'bouncy castle time' for the first time in a long time.'

Victoria was full of mischief, asking, 'Is there a re-run tomorrow?'

'No,' Nicola replied. 'My monthly has returned, but damn it was good.'

'Hum,' said Victoria. 'Perhaps I could…'

'No, you can't, and you know this. Uncle Adam has given you very precise instructions on how to look after yourself until everything returns to normal, which they haven't,' chided Nicola.

'I will ask Great Aunt Violet to fix you up with a full examination, as I know you are just a little bit of a long way off from being one hundred percent.'

Victoria became a bit glum, admitting she could feel better, but this wouldn't stop them from setting out on the great adventure to the other side of the Atlantic. Nicola said nothing. She knew Victoria was still having her bad moments and how hard she had tried to overcome them. Time would tell.

Chapter 13

The Yacht Recommissions at Goughal

THE DAYS to the yacht's departure passed quickly. The work of refurbishment neared completion except for the delivery of the new mainsail and spinnaker. Liam returned safe and sound from London but remained tight-lipped about his experiences. All that mattered was the debt had been cleared and he was free from additional worry.

This was more than the 'John the Baptist' situation. Just after lunch on that fateful Friday, Special Branch visited his emporium of turf accountancy to find one or two discrepancies, namely new fifty and twenty-pound notes whose numbers appeared on a list being held by the chief inspector.

His staff attempted to shield him from answering awkward questions, but his attempt to relocate via the back door had been thwarted by some rather burly policeman, who had obviously had a bad night. Or perhaps they were just plain violent bastards who enjoyed their job to the utmost.

According to unnamed sources, the arrival of the incriminating evidence had been blamed on an elderly French gentleman who visited Mr Baptist's emporium to collect his winnings and noticed the notes were too new to have been anything but suspicious.

So, Nicola remained happy, and so was everyone else. Lunch time arrived and Kerrigan's helpers arrived to remove the old mainsail from the mast. Not an easy task given its weight and the difficult to handle sail cloth. After some suitable Irish words of encouragement, the great sail was dragged onto the grass between the two guest cottages, and its many attachments removed.

Late afternoon, the spinnaker arrived and looked just grand in its red and yellow panels. Nicola directed operations to fit the furling gear to the tack of the sail, and hoist the spinnaker, whilst the others sought to control it as best they could in the early evening breeze. With the twin sheeting lines attached, fed through their respective fairleads, the sail was seen to be a thing of glory.

The operation concluded with Victoria using the yacht's powered winch to furl the sail around itself, which was carefully lowered, laid alongside the starboard guardrail, wrapped in its protective cover, and lashed in place ready for departure on the Monday morning tide.

With so few items remaining, everyone retired to Liam's cottage for a traditional meal, some traditional local poteen, and traditional homemade music made by the brothers Grunt, who were surprisingly expert musicians.

Victoria looked on this Irish fest with great interest. She delighted in new cultures and experiencing their way of life. Nicola kept a watchful eye on her friend's alcohol consumption as Vicky could become quite talkative after a few too many.

They retired late to the comfort of the yacht that had now become their home, this magnificent vessel with all its 'mod cons.' Victoria still could not bring herself to sleep in the main owner's cabin aft; in fact, she avoided it most of the time. The main guest cabin forward gave the same comfort, so little was lost.

Nicola always went to bed last, ensuring the ventilation scoops caught the night breeze and entry into the yacht secured. Victoria still had the occasional nightmares, with Nicola always to hand to wake her up, bring her around, and get her settled down again.

Next morning was Sunday morning. Myriam disappeared early with her brood to take Holy Communion at the local church, a longish thirty-minute walk away. The two friends woke to the peace and tranquillity of the harbour, with only the sounds of nature making its call. They lay late in bed; in the knowledge their day would be busy.

Nicola's friends from Wales were due on the afternoon tide. She had been happy to recommend the services provided by Liam and his family, hoping this would be the start of a new era for the nascent boatyard business. It certainly deserved to be successful.

The yacht looked splendid in its new colour. Nicola had grown to like the pale-yellow paint with its immaculate surface finish. All the sailing equipment had been serviced, the winches, so vital for shorthanded sailing were top-notch, and the few additions for which time had been found in such a busy period would add to the utility of the vessel's systems.

Mid-morning became the start of the expected busy day. First up came the sound of a wheeled trolley and the march of many feet as the new mainsail arrived alongside the visitor's mooring berth. Liam moved the yacht from the floating dock to the visitor's mooring berth and as the great mainsail was laid on the ground facing the correct way to install it on the mast.

Liam and brother Kerrigan argued about the best way to do this not so easy task. The new sail was stiff, but fortunately a good bit lighter than the old sail. The new sail had to be handled much more carefully, the Kevlar material always unforgiving when creased.

Eventually, the task was safely completed, with Kerrigan issuing a colourful range of instructions including strange expletives young children should not hear.

With little wind, Kerrigan hoisted the new mainsail to its fullest extent. It took a bit of a struggle to get the foot of the sail fed into the boom and all the cordage installed. When finished, Kerrigan moved back to the dockside, stood back to look at his new creation, and was very happy how it set.

'Well, Nicola,' said Kerrigan. 'What do you think? It looks perfect. There is a lot of power in this sail. You will have to be careful with your weather forecasts and timing to slab reef for less power.'

Nicola made to stand next to Kerrigan, saying, 'Not bad, let's see it with one reef in.'

Kerrigan shouted to his helpers and the within seconds, the great sail was reefed down into its 'lazy jacks'. Kerrigan explained the yacht had only two sets of lines for slab reefing, and asked if she wanted just one and two, or perhaps one and three slab reefs to be available.

'How much will the power reduce with two slab reefs?' she asked.

'Difficult to say without sea trials,' replied Kerrigan. 'This mainsail is a lot lighter than the old one, so your ship will stand better against all wind strengths. In the Caribbean it will be one thing or the other, so what you see should be OK.'

'All I can say, Kerrigan, is you have performed a miracle, thank you very much.'

Kerrigan welcomed Nicola's praise. He knew she was an experienced sailor who knew what she was talking about. Changing the yacht from a cutter to a sloop had been a good move for her purpose but he wondered if there were any other reasons for the change. He had his suspicions, but she had bought his silence.

With the lunch hour approaching fast, Myriam invited everyone to a barbeque outside the guest cottages. Cold beer placed in buckets full of ice were under temporary tables laden with good things to eat and savour. An interruption to the celebration of a project well done came in the form of three yachts entering the river up to the pool that was Goughal Harbour. The lead yacht flew the flag of a Welsh dragon; it was none other than 'Taffy' Madoc Kendrick-Jones – Commodore of the Welsh Cruisers Association, one of Nicola's best friends.

'Liam,' shouted Nicola. 'You had best tell them where to moor up;

there is little space alongside here.'

Liam went aboard the yacht, energised the VHF radio to call to the parade of welcome visitors. He was delighted Nicola had kept her word to pass the news about his shipyard to her friends.

The melodic voice of Commodore Madoc Kendrick-Jones boomed back and Liam suggested the two visiting yachts scheduled to be drydocked should moor for now inside the floating dock, and the yacht with the wooden hull should moor alongside Nicola's resplendent ship.

Soon the crews of the three visiting yachts were making introductions.

'Having a party are we?' boomed the Commodore 'We'd best bring our contribution ashore,' and sent his crew to scavenge for beers, steaks, and other foods they had brought with them.

'Gwyneth,' welcomed Nicola. 'So nice to see you again. I see you haven't found the volume control on your husband.'

'Darling, good to see you too,' replied Gwyneth. 'No, he broke the last one at the club's annual ball. He and his gang were terrorising visitors from London with their close harmony singing. Still, he's a good boy at home; despite thinking he's still able to chase the local talent.'

Gwyneth saw her husband fixed his eye on Victoria, who had emerged from her cabin dressed up in her version of Judy Garland in her 'Yellow Brick Road' outfit. Quite where the red shoes and the wig with the long brown curls had come from was a mystery to Nicola. Victoria was at her mischievous best, determined to put her past cares behind her.

'Victoria darling,' enthused Gwyneth. 'Come and give me a hug, you look good in that outfit. Be careful with the boys, it's been a long voyage from Wales. Some are still a trifle hung-over from last night's rugby celebration, England 16 – Wales 17, a close match. We were lucky, but I doubt if they will admit it.'

Liam looked on bewildered, 'Welcome to the land of the Welsh,' he thought, 'But had they brought treasure to humble Ireland and its impoverished inhabitants?'

'Gwyneth,' asked Nicola. 'How long did it take you to come over? Must be all of two hundred and fifty miles.'

'That's as the crow flies, but we had a shortage of crows. The weatherman promised a quick blast across the Irish Sea. We left at six last night, the wind dropped, and then filled in again from the south-west for a while.

We got half-way across and the damn wind veered to the West, so we had to beat to windward the last fifty miles. Good sailing though, at least we arrived on the tide.'

Victoria had met Gwyneth a few times before and just loved her

Welsh accent. It came over as strong, natural, and honest. Her husband was the same at home, when he reverted to Mr Madoc Kendrick-Jones, mind your manners and take-off your farmyard boots before attempting to pass any further than the vast kitchen with its Welsh slate floor.

Liam thought to leave the subject of commerce for later, but the Commodore collared him and forcefully requested a tour of Nicola's 'new' yacht, looking resplendent in its pale-yellow finish, newly varnished woodwork, and polished bright work.

Liam was happy to oblige, and the pair of them disappeared to talk shop, not before grabbing a few beers on the way.

Gwyneth didn't mind, she shuffled her two female friends to one side for some girl talk. Nicola slowed her down, and took her, with Victoria, to meet Myriam and little Rosie, who enjoyed being chatted-up by one of the Welsh crew.

Liam got down to the business of getting to know his new customers. He need not have worried. An enthusiastic Commodore shouted for his troops to come to look at Nicola's 'new' yacht and hadn't Liam and his boys done a wonderful job.

Kerrigan arrived and was quickly surrounded by the three Welsh skippers asking about new sails. Liam smiled. The time was coming for his elder brother to stump up some commission.

The party lasted until the food and the beer ran out. Victoria became quite tipsy from the wine and it was time for bed. Nicola had a long farewell conversation with Kerrigan, but Nicola had a long day ahead of her tomorrow, and Myriam headed Kerrigan 'off at the pass,' much to the amusement of brother Liam.

The Commodore moved his crew into one of the guest cottages, so as to have his yacht to himself and his wife. Liam thought to offer to lift the floating dock out of the water to prevent any undue rocking motion, but he concluded the Commodore didn't give a damn about anything, so he kept his offer for later.

The crew of the yacht moored outboard of Nicola's were more restrained in their behaviour with all the appearance of being strong Presbyterian church goers.

Happy all had gone well during the day, Nicola headed towards her favourite part of the day, bath and bed, and a good night's sleep.

Chapter 14

The Yacht heads for Port St. Peter, Scotland

MONDAY MORNING dawned bright and clear, pleasing Nicola no end. The weather forecast seemed favourable as far north as Dublin when the wind would veer to the North. So, an easy run along the Irish coast, followed by a beat to windward past the Isle of Man and then on to Port St. Peter.

Victoria cleared the breakfast things away, as Nicola secured the yacht ready for sea. Kerrigan offered to guide them down the river and spend twenty minutes aboard to fine-tune the new rig; an offer Nicola readily accepted.

Nicola was not one for tearful farewells, and in any case, by the time she was ready to slip, Liam and the Commodore were dashing around finalising the scope of work for the three Welsh yachts.

Victoria looked pleased to see Myriam involved, translating what was agreed on to the new worksheets she had prepared for the new way of working. The Commodore looked most impressed, so the exercise had been well worthwhile.

The busy shipyard came to a brief stop as Nicola sounded the foghorn to call everyone came over to say thank you and bon voyage. Victoria felt sad to leave, she had grown to like Ireland a great deal, but recognised the need to get the visit to Port St. Peter over and done with, and escape from the dangers in the UK. To get to sea and onwards to a new life.

Victoria steered the yacht down the river, followed by Kerrigan in the fishing dory, and as they reached open water, Kerrigan came alongside, tied up, and jumped aboard to help Nicola raise the mainsail. With the two girls taking control of the winches, he put the yacht through a series of manoeuvres on all points of sail to check the set-up of the yacht. He made a few minor adjustments and pronouncing himself satisfied.

Then, he gave both girls a big farewell hug, thanked them for all the help they had given the O'Grady family, and with that, he was gone. Nicola was keen to helm the yacht to know the new feel of her and after a short while pronounced it as good. She gave the helm to Victoria who quickly came to the same opinion.

The yacht set out on an easterly course, heading towards the turn northwards at Carnsore Point. With the wind almost directly behind, the yacht powered along in fine style, and four hours later reached the turn to the north-northeast, passing the busy port of Rosslare with its fleets of roll-on roll-off car ferries to Wales and Northern France.

With the wind now on the beam, and with one slab reef in the mainsail and a full foresail, the yacht made magnificent progress towards their destination at Port St. Peter. Nicola calculated their arrival time round about nine a.m. the following day. With the weather forecast giving the strong possibility of winds veering around to the north-west, possibly to the north, Nicola wished to make the most of the present favourable wind.

Kerrigan had advised keeping offshore due to the extensive inshore activities by the Irish fishing industry, busily trying to keep up with demand from restaurants all over the UK and Europe.

As the routine aboard settled down, Victoria set-up the autopilot, went below to update the logbook and shut down all the electronics. Nicola remained nervous about maritime patrol aircraft. The day remained clear, blue skies with occasional high and low cloud heading toward Wales.

Late evening, as the sun gave way to the night in a blaze of colour, the yacht passed well offshore from the magic city of Dublin. Vicky and Nicky had visited that fair city many times, all happy times. Shouldn't they repeat the process? A nice idea but the Irish were an inquisitive lot always asking searching questions about anything out of the ordinary. The arrival of a grand yacht, gleaming in its new paintwork would generate many unwanted questions, none of which had suitable answers.

As darkness fell, the two friends reverted to two-hour watches. The autopilot worked as flawlessly as ever. Victoria christened it 'George'. Victoria's grandfather had served in the RAF during WW2. 'George', was, of course, slang for the autopilot, and a good auto-pilot was worth two men on watch any day of the week.

The night watches passed peacefully, the clear weather held, and the change in the wind direction came four hours later than the forecast. This enabled Nicola to hold Northern Ireland close, and when the change did come, the yacht changed on to port tack for a straight run to Port St. Peter.

The entrance to Port St. Peter slowly came into sight. Victoria took the helm as Nicola energised the main engine and stowed away the mainsail. The port had a tricky entrance, and it became necessary to keep to the centre of the dredged channel, followed by a sharp left hook into a small but secure harbour.

As they passed an outer marker, Victoria handed the helm to Nicola, so she could furl the foresail. The tidal range in the harbour was substantial and entering the port on a rising tide considered a big bonus. They entered the port very slowly, with Victoria hanging on to the forestay, shouting back instructions to Nicola. The echo sounder showed sufficient water depth for their arrival, but Nicola noted their departure would be best at high tide to give a greater margin for safety.

THE YACHT ENTERED the inner harbour and found a berth with sufficient length. Victoria saw the rough dockside walls and dashed around putting out as many fenders as she could. Nicola spotted a familiar long wheelbase Land Rover, whose driver came over to help secure the long mooring ropes.

'Good morning Hamish. Is Violet with you?'

'Madam is in the shop collecting the mornin' papers,' he replied.

Then, the lady herself arrived at the dockside, looking down at the yacht.

'Should have brought my sunglasses with me,' cried out Great Aunt Violet, her Scottish accent long since overtaken by the many years spent in France during and after the war.

Hamish helped the grand old lady aboard. She looked very spritely for her many years but jumping in and out of large yachts was not a risk she wanted to take.

'Kettle on?' she asked.

Nicola went below with Great Aunt Violet to make themselves comfortable. Hamish disappeared to get the messages, or shopping as it is known in English, in the full knowledge the ladies were about to start an extensive conversation. His shopping trip and gossiping with the local traders would take as long as it took the clock to reach the magic moment of the day, 'opening time.'

Nicola and Victoria welcomed Great Aunt Violet with heartfelt feelings. It had been four long months since they had last met, the recent events being a mixture of good and unbelievably bad. Great Aunt Violet accepted a large mug of tea from Victoria and asked if there was any Scottish shortcake.

She looked around the spacious interior of this yacht, with its beautiful cherry wood finish, recognising it as a classic American built yacht, and American yachts only had cookies. She accepted the yacht's biscuit tin from Nicola and found something inside with a chocolate covering. That would have to do.

The conversation started on the difficult subject of their kidnapping. Victoria excused herself and went to the heads to wash her face, powder her nose, or whatever it took to miss this conversation. Her nightmares were slowly receding, and she did not need any reminding of the terrible events.

When she returned to the main saloon, Great Aunt Violet asked her to sit next to her and to raise her sports shirt and reveal her back. Her back had healed well, but the faint marks were still plainly visible. Great Aunt Violet said she was sorry, but she had to see the damage for herself. She didn't say why, but Nicola knew the examination would be important for other reasons.

Victoria went to the heads, as Nicola took the opportunity to show Great Aunt Violet the before and after treatment photographs taken by Uncle Adam. During the time Great Aunt Violet examined the photographs, she whipped out her mobile phone and texted a brief message to a waiting third party. Nicola asked if she was still working, only to be told 'every day', with no further explanation.

The conversation turned to the more pleasant subject concerning Adam's and Pamela's coming nuptials. Victoria returned to the main saloon and sparked up when Nicola asked her to recall the late evening's entertainment when a rampant Pamela had flung open her bedroom door when she discovered the spying activities.

Great Aunt Violet grinned like a Cheshire cat. She loved the account of the actual proposal of marriage. She listened with interest about the couple's plans for the future and the car story regarding Duke Marmaduke. She knew most of the details about the visit to Ireland thanking her for all she had done.

Great Aunt Violet turned to the vexed subject of the stolen money from the Manchester bank. Nicola gave her a brief run-down of what had gone where, telling her the new and unissued notes had been packaged as a spare sail, complete with an outer wrapping of sail cloth with a mainsail headboard, and forged shipping labels from one of the industry main sail makers; suitably weighted to sink rapidly should the need arise.

She told Nicola she did not wish to know anything about this toxic subject then asked Nicola to hand over all bank notes of whatever currency. Nicola didn't understand what she wanted to do.

'Nicola,' Great Aunt Violet answered her sharply, 'Used notes are not as untraceable as you think. Your Euros came from Portugal and a quick look will confirm where you have been. All your bank notes need to find new homes, to insulate you from the authorities, who are desperately trying to track your movements.'

Victoria went to the yacht's safe and brought all the bank notes to the main saloon table. Wearing a pair of thin plastic gloves, Great Aunt Violet counted out the notes faster than the best bank clerk.

'Thank you,' said Great Aunt Violet, 'Hamish will bring the money I have for you from the Land Rover. It's a mixture of UK pounds, German issued Euros and US dollar bills.

I also have new bank cards for your journey either side of the Atlantic. Documents for this yacht I can't get in the time available, but insurance cover notes I do have for you, and that's about all.'

Great Aunt Violet paused, then continued, 'You will need to be careful, and you may even get away with it. You're riding your luck Nicola, but you don't need me to tell you this. Mr Hackett does not yet know who you are, so you have a window of opportunity to get away from this mess.'

Nicola stayed silent and thought for a while. She told Great Aunt Violet once the yacht arrived in the USA, she would find a way of getting the authorities to figure out to whom the yacht actually belonged.

Great Aunt Violet said as far as anybody knew, nobody in the USA was looking for it, but yachts in the USA, could go unattended for an awfully long time.

'Nicola,' said Great Aunt Violet. 'Let me see these pop guns you inherited from the deceased.'

Nicola went to the main owner's cabin and returned with all three handguns. She broke each one open in turn, removed any ammunition, and handed them over. Great Aunt Violet looked at them with the recognition these were the best assassin weapons she had seen in a long time.

'Have you seen this type of weapon before Nicola?' asked Great Aunt Violet.

Nicola nodded her head, confiding she had examined an exact gun in her forensic lab in Oxford at the request of Special Branch. The findings were the weapon was part of a special order of twelve, believed to have been placed by a master criminal, and made with duplex steels for added strength and lightness. It had a perfect balance, fitted the hand beautifully, and when used close-up became highly effective, especially with head shots under the chin.

'One for me?' asked Great Aunt Violet. 'One could come in handy; you never know.'

Nicola retrieved two of the weapons, returned them to their hiding place, and returned with a handful of ammunition.

The conversation tailed off. Victoria went to the galley to make coffee. Nicola was not surprised Great Aunt Violet would not help her on the subject of the new and unissued notes. She was quite right of course.

Best to give the packaged notes the 'deep six,' the deeper the better.

Great Aunt Violet was surprised why Nicola held fast to her view these funds could be useful later on. She knew Nicola rebelled against common sense, and the bastards who had caused her, and Vicky, to lose the jobs they liked so much.

It started to get late. Lunch time, and with a highly recommend pub serving the best

Highland cuisine but a stone throw's away, it was time to rescue Hamish from the perils of alcohol. As they walked across to the 'The Conrad', another yacht slowly and carefully entered into the harbour. With no free berths available, the yacht circled around looking for what to do next.

Nicola excused herself, returned to her yacht to wave across the water for the other yacht to come alongside and moor up. She recognised the type immediately, one of the prettiest, British made, centre cockpit yachts in the marketplace, a Moody 44, in pale blue.

'You're OK to moor up alongside,' she shouted to the skipper. 'My paint is new so please use plenty of fenders. We'll be in the pub if you need anything.'

The skipper of the Moody shouted his thanks and said he would come and meet with them. The skipper sounded very American; now what would an American be doing in this part of the world with a very British example of maritime excellence?

'You're welcome,' she cried back as she dashed to catch-up with her Aunt and Victoria.

They found Hamish none too worse for wear in the public bar, just in time to manoeuvre him into the lounge bar where the lunch time menu would be more extensive. Great Aunt Violet felt hungry and wished to check out the daily special dishes. Nicola had an idea what was coming, but Victoria had never eaten in a Scottish pub with good food. The Scottish pubs she knew were Pie Pubs, fatty mince pie, gristly steak pie and worst of all mealy pudding pie, all with generally soggy pastry.

Great Aunt Violet scanned the menu and ordered for all four of them. The first course, 'Cullen Skink,' a traditional thick Scottish soup with smoked haddock, potatoes, with plenty of onions, preferably using 'finnan haddie'.

Next, she ordered a starter portion of local fish kedgeree, with white fish and prawns, all landed that very morning. The main course to follow, a wonderful dish of roast lamb with black pudding filled roasted apples, greens, and roast potatoes.

Nicola loved her choice of dishes, but Victoria looked confused. She became less confused when the landlord served everyone with a small glass of 'Black Isle' beer and a large dram of single malt whisky. This pub still served quarter gills, and EU mandated metrication could wait. Nicola explained this pub had always served a 'haf and a haf,' and always would do. The first 'haf,' the beer, traditionally included in the price of the whisky.

Great Aunt Violet was in a good mood and raised a toast to them for coming through some terrible times. Nicola handed her a present of a small carry bag. It contained small, sealed, plastic sample jars of human hair, labelled one to four. Great Aunt Violet guessed who the first three jars might just belong to, but her strange looked focused on the fourth jar. Nicola whispered in her ear a clue as to who it might be. Maybe, a missing Irishman?

Great Aunt Violet looked a little lost at this comment until Nicola told her the Irishman really hated being called, 'Paddy'. This narrowed it down to a couple of thousand Irishmen until Nicola added the level of violence it produced. A knowing smile slowly appeared on Great Aunt Violet's face.

Wee Jimmy, the waiter, served the first course; the soup looked and smelled magnificent, especially with the crusty home-made bread rolls. As they were half-way through their soup, the crew of the Moody 44 entered the lounge bar looking for somewhere to sit.

The adjoining table was populated by three drunken fishermen who'd long since finished eating. Great Aunt Violet sharply reminded them to take what was left of their 'pay' home to their families, or she would be having sharp words with their boat owner. They shuffled in the general direct of the exit, with only a fifty/fifty chance of making it. Wee Jimmy guided his best and most regular customers in the direction of safety, before hurriedly clearing the table for the Americans.

As they finished their soup, the Americans looked on at this strange local dish. Nicola finished hers and introduced herself as the skipper of the big sloop, which the American's had already christened the 'Yellow Peril'. The skipper's name was Hank.

'Hank the Yank,' thought Nicola. 'I wonder why they are here.'

Asking the usual questions, she discovered the crew had been hired to fly to the UK at short notice, obtain a yacht which could cross the Atlantic Ocean, get it fully prepared, then wait for further instructions. That was three weeks ago. Now they had finally received instructions to come to Port St. Peter, ready to sail immediately.

Great Aunt Violet looked at Hank, a regular kind of guy, a professional yachtsman, and his motley crew. There were two youngsters in their early twenties, looking like professional crew from the world of big yacht racing, probably in-between contracts. They were busy eyeing up Victoria, who pretended not to notice.

The third member of the crew was, she thought for a moment, yes, an ex-soldier, handy with any kind of weapon, if ever she saw one. Great Aunt Violet gently kicked Nicola's leg and nodded across the other side of the table. Nicola cottoned on and smiled.

'So, what good to eat?' Hank asked of Nicola. Time to have some fun.

'Well Hank, the soup is called Cullen Skink, basically a smoked fish soup, then there is liver and bacon on the menu, chicken livers BBQ style, cows' tongue in gravy, and Haggis, a heavily spiced mix of lambs offal and other bits and pieces.

The two younger members of the American crew appeared to be turning green and faced the prospect of going hungry.

Wee Jimmy passed with a large tray of speciality dishes for a group of oldies dining enjoying their monthly reunion of the Royal Navy's WWII 'Port St. Peter Mine Clearing Squadron.' The aroma of the food wafted throughout the dining room and smelt delicious. Nicola smiled and paused to let the American sailors watch this delicious food being served.

Hank spoke up, 'What's that dish?' he asked. 'It smells right good.'

'The dish consists of cooked lamb's kidneys, swimming in a rich thick brown sauce, served on top of a thick slice of fried brown bread. Absolutely delicious. It's called 'shit on a raft.' A favourite dish of Her Majesty's Royal Navy during World War Two,' informed Great Aunt Violet. Hank looked aghast, as his two younger members of his crew fled outside for some fresh air.

'Violet,' asked Nicola. 'You didn't tell me they had this delicious dish on the menu.'

'It's not; it's a special order for the navy veterans; for their reunion. There's only a few of them left and considering the way they smoke and drink whisky, it's no wonder we won the war.'

Hank decided he was having his leg pulled, quite severely in his opinion. Welcome to Scotland.

'OK ladies, you've had your fun, so what can my crew have to eat? They're dedicated 'surf and turf' eaters and apart from hamburgers, they know nothing else,' said Hank.

'Haggis hamburgers?' suggested Nicola, smiling.

'OK Nicky,' said Victoria. 'You've had your fun, now help the nice man with some boring food.'

Great Aunt Violet called Wee Jimmy and asked if there were any steaks? He nodded an affirmative.

'OK, the Americans would like four steaks, medium, with an egg on top, sunny side up, and lashing of fries, chips to you and me, plus a bottle of tomato sauce on the side. And give them some of the lager you call beer. And put it on my account.'

'This is very generous of you lady. You OK with this?' said Hank.

'No problem Hank, I own the joint, as you would say,' smiled Great Aunt Violet.

This was news to Nicola. Still, the pub was a gold mine. Visitors came from far and wide to eat and enjoy the atmosphere. In the summer it was chaos when the pub had to insist on reservations, just to bring order to the business.

The meal progressed. The main course proved to be the delight of the day. Nicola was full, and was unable to face a sweet course, no matter how tempting the menu. Victoria and Great Aunt Violet felt the same. Hamish attempted, with great determination, the sticky toffee pudding but could only manage to eat half a generous portion.

On the adjacent table, the Americans were making short work of the steaks, and even shorter work of three pints of beer each. Thirsty work; this waiting around. The truth became apparent. Their yacht had no decent chef aboard, and although they took it turns the results were mixed, to say the least.

Great Aunt Violet ordered three green teas and Hamish a large glass of water. As Great Aunt Violet sipped her tea, Hank, sitting next to her moved sideways to ask a few general questions.

He could see Great Aunt Violet was not just any old grandmother. In fact, he quickly learned she never had children or married, although she did have a long-term companion going back to her time in France during the war.

She expertly started to extract information from Hank now the lager had made him more relaxed. She discovered he was waiting for a rich American client coming up from down south. This would be London, of course, and he had his son with him, a child about eleven years old.

Hank bemoaned the fact he had hoped to buy a stronger yacht, more suited to the client's intention of sailing directly to the USA. Autumn had arrived, a fact the Atlantic Ocean was more than aware and the harsh weather season was not far away.

Great Aunt Violet discussed this with Hank. Shouldn't he drop south to go the long way around, with its warmer trade winds giving easy downwind sailing. Hank wished he could have purchased a yacht similar to Nicola's. These older yachts had good sea keeping qualities and it was not always the case they were expensive.

When Hank returned to this subject fifteen minutes later, Great Aunt Violet asked, quite bluntly, if he would like to swap boats. She had concerns Nicola's yacht was too big for shorthanded work, whereas the Moody 44 was pitched squarely at the shorthanded market.

Hank thought about it for a moment. Was this lady offering a solution to a problem that bugged him? An easy swap, could it possible?

Nicola moved over beside them both. A burning sensation in her ears told her she was being talked about.

'Nicola,' ask Great Aunt Violet. 'Fancy swapping your ship for theirs. It would be ideal for your voyage down to Palma, and then use the trade wind route across the Atlantic.'

Nicola looked at her in wonder, just where did this idea come from?

She looked at Hank and saw a man looking for a positive answer. She would hate to leave this magnificent sloop but the problems identified two weeks ago were still in the upper reaches of her mind.

The yacht had looked after them well. The voyage from Ireland had been a dream, the sailing was the best, but here was a chance to leave the murky past behind. Did the Moody have the correct paperwork?

'Hank, are you planning the direct route via Iceland?' she asked. Hank nodded his head positively.

'A good start,' thought Nicola, 'Now for some bargaining.' 'Can you manage a cash adjustment too?' she asked.

Hank nodded his head positively

Even better. Time to get down to brass tacks.

'OK Hank,' Nicola started. 'Straight talk, cards on the table?' 'There's a better way?' he replied.

'OK Hank, I can offer you one in number American built yacht that will give no problems when you arrive in the USA. Seventy feet overall, just refurbished, with new Kevlar sails. She has full navigation and communications suites; food and stores for nine persons for two months. Nine hundred litres of diesel, two water makers, twin channel auto-pilot which works extremely well and can handle any weather you're likely to experience.'

'Thanks. The Moody is equipped for trans-ocean sailing, more or less the same as your ship. It needs supplies which we've ordered and I can offer fifty thousand US dollars to make-up the difference.'

'I'm thinking more about a hundred and fifty thousand. We all know the price difference between the two yachts. You could set sail right now this minute if you wished.'

'Hum, can't reach this high, how about a hundred in cash. Nice crisp hundred-dollar bills,' said Hank.

'Do you have paperwork, bills of sale, registration, et al, for the Moody' asked Nicola. 'Yes, to the first, no names of course, the registration papers we have, but I've held back from submitting them due to, err, circumstances.'

The word 'circumstances' told Great Aunt Violet all she needed to know. There was a high-powered American financier from London, being actively sought by just about everybody. A fugitive travelling with a son, the child of eleven years old.

Her contact, a member of the UK secret service, had offered her a substantial payment if she should by chance meet this gentleman and 'baby' him out of the country.

A secret sea-voyage in a private yacht would be about the only way this person would make it away from the melee of attention from an ever-hungry media and the police authorities.

Apart from all that, Port St. Peter was on the correct side of the UK to make a vanishing trick come true. No wonder Nicola complained about constant aerial searching. The authorities were suffering from 'black yacht-itist,' but the search for the black yacht involved in the hunt for the Manchester bank robbers had been overtaken by more important matters

'Hank, come closer.' Great Aunt Violet said, 'Don't take fright, but I know what you are up too. Mr Douglas Chester Fairfield Jr. is coming to town, this town, and I'm the one to 'baby' you and your client out of the country.'

Hank looked shocked.

'Nicola will accept the offer, but you should know one thing, she has no paperwork for the sloop. If you go direct to the States, you do not need any either. Is this a problem?'

'There's a story to all this?' asked Hank.

'It's a best seller, but nothing for you to worry about. It is something for us to worry about. When you sail, do exactly, and I mean exactly, what I tell you. Just get two hundred and fifty miles out into the Atlantic without detection and you will just vanish in the vast expanse of the ocean. Deal?

'I guess,' said Hank.

'Good,' smiled Great Aunt Violet. 'Now we all shake hands and get to work.'

Victoria came to see what was up. She had been busy winding up the two younger Americans with her good looks and sweet baby voice. Nicola gave her a brief rundown of the proceedings and now came the time to get to work.

Great Aunt Violet took the account for lunch, initialled it, and slipped a twenty-pound note as a tip to her favourite chef.

As everybody arrived back at the two yachts, a discussion broke out about what actions to conduct first. Victoria suggested the obvious. The two yachts should be facing out to sea, so with all this manpower available, just tie the two yachts together and spin them around as one, leaving the big yellow sloop on the outside.

Hank went with the idea. He wished to leave as soon as his client arrived .

Long ropes were produced and in no time at all the Moody 44 found itself alongside the quay and the 'Yellow Peril,' a name which continued to find favour with the Americans, lay alongside ready to set sail.

As each crew moved their possessions between each yacht Great Aunt Violet asked Victoria to join her.

'Vicky,' she started, 'Can you wipe the 'past journeys made' memory from the GPS units on the big yacht. It will be terribly inconvenient for the information to end up in the wrong hands, or any hands for that matter.'

'Good idea. I'll see to it straight away,' she replied.

'And bring the charts of where the yacht has been too,' Great Aunt Violet shouted after her.

Hank came to Great Aunt Violet's side asking how to bring his client to the yacht. Great Aunt Violet asked for the details although she was sure the client would arrive at the disused airfield just five miles away. Hank became a bit reticent, so Great Aunt Violet helped him out. 'Hank, will a helicopter perchance make a stop at the airfield just down the road. What time?'

'Eight p.m. just after dark,' she was told.

'Good, I will ask my driver to take my delivery van and back it into the airfield entrance. Please arrange for the helicopter to drop your client as close as possible. The timing is ideal. The locals will be watching the football on TV, an 'old firm' game between the two premier Glasgow teams. Are you going to send your ex-soldier to do the duty?'

'And just how do you know this?' Hank asked.

Great Aunt Violet looked at him kind of queer, telling him she'd been in the game for longer than she cared to remember.

'Now then Hank, when you leave the harbour keep a westerly course for five miles to the middle of the North Channel. The tide will be with you. Then, steer north-northwest, raise all sail keeping well offshore from Rathlin Island. When its lighthouse appears on your beam you turn to the north-west and stay on this course until the Malin Head lighthouse appears just behind your beam, then you will be clear to move into the Atlantic. You must get clear of the Irish mainland before dawn, so get a move on.'

'Sounds easy. I'll just programme my GPS,' said Hank.

'Oh no you won't,' replied Great Aunt Violet forcefully, 'You must leave 'dead ship. No electronics, no radar, and no radio whatsoever. Every frequency is being monitored and reported. In fact, I recommend you cross the Atlantic in 'dead ship' mode. Maybe the occasional use of the hand-held GPS to check your position. Then, shut it down and disconnect the battery. You have no idea of the efforts being made to find your client, and if they find him, they will find you.'

'Gee,' said Hank, 'Sailing the old-fashioned way.'

'Don't worry. After a week search activities will be wound down. Rumours will be spread your client may have made it to Norway in a fishing boat. So, lesson 'Number One' is don't 'fuck-up'. Lesson 'Number Two' is remember Lesson 'Number One.'

As the daylight slowly faded away Nicola and Victoria kept busy making themselves comfortable aboard their new ship. Victoria liked the name, Moody Blue, and its centre cockpit. She thought it would be much safer being higher up with all sail handling controls much easier to reach. The winches were not powered, but she didn't think it would be much of a problem, as everything looked as though it would be much easier to work with.

Down below, Moody Blue possessed the two-stateroom layout giving plenty of comfortable spaces for a short-handed crew. Victoria scanned the internet finding many favourable comments. One website described the twin stateroom layout as the 'happy couples' layout. How she wished to be one-half of a happy couple, but that's why they were going to the USA, the land where, so everyone seemed to think, you could find what you wanted.

The two crews were relaxing aboard their respective yachts, resting, and waiting for the next event. The Americans became a bit nervous as the clock crept past seven o'clock and it did not seem to be in any hurry to reach eight o'clock.

Great Aunt Violet returned, followed by Hamish, carrying fish suppers for all, wrapped in issues of the 'Sporting Life' newspaper. Nicola wasn't hungry, but Scottish fish suppers were not to be refused. The Americans piled in giving their thanks by handing out cold beers all round.

As the clock reached seven thirty, Hank received a text message and waved over to Great Aunt Violet; now was the time to get moving. His ex-soldier crewmember made his way to the quayside, just as a scruffy, unmarked, van arrived, driven by Great Aunt Violet's driver.

Eight o'clock passed nervously and soon afterwards the faint sounds of a helicopter flying low over the sea was heard. Nicola wondered where it would disappear to. Who knows? Events were moving quickly. She found herself needing time to get a grip to become focussed on events yet to come.

TWENTY MINUTES LATER, the unmarked van returned to the quayside and reversed up to the Moody 44. The ex-soldier crewmember jumped out of the passenger seat, opened the rear door, lifting the client's son aboard Moody Blue, quickly followed by the client's luggage. Then, the man himself emerged dropping down onto the deck of Nicola's new yacht.

The new arrivals were ushered across Moody Blue on to the sloop and into the main saloon, followed by Nicola, Victoria, and Great Aunt Violet.

Hank made all the introductions as Mr Douglas Chester Fairfield Jr. accepted a mug of black coffee. The young man, David Chester Fairfield Jr. Jr. asked for a soda and was handed an own brand cola, which made him wince. Nicola was not surprised, she hated own brand cola too.

Nicola saw the young man looked hungry, asking him if he would like to eat something.

He told them lunch had been rushed due to . . . well, he couldn't say, best ask his Dad.

Mr Douglas Chester Fairfield Jr. said he was also hungry, so Hank sent one of his two young crew to the pub to get   ?

'Not so fast Hank,' said Great Aunt Violet, 'The pub has fed everyone here except for the new arrivals. Requesting more food means new arrivals and they are a noisy bunch in the Pub. Nicola, what's quick and simple in the freezer?'

'Irish stew, in packs of double portions,' replied Nicola.

Mr Douglas Chester Fairfield Jr. asked what the hell was Irish stew. Victoria giggled to tell him the stew was 'leftovers' from a farm slaughterhouse with the odd little boy's arm added for flavour.

'Sounds good to me,' he replied. 'As long as there's plenty of tomato sauce with a bread roll on the side.'

Hank smiled; he had quickly got used to the two girl's quirky humour.

Chester Fairfield Jr. kept a straight face as his son David looked up a little confused.

'It's alright son,' said his father. 'We will soon be heading back home and leave these crazies behind.'

Great Aunt Violet snorted, 'The last time I was in the States, crazies were in plentiful supply.'

'Yes Ma'am,' Douglas Chester replied. 'But they're American crazies and we understand them.'

Nicola left them to it. She took the stew from the refrigerator and soon had it heating in the microwave. She popped two bread rolls from the freezer into the small electrical oven sitting on the countertop. Three minutes later she served piping hot, delicious Irish Stew with tomato sauce.

The food was wolfed down, as Douglas Chester started to look around the main saloon. Everything seemed familiar asking Hank how he found this yacht. Hank explained it had found him. Great Aunt Violet engaged with Chester to give the low down on the current situation. Chester just nodded, said thank you, asking to be left alone with his crew.

The two girls returned to Moody Blue to settle in for the night. Great Aunt Violet told them she would return home, come back early the next day, asking Nicola if she could give her passage down to Southern Ireland.

She wouldn't say why, but Hamish had told her during lunch, Jus had left the day before in what he described as the company van.

From what little Nicola knew about Great Aunt Violet's business, it was clear another operation was underway, so she chose not to ask unnecessary questions. As the clock crept towards nine o'clock Nicola and Victoria went on deck. Their beloved yacht's engine was running as Captain Hank issued low key orders to untie the yacht and stow all fenders.

Nicola felt pleased to see the Americans had darkened ship, no light shone from the portholes or windows. With only the green and red navigation lights lit, Hank gave them a farewell wave, as he concentrated on getting this big yacht out of the harbour at the appointed time, just a few minutes after the start of the second half of the big football match.

The sloop eased itself out of the harbour, and with that, it was gone.

Chapter 15

Moody Blue Heads South to Palma

NOW HANK and his compatriots had departed, peace descended on Port St. Peter. Victoria completed a list of stores to victual Moody Blue for their journey south. The plan was coming together. Nicola received acceptance of their entry into the Transatlantic Rally for Cruiser's and now the correct documents could be submitted.

The bonus was Victoria appeared to be well, although slight doubt appeared in the form of Great Aunt Violet's close friend, Dr Fay, a specialist consultant in the field of gynaecology.

Despite Victoria's protest she was just fine, Great Aunt Violet remained unconvinced. She had great experience in this matter, most of it from the world war conflict in Europe all those years ago. She wasn't the only one who had suffered terribly at the hands of the Gestapo.

Dr Fay was very kind with Victoria. The comfortable double berth cabin underneath the centre cockpit became the examination room. Dr Fay came fully prepared and her examination was, to say the least, thorough, but for a change, the good doctor could not come to a hundred percent firm conclusion.

The signs of great damage were still just visible, but only because she knew what to look for. She saw whoever treated Victoria in the first place had done an unbelievably good job.

Still, Dr Fay was persuaded to give her a clean bill of health, as only time would tell. As Victoria restored herself to her personal comforts, Dr Fay presented Nicola with a large medical bag with a whole host of medications, the means to administer them and a range of test strips, including a folder containing instructions of what to look for, how to interpret symptoms.

Dr Fay completed a stocktake of the yacht's medical cabinet, wrote out a long list of general items, including specialist prescriptions, advising Nicola to get these items before setting sail. Nicola felt reassured. As a final precaution, she recorded the maritime radio stations who could connect her to a doctor-on-call for the marine world of shipping.

So, apart from some last-minute shopping for stores, collecting the charts ordered from the post office, a top-up of diesel from the local garage, and a delivery from a medical wholesaler, Moody Blue became ready to take them to the New World.

After a hectic day, Nicola checked the weather forecast, which remained favourable, took a hot shower, and headed for a good night's sleep. It did not take long before Victoria locked-up, showered, and joined her in the very comfortable double berth cabin.

Early the next morning Great Aunt Violet arrived on board. Nicola was up and about, ready for the day. Victoria wasn't. She didn't approve of dawn and couldn't remember the last time she actually wanted to get up early to see one.

Nicola welcomed her aunt with the hot cup of tea to start the day and made breakfast for herself. Violet had eaten; Victoria had no intention of getting up.

'How is Victoria,' asked Great Aunt Violet. 'Any update?'

'She's fine,' replied Nicola. 'We still sleep together; keeps her safe. I'm there if she has bad dreams. It keeps her calm about going to sleep, she is truly afraid of her nightmares. They have been bad, but slowly but surely she puts them behind her. A week ago she had the last one, but it wasn't very strong.'

'Time to be going Nicola, there's work to be done.'

Nicola finished her breakfast, dressed for the day on deck. She started the main engine, waited for Great Aunt Violet's driver to release the mooring ropes, waved goodbye, and headed Moody Blue out of the harbour into the North Channel separating Scotland from Northern Ireland. The wind felt chilly, coming from the greatly appreciated direction of north, giving an easy start to the voyage back to Southern Ireland.

As Moody Blue entered the seaway with Great Aunt Violet at the helm, Nicola quickly raised all sail then set course for the Irish coast. The voyage would take just under two days, depending on the weather and the tides. With the wind coming over the starboard quarter, Moody Blue picked up her skirts and reached her maximum speed, although the ride was a little bumpy in the strong following seas.

This was Nicola's first experience with the Moody, but it impressed her considering the stark difference from the 'Yellow Peril,' which she hoped had escaped safely into the vast Atlantic Ocean undetected.

Great Aunt Violet appeared to be enjoying her spell at the helm, demanding strong coffee on a regular schedule.

Victoria woke bright as a button, leapt into action, and dressed for the day. Nicola thought the words 'leapt into action' hardly applied; she was a slow starter to any day at the best of times. Still, she stood her turn in the galley, made hot drinks and snacks for all, and initiated the start of the seven-day stew pot.

As Moody Blue closed the coast south of Bangor, the seas calmed down as the tide turned to the south, aligning with the wind. This was grand sailing, and the Moody 44 made good progress. Nicola discussed who would keep each watch, as the Moody continued on what would be her maiden voyage.

The day passed without incident, and as night approached, the aerial traffic heading towards Dublin airport in the clear evening air was easy to see. With night came the expected drop in the wind strength. Fortunately, there was little commercial shipping traffic, and the local fishing fleets along the coast had long since called it a day.

Nicola stood most of the night watch, dozing off when the sea ahead became clear, hoping Victoria would be able to take over most of the day watch. Half-way through the night Great Aunt Violet came on deck. She couldn't sleep, so she came on deck to keep her favourite niece company with a large mug of coco.

Nicola welcomed the chance to get quality time with her Great Aunt. There was so much history to talk about, although she was not sure how much history would be revealed.

For a change Great Aunt Violet was willing to talk about many things, her service in the French Resistance, her long-term relationship with her companion, Jus William, and a little about her post-war record.

Nicola found certain areas of her great aunt's history were not going to be revealed; perhaps these were the sad parts where she or her companion in arms had suffered greatly.

She did discover a comprehensive history had been written of her life in France, and a trusted member of the security services had turned the details into a book. The book had been placed in quarantine until the UK and the French government could agree on its release, she assumed after Great Aunt Violet's death.

Great Aunt Violet did have a copy of the book, a very secret fact as no one knew she had it. Quite how she had obtained the copy was not going to be revealed, but chances were it was on a pin drive, an easy device to hide.

Nicola tentatively asked about her will and who would her executive be with the responsibilities to conduct her last wishes. Great Aunt Violet paused before replying. She told Nicola she was a wealthy lady but how wealthy was not going to be revealed.

Nicola would be well provided for, as would Uncle Adam. Her extensive properties had been formed into a limited company, and passed to the control of ex-service personnel, although her ownership had been retained. One of her long-term friends, a legal eagle of some repute, had been issued with definite instructions she knew would be carried out.

Nicola didn't press the subject, knowing Great Aunt Violet would tell her if and when she wanted to. Clearly, the upcoming mission to Southern Ireland played on her mind but she released few details. Suffice to say the east European mafia was attempting something really bad concerning the Irish National Stud near Kildare to the south-west of Dublin. Such was the level of the threat the respective governments had called for help, with the commitment to look the other way if matters went the way that was more than likely.

Nicola chanced her luck by asking if this operation would be 'a BB special,' where the badies would be made to disappear forever. Great Aunt Violet just smiled, muttering something about old times and what fun it was going to be. Nicola tried to keep a straight face, but it suddenly became clear why her great-aunt had just succumbed to giving her even the sketchiest outlines of her last wishes.

The pair of them lapsed into silence, enjoying the canopy of the stars in the night sky. Great Aunt Violet eventually returned to her cabin, the talk with Nicola having done her the world of good. As dawn broke, Victoria made breakfast of hot porridge and Scottish scones for everyone and went on deck to relieve Nicola.

Nicola did a quick hand-over, thanked her for her stint in the galley, finished her breakfast, and turned in for some much-needed sleep. The day passed without incident as Moody Blue kept up a reasonable pace in the cold northerly wind. Great Aunt Violet made herself useful and enjoyed catching up with Victoria for some extended small talk.

Victoria wasn't to know Great Aunt Violet simply needed to get to know her better, to catch-up on past events and gauge if her health had really returned to full strength. Victoria would have to be fully fit for the voyage from Ireland to Ilha Gran Canarias for the start of the Atlantic Cruiser rally to English Harbour in the Caribbean.

The day turned to night, progress remained acceptable, all remained well on board. With luck, the expectation was Moody Blue would arrive at Goughal early the next morning. Nicola and Victoria shared the night watches, taking turns of three hours each. Great Aunt Violet took over the duties as chief cook and bottle washer, showing she was still more than capable of doing the domestics.

Dawn broke as Moody Blue closed the shoreline. The wind remained favourable, but the rain returned to test the ability of the most modern sailing attire. It also turned colder.

Nicola had taken the precaution of investing in new offshore clothing during their stay in Port St Peter. She remembered the advice about keeping dry and warm from a Norwegian sailing chum of hers many years ago. Their approach to offshore clothing followed the well-worn maxim, 'There's no such thing as bad weather, only bad clothing.'

The radar was energised to pick-up the entrance to Goughal Harbour. Nicola felt pleased Liam had installed an unofficial channel marker with a radar reflector at the point of entry. There would be little difficulty getting Moody Blue into the harbour. Her draft was a lot less than the big sloop and the neap tide had an exceptionally small range for the time of year.

As Moody Blue entered the harbour, Victoria called-up the shipyard to announce their arrival, as Nicola dropped the mainsail into the lazy jacks. Moody Blue moored up alongside the finished jetty. Nicola saw Liam making his way around to greet them.

He was surprised when Great Aunt Violet bid him good morning and invited him aboard for an early mug of tea. She had things to talk about, important things. Liam bid her good-morning, said he was kind of expecting her to arrive, but not by sea. His first question, just what the hell was going on?

'It's like this Liam; the East European mafia are having a go at the Irish National Stud and the local race meetings. It's serious, very serious. It has been decided at the highest level to counter their activities by any means possible. Perhaps you can guess what this means. I have to ask you and yours for some very discrete assistance. Can do?'

Liam thought for a moment and asked at what level any assistance should be considered. Great Aunt Violet replied she needed observers, drivers, helpers on the racecourse and informers.

She didn't want any of his people involved with any violence, but if there were any suitable gunmen to act as back-up, she might consider using them in the last resort.

Liam looked a little confused, but Great Aunt Violet continued to give an overview of the criminal activities expected from the 'invaders,' as she called them.

The future of the National Stud and the long-term health of the racing industry was at stake. She had funds, generous funds, but stressed the activities she would be involved with would be outside of the strict interpretation of the law. Higher authority had agreed fighting the threat with one hand tied behind one's back would be unwise and one could always look the other way.

Liam, if nothing else was an Irish patriot. He and his like-minded contacts would be aghast at this threat, and if there was the chance of some reward for a little fun, so be it.

'One thing Liam,' started Great Aunt Violet. 'I am not here, and you didn't see me arrive. OK girls, sorry, but your stay in Goughal must be short, get any supplies you need as soon as possible but you must be gone.'

'Yes. Great Aunt Violet,' replied Nicola. 'We understand. Take care of yourself, and don't.'

'Don't what?' snapped Great Aunt Violet.

'Don't do anything dangerous,' replied Victoria. 'We both love you dearly.'

Great Aunt Violet thanked them for their kind words and took her baggage on deck indicating to Liam to help her disappear into one of the guest cottages whilst she prepared to leave for the area of operations.

Nicola couldn't think of anything they needed, as Moody Blue had supplies for at least two months. The two girls kissed their favourite aunt goodbye and prepared to sail. Nicola looked around the harbour; nobody else was up at this early hour.

As a parting shot, Nicola asked Liam how his business had progressed with the three Welsh yachts, to be told everything went well. They had promised they would return to lay-up for the winter months. The Welsh Commodore also promised to spread the word, and two tentative bookings had been received, so all in all, Liam was very grateful.

Victoria watched Liam disappear with Great Aunt Violet. Nicola untied Moody Blue and pushed her bow away from the jetty, jumped back on board as Victoria backed Moody Blue into the centre of the pool, and with the helm hard down, turned and headed towards the sea.

AS THE YACHT reached open water, Nicola raised the mainsail as Moody Blue turned south towards the Canary Islands. Setting all sail in the moderate south-west wind coming out of the Atlantic, Moody Blue headed quickly towards their future.

'Well, Miss Stanwick, said Nicola, 'We're on our way at last. On our way to the future.

Leaving all our cares and woes behind. How do you feel?' 'Relieved, happy to be out from under. Let's have some fun too.'

'Vicky,' said Nicola, 'Just one note of concern. How are you truly feeling? We will be going into the Atlantic. Our rhumb line course will take us close to the north-west corner of Spain. However, I wish to go further offshore, into deeper waters to keep clear of the shipping lanes. However, this takes us a long way from Oporto or Lisbon should you have a relapse and need medical treatment.

So, Vicky dear, you tell me what is best. You're holding up well, but Dr Fay couldn't come to a hundred percent firm conclusion, nor could Great Aunt Violet.'

Victoria looked downhearted at this review of her health. Problem number one, she could not refute it. Her good days were kind of OK, but her bad days, which she had hoped to hide, were not so good.

She looked up at Nicola and said, 'I don't know for certain; I'm still struggling to return to normal. I even forget what normal is anymore. I guess it would be best to steer a course that's kind of halfway. If we get past Lisbon, then I should be fine. If not Oporto or Lisbon are two ports within reach should the need arise.'

Nicola could see the anguish on Victoria's face; her trembling voice said it all. She knew Victoria would fight to the end.

'It's all right Vicky,' she said, 'You are doing your best, as always. We can use the route which suits you best. Don't worry if we have to hole up somewhere, so be it, your health comes first.'

Nicola's kind words put a smile on Victoria's face. The poor girl so desperately needed comforting. The recent past lingered far too close for comfort. Nicola went below to allow Victoria to come to herself. A spell at the helm would do her the world of good, suppressing her worries as she concentred on getting Moody Blue on track to the promised future.

And so it proved, after three hours on the helm Victoria had recovered her mojo, as she liked to call it, scanned the horizon for any shipping and slipped below decks to commence the daily domestics in the galley. Nicola had taken the chance to get some sleep and felt very relaxed when she was woken up for her spell on watch with a strong cup of tea, and a delicious salad sandwich.

'Feeling better are we?' Nicola asked.

'Never better,' came the reply. 'We are clear of the mainland, the weather is stable, the wind is Force 4 from the west, Moody Blue is sailing like a dream on starboard tack and talking of dreams I'm off to bed and hope to have none.'

Nicola rose from her berth, washed, and prepared for the next four hours on watch. She went on deck to find all was well. Back at the navigation desk, she quickly downloaded the latest weather forecast, which indicated a slowly falling pressure with an increase in wind strength.

Nicola checked the barometer chart and saw the forecast matched the recorded readings.

The wind direction would veer slightly to the north-west, so an easy four hours of satisfactory progress looked to be on the menu. And talking of menus, it became time to prepare the perennial pot of stew for dinner and subsequent meals thereafter.

Having completed the domestics, Nicola took a large cushion on deck to get herself comfortable for an hour of relaxation just watching the world pass by. As the sun slowly sank in the west, the end of a comfortable day's sailing arrived. Soon it would be time to wake Victoria for the next watch.

The routine aboard Moody Blue continued smoothly through the night and through into the next day. The watch-keeper updated the log every half hour as they progressed most encouragingly. If Moody Blue continued her daily average of around two hundred nautical miles per day, they would get to the Canary Islands with a week to spare.

The wind veered to the north as Moody Blue began to pass Lisbon, bringing with it a prosperous wind. Easy sailing with the foresail goose-winged out on the other side of the mainsail. It took a little fiddling with the auto pilot to keep the yacht square to the wind direction. Nicola had never experienced a 'Chinese gybe' and had no intention of starting now. A 'Chinese gybe' could be very violent because as the mainsail slammed to the other side of the yacht great damage could be caused.

Nicola elected to rig a 'preventer' line securing the mainsail boom on the designated tack. During the night, she felt safer with Moody Blue sailing on a broad reach with the auto-pilot set to keep the wind angle where she wanted it.

The further their progress to the south, the more moderate would be the wind. Victoria agreed with Nicola's edict, as controlling Moody Blue from the centre cockpit posed little problems, with a gentle gybe every few hours just to keep the yacht sailing around its designated rhumb line.

The following evening, as Moody Blue passed offshore from the furthest south-west point of Portugal, Nicola was resting in her cabin. It would soon be time for her to go on watch, to let Victoria get four hours much needed rest. Victoria had held up well, displaying no signs of any physical distress, and generally happy within herself.

She felt the yacht gybe over onto the port tack. Nicola nodded off only to be awakened by the sound of flapping sails and a change in the motion of Moody Blue, which felt as though the yacht had come up on to the wind.

Nicola quickly dressed for action, went on deck to find Victoria slumped in a corner of the centre cockpit her limp hand holding onto the steering wheel. She checked the auto-pilot to discover Victoria had reset the course to the south-east. She lifted her into her arms and cuddled her. Victoria moaned in deep distress. Nicola shone a torch on her face and was horrified to find how ill she looked.

'Oh, you poor dear. What's happened to you?'

Victoria looked up. She was crying, saying sorry but she felt so ill. Nicola's worse nightmare had come and instantly realised why Victoria changed course. It was too far to reach Lisbon for the specialist care she urgently needed.

Nicola realised the joint civilian-military hospital in Gibraltar would be their best hope. She knew the hospital had a specialist gynaecology unit. Uncle Adam had mentioned in passing a friendly rival of his headed-up the hospital complex.

She managed to get Victoria down below into her cabin, stripped of her waterproof clothing, and saw her jeans had a very dark patch in her pelvis area.

'Oh, not again. You poor girl.'

Nicola put her to bed, stripped her down to her underwear, placed a thick towel under her bottom and removed her pants. God the smell was awful. Nicola rushed back on deck to see if the way ahead remained clear. She could see no shipping, the radar remaining thankfully clear for the next hour at least.

Thinking quickly, Nicola formed a list of urgent actions. She removed Dr Fay's emergency bag from its stowage. Then, she filled a large basin full of hot water, added disinfectant and cleaned up Victoria as best she could.

After a hurried reading of the instructions, she inserted a multi-way infusion point on the back of her right hand and connected a bag of saline drip hanging from an overhead fixture. On her left arm, she attached the wrap-around armband and connected it to the portable blood pressure machine and took her readings. They were low, extremely low, and she noted them down.

Following Dr Fay's instructions, she compared the readings and findings with the written notes. The notes bid her inject two medications immediately. Nicola took a fresh syringe from its protective wrapper and injected both medications. Nicola waited for a few minutes and retook Victoria's blood pressure.

Slight improvement became apparent, but the notes did not inspire confidence. Further monitoring of the patient was necessary, but the notes made it plain medical treatment at a recognised hospital was an urgent requirement. Making her as comfortable as she could, Nicola headed to the navigation desk, searched Dr Fay's notes for the best wireless station to call, energised the HF radio, and set it to the right frequency to connect with Gibraltar Marine. 'Gibraltar Marine, Gibraltar Marine, Pan Pan Pan, this is the yacht Moody Blue, come in please.'

Nicola waited pensively, but after two further calls, Gibraltar Marine answered, 'Moody Blue this Gibraltar Marine, please state your emergency, over.'

Nicola replied, 'Roger Gibraltar Marine,' this is the yacht Moody Blue travelling from Scotland to the Canary Islands. We are a crew of two females, I am the skipper and my first mate is dangerously ill. Requesting any available assistance, over.'

Gibraltar Marine answered quickly in a calm professional manner, asking for details, age, and status of the patient and previous history. Nicola provided the details and referred Gibraltar Marine to Dr Fay in Scotland to obtain the necessary background. She advised her current position, the current weather, and they were heading to Gibraltar but expressed the opinion the patient would not survive the three-to-four-day journey.

The Duty Commander at Gibraltar Marine confirmed his understanding of the emergency and its level of urgency. He requested she stay on this frequency during the night and passed her a day frequency to use when the current night frequency faded in the morning. He also advised Nicola to continue monitoring the patient and ensured she took frequent food intake to keep her strength up.

Nicola felt relieved some action would be forthcoming and wondered what it might be. Moody Blue was a long way out from Gibraltar and she remained unsure if an SAR helicopter had the range to reach her in time.

What Nicola did not know, came in the form of previous planning by the military in Gibraltar to seek methods by which an extended SAR mission could be activated.

The Duty Commander began the procedure. Quite a few military personnel were going to have their beauty sleep disturbed. He busied himself making a long-distance telephone call to Dr Fay, the last medical doctor who had examined the patient.

A sleepy Dr Fay gave Gibraltar Marine a brief run of what she knew from her examination, but when she heard the medical details, she became wide awake, quickly confirming the patient's life would be in grave danger unless the patient could be brought quickly to hospital for specialist treatment. The duty doctor asked how much time they had only to be told twelve hours maximum, but more like eight hours.

The Duty Commander quickly consulted with Professor Samuel Samuelson, the director of the joint civilian-military hospital. Professor Samuelson knew the day would come when a similar emergency was declared. He listened to the data, quickly confirmed any action should be immediate.

The Duty Commander got down to his task, assessing his assets, and asking his team for the 'scores on the board.' The duty RN naval officer confirmed HMS Brecken Ridge was on patrol, monitoring the seaways leading to the Straits of Gibraltar in more or less a reasonable position to respond. He also advised the ship had a helicopter pad large enough to land an S61 Sea King helicopter, but it wasn't rated for such. However, given the helicopter would arrive almost empty of fuel, carrying no more than a flight crew, he didn't see a problem as long as the ship's captain agreed.

The duty RAF officer confirmed an S61 SAR helicopter was available, the good news being it had just been released from a long overhaul and was in tip-top condition. Its designated flight crew were on station and they could be quickly called to duty at any time.

The Duty Commander went to the situation board, marked the last reported position of Moody Blue and the position of the naval ship, quickly calculating distances and risk factor. 'OK team,' he called out, 'Let us consider this. We launched the SAR helicopter in stripped down mode, two flight crew, one paramedic and one winchman/rescue swimmer to go down on the wire.

The SAR helicopter will take-off with a full fuel load, flies to HMS Brecken Ridge, refuels, then, all being well the SAR helicopter should have sufficient range to connect with the target yacht, recover the patient and fly direct to Gibraltar base, landing at the hospital helipad. Any comments?'

The duty RN officer suggested the yacht continue on a direct course for Gibraltar, and HMS Brecken Ridge ordered to sail at full speed to get as close to this course line as possible. He knew the duty winchman had yachting experience, so he could be dropped aboard the yacht to help bring the yacht into Gibraltar, reducing the helicopter payload, thus giving a slight increase in range given the very tight margins this mission would be working too.

With no other comments, the Duty Commander confirmed his plan, ordered his assistants into action, whilst he called the Governor's office to advise the OIC HQ, British Forces Gibraltar.

Within the hour, the SAR helicopter, captained by Lt. Commander (Jock) Sinclair, a famous ex RN jet jockey, Lt. Boeing RN, RAF Master Sergeant Mike Wilkens, a veteran winchman of fifteen years' experience, and paramedic, Flight Lt Sheila Williams, a highly experienced RAF medic, set off on this vital mission.

The Duty Commander felt relieved at the quick reaction of getting this complicated mission away in such a short time in the middle of the night. He had been one of the main architects of the extended SAR helicopter reach programme. He was more than aware a lot of senior people were going to monitor the success of the mission.

Before he forgot, the time had come to contact Moody Blue to advise her skipper of the requirements of the mission. He took five minutes to relax and drink a much-needed cup of coffee to sound more reassuring to the skipper of the yacht, to give her hope and to advise her part in the mission, which would be all important.

The risk factor had been calculated but strong medical opinion told him to get the patient into hospital with no time lost, and there was none to spare.

The Duty Commander picked up the radio microphone and started his call, Moody Blue, Moody Blue this is Gibraltar Marine, come in, over.'

'Gibraltar Marine, this is Moody Blue go ahead, over.'

The Duty Commander picked up on the quick response and the sound of great concern in the skipper's voice.

'Roger, Moody Blue please take down the following details. An SAR helicopter departed Gibraltar base twenty minutes ago. It will fly to a RN support vessel to refuel; time for this leg is two hours twenty minutes. Their stop time is twenty minutes for refuelling and crew refreshment. The next leg to your yacht is calculated at forty-five minutes. We are allowing ten minutes maximum for recovery of your patient. Return flight time to Gibraltar base is calculated to be just inside their maximum range, using up to fifty percent of their 'emergency only' fuel capacity. copy?'

'Copy,' said Nicola

'OK, Moody Blue you must be fully prepared before, I repeat, fully prepared before the arrival of the SAR helicopter. The mainsail must be down and secured, mainsail boom stowed as far outboard as possible on the lee side. The mast backstay must be removed and brought forward past your centre cockpit. Your main engine will be running, so follow the directions from the helicopter commander on VHF Channel 16. If you can turn a boat hook into a static earthing rod this will help too.

The patient must be ready for transfer to the recovery basket, including waterproofs, a dry suit is best, with warm clothing underneath, head protection if you have it, and an injection point on the back of either hand would be useful. Try to bring the patient on deck to save time. Time is very much of the essence, so please be ready, we should be with you in about three hours, copy?'

'Copy,' said Nicola.

'OK Moody Blue please try to gain as much distance as possible towards Gibraltar. Every little helps, our margins are small, and we do not wish to waste time with a return refuelling stop, as your patient does not have that luxury. Over.'

'OK, Gibraltar Marine, I have noted all the details, everything will be ready, and many thanks,' finished Nicola.

'OK Moody Blue. One last thing. The SAR helicopter will leave their winchman to help you on the last leg of your journey to Gibraltar. God speed. Out.'

'Phew,' Nicola thought. 'Who would have thought? We are a long way out, but let us give thanks and get ready.'

Nicola returned to Victoria's side, gave her comfort, replacing the intravenous drip with a fresh bag. She monitored her readings and thanked god there seemed to be some improvement. She tried to wake Victoria with little success, but some recognition of her presence was there.

Her breathing remained very shallow. Nicola thought it best to use the limited amount of oxygen to help Victoria breathe. She pressed the oxygen mask to her face and set the flow to last as long as possible. The oxygen seemed to work, which became the bonus of the hour.

'Victoria,' said Nicola in a strong voice. 'The Navy is sending a rescue helicopter to take you directly to the hospital in Gibraltar. There you will recover in the hands of specialists. So, hang on for just a few more hours, do you hear?'

Victoria briefly fluttered her eyelids, which Nicola took as a good sign. This girl had spirit and this spirit would have to carry her for the next few hours. The number of hours seemed long, but then the Navy had responded more quickly than she could ever have hoped. Best to get busy topside.

As Moody Blue continued to the south-east Nicola found the wind becoming more influenced by the European mainland and had veered towards north-east. She reset the auto-pilot on the direct course for Gibraltar. The wind faded with the night, so she was able to shake out the one slab reef from the mainsail and set the sail for maximum power.

Nicola wondered who the winchman might be. Whoever he was, he just had his beauty sleep disturbed, and if nothing else, by the time Victoria had been airlifted to safety, he would be ready for a good breakfast.

The way was clear, Nicola checked the navigation lights were lit, then went below to switch on the radar and reset the radar detector for maximum range. Rummaging around in Victoria's cabin, she quickly put together the clothes she would need plus a set of waterproofs. She had a dry-suit, but it would be far too awkward to get her into it. The navy were not about to drop her into the sea, and if they did, well goodnight Vienna.

Nicola sat down near the galley to eat some more food and take a short rest. She took great care not to fall asleep. An hour later she checked on Victoria, saw some slight improvement in her condition. The HF radio burst into life, it was Gibraltar Marine and a Professor Samuelson speaking. They held a brief conversation about Victoria's life signs and received a few suggestions to prepare for the evacuation.

Thankful folks were thinking about the needs of the patient, Nicola stripped Victoria naked, performed a quick bed bath and dressed her in all the warm clothing she could find. She had no idea how cold it would be in the helicopter, but surely they would have blankets.

Still twenty minutes later, Victoria lay fully dressed, with the intravenous drip reconnected to the back of her hand still unmoving, breathing the last of the oxygen.

Nicola felt pleased with herself; with an hour still to go, she was ready. A quick look at the radar showed Moody Blue had little to worry about other shipping. Nicola returned to Victoria, sitting up so as not to fall asleep, tenderly stroking Victoria's hair.

Forty minutes later the radar detector started to beep. Nicola double checked Victoria was ready, with her documents, passport, Dr Fay's medical procedure, and some cash stuffed inside a plastic zipper bag shoved inside one of her many jacket pockets. Nicola rushed on deck to look for the helicopter, lit a red flare and held it up high.

The VHF radio burst into life, the helicopter would arrive in ten minutes and please could the red flare be discharged into the sea otherwise it would interfere with the helicopter crew's night vision headsets.

Nicola threw the flare into the sea, quickly dropping the mainsail into the lazy jacks. She clipped on her safety line and went forward to wrap strong tape ties to secure the mainsail, brought the boom hard over to the lee side of the yacht and tied the mast backstay down behind the boom.

'Three minutes, Nicola,' said the VHF radio, as she hauled on the foresail reefing line. With the engine running ahead at half speed, she requested further instructions from the helicopter.

Moody Blue please set your course with the wind at fifteen degrees off your port bow, over,' said the VHF radio.

Nicola set the course and searched around for the earthing rod.

Suddenly, Moody Blue was illuminated in a blaze of light by the helicopter's searchlights. The VHF burst into life, 'Winchman coming down.' The downdraft from the helicopter blades battered Nicola.

A metal wire with a weight on the end swung in over the port quarter. Just in time Nicola fended it off with the earthing rod. The winchman landed just behind the centre cockpit holding a recovery basket.

Nicola hauled the basket containing a large haversack into the middle of the centre cockpit. The winchman jumped into the cockpit to sling the haversack down into the main saloon. The winchman shouted out for her to hold on to the basket, where was the patient?

Nicola shouted out, 'The patient is lying in the forward master cabin.'

He disappeared below and two minutes later the winchman reappeared with Victoria in his arms. He quickly laid her in the recovery basket, strapped her in, and produced a spare protective helmet to fit on Victoria's head. Nicola bent over to Victoria and shouted into her left ear, 'Nicky, just hang on. The helicopter will take you to safety. When you wake up you will be alive and well.'

Nicola kissed her best friend on the forehead and saw a momentary flicker of Victoria's eyes. The winchman clipped onto the ring above the recovery basket and shouted into a microphone attached to his helmet, and then he was gone and Victoria was on her way.

'That was fast,' thought Nicola, 'Now what?'

Two minutes later, the winchman reappeared, unhooked from his winch line, waving the helicopter away. The helicopter-backed away to disappear into the night.

Peace returned to Moody Blue as Nicola unfurled the foresail, reset the auto-pilot to the course for Gibraltar, and throttled down the main engine to tick-over.

'Hi,' she said. 'Welcome aboard, I'm Nicola.'

'I'm Master Sergeant Mike Wilkens. Glad to be of service, how are you?' replied the winchman.

'Very tired and very concerned, but at least Vicky is on her way to the hospital. I hope she arrives on time,' mumbled Nicola.

'Be hopeful,' said Mike Wilkens. 'She is in good hands, the best. Any breakfast?'

The pair of them went below. Nicola put the kettle on and lit the grill to prepare a cooked English breakfast. She told Mike Wilkens to go forward to the guest master suite, make himself comfortable, and change out of his uncomfortable flying togs. As breakfast became ready, Mike reappeared in clothing more suited to life aboard an ocean-going yacht and sat down at the dining table in the main saloon.

'Early start to the day?' asked Nicola.

'You could say that. When was the last time you slept?' 'Can't remember,' replied Nicola. 'Probably forty hours ago.'

Nicola served breakfast, which they tucked into with scant conversation. As breakfast finished, Nicola asked Mike to get dressed for topsides so she could get Moody Blue back under full sail, show him the ropes, asking if he could stand watch for the next four hours. Mike looked tired, as well he might, but Nicola's eyesight was getting blurred, a strong indication she needed rest.

Mike hoisted the mainsail, as Nicola set to trimming both sails for what would be a blast reach towards the Spanish coast. She shut down the main engine, looked at the radar, which indicated no shipping ahead, and set the auto-pilot.

'Just update the logbook every half-hour, and if the coast is clear, you can relax and doze off until the alarm goes at the next half-hour. I'm told you have sailing experience, yes?'

Mike told her he regularly sailed with a Samantha Samuelson, daughter of the Hospital director, gaining various RYA courses certificates, including 'ocean crew'. This was welcome news to Nicola. At last, there would be some relief for the remainder of the journey. She wondered how Vicky was getting on in the helicopter, hoping above hope, her worries were over.

It was just as well Nicola did not know the events taking place in the helicopter. Lt. Commander Stirling, pilot flying, switched on his helmet intercom, 'Pilot not flying, you have the aircraft. I need to shake hands with an old friend.'

Lt. Henry Boeing replied, 'I have the aircraft on auto-pilot pre-set course at one two five degrees, over.'

'Thanks, Henry, let us see how the patient is doing,' came the reply.

Jock Stirling entered the cabin of the Sea King helicopter, slipped behind a temporary curtain to perform a much-needed relief into the communal bucket. He finished and knelt beside his favourite paramedic asking how the patient was progressing.

'Good news or bad news Shelia?' he asked. Flight Lt. Sheila Williams wasn't sure.

'The patient is kind of stable, for now. I think the intravenous drip is holding her in a stable condition, but there are signs I'm struggling to understand,' she replied.

'Bad signs?' asked the senior pilot.

'I think she is about to fall off a cliff. Her blood pressure is showing a slow decline, her pulse is the same. I've run out of the medication supplied with the patient; there's nothing left. Her face is death white, and I'm losing to battle to keep her body heat up, her temperature is hovering near dangerous. At this rate, she isn't going to make it, sorry Jock.'

'Let's look into this bag that came with her. What's this at the bottom, a removable panel?'

In the bottom of the medical bag, he found a plastic bag wrapped in insulation material.

Inside was a satchel of blood, type A+, the date taken, and the donor's name, the patient. 'Will this help?' he asked.

'Should do,' replied Shelia Williams. 'Judging by the smell, she has been leaking badly from her pelvis region, the nappy fitted aboard the yacht is wringing wet, and so she must be losing a lot of blood. Hang it up somewhere and let me connect the tube to the injection point.'

With the injection of fresh blood completed, Victoria's life signs showed a momentary improvement, but the slow decline continued.

'How long before we land Jock?' she asked.

'About fifty minutes on the approved route,' replied the senior pilot. 'She isn't going to make it. Jock, do something,' Shelia pleaded. 'Captain,' called Lt Henry Boeing, 'Can you come back to the cockpit.' Jock Sinclair quickly sat back down in his pilot's seat.

'What's up Henry?' he asked.

'We don't have sufficient fuel to continue on this course. This forecasted five to ten knots north-east wind has piped up to thirty plus and it's eating our lunch. My calculation shows our fuel reserve is now zero to minus ten minutes. We will have to overfly Spanish airspace, where we might just make it. How is the patient?'

'She isn't going to make it if we don't get her to the hospital in the next hour. How far out are we?'

'Jock, the direct route is thirty minutes, then we will land with fuel reserve at plus eight to five minutes. We're about to start flying on our fuel reserve in a few minutes.'

'Merda,' exclaimed Jock Sinclair. 'I've never lost a patient yet and now is not the time to start. There is one very pretty lady back there.'

'OK. Pilot Flying, set a direct course for Gibraltar Marine. I'll make the contact requests,' ordered Lt. Cmdr. Sinclair.

The helicopter changed course to head into Spanish airspace and an unknown situation. Spain had been upping the ante against Gibraltar at the diplomatic level, although there had been few problems on the ground.

'Gibraltar Marine, Gibraltar Marine this is ER-SAR-01, come in, over.'
'ER-SAR-01, this is Gibraltar Marine. Go ahead, over,' came the reply

'Roger Gibraltar Marine, declaring an emergency, Mayday, Mayday, Mayday, this is ER-SAR-01 declaring an emergency. We are now using our fuel reserve and must use the direct route over Spanish airspace. We expect to land with only ten to five minutes reserve remaining. Also declaring an emergency, the patient is very close to death, estimated at no more than forty minutes, over.'

'Roger ER-SAR-01, you are not cleared to fly over Spanish airspace, over.' 'Roger Gibraltar Marine, I will contact them immediately, out.'

'So far, so good,' thought Jock Sinclair. 'Let's hope they get busy. Now for the difficult part.'

Jock Sinclair switched his radio to the international air traffic control frequency and began. 'Spanish Air Traffic Control this is Royal Navy flight ER-SAR-01, declaring an

emergency, over.'

'Go ahead ER-SAR-01, state your emergency,' came the reply.

'Roger, Mayday, Mayday, Mayday, we are on an extended SAR mission, we are now using our reserve fuel. We have a patient very close to death, requesting the direct route to Gibraltar Marine, over.'

'Take your time boys, take your time,' thought Jock Sinclair.

'Time to landing Henry?' asked Jock Sinclair 'Twenty-eight minutes,' came the reply.

'Royal Navy ER-SAR-01, please state the patient's name,' requested the Spanish controller.

'Victoria Stanwick, age 31 years, over,' replied Jock Sinclair. 'Does she have her passport, over,' came the reply.

'Yes,' replied Jock Sinclair.

'OK ER-SAR-01, please contact air traffic control at 'Helipuerto de Algeciras' for overflying permission, on Channel Three-One, out.'

'Phew, that was lucky,' thought Jock Sinclair, as he switched over to the requested channel. He repeated the same procedure with Algeciras and received immediate clearance to fly direct to Gibraltar Base.

'Gibraltar Marine, this is ER-SAR-01, we are cleared to fly direct to Gibraltar base, landing in twenty-two minutes, please have Professor Samuelson's emergency team ready at the helipad. The patient will need emergency in-helicopter treatment, assuming she lives long enough, over.'

Jock Sinclair felt bad about these words, but the truth was the truth. He switched his helmet comms to internal and spoke to his paramedic.

'Shelia, twenty minutes to landing. The hospital emergency team will be on the hospital helipad to conduct in-helicopter emergency treatment. Connecting you now to Gibraltar Marine, please give them a concise update, over.'

'Roger Jock, go ahead,' replied Shelia Williams.

Shelia Williams updated the onshore team on the condition of the incoming patient. She felt pleased to pass sufficient details to make a difference. She heard the helicopter going quiet, as it commenced its high-speed descent to the hospital helipad.

Pilot Jock Sinclair wrung the maximum performance from his aircraft as he could. With two minutes to landing, he only had five minutes fuel left. He'd never flown to such tight limits before, but he remained optimistic he would succeed. He saw a batman at the back of the helipad, waving him in. The aircraft was flying too fast, time to pull up on the collective and bring the nose up for what would be a hard landing if he wasn't careful.

With the fuel alarm making one hell of a din, the helicopter came to a classic stop and drop landing. Safely on the ground, Sinclair waved to the waiting medical team to rush to the aircraft and get aboard before he commenced the helicopter blades wind-down.

Shelia Williams flung open wide the main door of the aircraft and helped pull everyone aboard. The medical team quickly got to work, as the pilot disengaged the main rotors from the engine. As the rotating blades slowly came to a halt, the helicopter's main engines shut down, rather quicker than the normal period to let them cool down sufficiently before shutdown.

'Phew,' whistled Lt Henry Boeing. 'That was close; well-done skipper.'

His skipper looked tired, it had been a long flight, and the responsibility of getting his patient back in time had been hard.

'Henry,' croaked Jock Sinclair in relief, 'Check-out what's going on in the cabin, and bring me only good news.'

Henry Boeing did as he was asked. He stood at the entrance from the cockpit for an agonising ten minutes, praying that things were going well. The medical team were hard at it, and the Professor looked concerned. The Professor could be seen giving urgent instructions to his daughter and her assistant.

Finally, their looks turned positive and a look of relief appeared on the Professor's face. The Professor looked around at Henry Boeing, gave him a well done, as his daughter waved over for the hospital stretcher cart to come to the cabin door to take the patient to the waiting hospital.

Chapter 16

AS MOODY BLUE continued on her course to the south-east, the wind, which had so nearly caused the SAR helicopter to have a life-threatening situation, decided to inflict itself upon the hapless yacht. Nicola was enjoying a stellar sailing experience when a heavy gust of wind momentarily overpowered the yacht.

Nicola couldn't control this wild lady, as she healed over to an alarming degree, the twin rudders fighting for grip with strong cavitation. Then, the yacht griped up into the wind, with all sails flogging in the violent tempest. Nicola could do little else but to rush to the main halyard to let the mainsail drop into its lazy jacks.

She tried to bear away, but with all way lost, she started the main engine to power her way out of trouble.

'Phew, that was exciting whilst it lasted,' thought Nicola. She saw dark clouds in the distance which could only be an impending storm and decided to take things a bit easier.

Moody Blue reached a point twenty miles offshore from the kink in the coastline called 'Tombolo de Trafalgar'. They stood the chance of arriving at Gibraltar in the next twelve hours, but first she had to deal with the oncoming tempest.

She reefed the foresail by fifty per cent, bore away and sheeted in the sail with the winch. It became a struggle, as the foresail looked close to being blown out. As long as she didn't let it flog in the wind, it should hold, she hoped.

Mike came on deck to lend a hand. He had been dozing in his bunk but had almost been ejected onto the deck when Moody Blue heeled hard over. He should have strapped himself in, but being this close to land, he didn't think it would be necessary. Another lesson learned.

Even with heavily shortened sail, Moody Blue made good time towards the headland of the Island of Tarifa, the turning mark to Gibraltar. The distance to run into Gibraltar would be greatly increased.

Moody Blue would have to beat into the teeth of the strong north-easterly wind. Nicola checked the chart, calculating the last leg would be at least eighteen nautical miles. This would be the first time she sailed the Moody on this point of sail in such a heavy wind.

With only a short distance to the turning mark, the oncoming storm confirmed its intent to increase to a strong tempest. Mike at least had some local knowledge and she asked his opinion. Clearly, the beat to windward into Gibraltar Bay was going to be near impossible. Few yachts would be able to manage such a journey, even if they wanted to.

Mike thought for a few moments then forcibly suggested it would be better to lay-up under the lee of the island and wait it out. Nicola could not agree more, the difficulty was getting there in the first place. She brought the main engine into service, but in the rising wind, it would be of little help.

There was only one thing for it, raise the mainsail heavily reefed and dispense with the foresail altogether. The problem was the mainsail reefing lines were not installed to reef the mainsail to its smallest size.

'Mike,' she shouted out above the wind. 'I need you to re-run the reef lines from the second slab to the fourth. Drop the boom into the cockpit area. It's an easy job for the outboard end, but for the inboard end next to the mast, you will need to be very careful and make sure you're strapped on for safety.'

Mike snorted at the word easy, but he had the strength for the task. He managed re-rigging the outboard end with some difficulty. The inboard end would need great care. Clipping his safety line to the nearest strong point, he laboured hard, hanging on to the mast for dear life as Moody Blue pitched and fell into the heavy oncoming seas. Eventually, he completed the task, dropped back into the centre cockpit to take a breather.

With the main engine running flat out, Nicola struggled with the helm to hold Moody Blue in position. Mike fully reefed the foresail and quickly hoisted the mainsail. It looked very small, hardly able to catch sufficient wind, but wind there was a plenty. With the mainsheet track let out to the fullest extent to leeward, he trimmed the mainsail in hard as Nicola bore away from the wind just enough to use its abundant power at the foot of the sail.

Moody Blue started to thrash to windward, but Nicola couldn't get the course she wanted to the land end of the small island. Keeping the yacht on this course would take them out to sea, into the main channel and greater danger.

'Ready about,' shouted Nicola, as she spun the helm to change tack on to starboard, to head Moody Blue directly for the shoreline. The angle to the wind was way above what she expected but closing the shore would be by far the best option.

As the yacht closed the shore the depth sounder indicated the slow reduction of water depth under the keel, Nicola chose her moment with care, bringing Moody Blue back onto port tack. Slowly but surely the yacht thrashed its way into the wind shadow underneath the Island of Tarifa.

The crew of Moody Blue were relieved to reach safety for the moment. Nicola ordered anchoring with a long a scope of anchor chain. The anchor could not be relied on not to hold but by maintaining a 'steaming watch, using the main engine on slow ahead, she hoped to be able to keep station until the worst of the tempest had passed.

There would be no sleep this night for either of them. The weather forecast gave only a brief gap in the weather. The next storm was due to come barrelling in out of the Atlantic from the west. If they delayed moving from their current shelter, Moody Blue would end up firmly on 'terra nova,' smashed to pieces on this unforgiving low shoreline.

Night came, as the violent wind howled overhead. Nicola went forward to feel the anchor chain, which was definitely dragging in the soft sand along this shoreline. She waved at Mike to power up the main engine, selecting half-ahead. The dragging of the anchor and its chain along the seabed stopped. Now there was nothing for it but to wait out the weather.

Mike went below to get food and hot drinks. Both fed, they huddled under the cockpit awning, as the long night slowly dragged by. By three o'clock in the morning, the tempest was clearly abating, but the weather coming from the Atlantic had made great progress, giving barely an hour and a half between weather fronts.

Nicola checked the radar and seeing her chance shouted out to Mike to recover the anchor. It had buried itself deep in the sand, and Moody Blue would have to run over it to break it free. A difficult problem showed itself. The tide had ebbed and there was precious little water depth under the keel.

Nicola edged Moody Blue forward as Mike hauled in the long anchor chain. At the point where Moody Blue was about to run over the anchor, the keel bumped the bottom of the seabed as the now rising swell started to make its presence known.

As the anchor broke free, Mike shouted to go full astern. Moody Blue came astern as fast as possible, the depth increased tantalisingly slowly. The swell running in advance of the new westerly wind dumped the keel a few times on the seabed.

In conjunction with the frantic manoeuvring, Mike made ready to make sail. Unfurling the foresail was an easy task, but he could only raise the mainsail as high as the top slab, hardly sufficient power to drive the yacht over the shoaling seabed. As Moody Blue healed over to the new wind, her keel left the seabed behind. Nicola spun the wheel to bring the yacht heading towards the extremity of the island which had given such welcome relief.

Under reduced rig, and with the main engine set to full ahead, Moody Blue powered down to the southern extremity of the island. The distance was barely two miles, but these two miles seemed to take an age. As the yacht rounded up to head north-east along the coast, the new wind started to hit with the force of a runaway steam train. Fortunately, the coastline gave some relief from the building weather, and Moody Blue was now running hot and hard before the storm.

Nicola gave the helm to Mike and ducked down to the navigation table to check on the distance to run before they reached another waypoint along the coastline, the need to miss its adjacent island, 'Isla Cabrita.' She shouted the new course to steer and slaved the radar display to the monitor at the helming position.

Mike steered Moody Blue with great confidence, keeping his eye on the depth sounder as he hugged the Spanish coastline for maximum protection from the storm. As their yacht passed the island on their starboard beam, Mike hardened up on the wind to head directly into the large bay towards the entrance of Gibraltar harbour.

The storm clouds were rolling in fast, as the wind rose to a new pitch. Nicola handed Mike a pair of goggles, the driving rain would soon make them indispensable. Halfway across the bay, the storm hit with full force, with the driving rain blotting out the outline of the Rock of Gibraltar. With the foresail now fully reefed, and with only a vestigial mainsail set, Moody Blue had too much power. Mike was having difficulties controlling the yacht as it crashed through the mounting seas.

Nicola shielded the radar display from the rain to see Moody Blue would not reach the north entrance with safety. She took a bearing to head to the south entrance and shouted the course correction to Mike. This new course brought the wind far close to being dead astern, Moody Blue rolled violently to windward, giving Mike a heart-stopping moment. They both hung on grimly; the yacht reached the point where there was nothing for it but to hang on.

A brief gap in the rain afforded a glimpse of the southern entrance, a minor course correction, a quick prayer, and hope to hell no other vessel was about to leave the harbour.

Moody Blue burst into Gibraltar harbour. Mike quickly rounded up to come under the protective wall of the main breakwater. As the wind whistled violently overhead, Nicola dropped the mainsail into the lazy jacks, breathing a sigh of deep relief. Mike held position under main engine whilst Nicola gathered herself together to consult the harbour directory to find exactly where the promised hospital berth might be.

The harbour master's launch came up to them, asked the usual questions, and then directed them to proceed to the north end of the harbour. Nicola prepared Moody Blue to go alongside, raking around in the depths of the centre cockpit seat lockers for fenders and mooring ropes that were not all tangled-up.

As Moody Blue approached the hospital berth, daylight struggled into being to help them go alongside and moor up. At the berth, Nicola saw a number of waiting persons, official and civilian.

The first official came from Immigration and Border Control, a freshman, new to the posting. He carefully checked Nicola's passport, which he handed back with as little grace as possible.

Sergeant Mike Wilkens only had his service ID which seemed to be a problem. It mattered little Mike told the official he was aircrew returning from an air-sea rescue mission. Mike saw the waiting RAF Land Rover and an increasingly impatient duty officer. Mike leapt ashore, waved goodbye and then he was gone.

The Customs and Excise man took little interest in a yacht crewed by a lone female. The hour was early, the weather was not improving, and his shift at the local airport would soon begin with the arrival of the first flight from London.

Nicola looked up and wondered where the entrance to the hospital was. A young lady with long blonde hair, hanging on to the lead of an energetic blonde-haired Labrador, asked if she was Nicola, and had she come to visit Victoria.

Nicola nodded, and the young lady introduced herself as Samantha, although she preferred to be called just Sam.

'Hi,' she called out. 'I am the daughter of Professor Samuel Samuelson, the director of the hospital. He would like you to come over as soon as you can. He wishes to bring your friend out of general anaesthetic and it would be best if she saw a friend first. Stops her having a shock. Daddy has kept her under since she arrived.'

'Is she OK?' asked Nicola. 'I had great concern when the helicopter lifted her from the yacht.'

'Yes,' replied Samantha, 'She is recovering well, but when she awakes we can see the true situation. Will you take long to get ready?'

'Two minutes,' as Nicola disappeared down below.

Two minutes later Nicola reappeared with a small backpack, locked up Moody Blue and climbed onto the dockside. The two ladies walked quickly to the side of the hospital, where the dog was deposited in the guard room. Samantha signed the security book for the pair of them.

An elderly lift to the sixth floor took its time, during which Nicola discovered Samantha held the position of senior nurse, specialising in gynaecology; soon take her exams to go to the university hospital in London to continue her studies.

Being a scientist herself, this all sounded jolly interesting, leading to the hope Victoria could recover much quicker than expected. It increasingly looked like the chances of getting to the start-line for the Atlantic Rally would be doubtful.

As they entered the hospital, it was easy to see its Royal Navy origins. At least the brown lino flooring had long since been replaced, and the dark green and white painted walls had been covered with a neutral texture, but the original steel framed windows, with only a single pane of glass in small squares, continued to endure, windows that could be found the world over, wherever the Royal Navy had been. Windows guaranteed to keep some of the weather on the outside and all the running condensation on the inside.

Samantha took Nicola direct to the 'intensive care ward' where Victoria was recovering from a long and difficult operation. Surrounded by a suite of the latest technology, Victoria had been kept under general anaesthetic in strictly controlled conditions.

A tall lean man, with greying hair and rimless glasses, introduced himself as Professor Samuelson. He was directing a nurse, as she prepared to give Victoria an injection to hasten the recovery process. He asked Nicola to take the hand of her friend and start speaking softly into Victoria's ear.

Nicola moved close to Victoria's head and whispered, 'Come on you lazy bitch, wake up,' which was not quite what the Professor had in mind. Victoria's face remained calm and enigmatic.

Nicola returned to the side of Victoria's head and whispered a repeat of her Elisa Doolittle routine would not be necessary, and asked for something saintlier, since she had, according to her information, visited the pearly gates, only to be told to 'naff-orft' by the Arch-Angel Gabriel.

Victoria smiled, opened her left eye, and looked hard at everybody. 'Oh no,' laughed Nicola, 'It's the mad staring eye, we are all doomed.'

At this point, Samantha started giggling, the nurse looked as if she seen it all before.

Professor Samuelson wondered just what the hell was going on in his hospital.

'It's OK Professor,' said Nicola. 'This banter is fairly normal. Some doctors take it the wrong way, but it means she, Miss Victoria Stanwick, in all her glory, is alive and well. Thank you very much for rescuing the Arch-Angel Gabriel from an interesting interview.'

'Can I sit up now?' asked Victoria. 'I've been a lyin' on my back, like a good little girl, for far too long.'

Professor Samuelson asked if the performance had finished, as he needed to check his latest patient, and he had a million and one things to do that morning.

'I believe so Professor,' replied Nicola, 'We've have been spared her Elisa Doolittle routine, which would have dangerous, as she would've burst into song, and she can't sing for toffee.'

Professor Samuelson smiled, turned around to the stoic member of his medical team, and said, 'Nurse, the screens, if you would be so kind.'

Victoria started giggling and muttered, 'Magic fingers time, oh lucky me.'

Nicola heard it but she was grateful nobody else did, as the nurse shuffled everyone away from Victoria's bed now hidden by the screens. The nurse pointed at the comfortable reclining chairs at the other end of the ward, to enable the Professor to get on with his examination.

Samantha came over to sit with Nicola. Nicola thought this strange. Samantha started a light general conversation, mostly about the difficult voyage to reach Gibraltar harbour. But the conversation soon turned to medical matters. Nicola quickly came to the conclusion her father had asked his daughter to see what information she could gather regarding the initial assault on his patient.

Nicola said she did not want to go into details at the moment, describing only their kidnapping on the waterfront in Wales, and the journey through hell. She had already told Sgt Wilkens the 'new' official version of what had happened in the expectation this story would have already been passed to others.

Nicola continued with the 'new' official story of the arrival of the yacht somewhere off the Atlantic coast of, as far as she could tell, Spain, or maybe Portugal, somewhere east of the headland at Faro, and how she rescued Victoria and sent the yacht drifting out to sea, with the three assailant's unconscious from an overdose of drugs, alcohol, and seasickness.

She also briefly described how she unfurled a foresail to take the yacht out to sea, as the severed plastic discharge pipes in the heads allowed the yacht to sink gently into the dark depths of the ocean.

Her description of the journey to Paris was also equally vague and who had helped them get to a private hospital. Nicola had almost finished this less than convincing discourse when a hospital orderly came in looking for a Miss Stranraer and did she know an M. Jus William from Paris. Nicola nodded an affirmative.

The hospital orderly ushered Jus into the ward.

'Bonjour chéri Nicola, comment allez-vous, heureux que vous l'avez fait à Gibraltar en bonne forme,' as he sat down at her side.

Nicola replied, 'Merci Jus Je vais bien, Victoria est assistée en ce moment par le Professeur Samuelson.'

Nicola turned around to Samantha, 'Oh sorry, we should be speaking in English, how rude of us, do you understand French?'

'That's OK,' Samantha replied. 'My French is almost non-existent. I spend my free time, what there is of it, trying to get my head around the local Spanish dialect.'

Jus removed an iPad from his rucksack which looked remarkably like the one Nicola had left aboard Moody Blue.

'I brought you this from Paris. You must have forgotten to take it with you,' said Jus. 'I have added the 'before' and 'after' photographs of Victoria's, and your, injuries. I think you did request them; the moment was very sad and such things are hard to remember and not too important at the time.'

Nicola took the iPad to open up the files containing the gruesome photographs. She noticed straight away they had been doctored to remove the easily recognisable interior décor of a Portuguese monastery, for somewhere else, a modern hospital ward in, say, Paris.

She was not disappointed. The 'before' photographs were untouched originals taken close up. The 'after' photographs showed both herself and Victoria a few days after the initial treatment had been completed, both standing in a corner with sunlight coming in from a side window.

Intrigued, Nicola expanded the 'after' photographs so show a hazy view of a city. She smiled to herself when the very faint outline of the Eiffel Tower could be seen in the distance. This background could only have come from the 'Tour Montparnasse'. Altogether, a nice touch and expert use of Photoshop software. Clearly, Great Aunt Violet had been busy adding detail to Nicola's escape story.

Samantha looked on, clearly eager to see the photographs. Nicola told her to understand the 'before' photographs were not for the faint hearted, and she should be aware of this. Samantha muttered something about they could not be too bad but waited for Nicola to hand over the iPad.

Samantha looked through the 'before' photographs in total disbelief. She started with the photographs of Nicola, with her huge black eye on her left side, the broken lip with one of the lower teeth almost through to the outside of her face, the huge bruises all over her body and legs, and between her legs. She felt sick to the stomach.

Nicola told her to take stock, then a deep breath before moving on to the photographs of Victoria. Samantha froze in horror then excused herself to go to the bathroom. Nicola heard the sounds of someone being sick. She was not surprised and almost joined her despite having seen the gruesome spectacle before.

Samantha returned, her face red with tears and shock.

'Are you all right now?' asked Nicola. 'I told you it would be a shock. Even now, I still feel unbelievably bad about the inhumane attack we were both subjected to.'

Samantha opened the 'after' photographs and whistled her surprise at the improvement in what she was told was just under seven long days and nights. First, the photographs of Nicola, asking just how so much progress in recovery had taken so little time.

Nicola gave her a brief outline of the aftercare, the remedial drenagem massages. This massage technique for faster recovery of deep injuries was one Samantha hoped to master.

Samantha moved with haste to the photographs showing the 'after' pictures of Victoria's damaged areas. When she looked at the photograph of her back, she just did not believe it and said so. Nicola assured her what she saw was correct.

Samantha pressed for details of this treatment, but Nicola could honestly say she didn't know the full details and the 'doctor', the Mother Superior, had used an experimental treatment believed to have come from the States, and being experimental, had kept the details to herself.

Nicola knew she had to be careful with her choice of words; the smallest slip could give the game away. She asked Samantha if she was satisfied; for her, she could give no more information, the photographs said it all.

Samantha asked if she could have a second look through the photographs and this time she managed to look at them more objectively. She would have spent longer but her father shouted for her to come to Victoria's bedside so he could give her an update on her condition.

Nicola had a quiet word with Jus regarding the photographs. Great Aunt Violet had been clever in anticipating the use of the photographs to bring substance to the 'what, where and when' discussion, now the subject was out in the open. If people came to their own conclusions it would be up to them. Best to say nothing.

Professor Samuelson left Victoria's bedside, collected a cup of coffee from the kitchen and sat beside Nicola. Nicola introduced him to Jus as her Aunt's companion. Professor Samuelson looked at Jus wondering just who the hell was he, clearly no ordinary member of the human race.

Nicola said she needed the ladies restroom and left Jus to work a little bit of French magic with a sceptical member of the medical profession.

As Nicola returned with a cup of coffee for herself and Jus she saw the two men in deep discussion over the photographs. The Professor was having difficulty in recognising the 'before' photographs with the actual person. Jus showed him the various faint birthmarks on both girl's to compare with the actual before him.

The Professor had not examined Nicola, so he asked Nicola into an adjacent examination room to look at various sensitive areas of her body to confirm his orientation. He asked Nicola if she would like him to give her a check-up, but Nicola thanked him but declined, saying everything was back to normal.

Professor Samuelson examined the 'after' photographs very carefully, looked up at Jus asking if they were taken in the Tour Montparnasse, because as far as he knew there was no medical clinic in that tall Parisian tower. Jus just smiled and suggested if the clinic was private, few persons would know about it. He added the clinic belonged to an organisation which always kept its secrets.

Professor Samuelson asked what organisation, only to be shown a security pass for an obscure department of the French Interior Ministry. Nicola poked her nose into the conversation, asking Jus if this was his secret service pass. Jus looked at her with his best poker face and told them both he could not reveal any more details.

Samuel Samuelson looked at the two of them, decided asking any more questions would be a waste of time, and made his excuses as Sylvia, his personal assistant, arrived with a clipboard full of unfulfilled appointments.

Nicola looked up at Sylvia and decided here was efficiency personified, a good looking brunet, wearing severe office attire. She spoke in short, clipped sentences. Nicola soon managed to make the connection with what she overheard in the corridor by two male ward assistances with the person in front of her, the 'Wicked Witch of the North.'

Samantha drew back the screens around Victoria's bed, inviting everyone to join with her and Victoria. Samantha noticed Nicola's interest in the Lady Sylvia, as she called her, and asked for an instant opinion.

Nicola turned around, looked at Samantha, and asked what she thought was going on. Nicola had very quickly picked-up on the tension between father and daughter regarding a new family situation. This, of course, was normal when one partner in a successful marriage had lost the other. For widowers, the difficulty of starting a new firm relationship had to negotiate the minefield of what the children thought, especially daughters.

Professor Samuelson had been a widower for nigh-on two years and undoubtedly suppressed his grief by overworking at the hospital. His nights would be lonely in the darkness of the night, and there existed the possibility he had been overprotective with his daughter. That they were very close stood out a mile.

Samantha would not reveal the level of any relationship which had developed. Her father, to be fair, had been very careful not to upset the family apple cart. Victoria sat back revelling in some interesting conversation. She had had quiet words with the Professor during the hour he had spent in his examinations. He had been kind, sensitive, and very professional. He responded with a few pearls of wisdom, allowing Victoria and her ever-active mind to come to various conclusions which needed to be checked out against real-time observation.

'They're deeply in love,' Victoria blurted out, 'Well she is for sure and your father is more than interested.'

The words hit Samantha like a bolt from the blue, asking how she could possibly come to this conclusion.

'It's the little things, Samantha,' replied Victoria. 'Like the meeting of their eyes when she showed your father the appointments on the clipboard, two professionals accepting each other's expertise to form a perfect team. That she fancies him is a given, a good-looking woman in her early forties looking for a husband, love, and children, not necessarily in that order.'

Nicola groaned under her breath. Victoria always came out with the line 'not necessarily in that order,' but she could be correct. Nicola envisaged Miss Sylvia in less formal clothing, a flared skirt just above the knee, revealing long slender legs, a loose comfortable silk blouse showing the outline of a dark coloured bra beneath, her hair up in a bun, in all she could 'dress to impress,' able to run any opposition to a distant second.

Nicola confronted Samantha with some wise words. She would

soon be going away to university; did she expect her father to survive lonely days and nights on his own. If the Lady Sylvia was anxious to look after her father, she should encourage the match; the pair of them were ideally suited.

Victoria joined in, telling Samantha life moves on. Her father was a young man in his prime, he needed love, he would yearn for sex, he needed a new centre point for the rest of his life, so why should she, his loving daughter not go with the flow, and get with the programme. The Lady Sylvia was not after her father's money, she had her own home, and she would care for her father.

Jus sat back, nursing another hot cup of coffee, wishing the 'no smoking sign' would vanish. This conversation had been most interesting, his two young charges doing all they could to help a young lady at the cusp of a successful career, but clearly struggling with deep family emotions.

'You're very quiet, M. William,' said Nicola. 'Want to join in the conversation?'

'What can I add?' Jus replied. 'You see, you understand all, you express your thoughts most clearly. Mademoiselle Sylvia is indeed an attractive woman, capable of great love and activity.'

'Are you telling me you fancy her, you old rogue?'

Jus sighed, and said, 'Mon chéri, I bound by advancing years to be grateful for my past conquests, and the love of your devoted aunt. However, let us pray le Professeur can match her ambitions.'

Samantha found her head spinning with such unusual conversation. She knew the time would come to flee the nest and had secretly worried about the consequences. And here were three almost complete strangers giving her the advice she knew she needed but was afraid to ask for. She suddenly realised she had no female friends to confide in. No wonder she had bonded so quickly with Victoria, this sweet nothing of a young woman who had talents she needed to explore.

Lunch time approached, with Victoria thinking she would be left on her own with prison, or rather hospital food, to look forward to. She started to feel very hungry; knowing full well her next meal of solids would be carefully controlled.

'If you boys and girls are thinking about lunch, you can forget about leaving me on my own,' she calmly informed. 'Just get me dressed and find a blasted wheelchair. Samantha can choose what's best, even if it's only soup.'

'I shouldn't really,' said Samantha, 'But you're right, the food in this place is very UK hospital. Daddy is out on his rounds; we can slip out the back door. The local 'greasy spoon' is not far away.'

'Greasy spoon'. Nicola hadn't heard this magic piece of Royal Navy slang in years, mostly from a long-lost father who had died on active service in the Far East.

'It's OK Nicola,' said Samantha. 'The local is actually quite good. The owner is a good friend, you can order almost anything if he has the ingredients.'

In no time at all, the hospital escapees assembled in the café known as 'la Cuchara Grasienta' in the forlorn hope the name in Spanish would improve the service. The owner, a Glaswegian gentleman, allegedly on the run from Interpol these last twenty years, proudly displayed a sign announcing, 'Good food, and good service, tomorrow.' A keep sake from the main stand cafeteria at the Celtic Park football ground in Glasgow.

He greeted his early lunchtime customers with a thick Glasgow accent almost incomprehensible to even the most informed 'Sassenach.'

Samantha greeted him like the old friend he was, ordered for Victoria, and asked around the table for their wishes. Spanish omelettes seemed to be the favourite, quick simple and a house speciality. Samantha requested the usual bottles of red or brown sauce would not be needed, but a communal mixed salad would be most welcomed.

Victoria's special soup arrived first, accompanied by savoury biscuits. The meal was served with strong tea. Jus requested an equally strong coffee, which exceeded his expectations. With the meal over, Victoria returned to her bed in a private ward, just before Professor Samuelson and Sylvia returned from their duties, slightly perplexed at the smiling faces before them.

It became time for Jus to cut loose; he had things to do. Nicola badly needed to catch up on some much-needed sleep. As they made to leave Victoria to her afternoon nap, Professor Samuelson invited Nicola to dinner at 8 p.m. should she feel able to come. Nicola thankfully accepted.

Back aboard Moody Blue, Nicola spent thirty minutes tidying up and making things shipshape. An official voice shouted down, asking for the skipper of the yacht. Nicola went on deck to be confronted by an assistant harbour master, intent on ruining her afternoon.

'You can't moor 'ere,' said the official voice. 'This is the hospital berth.'

'Yes, I know. Go and talk to Professor Samuelson. I am his visitor, excuse me I'm going to bed,' shouted an annoyed Nicola, who went below and slammed the main saloon hatch after her.

Nicola made her way to the main aft cabin, took a quick shower, and slumped into the comfortable double berth. Exhausted, she fell asleep instantly, grateful Victoria had been rescued in time and, thank God, was now on the way to a full recovery.

She awoke four hours later and remembered her invitation to dinner. She would have preferred to go back to sleep, but this would only result in her waking up in the middle of the night, unable to return to slumber. She ran the main engine for half an hour to recharge the main engine batteries.

She took stock of her food and water supplies and found all were much lower than expected. The hospital mooring berth did not provide services for yachts, so a move to the adjacent marina could wait until tomorrow morning. At least the annoying official had gone away, as she was in no mood to deal with a jobsworth like him.

Chapter 17

NICOLA LOOKED at her watch. The time had suddenly advanced to 19.45 and she was expected somewhere in fifteen minutes. It occurred she didn't know where this somewhere was.

She only had to find shoes, finish her make-up to be ready for whatever. A car screeched to a halt next to Moody Blue and the sounds of two voices heard followed by the sounds of shoes being lobbed into the centre cockpit.

'Anyone home?' called Professor Samuelson. 'Hope we are not too late.' 'Come on down below,' replied Nicola. 'Take care with the companionway.'

Professor Samuelson, followed by a lady in a pleated skirt showing off a very nice pair of legs, descended into the main saloon.

'Hi Samuel, Hi Sylvia, welcome to Moody Blue. Time for a starter, uma aperitif?' 'Good idea. Darling what will you have?'

Sylvia requested a still water, as she was duty driver for the evening. Samuel requested a stiff drink with a splash of water. It had been a long day. Nicola pulled out a bottle of brandy from under the main saloon table, poured two large glasses, and placed a bottle of mineral water on the table.

'Wonderful brandy,' said Samuel. 'Never seen this brand before.'

'It was a gift,' replied Nicola, without elaboration. The boxes of brandy had come from the black cutter, now a yellow sloop. This VSOP was well above even the best standard she had ever experienced. It occurred she should look for the details on the internet.

'Mind if I have a wander around your ship?' asked Samuel. 'It looks very comfortable.'

Nicola told him Moody Blue was the two state-cabin option, with a single berth next to the navigation table and one behind the galley for use at sea. This model was aimed squarely at the 'retired couples' market, and for her, a crew of three would be ideal, simply because 'George,' the twin channel auto-pilot, did most of the steering, and with only three persons aboard, supplies would last for a longer journey.

Sylvia looked on. She knew little about yachting and had no intention of starting. Golf was her game. She played to a handicap of four, of which she remained immensely proud. She spent time working on Samuel to take up the sport, but he remained fully committed to his hospital, something she was minded to slowly change over time.

Nicola showed Samuel around the yacht, the forward master cabin, with its very discrete décor, its adjacent on-suite, the workshop, and storage forward of the main mast, and aft, the main aft cabin, the engine room under the centre cockpit, and the galley.

He asked Sylvia to check-out the main aft cabin. Nicola saw Sylvia could see the possibilities of some discrete 'alone time' with her intended. Somewhere a couple intent on catching up on the good moments in life could escape to, say moored out of the way in a deserted creek at low tide, with only nature making its infernal noises.

Samuel moved close to Sylvia putting his arm around her waist to give her a quick hug. For Nicola, it was abundantly clear these two were in the throes of playing catch-up, just as soon as the coast was clear.

'Well, are we ready to go and eat?' asked Nicola who by this time had regained an appetite that needed feeding 'If it's your treat I insist on buying the drinks.'

'No, no Nicola, it's my invitation to dinner,' replied Samuel.

'Darling,' interjected Sylvia. 'You have invited us to dinner, which is food, nothing about who can pay for the drinks. Thank you, Nicola very kind of you to offer. Let's go.'

The threesome made it topside, Nicola locked up the main hatchway, and followed the happy couple over to her car. Nicola examined the car, a newish VW Golf GTI. 'Interesting,' she thought.

'Like my car Nicola?' Sylvia asked. 'It's quite special. V6 turbo-diesel, plus all-wheel drive.'

'What does it do?' asked Nicola, inquiring about how fast it might go.

'What does it do?' repeated Sylvia. 'It annoys every Porsche 911 ever made, and the occasional Ferrari. It's a wolf in 'town mobile' clothing. I have great fun with it. Samuel just closes his eyes in the knowledge his life insurance is up to date. Hop in the back Darling, you're travelling coach this evening.'

Sylvia was a good as her word, as she piloted the car out of the dockyard. Nicola could see she had the skills to master this excellent example of motor car engineering. The border crossing into the Spain caused little delay, and as Nicola sat in the front of this mid-sized rocket ship, it became obvious it could travel across the continent at a remarkable rate of knots.

Ten kilometres down the road, a discrete hotel came into view. The car park had few vehicles and the hotel restaurant looked to be occupied by 'early to bed' German residents.

The restaurant manager greeted them warmly, another nugget of information for the inquisitive Nicola. The hotel must be their hideaway from the toils of the big wide world. Nicola sensed this display of secrets had been triggered, but by what?

The evening meal came and went. Typical Spanish fare of delicious seafood and local meats, with a stunning sweet course made from a mixture of caramelised orange peel and lemon fruits, smothered in a local cream cheese.

'Nicola,' asked Samuel. 'Just what exactly took place in the ward after Sylvia and I started my rounds in the hospital.'

'What do you mean?' asked Nicola.

'Well, late afternoon, when we returned to the intensive care ward, my daughter, for the first time, greeted Sylvia with some affection. As grateful for the change in attitude as we both are, it came as a surprise,' answered Samuel.

'I guess Victoria saw all. Victoria being Victoria sought to have a word in Samantha's ear. Those two have bonded so fast it's like watching super glue at work. You could call it the 'blonde leading the blonde.' Samuel laughed out loud.

'I guess Samantha needed a soul mate, and along came the effervescent Victoria. She doesn't hold back you know if she likes someone,' replied Nicola. 'I hope she did well?'

'Definitely. Samantha has kept the tension between us quite high, but I couldn't understand why?'

'Can I suggest,' said Nicola choosing her words very carefully, 'Two strangers, that's Vicky and myself, saw something Samantha was trying not to see. She has the ambition to succeed, which means leaving home and the hospital. It will be a big step, but one she must take. She cares for her father very much but leaving him to a lonely life after she has flown the coop worried her too much, I would guess.

Victoria would have pointed out you two were coming together, and Sylvia would be more than capable of bringing happiness to her father, so why didn't she see this and let the relationship develop in the open, where it belongs.'

'Crikey,' said Sylvia, 'You're good. I thought you were just a scientist. Anyway, many thanks are in order, so the next round of drinks are on me.'

The manager came to the table with a special bottle of Cava, compliments of the management, expressing the hope his special customers had enjoyed their evening. This became the first time Samuel could see his favourite manager could lip read.

'The secrets he must know; interesting,' he thought.

The return journey was more tranquil, and for sure Nicola was not up to seeing Spain go by at warp speed. She sat at the back and let the two lovers in the front have their little moments of touching each other, holding hands and generally being as one.

'I have a guest room at my place if you want to stay overnight,' suggested Samuel.

Then, he received a call on his mobile, his daughter telling him she would spend the night in the hospital with Victoria.

'Was that Vicky giving you the all clear?' asked Nicola.

'No, it was Samantha telling me she is spending the night in the hospital with Victoria.' 'OK, best drop me off at Moody Blue. I have to move berth to the marina first thing in the

morning, and then you can drop Sylvia off wherever.'

As this news filtered into the consciousness of Sylvia's mind, the Golf GTI seemed to increase its speed back to warp speed plus one.

'Hum,' thought Nicola, 'Lucky them,' and smiled to herself, luxuriating in a job well done.

Chapter 18

NICOLA AWOKE at sunrise, looked at her watch and decided the sun had started far too early for her. She drifted back to sleep and only the sound of a busy world outside brought her back to the current year. Nicola took a long visit to the heads, including a quick shower, answered the call of nature, and attempted to get her hair fixed up out of the way. Breakfast took a little time, and once she had dressed, she was ready for the day.

First things first. Move Moody Blue to the Marina for the included services. She went on deck to see if it looked like a pleasant day. She started the main engine and collared a passing dockworker to let go the mooring ropes and heave them back aboard.

It took but a few minutes to motor to the end of the old naval dock and into the marina entrance. She tied up at the reception berth and called out for the manager.

The manager welcomed her to his marina, aware she would be arriving courtesy of a call from his old chum Professor Samuelson. He directed Nicola over to a reserved berth. It had all the services she needed, water and electrical power, close to the ablutions block complete with all mod cons; positioned as close as possible to the gate leading to the hospital.

A brief discussion about the daily rate resulted in a satisfactory compromise where Nicola would pay cash and the Marina would include all the services which went with the mooring berth.

Nicola spent the rest of the morning catching up on connecting the water and electrical supply, throwing a pile of washing into the commercial washing machine shore-side, and generally being housekeeper of the month. Later she went to the marina office to order a supply of diesel and on the way back to Moody Blue. Nicola popped into the marina shop for more coffee, fresh bread and other bits and pieces.

Satisfied with her domestic abilities, she stayed below for the rest of the morning and relaxed with the morning paper and a mug of coffee.

Nicola recalled the events of last evening. It occurred the Professor had examined Moody Blue more closely than expected. There had been discrete questions about safety equipment, where the crew slept during a voyage, who did what, what were the watch keeping systems.

Should she be hoping the Professor would let Vicky return to light duties aboard Moody Blue if he released his daughter Samantha from the hospital to at least take the five-day voyage down to the Canary Islands?

She switched on the yacht's computer, connected to the marina Wi-Fi, and looked through the 'crew wanted and available' websites. This late in the year, there would be very few people looking to crew a yacht crossing the Atlantic. Those that did were already in the Canary Islands, choosing which mega cruiser they wanted to take passage in.

Anyway, it was time for lunch. Nicola had arranged to meet with Samantha at the 'la Cuchara Grasienta'. They both arrived at the same time and discussed what delights might be on offer today. As they sat down the Glaswegian owner suggested fish and chips and did they wish baked beans or mushy peas?

Nicola inquired about the quality of the batter, only to be told he had been using his grandmother's gold star recipe for the last twenty years. Two fish and chips it was then. Samantha brought Nicola up to date. Her father had been seen floating on air around the wards and the Lady Sylvia had a smile like a Cheshire cat. Clearly, her night in the hospital fortress had resulted in intended consequences.

'And what time did you two stop nattering,' asked Nicola. 'About two a.m.?'

'Oh no,' replied Samantha. 'We were just getting into our stride then, I guess we fell asleep about four a.m. Oh! What a wonderful evening.'

'And night shift, can't think what you two had to talk about?' sniffed Nicola. 'Oh, men mostly,' giggled Samantha.

The arrival of the fish and chips delayed any other comment Nicola might have. The meal was special, served with fresh brown bread and really strong tea, navy style.

Nicola asked Samantha about Victoria's future, would she fully recover, enjoy a happy relationship with a husband, and produce bouncing babies. Samantha thought Victoria would indeed recover, but it would take time. Her core system had been under great stress.

During the morning, despite many complaints, Victoria had undergone an exercise programme to enable her vital systems to be monitored. The exercise had not been too strong, and the results positive. They would have been better had Victoria stopped complaining, but they now understood she didn't like formal exercise and never had.

'I'll have a stiff word in her ear,' said Nicola. 'She just has to co-operate or we'll get nowhere.'

After lunch, Samantha and Nicola retreated to the hospital to find Professor Samuelson having a fatherly word with Victoria. His efforts seem to be rewarded, but it was hard to tell.

He greeted Nicola and his daughter and excused himself due to a busy afternoon. Nicola sat beside Victoria and started to pass the time of day.

'OK Nicky, and when are you going to start telling me what I must and mustn't do?' she started.

'Can do Chuck. Now is a good time, or do you want to spend the next three weeks tied to this hospital bed? It's up to you,' replied Nicola with flat emotion.

'Well, that's all I need,' replied Victoria in a huff.

'Victoria,' said Nicola trying to find the words to sooth her discontent, 'Folk are trying very hard to get you to the level where you might, and I mean might, be released from the hospital in a few days' time. These exercise tests are designed to find the state of your health. Little point putting you back together, only to let you go swanning across the Atlantic Ocean and having another relapse. So, go with the programme, and let's get the hell out of here.'

'Huh,' responded Victoria, going into a deeper silent mump.

Sylvia arrived trailing a medical assistant behind her. 'Good afternoon Victoria, time for your herbal infusion, must keep your digestive system ticking over.'

Victoria was about to give Sylvia a two-barrel blast of invective but seeing Nicola's face rising to storm level she thought better of it. Victoria drank the herbal tea with little grace and slipped back down under the covers, wishing everyone would go away.

'Nicky, can you follow me please,' called Sylvia. 'The Professor wishes to talk with you.' 'Sure.'

As Nicola left the ward, she felt Victoria's eyes burning into her back. She put her right hand behind her with the middle finger pointing to the ceiling. Sylvia was full of the joys of spring telling her everything would be OK.

Professor Samuelson welcomed Nicola and Sylvia into his comfortable if chaotic office and served them both with delightful Moroccan coffee with Arab sweetmeats.

'A good start,' thought Nicola. 'I wonder what's next?'

'Nicola,' began Professor Samuelson, 'Miss Victoria is rebelling against hospital treatment, and it is not helping progress. She is quite well, very well, in fact. This morning's tests were positive, but if I keep her in the hospital her progress will reverse, she will regress.

The hospital is coming to the closed season and half the wards will be closed for refurbishment. Samantha needs to take time off. I owe her far too many days holiday. So, I propose the following. Samantha takes time off at your expense during the voyage to the Canaries. She will direct and keep Victoria strictly in accordance with a programme I am devising. When you reach the Canaries, Samantha will have sufficient holidays to take the voyage across the Atlantic, something she has always dreamed about.

She will also need to allot time during the voyage to her studies, as before and after year's end, she will sit her exams at the university. There is flexibility in the exam dates as she will sit the test on her own, courtesy of an old friend of mine who runs the study courses. Any questions?'

Nicola sat back and thought. This looked like an offer she could not refuse, but best to take stock first.

'What did you have in mind regarding remuneration to the Canary Islands?' asked Nicola. 'I thought two hundred Euros a day would be about right, say five days?' replied Professor Samuelson.

'Is this negotiable?' smiled Nicola. 'Possibly,' replied Professor Samuelson.

Nicola looked at the Professor and his lady love, both looking slightly anxious as to the result of this conversation.

'Well. I guess you are looking for a package. My thoughts, my suggestion you understand, say a thousand quid cash before we sail, full board and incidental expenses in port, plus fifty US dollars a day the minute we sail from the Canaries to cross the Atlantic, and a one-way air ticket home to London.'

'So, you haven't been thinking about this before?' suggested Professor Samuelson. 'No, not really,' smiled Nicola, knowing full well both parties were on the same page. Sylvia broke into the conversation and sweetly said, 'Nicola, it's a deal, thank you.'

'Well, Madam Victoria will be pleased. I would like to depart Thursday evening after dark.

Is this OK with you Samuel?

'Yes, assuming I can give Victoria the all clear in the morning. By the way, Miss Victoria hasn't been acting up just to get out of here, I hope.'

'Oh no. This is normal. She just hates being ill, stuck in bed, when she has plans that are about to slip away.'

Nicola went to Victoria's bedside, with Samantha trying hard to get her to complete a small test procedure. Samantha was about to lose her patience when Nicola butted in the mounting tension.

'OK, you two, this is your Captain speaking. We sail at midnight on Thursday. Miss Stanwick, if you do not complete these bloody tests today and tomorrow, you will be left behind. If by any chance you do make departure with Moody Blue you will be required to adhere to all instructions by the ship's doctor. Any goddamn questions?'

'Pardon,' asked Victoria. 'Did I hear you correctly?'

'Unless you're hard of hearing Miss Stanwick, you did. Now I have to leave you two shipmates to get matters in hand before Thursday.'

Nicola left the ward smiling to herself. The time had come to do a little banking. With a hundred thousand US dollars aboard Moody Blue which could be considered a problem with the authorities ever watchful for bandits smuggling things they shouldn't.

It didn't take long to walk back to Moody Blue and collect half of the US dollars, and almost all of the UK pounds, which were always difficult to use abroad anyway now everyone had added the mighty Euro to the list of currencies most tradable on the street.

It took a while to find her bank in Gibraltar's busy main street. She wondered why the Spanish appeared to be in such a hurry to get their hands on the Rock when nearly everyone she saw in the street had come from Spain. Clearly, the ongoing political game between the two governments was the usual distraction from the sad fact Spain had zero chance of matching the efficiency of Germany.

Some years ago, a friend of hers had imported a British car from the US to Spain and it had taken ten months to get the paperwork sorted out without backhanders. For her, Spain revelled in the competition with Portugal as to which country could take the longest amount of time, with the maximum number of jobsworths, to complete even the simplest bureaucratic procedure.

By contrast, her British bank excelled in providing efficient service. Clearly moving money around the planet was an easy and profitable business. Nicola checked her debit and credit cards would work in the ports and locations in which she hoped to arrive.

Banking complete, Nicola found a discrete café in which to indulge in some tasty pastries complete with a cup of Kenyan coffee. She even got chatted up by a passing handsome stranger, despite her hair being nowhere near her usual standard. Coffee break over, Nicola headed towards a recommended hairdresser for two hours of luxuriating attention to her hair and what was left of her nails.

On her return to the hospital, Nicola was met by two blonde ladies seeking confirmation of the intended departure on Thursday midnight. Nicola smiled and referred them to Professor

Samuelson and his P.A., both of whom had called it a day and vanished from the hospital on unspecified business.

A secretary brought Samantha a note from her father detailing what had to be done and the additional tests to be carried out. He had also specified a slow workup in the hospital gymnasium so Victoria could restore a measure fitness to cope with life aboard a yacht undertaking a deep-water sea passage.

The Professor's note, once it had been shown to Victoria, resulted in much muttering under her breath, but if she wanted to escape this was the bloody tunnel she would have to dig. So, after a satisfying day, Nicola returned to Moody Blue for a quiet night listening to the radio and catching up on a good book.

The next morning heralded the start of another busy day. Moody Blue needed re-victualing for the voyage to the Canary Islands and the cruiser race across the Atlantic Ocean. After a frugal breakfast, Nicola sat at the main saloon dining table with lists of what went before, updated with what remained, producing a shopping list of some considerable size.

Moody Blue still had a sufficiency of booze, although Nicola was not concerned about alcohol aboard. The voyage to the Canaries would be fast. There would be little leeway regarding the need to check-in at race control and satisfy the safety check. The food list took a little time to update, and after a quick coffee she wandered over to the marina office to place her order.

On her return to Moody Blue she stopped at the marina supply shop and gave them a list of ropes and fittings she needed, paid for them, and asked someone bring everything over when ready.

During her inspection of the yacht's storeroom, Nicola found, of all things, a new asymmetric spinnaker complete with an installation kit to modify Moody Blue and how to set it up ready for use. She phoned the marina workshop becoming pleasantly surprised when the technician said he could come straight away.

Late morning the fuel truck arrived. The Spanish driver quickly checked the yacht's fuel tanks were clean and then completed refilling. Duty-free diesel resulted in a good price, and no, the driver could not accept her Amex card, but slyly informed a reasonable discount for cash. She wondered if he had relatives in Oporto.

The marine technician arrived, looked at the work involved, and quoted a price which Nicola thought reasonable considering she was in a hurry.

Whilst the technician worked on deck, Nicola decided to rake around the yacht's storeroom to see what other goodies she could find. Someone had been busy, as she found a list of items in the workbench drawer, and all in all, there was more than a sufficiency of spares, especially for the auto-pilot, 'George,' used mostly during the night.

Next, the marina delivered her order of ropes and other stuff, and Nicola set too rigging a third reef line for the mainsail. She lubricated the mast's mainsail track, then there seemed little else to do. Time for another coffee shared with the marine technician, a young eager sort of guy in his early twenties, who had noticed, more than once, Nicola looked very trim in her short shorts and a sports shirt with two top buttons undone.

Nicola smiled and went below closing the main hatch behind her. Her cell phone rang, 'Good morning to you Professor,' she answered, 'An evening farewell dinner at Sylvia's place. Is this an 'all hands-on deck' evening, super, eight p.m., can do, send a taxi for me, thanks,' and then she rang-off.

Nicola made lunch for herself and a sandwich for the marine technician. The work had progressed well and it wouldn't be long before the new spinnaker could be hoisted and its control lines checked, lowered, and stowed away in its protective cover alongside the starboard guardrails.

After lunch, Nicola wandered across to visit Victoria and see how Team Samantha was getting on.

'Hello stranger,' came the grumpy greeting from her best friend. 'How is she doing Samantha?' asked Nicola.

'Very well actually when she's not gritting her teeth and complaining under her breath,' replied Samantha.

'That's my girl. She never gives in, thank goodness. By the way, do you have the correct offshore protective clothing for long sea voyages?' said Nicola.

'I think so, got a list for me?' replied Samantha.

'Well, as a minimum, chest-high trousers, storm jacket with hood and goggles, thermal undergarments, a certified survival suit and lifejacket with beacon, and footwear to match,' replied Nicola.

'Ah, This is quite a list. I had better get busy, thanks.'

Victoria called Nicola over to her, asking if they were really sailing Thursday evening.

Nicola smiled and told her it was not April Fool's day and why wasn't she happy? 'Thank Christ for that,' muttered Victoria.

'No Vicky, you should thank everyone around you. Stop being a pain,' counselled Nicola. 'Excuse me I need to talk to the Professor.'

Nicola found Professor Samuelson in his office. His desk seemed remarkably clear, a new event for sure.

'Hi Samuel, moving out?' asked Nicola.

'Just preparing for the new era thanks to you. You must come again. Anyway, how can I help you?'

Nicola pulled out a thick envelope from her shoulder bag and handed it over.

'Ah, thanks very much, used notes I trust, no recurring numbers,' said Samuel smiling. 'You been talking to that crooked cop Collingwood have you. I think I smell the remains

of his exotic aftershave. Did he just disappear out of the back door?'

'Guilty as charged,' said Samuel. 'By the way, dinner tonight, seven p.m., Sylvia's place, here is the address.'

'Who's invited?'

'You three and us two. A 'bon voyage' dinner would seem to be appropriate for the occasion. It's a big step for me, Samantha, and I guess Sylvia. Nothing formal. Sylvia is a good chef. In fact, she's busy preparing as we speak. I rarely visit her place, so it will be nice to relax and be waited on for a change.'

'Shouldn't you be helping peel the spuds and do the washing up?'

'Goodness me, no,' replied Samuel, 'she has a domestic who does all this for her.' 'Oh really,' thought Nicola.

'OK Samuel, look forward to it. I must fly,' and with that Nicola headed back to 'Moody Blue.'

Late afternoon, Moody Blue was invaded by Samantha and Victoria. Samantha wanted to check out the facilities, wishing to feel comfortable with what to bring on the voyage.

Nicola advised only two suitcases, which would be the limit when she flew back to Europe when her adventure had finished. Nicola said she could leave her sailing equipment behind, and she would ship it to her later on.

Victoria opened a large shopping bag. Nicola didn't know the store but guessed, correctly, she had been shopping. With a flourish, Victoria produced her version of a typical Moroccan evening dress in stunning colours which came just below the knee. The colours matched her blonde hair and her pale complexion. Someone was out to upstage everyone, and Nicola hoped she wasn't about to turn a farewell dinner into a 'Vicky special.'

The three girls relaxed taking it turns to get ready for the dinner party. All three were interested to see Sylvia's home. A taxi arrived at the requested time. Nicola handed the driver the address, who seemed impressed.

The taxi arrived at a beautiful late 19th-century brick house of extensive proportions. Sylvia's maid answered the door, showing them into a huge lounge with its impressive external manicured terrace with mature trees and private swimming pool.

Sylvia welcomed them all into the large, fitted kitchen with its adjacent dining room.

'Like a quick tour?' she asked, guided them around her elegant home and then to the terrace to show the house's elevated position with magnificent panoramic views over the Straits and the Bay of Gibraltar.

Nicola saw Sylvia's home had retained all its original features, with its real marble fireplaces and asked the history of the property.

Sylvia said her late father bought it from the Admiralty when he was posted to Gibraltar as a Captain RN in charge of operations. Her father hated naval accommodation and turned a large bequest from an ageing aunt into a desirable, and now valuable, residence.

Samantha looked stunned. So little did she know about the lady her father had chosen to be his new love, for this was what she plainly was. The Professor's house belonged to the hospital. It had space, four bedrooms and all the facilities, but none of the Victorian decorative features of this comfortable original house.

Sylvia explained the property was originally the residence a Royal Navy Admiral or the Consul General, the history had never been confirmed. All she knew was she loved its style and adored its comfort and status.

Dinner turned out to be a memorable affair. Sylvia was clearly at one with the art of cooking good simple Spanish food, with Tapas the favourite starter. She also served some very good Spanish wine Samuel had never seen in the local wine shops. When the time came for coffees and sweetmeats, everyone repaired to the terrace and slumped in some very old, very comfortable leather armchairs.

The view of the harbour, the city below them, and the passage of ships through the Straits, all served to enhance the evening.

Samuel saw everyone sitting very comfortable close to each other. Nicola had the ear of Sylvia. Samantha and Victoria were nattering away at high speed and Samuel preferred to watch. He beckoned Sylvia's maid to serve a glasses of chilled white wine and called all to order.

'First of all,' he started, 'A big thank you to Sylvia for a wonderful dinner, now a few words. Just a few days ago Vicky was rescued and landed at my door. We are all blessed she made it through to a full recovery. Vicky, you have done very well, but I caution you, most sincerely, another relapse I doubt you will survive. So, Samantha, you are charged with directing Vicky so she will live happily ever after.

Now, Samantha and I have survived the last two years, it's been very difficult but we have both found what we are looking for to enable us to move forward. We keep our memories, of course, but now we will make new memories, happy memories.

By the time you three have crossed the Atlantic Ocean, which is no mean feat even in this day and age, you will be more confident, a more assured person, more able to reach the highest level of your profession and have a good life. So, Samantha, you must study during the voyage, my tutor will test you when you sit his exams. He expects you to do well, but only very well will do.'

'Nicola,' he continued, 'In such a short time you two girls have become dear to all our hearts. Sylvia and I have learned to work together, and now with Samantha's blessing come the difficult part of learning to live together. I expect success, but nothing is taken for granted. So, I now propose a toast. 'Here's to us, bon voyage, which starts for everyone here, first thing tomorrow.'

Sylvia loved the speech, as Samantha rushed to her father to give him a big hug, with tears of happiness in her eyes. Nicola and Victoria joined in the hug fest thanking him and Samantha for everything.

Sylvia went to Samuel's side and whispered how she loved his words and could she book the next session of kissing and cuddling. His reply quite typical when he whispered, 'Let's see what we can do. It's getting late, another round of coffees to get them sobered up a little, then perhaps you could call a cab.'

The next morning, a cold front arrived with the month's supply of rain. It looked like it also had last month's supply included. The wind fell away at midday, bringing that joyous type of weather, so beloved by the British, drizzle.

Professor Samuelson arrived late at the hospital and so did Sylvia, a fact noticed by almost all the staff. Both were in a seriously good humour, leading to confirmation by many, as to what may or may not have occurred. Samantha spent the night on Moody Blue and both she and Victoria came to the hospital to collect their possessions for the voyage.

After a lengthy farewell to all the staff, the two crew mates grabbed a lift back to Moody Blue to find Nicola loading the last of the supplies and paying off the marina technician and the marina manager for all outstanding dues.

By late afternoon, Moody Blue was ready in all respects to go to sea, but Nicola still wanted to leave at midnight. Samantha and Victoria thought they should at least sail in daylight, or what was left of it. Nicola stood her ground, amongst much muttering from her crew.

She didn't want to cause worry by telling them she thought the yacht was being watched, but as the drizzle started to turn into a slow steady downpour, her cell phone picked up a text message from Jus informing the watcher, so there was one, had taken the rest of the day off, and was unlikely to make it the next day either.

'What a shame,' thought Nicola.

'All hands-on deck prepare for going to sea,' shouted Nicola. Victoria pointed out it was raining too hard, now she wanted to wait.

Nicola issued her orders, 'Victoria stay below, switch on the radar and keep watch. Samantha, soon as you're ready, bring Moody Blue tight to the dock on the midship's mooring line, then go ashore to let go the other mooring lines.'

Nicola started the main engine and raised the centre-cockpit awning. Nicola let go the one remaining mooring line and motioned Samantha to push the bow away from the dock and hop aboard.

Moody Blue moved from the dock and slowly gathered way. Nicola struggled with the driving rain to see the way to the north exit of the main harbour. Moody Blue passed silently into Gibraltar Bay. There was little wind. Nicola continued south under power as though to clear the tip of Gibraltar and then turn east, on the previously announced direction of Palma.

As the tip of Gibraltar fell away in the gloom, Nicola kept her course to the south to enter the shipping lanes. As Moody Blue reached the shipping lanes, her course quickly changed to the south-west.

The wind started to fill in from the north. Samantha made all sail and sat beside Nicola, double checking the radar display for ships likely to become a hazard. Visibility remained poor, which suited Nicola, and after an hour the wind filled to its forecasted strength as Moody Blue powered ahead on a broad starboard reach. Now the three girls were at the start of their big adventure.

Chapter 19

On the High Seas to the Canaries

THREE DAYS out of Gibraltar and Moody Blue had made good progress. All things being well she would arrive in Gran Canaria in time to check-in at race control with a day to spare.

The three girls were working well together. Victoria was adhering to Samantha's instructions, although there were times when Nicola thought Victoria's daily examinations were taking too long. An excess of giggling was detected as Samantha did her work.

That Victoria and Samantha had totally bonded together was a given.

The voyage went well and on the penultimate day before the arrival at Gran Canaria, Victoria had the afternoon watch. The sun had long since started its slide towards the distant horizon. Ahead she saw a large sloop, about sixty-five feet overall, proceeding on the same course, but at a much lower speed. To her, something was not right, but why she felt nervous about the stranger she could not say.

Victoria heard Nicola below preparing for another double dog watch. Nicola poked her head out of the main hatchway, asking if Victoria was OK, and would she like a cup of tea. Nicola came topside with the promised refreshments and sat beside Victoria. She reached into the seat locker, took out a pair of high-powered binoculars and trained it on the distant yacht.

'You're nervous about this yacht Vicky. What'd you see I should?'
'Doesn't look right,' replied Vicky. 'Can't say why.'

'Come up on your course twenty degrees, let's pass well to windward,' suggested Nicola.

As Moody Blue altered course Nicola trimmed the mainsail and the asymmetrical spinnaker.

Ahead, Nicola could see strong rising billowing clouds, indicating an approaching squall. Tropical squalls could be extraordinarily strong. If a yacht did not prepare, trouble would come with a capital 'T.'

The wind remained strong, about fifteen to twenty knots from astern. Fortunately, daytime squalls could be clearly identified by their tall clouds with a flat, dark base, often with a dark slab of rain visible underneath.

Moody Blue started to pass the stranger well to windward. The distant yacht, also flying a very flat spinnaker started to come up on the wind to chase after them. It was at this point when Nicola understood Vicky's feeling of unease.

Nicola shouted for Samantha to come on deck. For the moment, Moody Blue had the legs to keep in front of the stranger, but if both yachts came hard on the wind, the stranger would quickly overtake.

A sleepy Samantha arrived in the centre cockpit and asked to take the binoculars and tell what she could see. Nicola was shocked to hear that three naked males, at the bow of the stranger, in very close formation all facing the same way, enjoying some late evening buggery. The lead male was bent over, hanging on to the bow pulpit, whilst the other two were engaged in synchronised 'bumps a daisy.'

'Looks like a grammar school end of term outing,' quipped Samantha.

Nicola ordered a sharp course change to come up on the wind as close as possible to keep the asymmetrical spinnaker flying. As the following yacht changed course to follow, one of the three crew lost his balance and fell overboard.

Nicola hoped his recovery would give them chance to make a getaway. Her hopes were dashed when the yacht did not even slow down, as the overboarded crew member grabbed a trailing rope and hauled himself back aboard with seemingly no effort what's so ever.

'Oh no,' thought Nicola. 'These bastards are high as a kite on some designer substance, and I think I know what it is.'

'OK Vicky, Samantha, let's try this. See the dark cloud in front, it looks like a tropical squall. We need to reach it before they get to us.'

Vicky started the main engine at full throttle. Nicola shouted, 'Samantha, I'm going to furl the 'kite,' then release the foresail reefing line and wind on the foresail sheet. Vicky, when that's done, come to windward and head for the squall. Just as we reach the squall, Samantha you drop the mainsail into the lazy jacks as I reef the foresail, got it, everyone.'

'Then what?' asked Victoria.

'With any luck, they will run into the squall with full sail and the squall will rip them to pieces,' replied Nicola, 'Here's hoping.'

The strange yacht was catching them fast, but its helm did not appear to understand the weather into which he was steering.

'Ready, go,' shouted Nicola, and within seconds Moody Blue was heading close hauled into the oncoming squall at full speed. The pursuant yacht faithfully tried to follow, which was now very close. A crew member was waving a very recognisable bottle of brandy, yelling, 'come and get it.'

As the squall hit both yachts, Moody Blue suddenly stowed all her sails, as she powered away on the main engine into the darkness of the tempest. Nicola heard a mighty crash as the pursuant yacht lost the top of its mast, the mainsail dropping over her crew on deck. The wind vortexed, the pursuant yacht got caught in a slam dunk gybe, its boom swept over its cabin roof knocking over three crew members who dropped lifeless on to the deck.

Moody Blue continued on its way to safety. As the squall abated Victoria steered the yacht back on course for Gran Canaria. Nicola and Samantha cowered under the cockpit awning to protect them from the driving rain.

The crew of Moody Blue looked around as the weather cleared to see the pursuant yacht lying helpless in the water. The broken mast section swayed dangerously over the heads of the crew as they struggled to get their ship into some semblance of order.

Victoria steered Moody Blue off the wind to enable Nicola and Samantha to set all sail. Nicola went below to find her satellite phone. Pushing a fast dial button, a voice answered immediately.

'Speak Nicola,' it said.

'Great Aunt Violet, we are twelve hours out from Gran Canaria. We came across a larger yacht. As we started to overtake it, its crew attempted to close and board Moody Blue.

Mancurians; same as Mr Stone Dead. I feared a repeat of what Vicky and I went through before. I saw the same physical strength in a crew member who fell overboard and hauled himself back on deck as though he weighed nothing. He even had a bottle of brandy waved at me, the same as the one I gave to you.'

'So?' asked Great Aunt Violet.

'Did you run any tests on the sample of the substances I gave to you?' asked Nicola.

'Yes. It had some hallucinogenic properties, but nothing to bring about the dreadful behaviour you suffered from.'

'Aunt, check the brandy. It's very rare, it has a marking 'NS' somewhere on the label. The mark 'NS' stands for North Slope. It is a speciality of the distiller, with very limited appeal, so it's not being sold to the connoisseurs or collector's market. Therefore, it has other properties. As a wild guess, if it is mixed with other drugs it produces a product which turns a sex maniac into an unstoppable monster.'

'Let me get your suggestion straight. Two unwarranted products, which have not been classed as dangerous, when combined, turns into a single product which does?'

'That's right,' shouted Nicola. 'Think of the consequences, it's a gold mine for those supplying known molesters of young persons or anybody else they can get their hands on, like Victoria.'

'Oh my God, what have we discovered, you OK?'

Nicola gave her aunt a quick rundown on events and they were now sailing at full speed into the night.

'I'd best get busy. That yacht still afloat Nicky?' asked Great Aunt Violet. 'Yes,' said Nicola.

'Best get the Spanish Navy to bring them in. I'll talk to my contacts in Whitehall. I'll send Jus straight away. Better still, I'll come too. The Spanish have good facilities on the islands, time to make use of them. Stay safe.'

And with that, she rang-off.

'Well, things are moving fast.' thought Nicola.

Moody Blue now sailing fast on the direct course for the port of Las Palmas, tentatively returned to its normal routine. Victoria was sent to rest; she had been on watch far too long for Samantha's liking.

Nicola reset all sails as the wind fell away at the onset of dusk. Having given Victoria a quick check-up and finding all was well, Samantha set to in the galley to prepare the evening meal. Nicola came below from the cockpit and sat at the navigation station. She heard the radio calling for assistance from the yacht which so nearly caught up with them. Nicola had no intention of returning to give any assistance. She knew when the crew of this yacht started to come out of the stupor they were in, bad things could happen. She had seen it all before.

THE REMAINING VOYAGE to Las Palmas passed quickly and Moody Blue arrived in the early morning just after sunrise. The yacht registration dock for the Cruiser Race to the Caribbean looked as though it was open for business. Moody Blue checked-in, and after the safety inspection had been completed, the race documents were signed off and returned to Nicola.

Vicky looked around for a berth where they could lay up. Going alongside a French yacht looked the best option. In fact, it looked like they were being invited to do so.

Now to get rested and re-supplied. The local traders were keen to oblige, providing an excellent service for fuel and supplies. A technician from the local marina supply shop came aboard and offered Nicola an inspection service to check-out the mast, the standing rigging, and all the items of running rigging. She gratefully accepted this offer as it would be good to have one less chore to carry-out.

Halfway through a much-needed breakfast, a familiar voice asked if he could come aboard. 'What brings you here so early Mr Bernard Collingwood, famous leader of HM Branch Special. What can we do for you today?'

'A strong coffee would be a good start, and a detailed explanation of just what the fuck happened late yesterday afternoon. Excuse the language, but I've just arrived from Gibraltar by military aircraft, and I find myself in the middle of a shit storm,' replied a testy Commander Collingwood.

'Well, the good news, dear Bernard,' cooed Nicola, 'Is we escaped with our virginity intact, what's left of it anyway. A certain yacht, loaded with sex maniacs, in a state of mind very similar to the late Mr Stone and his two cohorts, attempted to board this yacht to carry out the same attack very much like the one Vicky and I survived the last time. And afterwards…'

'After you called your famous Great Aunt Violet,' interrupted Commander Collingwood, 'A lady who then pushed panic buttons over most Europe in general and Interpol in particular.'

'Well,' Nicola calmly continued, in speaking to Great Aunt Violet, it suddenly occurred to my scientific brain, just what the hell is going on. Did you or your science people stop to think how Stone and his chums carried out such a horrendous attack on us two girls over such a long period of time?

No, you didn't. You are too busy trying to chase down lousy few quid from the Manchester robbery instead of opening up your closed mind as to what's going on in the big wide world.

My research at Oxford University was starting to get too close. Then, I got the bums rush out the bloody door. All the information I sent to the relevant police departments was ignored, buried in some deep in-tray. No wonder the hoods of the world call the police 'Plod.'

Nicola continued, her voice rising in anger, 'I have developed a thesis Great Aunt Violet agrees with. She has tested the samples I took from the black yacht we were kidnapped on, and by the way, we haven't bothered sending the results out until we know which one of you Plod persons is competent to use it.'

Commander Collingwood sat stock still, shocked at being spoken to like an incompetent office boy. He tried to speak but Nicola stared at him in livid anger, daring him to say anything.

'Bernard, my thesis is Harry Hacket enterprises, the organisation leading this attack on European institutions, as you know full well but won't admit too, has or rather is, bringing a product to the speciality market of sexual excess.

Let us call it the 'Emperor Caligula' programme, a product comprising of two different, benign products, ones which will not worry the drug enforcement agencies, and when combined, produce the most tremendous urges in the male sex maniac where all civilised behaviour vanishes and brings about the prolonged and violent attacks on their victims.

Now you know why there are increasing incidences of young persons, of both sexes, disappearing, usually forever. Pound to a penny, the yacht the Spanish Navy are bringing in will reveal whether or not my thesis is correct. So, let's get our sorry act together, appoint someone as overlord for what will be a big investigation.'

Before the Commander could reply, two other gentlemen made themselves welcomed aboard Moody Blue. The first, an old friend of Nicola's, Professor Rodriques Fernándo, Head of the Spanish Forensic Science Department in Madrid. The other, a Sr. Rodriques M. Fernández, a Comisario Principal, Grupo Especial de Operaciones (GEO), a tough looking senior officer in the Spanish CNP, and eldest son of Sr Rodriques.

After introductions, Sr. Rodriques got down to business. He quickly sketched out what he thought was going on that fateful morning and asked for any updates. The Commander told him Dr Stranraer had a thesis, and if proved correct, then all hell was going to break loose unless it was contained.

He outlined a number of actions, all of which would require the Island's Governor General's approval. It took but a few minutes for the Commander to outline Nicola's thesis. What surprised him was her thesis was accepted, almost as old news?

The Comisario Principal told everybody he would take charge of the unfolding operation and agreed the start of the Cruiser Race, due in just under thirty-six hours, should be delayed by twenty-four hours. He took it upon himself to deal with Colonel B. Limperson, the CEO and owner of the race event.

Events started to unfold at a rapid pace. Inspection teams were rapidly formed to begin the inspection of the cruiser fleet, starting with the larger yachts.

Nicola found herself in the first team, along with Commander Collingwood, as it headed offshore to inspect a magnificent seventy-foot yacht owned by a minister of Her Majesty's government, Sir Nigel Stock.

Nicola had heard of this Nigel Stock before, none of it good. On TV he came across as a blowhard. His ministry was considered to be poorly organised, and despite a number of social scandals, he always survived censure.

As the fast patrol boat reached its first target Nicola saw this inspection team consisted of two tough looking heavily armed Spanish marines, two plain-clothed individuals with suspicious bulges under their black military jackets, two custom officials, the Commander, and a senior member of the Spanish GEO, complete with his impressive uniform and badges of rank.

Clearly, this team had the capability to deal with all that it might encounter. As the fast patrol boat reached the target yacht, the Spanish GEO operative shouted a request to come along side and board. The captain of the yacht told them to 'bugger off,' as the Minister did not wish to be disturbed.

The fast patrol boat slammed alongside, the Spanish marines jumped aboard, took over the cockpit of the yacht, their sub-machine guns at the ready. They were quickly followed by the two anonymous plain-clothed members of the inspection team, guns drawn, who disappeared down below to take over the main saloon. Shouts and abuse were heard and quickly quelled.

The rest of the team made their way below, only to be confronted by a furious Sir Nigel, demanding to know why his early morning had been so rudely interrupted. The Spanish GEO shoved him aside and ordered him to sit down and remain silent. Here was a tough member of the Spanish 'Brute Squad,' an organisation not dedicated to patience when dealing with high-level suspects.

The yacht's captain was ordered to assemble all persons on board, with their documents and the ship's papers. Sir Nigel started demanding what he saw as his rights as a British minister, only to be told, he was in Spanish territory as a private person, his official status as a member of a friendly state had not been registered beforehand.

With the situation under control, the two customs officials started their examination of the yacht. Nicola went forward with one of them, as she was keen to look over such a fine and expensive vessel. This yacht had all mod cons, clearly the result of a high-value yacht builder.

Nicola followed the customs officer to the bow of the yacht. The customs officer held a strange electronic instrument used for searching the dark corners of any maritime vessel. The crash bulkhead at the bow had an access hatch into the chain locker. The instrument gave a warning signal; the customs officer removed a hand tool from his waist bag and started to undo the fixings on the access hatch.

Both he and Nicola were shocked to find two young person's inside this void in the bow section of the yacht. Locked in an airless and pitch-black space they cowered in fear at the sight of the customs man. He gently coaxed them out of the void, the two persons rubbing their eyes in the new light. One was a female, about fourteen years old, the other a boy about the same age. They looked similar, surely not brother and sister?

Nicola called the Commander forward to see his worse fears come true. Commander Collingwood felt rage building, struggling to control it. Nicola put a hand on his shoulder and told him to count to twenty, then another twenty should he need.

The two young persons showed signs of physical abuse. He ordered the customs man and Nicola to hang fire for a moment and not make any unnecessary sounds. He motioned the two young persons to sit down and not to make any noise. The Commander went aft one compartment, opened a skylight up onto the foredeck to make a radio call on his handheld radio.

Within minutes, another RIB slammed alongside the yacht, as two members of the Island's Spanish forensic team dropped through the skylight, dressed the two young persons in thin white forensic coveralls, and bundled them topside and dropped them into the waiting RIB, which roared off at great speed.

The Commander returned to the main saloon, nodded at the plain clothed members of his team, took his own weapon from his jacket pocket, telling everyone to remain very still in a voice which brooked no discussion.

Sir Nigel looked in panic and wondered what was next. He did not have to wait long.

'Sir Nigel,' started the Commander, 'You and your crew are under arrest. Anybody makes a move you will be shot, dead. The word 'dead' was spat out in great venom.

The Commander called the two Spanish marines down into the main saloon and ordered the two plain-clothed members of his team to restrain the crew members using strong cable ties. Sir Nigel, struck dumb by the realisation of what happened, said nothing.

The Commander went over to the Spanish GEO officer to confer. They quickly agreed Nicola, the Commander and his two plain-clothed members would take the yacht a short distance up the coast to the Spanish Naval base and the Spanish GEO officer would take the rest of his team and continue inspecting the other yachts close by.

Before anyone made a move, the second customs man returned from the main owner's cabin with a case of brandy, and what he called a large bag of 'Bolivian baking powder.'

'Fancy that,' thought the Commander, 'This is too easy.'

Sir Nigel's face dropped; then started accusations this latest find had been planted on his yacht. The Commander looked at the doubtful package, only to be told by the customs officer this was Grade 'A' cocaine, and if cut and sold on the streets of any European capital, would fund his department for a quite a long time. Nicola took a small sample on the end of a spatula and inserted it into her portable test kit. No doubt it was high grade.

With the crew of the yacht and its owner sitting uncomfortably trussed up in the main saloon, the Spanish officers disembarked, leaving Nicola to return to the cockpit, start the main engine to slowly bring the yacht over the anchor chain. It took a while to reel in a lot of chain, but soon the yacht was free, heading towards the Spanish Naval Base. One of the patrolling Spanish Navy's coastal vessels moved over to challenge them, but it took just a quick radio call to let them proceed on their way.

'Guess you know how to drive one of these big beasts, Nicola?' stated the Commander. Nicola stared him down, would this man ever give up on questioning her about the past?

She was not amused.

'I can't think, for the life of me, why I bother to help you, Bernard. You're just a f**kin' pain. I'll leave you to it when we get to the base,' snarled Nicola.

The Commander tried to mollify Nicola, but he knew he had spoken in error. Nicola told him not to gaslight her, then ignored him to concentrate on steering the yacht into the Naval Base. As the yacht moored alongside the harbour wall, Nicola was surprised to see Great Aunt Violet waiting for her.

Great Aunt Violet's cheery welcome did little to make Nicola feel any better with the situation. She felt tired, stressed, unemployed, and the more she did for this Commander the less he seemed to respect her. If he could not get it into his thick skull both she and Victoria had been through hell, she was off.

Great Aunt Violet asked Nicola what was wrong. Nicola vented her feelings about the subject in hand and demanded transport back to 'Moody Blue.'

'Bernard,' shouted Great Aunt Violet. 'Have you upset my Nicola.' 'Afraid so Great Aunt Violet, I do apologise,' replied the Commander.

'You two had better kiss and make-up, there's a hell of a lot of work to do here,' stated Great Aunt Violet in no uncertain terms.

Nicola jumped ashore, stating in no uncertain terms she would make her own way back to Moody Blue. She was tired; needed a decent breakfast, despite it being almost lunchtime, and some sleep. Great Aunt Violet gave the Commander one hell of a dirty look and went down below to look at what he had brought her.

The Commander gently asked why she was taking charge; he was the ranking official. Great Aunt Violet turned around to face him and told him bluntly the Commissioner, his boss of Special Branch, Anti-Terrorist Section had requested her assistance. This was news to him, but he chose to wait his moment until later.

Nicola arrived at Moody Blue went below to discover Victoria and Samantha being entertained by Jus. His welcome was full of praise of what she had achieved in such a short space of time.

Nicola replied, 'Thank you, Jus. I meant what I said. I need breakfast and bed. Samantha please make me a simple omelette whilst I have a shower, toast on the side, with yummy tart marmalade and strong coffee.'

Victoria asked Jus what was going on? Jus told her Nicola's 'favourite' police person had just reached, in his usual manner, the highest point of her nasal passage and 'Et elle avait jeté un grand strop.'

Victoria giggled, knowing full well, an upset Nicola was one person to gently humour until she calmed down. Samantha looked on, wondering just what on earth happened, but she decided to refrain from asking any unnecessary questions.

Jus bid them 'Un bref adieu et il les verrait plus tard,' and disappeared once more into the fray.

As she munched through her breakfast, Victoria told Nicola she wanted to go ashore and look at the shops. Nicola waved her away, telling her to be careful, and told her to take one of the Frenchmen from the adjacent yacht for safety.

'Oh goody,' thought Victoria. 'The young one, about twenty-five years old. He's quite yummy.'

As Victoria departed, Nicola shouted after her not to get too close to her French escort except in an emergency. Victoria giggled to herself, 'I can soon find an emergency if I need one.'

Nicola headed to her comfortable bed and soon fell into a deep and undisturbed sleep. Samantha stayed aboard, conscious of the fact she was behind in her studies. Outside the noise of a large fleet of yachts continued, their crews enjoying another day in harbour, with another night on the razz to come. Fortunately, their behaviour remained civilised, which made a change.

EARLY EVENING SAW the tranquillity of Moody Blue disturbed by the arrival of Colonel B. Limperson, universally known as Col. Blimp. He was a large man with florid skin, a plumy false posh accent, and a huge blonde handlebar moustache with which he was obviously born. Trailing behind him, Samantha saw a strange looking woman, medium height, in her late forties, ghastly make-up and bright ginger hair. She smiled to excess, the falsest smile on record. Quite what this colour-coordinated duo of hideousness wanted; Samantha could only guess.

Col. Blimp asked to speak to the captain of Moody Blue. Samantha told him the skipper was sleeping and please could they come back later. The Colonel raised his voice, something he was well known for in the Army Catering Corp.

Civilians ignored him unless they wanted something. His voice could penetrate concrete lined steel plate. In this case, it woke Nicola, who was not best pleased. She needed the loo, so she elected to see what was what, so peace aboard Moody Blue could return.

Col. Blimp recalled Nicola had requested a 'crew available' list when she posted her entry in the cruiser race. Nicola recalled she had faxed him with a 'crew no longer required' note before Moody Blue departed from Gibraltar. The Colonel told Nicola he had never received the fax, which led Nicola to open her race file folder to produce the fax machine message receipt.

An impasse appeared imminent as the Colonel insisted event rules stated the race committee could insist on a yacht taking additional crew if it thought the yacht in question was either under crewed or short on experience.

Nicola held her temper. This man was not the brightest button in the box, but a full-on frontal rebuff would probably fail. She reminded the Colonel she had many years offshore experience and had won many prestigious cups. Samantha has just completed a qualifying voyage from Gibraltar to gain her RYA Offshore Skippers certification, and Victoria, who was admittedly a new girl, had learned quickly and become a valuable watch keeper.

Altogether her crew had trained and gelled, were comfortable with each other, and it was far too late to bring an unknown person into the crew.

The Colonel handed Nicola the woman's sailing C.V. on his company notepaper. Nicola paused and changed tack. She told him to save time later on she would complete an onboard pre-registration of this new crew person and asked she come below and bring her passport with her. This raised two sets of eyebrows, but Nicola insisted full details of a new crew member were required by her insurers.

The two of them went below to the navigation desk. She made a copy of the C.V. giving it to 'Ms Ginger' as she would be known, placing the original in her file. Nicola thumbed through her passport; then scanned all the pages.

She offered Ms Gwyneth Stoltz, for that was her name, a glass of water, which she accepted. Whilst Nicola completed her work, she noticed out of the side of her eye Ms Ginger closely examining the interior of the main saloon, and more importantly, her eye had fixed upon the spare mainsail package stowed under one of the padded bench seats at the far end of the cabin.

This package, which up to now had attracted no attention from anybody, contained the tiny secret of the unissued bank notes. As Ms Ginger's head turned to see if she was being watched, Nicola completed her scanning, handed back her passport and requested their return to the centre cockpit.

'OK Colonel, I think everything should be OK, perhaps if Ms Gwyneth could return tomorrow, say just after 10 a.m., bring her things, we will take matters from there. I will complete your crew acceptance form later, and get it to you before we sail, which will be before midday tomorrow.'

'Can't she join your crew now,' asked the Colonel, 'She has everything with her.'

'Sorry no,' said Nicola firmly, 'I need to re-arrange our accommodation. Her cabin is a storeroom at the moment. Ten-thirty a.m. tomorrow morning, OK?'

The Colonel was not best pleased, but he had achieved what he had set out to do, and a brief retreat would do little harm. As the Colonel and Ms Ginger disappeared down the jetty, Samantha asked, 'Nicola, surely you are not going to bring that dreadful woman aboard as crew?'

Nicola smiled a serene smile and asked Samantha to come below and sit at the main saloon table.

'Now Samantha, using this fingerprint kit, which I just happen to have in my special drawer; hold this glass at the bottom and the rim, whilst I dust for fingerprints. Excellent, now I use the fingerprint tape to cover the prints and transfer the prints to this special white paper.' With the fingerprints safety attached to the white paper, Nicola took the paper to the navigation desk and scanned the results. Then, she took out her smartphone and called Great

Aunt Violet.

'Hi Great Aunt Violet, how are you getting on. Making progress examining these two yachts?' asked Nicola.

'Three yachts. The Spanish GEO brought in another candidate and now I'll be here half the night, and you?' replied Great Aunt Violet.

Nicola brought her Aunt up to speed on the latest developments and asked for help. She told Nicola to email all the scanned material and she would get right back to her. Great Aunt Violet did explain a ginger haired woman had been seen skulking around the naval base but had been evicted by dockyard security police.

IT HAD BECOME too late for Nicola to return to her bunk. While she waited for Great Aunt Violet to return her call, she set about making supper. As the sun began to set, the sound of advanced giggling could be heard. It was Victoria on her way back to Moody Blue with her escort, a rather flushed Frenchman. The sounds of prolonged goodbyes were heard, followed by Victoria tripping over the centre cockpit combing and falling into Moody Blue.

Nicola stuck her head out of the main hatch, worried in case Victoria had hurt herself. She need not have bothered, Victoria was lying there, giggling, and attempting to raise herself and come below.

'I trust we are not inebriated?'

'No, not really, I'm just a happy little pussy cat,' giggled Victoria, 'I had a great time, lovely lunch and some French wine and a successful shop. What a nice escort you fixed me up with. Pity my usual has restarted otherwise…'

'More like a cat with a pussy,' opinioned Nicola. 'Meow,' said Victoria.

Victoria managed to raise herself off the deck, tidied herself, and followed Nicola below. Nicola asked, 'What's in the big shopping bag?'

'Lady's monthly items,' said Victoria, her fit of giggling slowly petering out. 'What's new?'

Nicola told her about the red-haired monster and Colonel Blimp. Samantha joined them, slightly cross about the lack of peace and quiet to get her studying completed.

Nicola's mobile phone rang. 'Nicola, it's Great Aunt Violet. The woman is a complete fraud. She is an insurance recovery agent; good at getting results by fair means or foul, generally foul. The passport is not hers, her real name is Ms Gwyneth Jones, and my guess she is somewhere on Mr Hackett's list of supporters. Despite the implied Welsh name, she comes from north England somewhere. And as for her sailing C.V., it's up there with the world's three biggest lies.'

'I see Great Aunt Violet, many thanks.'

'So, what are you going to do?' asked Great Aunt Violet. 'Oh, I'll think of something, catch you later.'

Supper time arrived; Samantha served asking Nicola for her next move. Victoria also asked for more details, but Nicola suggested she would sleep on the problem and invent something really cunning.

The next morning, the three girls rose later than they planned, as Moody Blue had been fully prepared the day before. Samantha felt excited at the prospect of the forthcoming adventure.

Victoria seemed to be taking it all in her stride, leaving Nicola to worry about the few last details. Nicola had a long chat with Great Aunt Violet on the phone who told her the three yachts brought into the Spanish Naval Base had been stripped, fingerprinted and what a haul had been collected.

Nine young persons in total had been rescued from the yachts from the Cruiser Fleet. Five had come from the three arrested yachts, the rest from the yachts in the marina or anchored offshore. Five were in reasonable shape, the others were in hospital. The press had been kept in the dark, although rumours were circulating at light speed around the fleet

The good news came when Great Aunt Violet told Nicola Moody Blues part in the proceedings had been kept very hush-hush. The crew of Moody Blue remained relaxed.

A loud 'Co-eee' heralded the start of the day's proceedings. Samantha asked where on earth her horrible accent originated. Victoria dryly suggested Manchester, the canal, the bottom off. Nicola was impressed. Victoria was back on form, about time too.

Nicola grabbed a sealed envelope from the navigation desk and went on deck.

'Good morning,' she cried out to Ms Ginger, hideously attired in her version of designer yachty kit.

'Drop your two bags into the centre cockpit. I'm afraid I must ask a favour. This envelope contains the Colonel's crew acceptance form. I cannot sail unless he receives it and I need a receipt as well. Hope you don't mind; my crew are busy getting ready to sail.'

Ms Ginger was not best pleased and looked around to see if anybody could run a quick errand, but all was chaos at this late hour prior to the start of the race. The cruiser fleet was on the move and time was becoming short. She grabbed the envelope and set-off at the trot to the race office.

Nicola called Samantha on deck, told her to follow at a distance and when she started to return, come back quickly. Samantha did as she was asked, as Victoria came on deck to ask what was next.

'I need a quick look in her designer carpet bag, see the combination lock,' said Nicola. 'It will take ages to find the combination' replied Victoria.

'Watch and learn my girl,' counselled Nicola.

Nicola took a close look at the number wheels of the lock and saw a very faint mark between two of the numbers. She spun the other wheels and found the same faint mark. Having lined up the wheels with the same faint line, she slowly spun all four of them together and the lock opened. Victoria was impressed.

Nicola donned thin forensic gloves, opening the bag to find a side pocket which revealed a current valid passport.

'Somewhere in this bag will be a hidden pocket,' muttered Nicola, 'Should be down the bottom somewhere.'

Nicola found the hidden pocket, removing the false passport she'd scanned yesterday, swapped it for the real passport, and stuffed a thick piece of cardboard in the hidden pocket.

'Nicky, Samantha is on her way back,' cautioned Victoria. Nicola put everything back as it was and closed the bag.

'Vicky, take these two bags to the coloured gentleman over there and give him this fifty Euro note. He knows what to do,' asked Nicola.

Victoria did as she was asked, as Nicola started the main engine. Samantha arrived in a hurry, went to the forward mooring line, cast-off and stepped lightly onto the bow. Victoria did the same at the stern, pushed the stern of Moody Blue away from the jetty and hopped aboard.

Nicola brought Moody Blue astern, spun the wheel, engaged forward drive, and set off after the other yachts. Just as a frantic Ms Ginger came into view, Moody Blue slipped behind a sixty-five-foot cruiser from Finland.

'That was cute, said Samantha, 'Well done.'

Chapter 20

MOODY BLUE POWERED into the open sea at full speed. Victoria checked the GPS, calculating their arrival at the start area with six minutes to spare before the five-minute gun, the signal when all competitors must switch off their engines.

Nicola surveyed the start line and saw it had a clear bias to the far end, away from the committee boat, assumed to be Col. Blimp's motor sailor. Best to stay away from the committee boat end. With thousands of miles to the other side of the 'pond', Nicola did not see the point of getting mixed up with any adventures on the start line.

Moody Blue found herself slowly coming up to the far end of the start line. Nicola made certain they were seen, recorded by the deputy race officer and crossed the start line correctly. Now they were on their way. Nicola put Moody Blue on the opposite tack, crossed behind the fleet to get up to windward and keep out of the way of the anxious.

The wind had yet to settle down. With so many yachts fighting for their share, it had great variance over the general path to the open ocean. Samantha could see Nicola called her strategy correctly.

As Moody Blue reached the last extremity of the island, she saw the fleet engaging in pointless and sometimes reckless manoeuvring, whilst they were sailing in clear air and even clearer water. It occurred to her Moody Blue had company, the French yacht they had shared the berth with. Victoria asked if they were being followed, but Nicola put on her Mona Lisa smile and said nothing.

During the evening, after Victoria completed the chores in the galley, she joined Nicola who had the first of the evening watches.

'Nicola, we didn't receive any more aggravation from Col. Blimp. I thought he would rush offshore and dump the bitch on our foredeck. Just what did you tell him in the letter you had 'muppet face' take to him?'

'Quite simply Vicky, I put the fear of god in him. I told him all the documents I received, had been couriered to my legal eagle in London, and I was going to sue him for a hundred grand.'

'Who's your lawyer in London, not Miss Susan at Susan Grabinar & Runnimead?' asked Victoria.

'Yep, the Lady Susan. Who hasn't lost any case she has taken on in the last twenty years,' smiled Nicola. 'She met this stuck-up twerp some years ago, filed him in the 'must bring this idiot down to size one day' file, and now she has the chance.'

'So, what did you do with the passport you nicked?' ask Victoria. 'Err, what passport? I gave everything to Great Aunt Violet.' 'You crafty bitch,' laughed Victoria.

'Meow,' replied Nicola. 'Now let us go sailing.'

The crew of Moody Blue settled down reverting to their usual watches. Now they were sailing in clear water. The auto-pilot soon pressed into service, leaving Victoria on watch, with Nicola and Samantha taking time off to get rested before sharing the night watches.

Nicola enjoyed the night watches the most, the clear sky, pocked with stars, nature's ultimate glory.

Samantha preferred the morning watch, from four am to eight am. Sunrises fascinated her. She possessed a diverse collection of photographs as the sun first broke the horizon. She hoped to take a photograph for each day's sunrise during the passage to the Americas.

SIX DAYS OUT Samantha noticed the French yacht was continuing to accompany Moody Blue. She had never been this far offshore before, alone in the middle of a large ocean. For some reason, the feeling of isolation gave her the feeling of insecurity. The insecurity factor, she assumed, was one reason why the many cruisers races held around the world had such popularity.

This race had just under a hundred and thirty yachts taking part, but the French yacht remained the only one she had seen. The French yacht seemed to be deliberately keeping them company, one of those sexy French designs which should have been miles in front by now.

However, the fleet stayed connected by radio, although some yachts had satellite communications. Each yacht communicated its daily position at midnight so the organisers could update the race website. A valuable safety feature this may be, but yachts with a greater interest in race position used the website to gain valuable knowledge of where the best weather conditions existed.

Samantha also noted the position Moody Blue posted each day held her at the front of her section. She saw the attention to detail to keep Moody Blue in the groove, even though Moody Blue could not be considered a racing yacht by any means.

Still, Samantha had to admit she had come to love being at sea, with two persons who would always be best friends. She welcomed the change in her life. She had to admit to herself she had remained a little too long under her father's wing. The death of her mother, through illness, had kept them together, but the future had well and truly arrived, and she felt glad to be in the right place at the right time.

Victoria, on the other hand, concentrated on getting physically fit. She'd had it with being in the hospital, being worked over, struggling to regain her health. As the time passed by, so her bad memories faded away. Her nightmares slowly ceased and she came to terms with the moment when she ended someone else's life.

She felt the need to reduce her 'Little Girl lost' act. Giggling would become reserved for private moments. Still, when she met someone who made it clear she was little more than an attractive female with only one use she would still use giggling to lead the person on, before she dropped the hammer on him. She examined the urge to always have the 'little gun' about her person. It made her feel safe and unsafe at the same time. Its use could bring more problems than it solved and she knew the police didn't like the public doing their job for them.

Victoria liked the freedom of being at sea. When the other two watchkeepers were sleeping during the day, she enjoyed steering Moody Blue with no clothes on, wearing a large Mexican style sombrero. Careful not to get burnt by the sun, she chose her moments with care, generally when the sun rose and when it set. She asked Samantha to massage her back with lashing of vitamin loaded oils once a day, and slowly, oh so slowly, her skin lost the marks of her terrible ordeal.

She'd become stronger too, enjoying the hard work of adjusting the sails, just as Nicola had taught her. She even read a book entitled, 'sailing for beginners,' enjoying the strange language.

THE VOYAGE OF Moody Blue continued smoothly, the routine fixed by necessity, common sense, and good seamanship. The expected transit time should be just under two weeks. The first week passed quickly. Nicola saw the time remaining would disappear very quickly, and there was the small matter of what problems would occur when they arrived at their destination, English Harbour.

She re-read the race instructions to understand the procedure for finishing the race, which mandated competitors to arrive at the tip of a peninsula, sail inside a mark of the course located just offshore and radio their finishing time to the timekeeper who would be manning a caravan located on the beach.

When each yacht finished, they should sail the remaining five miles along the coast, and radio to the harbour master for instructions to complete arrival formalities at the Immigration and Customs House, and then where to moor or berth.

'Seems easy enough,' thought Nicola. As she was about to use her satellite phone to get the latest updates on positions in the fleet, a text message arrived from Great Aunt Violet telling her to finish the race as instructed, then look for a fishing boat flying a flag with a lion on it.

Also, Samantha must be ready to go ashore for one night, and 'a friend,' this could only be Jus, would come aboard and take matters from there.

Nicola had already calculated their arrival time, at some time between five to six a.m. the next morning and texted back the information. She wondered what this was all about.

The next morning, a sleepy Samantha took breakfast well before she felt like it. She had doubled up on the watches to give Nicola more time to prepare for whatever. Victoria had risen early to cook breakfast and to see the duty helm, Nicola, fed and watered.

Moody Blue reached the finish mark at five thirty-six a.m. precisely, as Nicola set the auto-pilot to take the yacht on a direct course for English Harbour. Victoria attempted to radio in their finishing time to whoever manned the finish mark caravan on the beach, but without success. Finding a signal from the local telecommunications company, Nicola settled for sending a text with the finishing time, direct to the principal race officer.

Dawn broke with a fabulous sunrise. Two miles in front, Nicola could see a fishing boat loitering at the halfway point to the harbour. No other vessels were in sight at this early time of the day. As Moody Blue approached the fishing boat, it picked up speed and made to approach quickly. Nicola eased the mainsheet as the stranger prepared to come alongside.

'Fenders, starboard side,' shouted Nicola, as she brought Moody Blue into the wind and waved the fishing boat alongside. She saw the flag with a lion on it, so at least things were going to plan. Jus appeared from the wheelhouse and bid them all good morning.

Nicola cried out, 'Hello Jus. What gives?'

Jus called out, 'Ask Samantha to come quickly, no time to waste.'

A confused Samantha made the transfer to the fishing boat, carrying a 'day' bag with essentials. Jus gave her brief instructions; to land, clear immigration, and customs, then she would be taken to a pleasant waterside hotel with comfortable bed and all she needed for the day. She should be able to return to Moody Blue in the evening or simply stay in the hotel for the night.

Jus made it abundantly clear she should give no information about anything to anybody, but for her information Nicola had to urgently visit Ile Française, just thirty kilometres away to the east, to sign important documents at the La Banque Française des Caraïbes by lunchtime.

With that, Jus made it over to Moody Blue and waved the fishing boat away. 'Bon jour Jus, café monsieur?' enquired Victoria.

'Oui s'il vous plaît,' replied Jus as he indicated to Nicola to change course and make all sail. Nicola left him to his coffee, letting Victoria fuss around him with fresh croissants she'd baked late last night. With the trade wind now firmly just forward of the beam Moody Blue raced towards the next event of the day.

Nicola set the auto-pilot, asking Victoria to keep a look-out whilst she went for a much-needed shower and to wash her hair. She assumed she would be going ashore, so getting freshened up and presentable became a priority.

When she returned to the main saloon, she found Victoria had disappeared up forward to complete the same operation, leaving Jus to get on with whatever he had planned for the day.

By this time, Jus had removed the toxic package from its stowage position from under the main port bench seat at the front of the cabin. Nicola looked on, waiting for some idea of what would happen next. Jus looked up explaining a new sail, packaged in exactly the same way, was waiting at the Zona Franca warehouse on Ile Française.

On arrival, he would collect it, and bring it aboard. Then, he would return the package before him, using the excuse the delivered package had been marked as a mainsail for a Moody 42, and Moody Blue was a Moody 44. The toxic package would then be returned to the duty-free depot and 'lost' in their quarantine storage, to be collected by others at a later date. He would pay the storage fee upfront and the only way to find Nicola's package would be with a reference number.

Nicola thought about this for a moment then asked when could she recover her package?

Jus told her the package remained dangerous and much later would be best. Nicola asked Jus if he was expecting trouble when Moody Blue docked at English Harbour.

Jus smiled, confiding he was setting a trap and all she had to do was to go with the flow. Anyway, after the switching of the packages, Jus told Nicola they would visit an old friend, the manager of the local branch of La Banque Française des Caraïbes and asked her to remove all the cash she had aboard so it could be exchanged for new notes issued by the French bank.

Before Nicola could ask what the hell for, Jus told her she had a lot of cash aboard 'Moody Blue. The new cash would be seen to have originated by a withdrawal from the French bank, enabling Nicola to explain the origins of said cash, complete with official receipts, when Moody Blue docked at English Harbour.

'Anything else?' asked Nicola.

Jus asked her to rent a safety deposit box to store two other packages he had with him.

Then, they would enjoy a truly excellent lunch at a local fish restaurant.

Victoria returned to the fray, looking all prim and proper, eager to understand the day's events. Nicola said to ask Jus as she needed to return to the cockpit get her head around all she had been told.

Back at the helm, Nicola disconnected the auto-pilot and eased Moody Blue on to a new course to take them directly to the Zona Franca on Ile Française. This duty-free warehouse received goods and equipment from around the world, supporting the movement of spare parts for the marine trade.

The switch, as Nicola preferred to call the change-out, was a cute idea. She wondered who had dreamed it all up. She guessed she wouldn't have far to look, but who was setting what trap for whom? It all seemed very strange.

Still, the wind remained a cracking Force 5 and Moody Blue was charging along in fine style. So enjoyable did this experience seem, Nicola reached into a cool box in one of the bench seat lockers to remove a cool refreshing designer drink, mostly comprising of gin and tonic.

The arrival at the Zona Franca jetty occurred just after 10.30 a.m. Nicola called Victoria to help with mooring Moody Blue. She saw a depot storeman waiting at the side of the jetty with a handcart containing what looked like a sail in dense pack form. With Moody Blue safely alongside, Jus went ashore, greeted the storeman in a familiar manner, and signed off on the paperwork. He bundled the new mainsail aboard and stowed it down below. The storeman sat on his hand cart smoking an unfiltered Gauloises, its aroma spreading far and wide.

Jus returned to the cockpit with the toxic package and took it ashore complaining in high-speed French to the storeman, who simply shrugged his shoulders before setting off back to his office with Jus by his side. Five minutes later Jus returned, gave Nicola a receipt and set about un-mooring Moody Blue.

He pointed to the direction of the Immigration and Customs pier and went below for another coffee and a cigarette. Nicola shouted for Victoria to bring their passports. Their arrival at the Immigration and Customs pier was met by polite questioning, in French, why they had not checked-in first?

Nicola shouted to Jus to use his charm on the French official. Jus appeared in all his sartorial elegance. Clearly, the day's main event had yet to commence. Nicola collected her trendy, 'Must have in the locker room' crew bag, filled it with the yacht's cash and waited for Jus to smooth their path to the bank.

The Immigration and Customs official accepted the two girl's passports, to be returned on departure. Jus waved an official looking pass, which seemed to greatly impress the official, who saluted and waved them on.

It took but a short walk to the bank along original colonial French streets recently refurbished for the benefit of tourists. Chic bistros were everywhere, bursting with business from the hordes of tourists.

The bank, built in the 1890s, retained its exterior charm. Inside, the décor had the calm timeless quality the French excelled in. It reminded her of the time she had spent in Haiti.

The bank manager, one M. Marcel L'Herbier, welcomed the trio into his office. Clearly, he was an easy winner of the best dressed French bank manager competition, from the two-carat diamond pin securing his very expensive silk tie, to his handmade Italian shoes. Here was a man who would never give you the name of his tailor.

He greeted Jus like a long-lost son and when he clapped eyes on Nicola and Victoria the charm began like a deluge from a large waterfall. The amazing thing, to both Nicola and Victoria, everything about the man was totally genuine. They sat down and were served delicious Brazilian coffee, in delicate bone China.

To business, Jus explained the focus of their visit. Nicola handed over her stash of cash. A functionary arrived, wearing white gloves carrying a portable counting machine. Money counted, Nicola looked at the proffered receipt, as she decided the best split between receiving new US currency and new EU currency.

The functionary backed his way out of their presence and left them to continue with their small talk. Jus elegantly flipped his 'reverso' wristwatch to check the time, giving M. Marcel L'Herbier the cue to ask if their business had concluded.

Nicola requested the rental of a safety deposit box. A secret button under the desk of M. Marcel L'Herbier summoned the return of the functionary, the two packages Jus had brought with him were taken away and within minutes the functionary returned with the client key.

'Excellent,' M. Marcel L'Herbier exclaimed, 'And now for an excellent lunch.'

The restaurant was but a few steps away. Nicola saw it was everything a colonial French restaurant should be. If it had been located in Paris, one would not have entered without the security of a fully loaded gold credit card.

The speciality each day was the best fresh fish that ever existed, served in a variety of special sauces. The white wine was new to Nicola. She noted the name down to enquire its availability from Duke Marmaduke. The price would not matter, the wine clearly communicated the maxim, 'if you can't afford, don't ask.'

The lunch clearly could have drifted on until the sun commenced its regular descent to the horizon, but Jus expertly brought the proceedings to a close, and with back-slapping goodbyes all round, the trio headed back to Moody Blue.

Victoria collected their passports, as Nicola prepared Moody Blue for a fast blast reach back to English Harbour. Before the yacht cast off, a security van arrived with their new bank notes, complete with a certified copy of their individual numbers. Nicola signed for the delivery, stepped aboard surrendering the helm to Jus who stripped off to his briefs to catch, as he called it, the sun's rays at their best. Nicola and Victoria left him to it as they headed for the comfort of their cabin and a late afternoon nap.

TWO AND A half hours later Moody Blue reached a position offshore from English Harbour. Jus roused Nicola to take over the helm, who badly needed another four hours sleep. Nicola took the helm in time to see Jus disappear into a fishing boat positioned on the blind side of the yacht.

Confused, she set the auto-pilot so she could pop down below, made a mug of coffee, and rouse a complaining Victoria.

Their arrival at the HM Immigration and Customs jetty was met by an unusually large number of persons, including the expected immigration and customs officer, a police superintendent, and others. Nicola thought she saw the person she did not wish to see, the woman with the red hair.

The immigration and customs officer came aboard, very politely carrying out his duties. He returned to the jetty to speak with the police superintendent, shaking his head. He stood to one side, as the police superintendent stepped aboard.

'Are you Miss Nicola Stranraer?' he asked. 'I have come to serve a search warrant of your yacht.'

'It's just been inspected. So, let me see the warrant,' replied Nicola with little grace.

She read the warrant, taken out by a private entity seeking redress for loss of assets. Clearly, someone had been browbeating the local magistrate on a trumped-up charge. She doubted if it was strictly legal. Victoria took the warrant and gave it a penetrating examination.

'Officer,' Victoria said, 'This document is incorrect. In the first place, it has basic errors. In the second place, it is totally incompetent. It mentions we participated in a major robbery in which life was lost. We were victims of the aftermath of this robbery, a fact recorded in UK police files.'

The police superintendent leant forward to re-read the document over Victoria's shoulder, she turned her head and whispered, 'Don't you know your being set-up by the ginger tom at the back of this crowd. She is the instigator. You should know she is an insurance recovery agent and a bent one at that. She's after her ten percent and has no scruples on how she gets it.'

The police superintendent recoiled from the accusation and was not best pleased. Before he could respond, a tall, elegant man, dressed in typical lawyer's attire intervened. It was Jus reincarnated from his previous role as a master mariner.

Speaking in penetrating and precise clipped legalise, he destroyed the validity of the document and demanded the matter be dropped immediately or referred to the magistrate who had signed off on the warrant.

The police superintendent wavered, but Nicola, having received a telepathic communication from Jus, offered to kill the subject under the following 'suggestion,' the Customs officer should re-examine the yacht, supervised by the police superintendent and her lawyer, and nobody else. The examination should only concern a large packet of the alleged bank notes.

Now Nicola knew why on the return voyage, Jus had asked for two packets of the Euro notes be opened and spread along the top of the main saloon table. The smell of printer's ink from the new notes would infuse itself into the main saloon. The police superintendent seeing an easy way out of the impasse, agreed, much to the annoyance of Ms Ginger, who had forced her way to the front of the melee.

Before anyone could stop her, she jumped aboard Moody Blue disappeared down into the main saloon and started to pull out the spare mainsail package stowed under the main saloon bench seat.

'Here it is you dumb bastards,' she shouted. 'Now let's see what is what.'

The police superintendent ordered two of his officers below to restrain the woman and drag her sorry arse topside. He was fuming; this event could spin out of control.

The customs officer applied his sensing machine to the sail package now lying on the deck of the main saloon. He confirmed the sail package was, in fact, a sail. With loud dog's abuse coming from a restrained Ms Ginger, the sail package was taken topside and laid on the roof of the cabin.

Nicola explained the spare sail had been vacuumed packed to form a 'brick'. It saved taking up too much space. She carefully opened it up to reveal what it was, a spare mainsail. Everybody went quiet, the police superintendent counted to ten, suppressing his anger and ordered the cause of the problems to be arrested.

The Magistrate, a deputy on short-term assignment arrived, ordered everybody involved to sit down quietly in the centre cockpit, whilst he asked Nicola a range of questions. Had she been to Ile Française? What did she do there? And why?

Nicola told him yes, she had visited Ile Française and visited the bank. The Magistrate asked what she did at the bank. Nicola replied, pointedly, 'Banking?'

The customs officer brought Nicola's receipt for the safety deposit box. The Magistrate sensed he was being jerked around, looked very unhappy, and ordered this enquiry would conclude at Ile Française tomorrow morning. He would make all the necessary arrangements. Nicola and her lawyer should present themselves at the local airport at 9 a.m. tomorrow morning.

'What fun, I hope this is what Jus had in mind?' thought Nicola.

THE NEXT MORNING, a government helicopter took-off prompt at nine a.m., made the short flight to Ile Française, landing at the port helipad close to the port's immigration and customs office. The French officials were waiting and collected the passports of everyone they considered civilians, as opposed to bone vide government officials. The Ms Ginger woman was not best pleased with having her passport removed from her person, but she had little choice.

The group made short work of marching to the La Banque Française des Caraïbes, where M. Marcel L'Herbier stood waiting for them. The bank had yet to commence its daily routine.

M. Marcel L'Herbier undoubtedly wished to get this unwelcome visit done with as quickly as possible.

He bid everybody sit down in the bank's meeting room, offered everybody warm water to refresh themselves as the meeting room coffee machine was pointedly not working.

The police superintendent started the proceedings by requesting M. Marcel L'Herbier to confirm Nicola's receipt for the new bank notes was indeed genuine. M. Marcel L'Herbier looked at him in pure disdain, as though the question was beneath his dignity to answer.

After a poignant pause, he told the police superintendent the document was on bank note paper, it had his signature, so what was the question?

The police superintendent passed the document to M. Marcel L'Herbier, who looked at, countersigned it, and flicked it back at the police superintendent, his displeasure on full display.

The next question concerned Nicola's rental of a safe deposit box. M. Marcel L'Herbier threw his hands up in horror at the question, reminding everybody the contents of a safe deposit box could only be known by the client.

The Police superintendent handed M. Marcel L'Herbier a little used inter-governmental request for the safe deposit box to be opened up under new EU rules concerning serious crime and terrorism. At this juncture, M. Marcel L'Herbier became livid but Nicola thought he was overdoing his play-acting part of the proceedings.

Jus looked on with calm, like a film director who could see the current scene being played out to perfection.

An impasse ensued; the climate in the meeting room reached an all-time low. M. Marcel L'Herbier looked at Nicola for the way forward, because, after twenty-five years as a manager, under no circumstances would he violate the trust of a client.

Nicola removed the safe deposit key from her person and threw it in disgust on the meeting room table with the words, 'Help yourself, if you are that bothered.'

M. Marcel L'Herbier summoned his functionary, gave him Nicola's key, and bid him bring the subject safe deposit box. At this Ms Ginger started to get very excited, as Nicola smiled a deep inward smile.

The safe deposit box arrived and the package removed. Jus as Nicola's lawyer, said he would open the package.

Expectations around the table were high as the package was opened, but what cascaded onto the table was a large number of miniature ginger haired poodles, with their little legs flailing about making the most awful yapping sounds.

M. Marcel L'Herbier burst out laughing, Nicola smiled. Jus looked like he had just been dealt the best poker hand ever. The police superintendent fumed as never before, and as for the Magistrate; his face dropped as he realised the import of the morning's events. Ms Ginger died a death, her face one of total bewilderment. Nicola almost felt sorry for her, but hell no, she had it coming.

A chastened Magistrate and his police superintendent bid M. Marcel L'Herbier their profuse apologies, making smartly for the exit with unseemly haste, their embarrassment too hard to bear.

The return of the group to the waiting helicopter took little time, but at the Immigration and Customs office, the Magistrate received another shock, as Ms Ginger was arrested on charges of using a false passport in the name of Ms Gwyneth Stoltz. Somehow, the French authorities were in possession of her real name Ms Gwyneth Jones, wanted for questioning over various offences throughout Europe. Nicola wondered just how this latest twist had come about.

The flight back to English Harbour took little time, with few words spoken by anybody. The helicopter landed at the Governor General's residence and its extensive grounds overlooking a private beach. As the helicopter landed, Nicola saw Moody Blue had been anchored close to the Governor's residence.

As the passengers alighted, two of the Governor's staff approached the Magistrate to politely escorted him from the premises, apparently on his way to the international airport. Jus said it was time to disappear, adding that Victoria and Samantha had been taken to the Governor's residence.

The police superintendent made his excuses and took the offer of a lift back into town.

The Governor himself came to greet his guests. 'Nicola my dear. How spiffing to see you again.'

Nicola smiled. Sir Henry Brooks was a former RAF Air Vice Marshall with an interesting operational history. An elegant gentleman, still very fit, he came complete with RAF handlebar moustache and sporting a full head of white hair.

He looked like the all-original colonial masters of the British Empire, but under his bushy eyebrows came the sharpest mind Nicola ever had the pleasure to meet.

Sir Henry greeted Jus like the old friend he obviously was and guided them to his office just inside the main entrance of the residence. He sat them down. A servant provided cold water in crystal glasses and hot strong coffee.

'Now Nicky. Do tell me all.'

Nicola gave him a brief rundown on this morning events, adding all seemed to go to plan. 'Excellent my dear, just excellent,' replied Sir Henry.

Jus added a few extra observations, but otherwise, he had little to say. Nicola leant forward to Sir Henry and asked, 'OK Henry, just what was this morning's road show all about?'

Sir Henry paused for a moment, then, in a low voice he answered, 'Nicky, big secret, but this is the start of the push-back against Harry Hackett'

'The woman, known as Ms Ginger, is a big friend of the late Mr Stone's sister, who is in police custody as you know. Now we have Ms Ginger, and we can work around them to get more information. But the real intent is to keep Hatchet Harry off-guard. We do not know if Ms Ginger has made the connection between you two and the Manchester robbery, I hope not. In which case we have time, but if not, things will move forward faster than is wished.'

Sir Henry's wife, Lady Margret, arrived in Sir Henry's office. Lady Margret was the daughter of Lord Richardson, deceased, coming from a wealthy American family in New York. If Sir Henry was the smart one, Lady Margret was never far behind.

'Henry, you are hoarding our guest. Nicola so good to see you again, must be what, five years or more?' she said.

'Six and a half actually,' replied Nicola. 'Do you have my crew with you?' 'Yes, they are examining my art collection with Malcolm,' she replied. 'And who is Malcolm?' asked Nicola.

'A good friend. Real estate developer, an up-and-coming young man, you'll like him.' 'Margret,' started Sir Henry, 'Run along, it must be lunch time. I need a few words to finish.'

Lady Margret hurried out, as Sir Henry closed the door behind her.

'Nicola, I have a big favour to ask. Can you give Malcome passage to Miami; it's quite important.'

'I wasn't thinking to go to Miami just yet, what gives,' replied Nicola.

'Nicola, you will be sailing tonight, at six-thirty p.m. at the latest. There's a bit of a flap coming and you will be best out of it,' confided Sir Henry.

'What sort of flap?'

'Well, it's top secret, so I take for granted your confidence,' replied Sir Henry. 'There is a revolution being activated by international bad persons who have been fomenting unrest amongst the natives. Some seem to think the current management is too colonial, too backwards looking, all the usual accusations. The money men, who set-up here three years ago to take advantage of new tax rules, smell the opportunity for more, and what's worst the criminals are linked to our man in Manchester.'

Sir Henry continued, 'So, tonight, at 7 p.m., the island will go into lock-down, which is why you will sail before. It's going to be violent, but I have resources coming. A hundred Royal Marines will land on the southern tip of the island at dusk. The Para's are flying in sixty plus in the north. I already have a detachment of SAS guarding my residence, although they are well hidden. In fact, two of them are on your yacht, which by the way has been refuelled and rearmed.'

'Rearmed Henry, do you mean replenished?'

'Sorry, slip of the ex-RAF tongue,' replied Sir Henry. 'Commander Collingwood may be here before you depart, you two can shake hands and make-up.'

'Maybe not,' replied Nicola. 'I've had it with him.'

'Well, you will if for no other reason he will be the civilian face of the operation both here and in the UK against Harry Hackett, using the armed forces as best he sees fit.

This is serious Nicola; this is a no prisoners operation,' said Sir Henry, his voice dropping to its most threatening best. 'This is why I have Jus here, with his best men, currently taking the sun on board one of the recently arrived cruiser yachts. Now you know why this conversation has not taken place.'

'What conversation, Henry?' replied Nicola. 'Good girl, lunch time.'

Sir Henry, Jus and Nicola made their way into the main dining room to be greeted by a lavish Caribbean lunch. Victoria and Samantha had already tucked into the delicacies and of course, the rum punch bowl. Lady Margret prepared to serve but first guided her guests to their allotted seat places, putting Malcolm between Nicola and Victoria.

'Welcome everybody,' started Lady Margret. 'This is Malcolm Richardson, no relation, the rest you all know, so let's get started.'

Lunch became a roaring success, with everybody finding common sympathise with each other. For Samantha, it became a revelation. She had never enjoyed such high-powered company. Now she could see one of the attractions her father had for the Lady Sylvia.

Best of all came the seduction of Malcolm. Victoria could see Nicola had been smitten, and if she was not mistaken, his light had illuminated too. Victoria started to flirt with him, as Nicola watched. Malcolm thought he was being set-up with Victoria; certainly choosing either lady would be a pleasant challenge.

However, Malcolm soon figured it out. Lady Margret had targeted Nicola for his attention, and after all, she was the skipper of the yacht taking him to Miami.

Malcolm came from New York, reasonably well connected, and had made a name for himself in real estate. Starting off small, he had slowly but surely built an excellent reputation. He knew Lady Margret quite well, but who didn't in the small circle of influence in New York's inner social class.

He had found an ideal piece of land on the north side of Miami, an area of wasteland avoided by others. The main problem was the title. It existed but where?

By luck and a lot of hard work, Malcolm had found the owner with the title, an English recluse, whose ambition had been, for many years, to set up an English Colony. This jived with Malcolm, something new in the Florida real estate industry was needed, an English Village, American style, could be a good business opportunity.

He had broached the idea with Lady Margret. She had an English husband and distant English family somewhere in Oxfordshire. Lady Margret liked to invest in interesting projects, of which real estate was her favourite. The rich always had the feel of real estate, generally shunning the so-called smart money that was the stock market casino.

Now, he had taken the opportunity to visit Lady Margret with his broad outline of a project with four hundred properties complete with full central facilities for the new house owners. The district where this opportunity existed could in no way be described as fashionable, but this was where clever marketing came in. It was all there to be seen. Malcolm had raised the basic capital but had to admit cash flow and working capital looked kind of tight.

Lady Margret had gone through the proposal with great care and saw the opportunity. But the proposal lacked two things, the sufficiency of working capital to fund the daily ups and downs of what was going to be a major project, and a lack of high-level management, people she knew and could trust.

During their conversations, she had not mentioned the subject of management. She did not have her own people in the USA and was at a loss to know what suggestions to bring to the table. Then Moody Blue' unexpectedly turned up.

That morning, Lady Margret and Malcolm had revisited the subject. The way it was shaping up looked like she would invest twenty percent in the new venture if Malcolm would consider the services of Nicola and Victoria.

As the lunch slowly came to an end, Malcolm leant over to Nicola to ask if he could take passage with her to Miami. He explained briefly about the big decisions he had to take. He needed the solitude of the sea to collect his thoughts. Malcolm liked the look of this lady and hoped upon hope to get the opportunity to know all about her.

Nicola thought he was a very kind person and told him so. It would be a pleasure to have him aboard; had he heard they were leaving at 6.30 p.m. This was news to Malcolm but it wouldn't take him long to get ready.

Nicola smiled to herself. Some years ago, Lady Margret had tried making a match with the son of a friend in New Jersey. At the time, Nicola had reached the pinnacle of her career and refused to be distracted from making her new position a success. Now, Lady Margret might just have scored a hit.

Nicola thought Malcolm had questions to ask, so she took him to one side. 'Penny for your thoughts?' she asked.

Malcolm gave her a run down on the project in Miami and the position he thought Lady Margret had taken up. Nicola thought Lady Margret had been somewhat presumptuous, but this was her style. Nicola took Malcolm's hand and told him not to worry about Lady Margret, she had flown kites before.

She quietly told him her professional background and her hopes when she reached the USA. She told him Victoria was like-minded, so an opportunity of working together seemed a very attractive idea.

They could discuss matters on the voyage north, perhaps on the third day when everybody had settled down with each other. Nicola took the time to extol the virtues of Victoria; her CV was one of the best in the business when it came to big projects.

During Nicola's conversation with Malcolm, Lady Margret collared Victoria and brought her up to speed with her thoughts. Victoria dived into the subject headfirst.

'Lady Margret,' she asked. 'If you are thinking to take twenty percent of Malcolm's project, is this twenty percent of the first of the four phases, or all four. Have you a figure in mind, any numbers?'

Lady Margret replied she hadn't got this far, thinking more detail would be needed. Victoria pointedly asked if she was considering a cash injection or the provision of credit. Again, Lady Margret was not sure, which was why she wanted to talk to her first.

'OK Vicky; let us leave it for now. It's time for us ladies to go for a swim.' 'Our swim kit is on Moody Blue replied Victoria.

'Skinny dipping all round then,' Lady Margret called out to Nicola and Samantha. 'Come on you two, chop chop.'

The four ladies made their way down to the residence swimming pool, where two female staff were waiting with screens to disrobe behind, with large white fluffy towels to get dry with.

Sir Henry took this as his queue to collect Jus and Malcolm to steer them into his hideaway, his snooker room complete with a close to priceless elegant Cox and Yeman antique snooker table, comfortable leather armchairs and a servant nursing the best supplied cocktail cabinet this side of the Atlantic Ocean.

As both parties enjoyed what remained of the afternoon, the clock ruthlessly headed towards the time when afternoon tea should be served in time to enable Moody Blue to set sail before the main event of the evening.

The ladies were just about to finish their swim, complete with lengthy synchronised talking, when their men folk sauntered down to the pool to see how they were getting on. Lady Margret wasn't that bothered about modesty, so the crew of Moody Blue were not bothered either.

Sir Henry had seen the view before, as had Jus but for Malcolm, this was a new experience in old style European culture. Still, nobody blushed or got flustered. As the ladies regained their modesty, Sir Henry's Chef de Service, on the veranda, struck the dining room gong to announce afternoon tea had been served.

On the walk up from the swimming pool, Victoria asked Nicola were they really leaving at six-thirty p.m. Nicola confirmed the necessity, but without any detail. Victoria muttered something to Samantha who told her something hush-hush was going on.

Victoria pressed for more details, but all Samantha could tell her was she had spotted quite a few Special Forces soldiers in the grounds, to ensure their skinny-dipping experience remained a safe experience.

Victoria asked how she knew this, only to be told Samantha had been working in military hospitals long enough to spot these odd events.

As the afternoon tea came to an end, the time came for heartfelt goodbyes. Sir Henry had to jolly everyone along, as goodbyes could take a long time. As Nicola and her party reached the beach, she saw Moody Blue was very close to the shoreline. A flat-bottomed work boat soon transferred their belongings. The two soldiers in plain clothes silently slipped away and Nicola sent Samantha up forward to recover the anchor.

Within minutes Moody Blue had cleared the bay and entered into the deep blue ocean. The sun started to hide behind the mountains as dusk fell quickly. With full sail set in a reducingtrade wind, Moody Blue commenced her adventure towards the United States of America.

Chapter 21

The Journey to the USA Begins

THE CREW of Moody Blue settled down for the last leg of their journey to the USA. Nicola said she would stand the first and second dog watch, then the middle watch, doubling up with Malcolm, if Victoria would take the first watch, and Samantha stood the morning watch.

Victoria and Samantha headed to the forward master cabin to sleep off the excesses of the lunch and the afternoon tea. Nicola and Malcolm settled down to get Moody Blue on track, past Ile Française and out into the ocean.

As Moody Blue cleared the island of English Harbour, the radar detector became active. Nicola switched on the radar. A number of ships could be seen near the southern tip of the island. Malcolm asked if she had any idea who they were because their echoes did not look like fishing boats or local inter-island craft.

Now they were clear of English harbour, Nicola was able to tell Malcolm; it could be a British invasion force. Malcolm asked what the hell was going on. Nicola told him Sir Henry had babied them out to sea in advance of a total lock-down of the island.

She explained the basics but confessed she was more worried about Sir Henry. He was a good friend, but a military man through and through. He would lead his men from the front, and he'd confided he had been practising his firearm skills.

'As Sir Henry told me,' confided Nicola, 'The Royal Navy is landing Royal Marines and support troops on the southern tip of the island, and paratroopers are being dropped on the north end of the island. He has a large detachment of SAS guarding his residence, the airport, the radio station, and the power plants. Jus has also received, via the arriving yachts in the cruiser race, a number of his operatives.'

'So, we are very lucky to be on our way,' continued Nicola. 'If anybody asks, we departed from Ile Française to get Samantha back to the UK for her exams. I believe you have important business to attend to in Miami as well.'

'I guess we're well out of it, whatever it is,' commented Malcolm. 'What else do I need to know about apart from radar and radar detectors?'

Nicola took Malcolm down below, showed him the GPS, updated their position, and set a waypoint two miles to the south of the Ile Française southern lighthouse.

'When we reach the waypoint,' said Nicola, 'The GPS will give a signal. Then, we reset our course out into the Atlantic, add another waypoint to keep Moody Blue clear of the other islands, then it's a straight run into Miami.'

Nicola felt pleased Malcolm had a good idea of what to do and how to do it. They both returned to the cockpit. Malcolm was keen to take the helm. Nicola let him settle down behind the large steering wheel, went below, returning with two large mugs of coffee.

'Any ginger cookies,' asked Malcolm, only to be told Moody Blue only had ginger snaps, which Nicola fetched in the galley biscuit tin. The tin had the word 'biscuits' on the lid.

'Nicola,' asked Malcolm, munching slowly at one of Britain's favourite biscuits, 'How come ginger cookies are called ginger snaps.'

'Good question,' replied Nicola. 'I have no idea; ginger snaps have always been called 'snaps.' I guess being crispy, they make a sound when broken in half. The real secret is how to dunk them in your hot drink, without the wet portion falling into the mug.

Great minds have developed precise calculations on the optimum number of seconds, but I always use the words 'one-two,' spoken quickly, seems to work. They can also be called 'ginger nuts,' just in case you get confused, as Moody Blue has both types aboard.'

Malcolm shook his head. Clearly the British, or in this case the English, had words which were a complete mystery, and here he was in the middle of the ocean, not quite at her mercy, but something told him they were going to get along just fine.

He vowed to use his time aboard this fine yacht to get his head around all he had learnt from his visit to see Lady Margret and the simple way she had brought Nicola into his life.

'I wonder just how this is going to pan out,' he thought.

The two 'dog watches' passed easily enough, Victoria arrived on deck to stand the first watch to take them up to midnight, when he and Nicola were due to stand the middle watch.

He was going to be alone with an English lady through the night until 04.00 hours. He wondered what they would do to pass the time. Steer the yacht and keep a good lookout he guessed.

Two hours later, Moody Blue cleared the Caribbean islands. The trade wind remained a constant twenty knots over the starboard quarter. This was easy sailing, maintaining an easy nine knots. The centre cockpit offered a pleasant environment for the two watchkeepers. The warm wind meant waterproofs could be shed and they could relax in comfort.

As the clock approached two thirty in the morning Nicola, who had the helm, felt the temperature drop, a sure indication rain was on the way. One of her favourite treats was to strip off to enjoy an unlimited freshwater shower. Ideal for her hair maintenance plan. During the crossing of the Atlantic, the sun had bleached her hair, leaving it with streaks, not good.

Malcolm had gone below to make yet more coffee, but he had been gone awhile, no doubt having a quiet snooze for half an hour. As the heavy rain started to fall, Nicola checked the radar, saw it remained clear, switched on the autopilot, stripped off to her knickers and commence a heavenly freshwater shower.

She ladled water from a bucket to get her hair soaking wet, pouring a great deal of silky shampoo over her head. Extracting a natural sponge from her wash bag, she smothered it with fragrant body wash and began to soap herself down. The sensation was luxurious. The next sensation occurred when Malcolm arrived in the centre cockpit of Moody Blue to find a very attractive almost completely naked lady, covered in soap suds, looking at him with concern, or perhaps not. Could it be the realisation of an interesting idea?

Nicola bid him to close the main hatch to the main saloon and join her in this magic ritual. Nothing ventured, nothing gained, Malcolm stripped off, and soon he found himself covered from head to, well, just below the knees, in the same luxurious soap.

Nicola backed him up against the closed main hatch with the words, 'Hello sailor, come here often.' Her body pressed into his.

This was nice. Best go with the flow. Nicola planted a big kiss on his lips and his response was immediate. They kissed some more. This was exciting sailing, as Moody Blue provided the swaying motion two naked bodies were more than happy to receive.

'Malcolm,' Nicola whispered in his ear. 'Is this a gun in your underwear or are you enjoying the moment.' Malcolm adjusted his underwear, removed hers, and soon their two bodies were as close as they were ever going to get.

They stood, locked in a wonderful embrace until nature took its course. By this time, the rain had washed away the luxurious soap. Nicola asked

Malcolm to rinse her hair with the fresh water in the bucket.

The rain stopped, Nicola raised the cockpit canopy, handed Malcolm a clean dry towel and a pair of white disposal overalls to slip into when he had dried himself. The sky cleared and the moon came out to bathe the cockpit in a silky light.

Malcolm thought about fetching the coffee he had managed so easily to forget all about. Nicola handed him an opened bottle of a designer drink, a delicious mixture of slightly effervescent vodka and autumn fruits.

'That was lovely Malcolm,' Nicola purred. 'Nice kissing technique.'

Malcolm felt pleased. It had been a long time since he had received compliments on his kissing. His skin felt smooth and silky and his dark hair much refreshed.

Samantha burst into the cockpit, wondering why the main hatch had been closed. Nicola told her the yacht had passed through a lot of rain which would have gone into the cabin.

She returned with a coffee tray with steaming cups of coffee and the ship's biscuit tin. Malcolm slipped down below to the main aft cabin, as Nicola gave Samantha the duty watch handover.

Seeing all remained calm, Nicola followed Malcolm into the main aft cabin, slipped under the single cover, turned him over, snuggled into his back, and fell sound asleep.

The morning watch passed to the forenoon watch, as Samantha headed for some much-needed shuteye after a brief handover to Victoria. The wind had freshened a little with the coming of the new day and she chose to put in one slab reef just to keep Moody Blue at her peak of tranquil sailing.

Halfway through her watch, the radar detector started its annoying beep. She scanned the horizon, but the morning haze prevented her from seeing the source. The instrument told her the target ship appeared to be coming at full steam ahead, from the port quarter.

Out of the morning haze a US Coast Guard Cutter appeared, signalling Moody Blue with a Morse code message. Victoria couldn't read Morse code, barely knew of its existence. As the Coastguard ship drew close, Victoria waved at it, and then went below to make coffee.

She heard Nicola getting up in the main aft cabin, knocked on the door, and told her there was a Coastguard vessel close by, flashing a signalling lamp at Moody Blue.

'Vicky, is the VHF radio switched on and slaved up to the cockpit?'

Victoria gave a quick squeak, a giggle, and dashed back to the helm, switched on the VHF radio, and waited for someone to call.

'Unidentified yacht, unidentified yacht, for the last time come in please,' blared the radio. Victoria who only knew how to use a smartphone picked up the handset, and shouted,

'Hello.'

An annoyed voice from down below shouted out she had to press the lever on the handset to speak. It was Nicola, knowing full well she would have to leave her comfortable berth and come on deck.

Victoria tried to respond by pressing the lever on the handset, shouted a 'hello,' but heard nothing. Nicola arrived, told her only to press the lever on the handset to speak, then let it go to hear the other party. Victoria handed Nicola the radio handset, muttering why couldn't a phone be a phone anyone could use.

For the life of her, Nicola couldn't remember for the life of her why she hadn't shown Victoria how to use a two-way radio telephone.

Nicola called the Coastguard Cutter, 'Come in Coastguard, sorry about that, my crew only knows how to use Facebook. How can I help you?'

The pause at the other end of the radio call was palpable. Then, the person replied, 'Is this the English yacht Moody Blue and do you have a crew member named Samantha Samuelson, over?'

'Roger, this is the yacht Moody Blue who wants to know about any of my crew members, over?'

'This is Commander Keyte, US Coastguard vessel Waverider. I've been ordered to find this person, believed to be on your yacht, and fly her to Miami. Her father has passed this request via the UK Embassy in Washington, and I drew the short straw, over?'

'Roger Waverider, wait.'

'Vicky,' shouted Nicola. 'Make yourself useful and bring up my sat phone.'

The sat phone arrived, Nicola switched it on, waited for it to find a satellite and pushed a fast dial button.

A voice answered, 'Samuelson here, speak.'

'Samuel, it's Nicky, we are thirty hours out from Miami. I have a US Coastguard Cutter who wants to kidnap your daughter. Can you confirm?'

'Oh, Hi Nicola, yes I need her in London soon as possible. I've been called to an urgent case in Buck House. Can't give the name. Can do, all the arrangements have been made?'

'Of course, just had to check,' replied Nicola.

'How was the voyage, did Samantha do well,' asked her father. 'Very well. She's sleeping, best get busy, goodbye,' said Nicola.

Samantha dragged herself out of her berth, and unusually for her, started complaining at length. She sat at the main saloon dining table and was handed a mug of fresh tea and the ship's biscuit tin.

'Sorry to wake you,' said Nicola. 'Your father needs you in London PDQ, there's a US coastguard ship waiting to fly you by helicopter to Miami International, where you will be met by someone from the UK Consulate and given a first-class ticket on the first available flight.'

'What on earth does Father want me for?' asked Samantha.

'No idea, something about an urgent case in Buck House. I guess we know what this means,' informed Nicola. 'Guess it's a chance to become famous.'

'Or infamous. I best get ready,' said Samantha wearily.

Ten minutes later she was packed and ready to go. 'Got everything, passport, money, credit cards?'

Samantha muttered a yes, and could she leave her sailing togs behind, and have them sent on?

Nicola said this would be no problem and handed her an envelope of cash. 'OK. Let's go,' said Nicola.

Nicola ordered Victoria to bring Moody Blue up on to the wind and keep way on, whilst she deployed the fenders. The Coastguard sea-boat came alongside and a young midshipman heaved a sail bag aboard and followed it immediately.

Samantha's kit quickly made it into the sea-boat, as she carefully followed. With blown kisses and shouted farewells, the US Coastguard sea-boat headed back to the mother ship. Its recovery was smooth and professional, as was Samantha's transfer into a waiting helicopter.

Nicola looked the young midshipman up and down and asked, 'What gives.'

'Good morning Ma'am, my Captain sends his compliments and suggests you could use a replacement. My name is Midshipman Ricky Felts,' said the midshipman.

'Ricky Felts, the East Coast J-90 champion?'

'The very same,' smiled Ricky Felts. 'It's a pleasure to be aboard.'

Malcolm arrived on deck, his sleep having been disturbed beyond endurance, clutching a mug of coffee. He looked at the midshipman.

'Ricky Felts, what in God's name are you doing here,' he asked. 'You know this guy?' asked Nicola.

'Sure. Hot shot sailor from Key West. Welcome aboard Ricky. Want to go sailing?' 'Yes sir,' replied Ricky Felts.

'Good, then I can go back to bed. Nicola come; you need your sleep.

Victoria, Ricky will keep you company for the forenoon watch, just teach him all you know,' smiled Malcolm, as he returned to the main aft cabin with Nicola right behind him.

Victoria soon got Moody Blue back on course and set the autopilot for Miami.

'Bring your kit down into the saloon, I'll make you a coffee, I sure as hell need one,' said Victoria.

'Yes Ma'am, love a coffee, any cookies?'

'Only biscuits,' smiled Victoria. 'Please don't call me Ma'am. The name's Vicky, and you had best fill in the ship's logbook, including name, rank, address and evening telephone number if you please.'

Ricky smiled a big smile; here was a pretty girl with humour. He guessed she would spell humour with a 'u.' He liked the Brits, especially this one.

Victoria started to tell Ricky what ship this was, but he asked if this Moody 44 was the twin master cabin model, with a deep-water fin keel and twin rudders?

Victoria replied, 'If you can guess the serial number, you can have a second biscuit.'

Ricky laughed out loud, asked where he could change into relax rig and get topside to take a spell at the helm. Victoria showed Ricky the spare cabin, asked him to make himself at home and offered to rearrange it from a storeroom into sleeping quarters later on.

While Ricky changed into his sailing togs, Victoria updated Moody Blues position on the chart and calculated the distance to run. By her reckoning, they should arrive in Miami sometime late the following morning, but where they should land, she had no idea, hopefully, close to a shopping centre so she could stock up on ladies' items, make-up and visit a decent hairdresser.

Ricky took the helm and started to enjoy himself. Victoria remained below getting the day's work in the galley out of the way. Taking food into the USA was always a problem, so she prepared a slap-up meal for the evening. Jobs done, Victoria went topside to work on her tan, remembering at the last moment she would actually have to wear some form of swimming costume.

As the sun began its slow descent into the sea, Nicola, then Malcolm, arrived on deck, to see what progress Moody Blue had made during the day. The sky remained clear, and the paths of international airliners making their way to Miami were very clear as the sun shone upwards into their contrails.

Nicola handed Victoria a light robe to put on, suggested she take a shower and smother herself with after-sun cream. Victoria disappeared below as Nicola took the opportunity to become better acquainted with Ricky.

She discovered he had taken the opportunity to take a ride into Miami so he could attend a race qualifier event in two days' time. Clearly, Ricky had contacts in the US Coastguard service which allowed him to advance his racing career at the same time as his naval career.

AFTER THE EVENING meal, Ricky offered to take another spell on watch, so the three of them could conduct a meeting and come to an agreement on how the management of Malcolm's new project should be set-up.

To Malcolm's relief, the two girls were thinking along the same lines as he was. They all understood precise demarcation of responsibilities would be needed, given their close relationship with the Lady Margret. Their arrival into his world appeared heaven sent.

Victoria insisted the blossoming relationship between Malcolm and Nicola be discussed. Even that went well. So, an accord between them became the subject of a single piece of paper, describing Malcolm as the CEO and Construction Director, Victoria as CFO and Planning Director, and Nicola became the Director of Sales and General Management. Nicola and Victoria would be paid by receiving shares in the company, as Malcolm informed them he would not be drawing a salary for some time.

The meeting adjourned. Nicola set the watches for the rest of the evening and night. As Moody Blue started to close the American coastline, the watches would have to double up, starting with the morning watch. Ricky's close knowledge of the area was about to become most valuable.

After breakfast Nicola found a mobile telephone network to complete the arrivals procedure on the US Customs and Borders Protection website. Nicola made sure she had the letter given to her by Sir Henry to smooth the path through the American bureaucratic system.

As Moody Blue entered into Miami harbour a patrol boat came alongside to challenge them. Again, Midshipman Ricky proved what a useful man he was to have aboard.

Moody Blue went alongside Terminal 'H' flying the yellow 'Quebec' flag and awaited the arrival of the US Customs and Borders Protection officers.

Despite the odd circumstances of the crew of Moody Blue the immigration official had sufficient leeway to sign-off on the paperwork with little delay. Nicola waved goodbye to Midshipman Ricky as he rushed away to his next racing commitment.

A US Customs official followed to ensure no contaminating foods were brought ashore. Nicola took the official below and showed him what little food remained aboard. The customs official could see the skipper of this yacht had done her homework. He limited his actions to the disposal of the fresh foods and issued a caution regarding the frozen foods.

He wondered why a British yacht had so much produce from the USA. He wasn't the only one until Nicola remembered Moody Blue had been provisioned during their all too brief visit to English Harbour. Sir Henry had obviously been thinking ahead.

As the customs official went on his way, Malcolm asked the girls to be ready for a little jaunt. Malcolm took Moody Blue under power into Biscayne Bay, northwards to the marina where he had a favoured berth in front of the marina main office.

Victoria felt almost at home in the enclosed waters of Biscayne Bay. She could see built-up areas with shops, hairdressers and surf and turf restaurants, all under the general description of civilisation. Being at sea was all very relaxing, bad weather notwithstanding, but all she saw here was an opportunity to indulge.

Nicola saw her friend coming alive. To some extent she felt it herself. She felt good about her arrival but decided not to pester Malcolm about minor details, like where they would they live, and other matters. She was falling in love with Malcolm, but there was a way to go, and both Vicky and she would not be taking anything for granted.

Moody Blue arrived at the berth which would be her home for some time. 'Where are we off to Malcolm?' asked Victoria.

'You'll see,' he replied. He left Moody Blue and returned with an ageing Ford F-150 truck. Clearly, it had undergone a full refurbishment. It was Malcolm's pride and joy. They all bundled themselves aboard, with the two girls sitting on the front bench seat.

The truck made its way onto the main highway northbound, then dropped down onto the frontage road, hooked a left under the main highway, and went back up to the elevated main highway, southbound.

Malcolm asked Nicky and Vicky to keep a sharp lookout to the west. Coming into view was the extensive area of land which was his pet project.

'That's a lot of land Malcolm for four hundred properties,' said Nicola. 'Looks like room for many more.'

Malcolm replied, 'My studies show this is the most profitable layout.

It gives customers space for which they are more than prepared to pay for. The officials at city hall have limits on house density in this area for a variety of reasons and allows for an easier build programme.'

Nicola was impressed with his answer. She also realised there would be a lot to learn. Victoria remained silent. She studied the diagram of the basic layout on her lap to relate it to what she saw.

The truck left the highway, dropped down to the frontage road, and followed a side road leading to the entrance of the site. An elegant brick wall in mock London Brick framed an impressive entrance. Flowers and ornate bushes decorated the entrance in an attractive manner.

Malcolm admitted he had copied the entrance from a stately house in Wiltshire, England, but blowed if he could remember the name. Nicola thought it looked familiar but couldn't put the name to it either.

Inside the entrance, on a large, elevated area of ground stood a single four-bed property, complete with a large double garage. The garage doors mimicked two bay windows. Seemingly Malcolm reckoned a country house in an English country setting would not have a double garage at the front of the property.

No way would Americans want their garage at the rear of their home where they expected the swimming pool and barbeque to be. The double garage had a 'granny apartment' built over it, another valuable feature.

First impressions were good, Victoria said she admired the frontal aspect of the property but commented it did not look as authentic English as she would like but realised this was Florida and just the suggestion of good olde England would probably be sufficient. She put her mind to alterations which could enhance the olde world impression without increasing too many additional costs and build time.

Malcolm took them inside the house. The two girls found the interior to be modern, light and airy, warm and comfortable all at the same time. They found a dream kitchen, with adjacent utility rooms, fridge-freezers with the capacity to feed an army, and all the household goods one could wish for.

Upstairs, Malcolm showed them the two master en-suites at either end of the landing, with two smaller bedrooms in between sharing a central bathroom. All the rooms had lady's delight, ample cupboard space. The upstairs landing even possessed an alcove, complete with comfortable settee.

Nicola asked Malcolm how much the vast expanse of thick carpeting had cost, only to be told the supplier had offered a freebee if he could be considered for the contract to supply the whole project. An offer Malcolm had gladly accepted.

It turned out most of the furnishings and fitments had been supplied on a loan basis from existing suppliers from his last project. Clearly, the thought of being involved with a project including four hundred properties had strong financial attractions.

The three of them made their way downstairs to the lounge where a Portuguese lady from Angola, in her mid-fifties, called Rita, was waiting with coffee and refreshments. Malcolm introduced her to Nicola and Victoria. She had worked for him these last three years after her husband had run out on her and left her destitute.

Malcolm relaxed, asking for first impressions. Both Nicola and Victoria said they were impressed, but perhaps they needed more time to be objective. This led nicely into Malcolm's next conversation.

'Well girls,' he started, 'My idea is for you to move in and take up residence. You can use the second master en-suite at the far end of the upstairs landing. Rita will look after you and it will also give a nice feeling to the house. If you know the 'It's good to live here feeling,' then you can give customers the more personal touch.'

'Nice idea Malcolm,' replied Nicola. 'But there's only one bed, all be it a very big bed.' 'No problem,' replied Malcolm. 'The bed is two queens put together, easy to divide them.' 'How about visitors when you show clients around?'

'Yes, I've thought of that. I'll have the door split into top and bottom. During the times of showing, the bottom half can be locked, but clients can still look in, what do you think?'

'Could work, let's give it a try and see how it works out. Time is marching on so perhaps we should bring our things up from Moody Blue before the traffic hits rush hour. By the way, where are the offices you mentioned; in and above the garage?' asked Nicola.

'That's right,' said Malcolm, 'I'll show you later. Let's get a move on.'

THE JOURNEY TO Moody Blue took little time. In no time the two girls had loaded their personal belongings into the back of the truck, and securely locked-up Moody Blue for an extended period of rest.

The return to the show house much took longer than expected. Clearly, rush hour in Florida was the same as everywhere. By the time the three of them had unpacked their luggage and tidied themselves up a bit, time had left them behind. Victoria was hungry, tired, and close to complaining. Nicola was not in the mood to have Victoria complaining.

Matters were not helped when Rita told them she had only purchased food for tomorrow's breakfast. Nicola was not in the mood for home delivered pizza or Chinese. They were located too far from anywhere. The distance would result in delivered meals being cold.

Malcolm suggested going to the 'hole in the wall,' just a short distance up the frontage road. This outlet served the local community, mostly made up of African-Americans and Cubans. It was quite safe, just needed to dress down. Nicola looked at Vicky, who was as dressed down as ever she saw. Scruffy was the word, kind of attractive in its own peculiar way.

The trio set off quickly arriving at 'Matt's Diner'. They met Matt, a redneck and someone who had never heard of the word diet. He must have eaten more food than he ever served. Still, the place had a semblance of hygiene and whatever was cooking smelt really good.

'Beer, anyone?' asked Matt.

'Is the Pope a catholic?' replied Victoria dryly, thereby introducing Mr Matt to something new, English humour.

Three beers later, and after a quick perusal of the dog-eared menu, Nicola decided on a Spanish omelette, with a plate of hash browns on the side. Victoria stuck up two fingers, which Mr Matt took as a doubling of the order. Malcolm ordered a hamburger, no cheese, heavy on the fried onions, tomato, and chunky fries.

'Haute cuisine or nouvelle cuisine?' asked Nicola.

Malcolm smiled. He was warming to Nicola very quickly, whatever she said just did it for him.

'I guess it will be a stunning combination of the two,' he offered. Victoria complained about the weak beer; a remark Malcolm expected. 'Matt, u' got any of that dark Boston beer? Best bring three bottles.'

The familiar dark brown bottles arrived. Victoria drained hers in record time. Last night's watch-keeping aboard Moody Blue had drained her. She needed something stronger.

Victoria shouted out, 'Mr Matt, bring me a 'number fourteen' and plenty of ice on the side,' which was the first time Nicola knew she liked bourbon whisky. Mr Matt quickly brought a glass full of the amber liquid, smiled at Victoria and asked if anybody else wanted to get down to business?

Nicola stuck-up two fingers and Malcolm suggested next time the back of her hand should face her, just in case.

The food arrived, hot, steaming, and delicious. She took a hot roll on the side then ordered coffees for all. The meal, quickly consumed, ended with another round of 'number fourteen's. Malcolm suggested they get return quickly before the local police patrol came for their evening meal.

Nicola felt relieved to return to their new home. Tiredness had crept in quickly and bath and bed became a priority. Victoria headed straight to bed, curling up fast asleep. Nicola draped a blanket over her and turned off the lights. She went downstairs to find Malcolm and thanked him for everything. He put his arm around her waist, thanked her for coming into his life asking if there was anything else he could for her.

Nicola gave him a big kiss, thanked him again, but she really did need to wash and get some sleep. Malcolm told her he would stay this night. His home was empty and Rita had prepared a bed in one of the other bedrooms. Nicola felt tempted to ask which one, but for her, lights out would be lights out. Tomorrow would be another day.

Chapter 22

A New Life Begins in the USA

NEXT MORNING Nicola and Victoria rose late and by the time they struggled downstairs Malcolm was long gone into his commercial world. So, whatever happened during their first full day in the USA would be dedicated to recovery.

Rita served a waist busting breakfast, causing Nicola to vow she would limit this treat to once a week. Victoria ate like a hungry hog, devouring everything put down in front of her. She had heard about breakfasts USA.

'Hey, fatso,' called out Nicola, 'This is your third plate of waffles. You goin' for the world record.'

Victoria replied if Nicola needed the bathroom now would be a good time, only to be told the show house had any number of bathrooms. Victoria decided to have a nice long bath, to soak away all the aches and pains caused by an active life aboard a modern yacht.

Rita gave her a large bottle of luxury hair shampoo to let the repair work began. Nicola went downstairs to catch-up on getting accustomed to the show house.

Rita brought more coffee. Nicola asked her to take ten minutes to give her the latest news. Information on where they were and what was what. The ten minutes lasted at least an hour and it occurred Victoria had become silent in whichever bathroom she had commandered. Rita went to see, returning to say Victoria had dozed off in the bath and her skin had become all wrinkled. Now began the task of fixing her hair and Rita figured it would take a long time.

'I would delay lunch until much later,' advised Nicola.

After lunch, Rita showed the two girls around the office spaces in and above the garages. At ground level, the area had been laid out in open plan, with desks, a meeting table, sofas, and the usual coffee machine. Above, lay the executive's office, a secure meeting room, and a strong room to house the computer systems which ran the site.

The main office in the downstairs garage displayed a large wall map of the planned development site and various charts alluding to the

245

envisaged construction programme. The site was well laid out; the four hundred properties divided into four villages called, South Leigh, West Leigh, East Leigh, and North Leigh.

Victoria asked if anybody knew the old English meaning of the word. Nicola looked at her with a blank look, but the internet suggested the word derived from a meadow, with or without heather, a glade, or a sheltered location.

Given Florida's history on visiting hurricanes, Nicola fancied the last explanation would be appropriate. She wondered if the construction of these properties would feature storm protection.

The site layout looked simple enough, with each village having a central corridor for the inclusion of a strip park, with trees, bushes, and gardens for decorative plants. Around the perimeter of the whole site would be an access road, initially used for construction traffic. The plan showed the perimeter fence to be planted with a mixture of trees and bushes.

To the east lay the elevated main highway with its low-level frontage road. The main entrance to the four villages had been located on the east side. There were two entrances, one either side of the show house which would eventually become the clubhouse, with gardens, swimming pools and other sports facilities.

A curious impediment to the layout in North Leigh appeared to be a natural stream running west to east through the site. It mattered little, as the master plan showed the order of progress, with East Leigh the first phase, and North Leigh being the last.

Along the east perimeter, north and south of the main entrance complex, Nicola saw two spare pieces of land. Victoria pointed out these two sections of land were seemingly going to lie fallow, or perhaps be planted with trees and gardens, supposedly to add to the attractive appearance of the development from the elevated main highway. She started muttering to herself, which left Nicola wondering what bright ideas were formulating in her ever-active cerebral processes.

Rita asked if they would like to come with her to go shopping to stock up on food and kitchen supplies. Nicola asked if they could swing by Moody Blue to collect the remainder of their personal items.

By evening, Malcolm managed to make an appearance at the show house, apologising for his absence. He asked his two guests how they were settling in and was there anything they needed? Nicola mentioned transport. Clearly, a vehicle of some sort would be fundamental to life in the USA. She was pleased a long-term hire car was to be delivered first thing the following morning.

Malcolm dashed to his office to collect the papers he needed for the evening meeting, for which he was running twenty minutes late. Blowing kisses at everybody, he dashed out into the night.

Victoria asked Rita if this was normal, only to be told normally Malcolm did finish work at six in the evening most days, but important matters were coming to a head and he had a great deal on his plate.

The two girls were OK with this, especially Victoria, who knew any project start-up was a busy time. After their evening meal, they retired to their spacious bedroom to get themselves organised for the new day.

This new world felt strange; everything seemed to happen very fast. Was this the secret of life in the USA? Who to love; who to trust; and who to be wary of, all figured in their thoughts? The chatted until two a.m., but at the end of their conversation, they agreed they had probably landed on their feet.

The next morning came with cooling rain.

'This is more like it. Now for the morning commute from the bedroom to the breakfast table and then the office.' thought Nicola.

She found breakfast waiting. Victoria started a discrete conversation with Rita about the amount of food on the table. Slowly, but gently, it was agreed America had a lot of great breakfast dishes, but Nicky and Vicky knew full well they were in the 'getting married' market, and slim ladies had the advantage.

Malcolm arrived in his usual hurry. Fortunately, the two girls were only nursing their second mug of tea. Malcolm asked for an exchange of ideas, suggestions regarding the design, and outfitting of the show house. Nicola offered a few and Malcolm jotted them down. The real discussion came regarding finalising the price list. Nicola passed. This was Victoria's area of expertise.

Victoria pulled a paper out of her folder with her suggested version of pricing. She thought if the lower price covered the basic construction price complete with a standard low-level fit-out included, known as the 'must haves', then the 'would like to haves' would be priced as extras.

The client would be shown the show house and its extensive top-end fit out. Then, assuming a sale, the client is taken to a property in its 'non-fitted out' stage, and the client presented with a 'self-build' tabulation for them to agree and sign for.

'It will be like just like choosing extras on a new car purchase,' said Victoria.

Malcolm studied her proposal, shook his head, but before he could ask the obvious questions, Victoria piped up, 'It will give you somewhere in the region of fifteen per cent extra income, depending on the effectiveness of the salesperson.'

Nicola thought she was being set-up. She guessed sales and sales promotion would be the biggest part of her involvement in the progress towards success as Victoria smiled at her sweetly.

Other matters were discussed, the main one being US visas. Their allowance of ninety days would soon pass and messing around with US immigration regulations was not on Nicola's 'must do' list. Malcolm knew a visa attorney and promised to look into the subject.

AND SO, TWO weeks later, good progress on all fronts had been achieved, and a date set for the grand opening and afternoon reception of invited dignitaries, friends and potential clients who had logged into the development website.

Nicola's relationship with Malcolm grew at a steady pace. They were good working together during the day, their evenings both relaxing and enjoyable. Nicola restricted her alone time with Malcolm, aware Victoria was still struggling to leave the past behind.

Although they were sharing the same bedroom, Nicola wondered when it would be possible to let Victoria sleep in any bedroom on her own. Her nightmares had subsided to almost nil, but Nicola's presence in the same bedroom continued to give Victoria much-needed comfort.

Nicola admired Malcolm for being so understanding. She mentioned Victoria would soon need a man friend. One who could be trusted to behave as a kind gentleman and to take on board her unhappy past.

Nicola told him the basics of their story, even showed him some of the dreadful photographs. Malcolm did not press the subject, and even now, Nicola found it hard to give any graphic details. The photographs said it all.

The problem would come when Victoria's man friend would have to be told, and he would have to give a cast iron guarantee never, ever, to talk directly to Victoria about her dreadful suffering.

The run into 'Launch Day' proved hectic, but a strong effort by all concerned brought the open day to readiness. Nicola and Victoria were impressed by the number of people who turned up, even if it was a Friday afternoon event.

It made the investment the pair of them had in new outfits well worthwhile. Vicky's motto of 'Let's dress to impress' started to pay dividends. They chatted with Malcolm's friends and his contacts in an easy and confident manner. Folk were impressed. Malcolm had brought two lovely English ladies into his premium development.

Malcome soon discovered his two girls were on top form as they gently manoeuvred guests into becoming clients, and half-way through the afternoon, six properties had been signed up and three more became firm promises.

For Malcolm, this was like a dream come true. He had been very nervous on how the afternoon would turn out and how the achieved house sales stood up against the expensive marketing forecast.

Just as the afternoon started to wind down, an impressive man arrived with his PA.

Malcolm had been hoping this person would fulfil his promise to attend. And here was the man himself, Captain Benny 'Jets' Vincens, CEO and major shareholder of a substantial Florida corporate conglomeration.

Capt. Benny 'Jets' Vincens was a class act; everybody agreed with the description. Always well dressed, well mannered, the consummate businessman, with medium height, a strong athletic stance, piercing blue eyes, and a full head of distinguished dark hair. He could be any age, but rumours put him at somewhere in his early forties.

Nicola stood next to Victoria as Malcolm made the introductions. Victoria grasped Nicola's hand. Nicola felt a bolt of energy flow between them. Victoria stood transfixed, not knowing what to say. Nicola welcomed Benny on behalf of them both. He too felt the change, but surely, she wasn't dumbstruck.

Nicola did the talking, wondering what to do next. She kicked Victoria's ankle asking her to say something. Victoria giggled a 'hello' and fell silent.

Nicola explained Victoria had become rather shy and perhaps it would be best to sit down in the armchairs while Rita served refreshments. Nicola nodded at Rita to serve her favourite party drink to everyone, a refreshing Pimms No.1, complete with canapés.

Rita cottoned on to Victoria's predicament and flashed her eyelids at Nicola. Nicola nodded back and watched as Rita discretely added extra gin to Victoria's glass.

Malcolm started to give Benny the run down on his upper-level management team. When Benny was told Victoria was his finance specialist and overall planning controller, he looked hard at Victoria.

Nicola whispered something in Victoria's ear and Vicky started giggling. Nicola's next whisper brought streams of laughter which only stopped when Nicola dug her elbow hard in her ribs.

'Vicky,' said Nicola, 'Say hello properly to Capt. Benny. He is our next-door neighbour.

He lives in the big mansion up on the hill at the north end of Malcolm's land.'

Victoria didn't move a muscle for thirty seconds, just flashing her eyelids at everyone. She finished her drink in record time, returned the glass to Rita for a refill.

Then, she spoke in her best Black Isle English voice, 'Mr Benny, how dooo you doo, I am so very pleased to have met you,' her flashing eyes fixed firmly on his. The word 'you' had an interesting accent.

'Christ,' thought Nicola. 'She's fallen head over heels for this guy.'

Victoria sat very still; her gaze fixed firmly on Benny. Nicola came to the rescue with welcomed small talk. She looked over at Victoria. She knew her best friend was a very good-looking lady, but her face was flushed, highlighting her skin tone. Her eyes sparkled; her face serene. Victoria's beauty was unparalleled.

Benny leant over to Nicola's side and very politely asked, 'Does your friend speak?'

Nicola replied, 'Unfortunately yes. She has a range of different voices to go with her Jekyll and Hyde character. You have just heard her 'Black Isle' English, located in North Scotland. The local population speak accent-free English, very natural. If you stop, say a council worker sweeping the streets to ask directions, the reply will be quite different from the strong Scottish accents of the surrounding districts.

Then, she has her 'Eliza Doolittle' voice, which is a scream, and her famous Margret Thatcher voice, which is scary.

She also has a very calm and dignified voice which she uses when she is conducting, say a monthly meeting on a major construction project, where she will quietly strip the lazy, the incompetent, the dishonest, and any other waste of space, to the bone. She can put the knife in their back and they would never know until the pointy bit stops their tie from waving about. I witnessed it once, scary stuff I can tell you.'

'But Nicola, she giggles too much, she must be old enough by now?' enquired Benny.

'Ah, that's her 'not very sure of herself' default position. Until she makes up her mind whether to be a Jekyll or a Hyde. She's quite charming really,' replied Nicola.

Malcolm sat back. He was enjoying the show, for show was what it had become.

'So, Malcolm,' said Benny. 'These are your two superstars. Nice work. I hear you are romantically involved with Nicola, sleeping together are we?'

'Sleeping! Adjective: description of the noun, to sleep,' replied Malcolm, 'However, 'slept,' past tense or past participle, afraid so. At the moment, they both share the same bedroom for very good reason, and so I am celibate for the moment. But I live in hope.'

'Hope for what?' Benny enquired mischievously.

'Vicky finds a suitable boyfriend. I think you have been chosen. Best run for cover if I were you,' replied Malcolm.

Benny looked Victoria in the eye, smiled and said, 'Thank God I don't do athletics.' Nicola said nothing. Just where all this banter was taking everybody?

'Victoria, say something.'

'Mr Benny,' asked Victoria, in her little girl lost voice, 'Can I ask you a question or two?' 'Of course,' he replied.

'Are you married; have you ever been married; would you like to be happily married in a monogamous relationship; is there any history of madness in your family going back six generations; did you pass your last insurance medical with flying colours; do you snore when sleeping; are you kind to the animals, namely cute little dogs that go woof, and do you want children before you get too old to have them?'

Nicola almost fell out of her armchair laughing. Malcolm followed suit and Benny just sat there stunned.

'Better have another drink, old man,' said Malcolm. 'So, what are the answers?'

Benny did as he was bid. Boy did he need another drink. He smiled a big smile; this was surely a massive wind-up. It was becoming a fun evening and the two ladies were quite enchanting. He finished his next drink, only to find a smiling Rita refilling it. She was enjoying the show, the same as everybody else.

Benny finished his third drink. 'These Pimms are quite strong,' he thought.

'OK Vicky, hope you don't mind me calling you Vicky. Eight questions eh? Well, let's see.' Benny paused.

'The answers are,' he said counting on his fingers, 'No, No, Yes, No, Yes, No-I think, Yes, and Yes.'

Victoria stared at him. This was her man, hells teeth, the light is shining brightly.

'In which case,' started Victoria, in her most heartfelt voice, 'You are this afternoon's lucky American, congratulations.'

Nicola spoke, 'Victoria will you behave yourself.'

Benny replied, smiling, 'I think she's deadly serious Nicky, and I've only been here less than an hour. OK, let's see where this will take us.'

Malcolm remembered the almost forgotten opening day. 'Whoops, back to work. Nicky, can you help me do the tour of our guests, and if there is no other business, best to see them on their way.'

Nicola left Victoria sitting with Benny. They seemed to be chatting amongst themselves simply fine. Victoria had played her hand a bit over the top. But, on the other hand, it would need an exceptional performance to get the attention of such a man.

A good-looking man, nice manners, and delightfully rich. Hopefully, he would be bored with the gold diggers of this world, looking for someone with substance. He had answered the last question with some gravitas. Was he really looking for a family?

With the last of the guests finally gone, Malcolm slumped down on his sofa in time to receive a much-needed coffee from Rita. Victoria requested two coffees and one for Nicola.

'Congratulations Malcolm,' said Benny. 'A successful afternoon I trust?' 'Nicky, what's the score? I think we did quite well.'

Nicola replied she had eight firm offers, to be signed off as soon as the paperwork was ready, and ten strong indications of interest, which she would follow-up as soon as possible. She also had confirmation from the Lady Margret as to her true intentions.

Nicola always knew the Lady Margret would delay in becoming a shareholder in the business. To be fair, both Nicola and Victoria had struggled to find the format for an agreement which would match her thinking. Nicola proposed she should buy a number of properties per one million dollars at the standard specification.

Nicola and Victoria would set-up a local LLC company to manage the rental and management of the properties for a suitable fee. This proposal would bring the Lady Margret on board, enhance the backlog of properties to constructed, and give them a business to obtain US business visas, which looked like the quickest way to go.

Malcolm looked impressed, asking how many millions of US dollars the lady could invest. Nicola reckoned at least two, depending upon price, maybe the five million she had so extravagantly suggested in English Harbour.

'We had best come up with a figure soon then,' suggested Malcolm. 'Victoria can you work your magic on a spreadsheet soon.'

'Of course,' Victoria replied. 'It's going to be somewhere in the region of three properties per million dollars, with one, maybe, two years free condominium charges to sweeten the deal.'

'Time for a wee celebration,' suggested Malcolm. 'I'll get some drinks organised; there's plenty of snacks left over.'

'We can do better than this,' said Nicola, 'I would like to introduce you and Benny to a special wine we brought across the Atlantic. It has a special story.'

Victoria asked Rita to bring the bottle of wine resting on the sideboard since the previous evening. She wondered how the wine had travelled across the Atlantic. Sr. Vicente, when he discovered the two girls were going to take a case of his special wine aboard a yacht, had winced, declaring a sea voyage would bruise the wine and would require a lot of TLC before drinking.

Rita returned with the art deco bottle, opened it, and left it to breathe a little before serving. She retreated to the kitchen only to return with fresh wine glasses and tumblers of ice-cold water.

Rita served the water first and then the wine. Malcolm and Benny drank the cool water to prepare their taste buds for a new experience. They examined, then sipped the wine and waited to come to a conclusion. They agreed it was a special wine. Benny asked if it was a garage wine. Nicola smiled a yes at him.

'What would you say would be the retail value of this wine?' he asked.

Now here was a question which interested everybody. Nicola and Victoria only knew the selling price Duke Marmaduke had suggested. What would be the price this side of the Atlantic?

Nicola turned around to opinion such a wine in the USA collectors' market would be plus two hundred US dollar a bottle.

Malcolm's mouth fell open. Benny said nothing. They both repeated the procedure to re-taste the wine. Benny requested a refill, closely followed by Malcolm. Their glasses quickly drained for the second time. Nicola nudged Victoria in the ribs with her elbow, leant over and whispered in her ear, 'Count to twenty, and let's see what happens next.'

Rita looked across the room at the two girls and saw them plotting and whispering. What secrets were they sharing? She took another deep sip of the wine and a big smile spread across her broad face.

'Are you two gentlemen going to take these two lovely ladies out for dinner, or what?' asked Rita forcefully.

Rita had counted the number of Pimms No. 1 they had consumed and now they were on their third glass of Nicola's special wine.

'You want to step out Benny?' asked Malcolm. 'Rita can put together some very tasty Portuguese dishes, perhaps a side salad, with ice cream to follow.'

'Works for me my good friend,' said Benny in an increasingly mellow mood. Nicola nudged Victoria again, whispering, 'Tonight will be someone's lucky night.' 'Nicola darling,' said Malcolm. Victoria started giggling.

'What's up with her?' he asked.

'Oh, nothing,' said Nicola, trying hard not to start giggling too.

Benny asked if Nicola had any more of the wine. Victoria answered, 'Well Benny, we shipped a whole case with us when we left Portugal. Nicky's great aunt has two bottles, I gave one to Sir Henry in English Harbour, and this one is finished, so we have eight bottles left, with one upstairs. The remainder are resting on Moody Blue.

Benny decided they would stay in. The evening had promise. So little did he know? Nicola suggested they slow down a little. Yes, the wine was strong, but she chose not to elaborate any further.

Rita smiled to herself and set off for the kitchen. Benny asked Nicola for details of the wine, how much was there, could one purchase more? Nicola told him the vineyard had sufficient for roughly ten thousand bottles or eight hundred cases but two thousand bottles were going to be laid down in monastery cellars for at least five years, maybe longer.

Her Uncle Adam's good friend, one Duke Marmaduke, in cahoots with a Mr Prince Eugen, had purchased the entire safra and paid a deposit for the next year's safra.

Benny gently asked if she could acquire ten cases. He confided one of his businesses specialised in selling upmarket food and drink products to a discrete clientele.

Nicola took a few moments to explain the tripartite set-up between the Lady Pamela, who owned the vineyard 'Quinta de Souza Henrique do Douro,' Augusto 'de Oliviera, owner of the 'de Oliviera Port Ltda, and Mr Duke Marmaduke, a resolute retailer of classic wines to the nobles, gentry, and mug punters of this world.

'So, my dear Benjamin, if I put you in contact with Mr Marmaduke, you will get exclusive access to his sources of supply, can't say fairer than that.'

'Thank you very much Nicola. This would be very much appreciated. One question, what is the cost of this 'vin de garage' in the UK?

Nicola smiled sweetly and said, 'One thousand British pounds per case of twelve, net, plus tax if applicable or unavoidable, and delivery.'

'You have got to be kidding,' he replied.

'No Benny. Garage wines, low production, the highest quality, seriously high prices. Most go to collectors, usually as a financial hedge against movements in whatever market they were trying to plunder. This wine has other qualities, but I will leave you on your voyage of discovery.'

The last statement should have been a warning, but Benny had reached a level of tranquillity he rarely achieved.

'Anyway, Vicky and I will go and change out of uniform, into something more, err relaxing. We won't be long.'

Nicola took Victoria by the hand and took her upstairs. Victoria started to ask questions about the remainder of the evening, but Nicola soothed her concerns suggesting she take a twenty-second shower, not get her hair wet, and dress quickly.

'Are we hunting tonight Nicola?' asked Victoria.

'I am, and you should too. He really likes you, and you really like him, so don't fuck up, please.'

During the interval, Malcolm had a quiet word with Benny, just as Nicola had asked him to. Malcolm was worried his words may affect the moment.

FIFTEEN MINUTES LATER, and an all-time record for sure, the two girls descended the staircase in matching red and black, party dresses, stopping just above the knee, vee-neck, complimented by moderately high heel ankle strap shoes, matching earrings, and necklace. With their hair up and minimal make-up, their mid-Atlantic suntan was there to be seen.

Malcolm almost dropped his drink. Benny just looked, not knowing quite what to think. Nicola placed a second art deco bottle on the sideboard, fetched fresh classes, filled them up and served everybody with fresh wine and fresh chilled water from the ornate crystal glass decanter.

Glass in hand, Nicola eased herself gently onto Malcolm's lap and put an arm around his neck.

'Is this the killer blow?' he asked, smiling.

'Prepare to be reborn, Darling,' she replied and gave him a big kiss.

Victoria moved to sit on Benny's lap, apologised for being forward, put his free arm around her shoulders, stating this was the best seat in the house to watch Malcolm and Nicola for whatever came next. Benny felt her cute bottom on his knees. She felt and smelt wonderful; he wasn't about to complain.

'Malcolm,' said Victoria, 'When you come up for air; remember your lines.' 'I haven't got any lines,' he replied.

'OK, after me,' said Victoria. 'Nicola darling, I love you very much and I want you to be my wonderful wife. Say it slowly and with meaning.'

Malcolm looked helplessly at Benny but received no support.

'Just say the words, Malcolm, you may as well. The end of a good day.'

'And the start of a good night. This wine is working very well,' thought Nicola. Malcolm said the words. Word perfect, he even meant them. God this felt good.

'Is there a ring Malcolm?' asked Benny. 'My spies tell me you have been visiting certain jewellery shops.'

This was news to Nicola. Malcolm said he had indeed been looking in certain jewellery shops, for a tie pin, to which Benny replied, 'Bullshit,' here is a ring, it should fit. Take the lady tomorrow to choose her engagement ring unless you have a family heirloom to recycle.'

Victoria took the ring; it was made of shiny brass. She handed it over to Malcolm supervising the fitting of the ring on to the anointed finger. She quickly returned to Benny's vacant knee.

'Congratulations old man,' said Benny. 'Well done, you two are a perfect match.' 'Well thanks, Benny, now it's your turn.'

Victoria turned to face Benny, her eyes wide open, her lips ready to pounce, with hurry-up written all over her face.

'Are these spontaneous and unplanned moments, Malcolm,' asked Benny.

'Absolutely, a man of your advanced age cannot afford to waste time and a wonderful opportunity,' smiled Malcolm.

'I hardly know the girl,' countered Benny.

'Victoria comes pre-approved. We have sailed the seven seas together. Spent midnight watches discussing all manner of interesting subjects,' chided Malcolm. 'She can match you for sure.'

Nicola smiled in approval, stared at Benny, and simply said, 'Just say the words, Benny, become a happier man.'

Benny took another sip from his wine glass. Nicola whispered to Malcolm he was hesitating. Malcolm whispered Benny was just weighing up his options.

'He doesn't have any,' whispered Nicola.

'Victoria, darling,' started Benny, 'Would you like to accompany me to my jewellers tomorrow?'

Victoria uttered a sharp squeak.

Malcolm told Benny, 'Just say the words man. Today, tomorrow, next week, it's a goin' to happen. Don't delay, be brave.'

Benny took a deep breath, 'Victoria. My darling, I wish to solicit your heartfelt approval of my sincere and honest proposal of matrimony, to have and to hold, on a regular basis, give me heirs and love me forever?'

'Gosh, blimey, cor blimey lov' a duck,' said Victoria. Eliza Doolittle had returned. 'Vicky,' shouted Nicola across the room.

'Dearest Benny,' started Victoria, in her best natural voice, 'Excuse me. The answer is YES, you wonderful man, kisses coming.'

'Supper is served,' called Rita. 'If you're hungry that is?'

Malcolm and Nicola rose. The evening was running out fast, time to progress matters. Victoria struggled to release herself from Benny. Benny was in a world of his own, but he felt Victoria holding his hand, taking him to the table.

Rita collected the half empty wine glasses to put them out of the way on top of the sideboard.

'You folks best drink the cool clear water before retiring rather than drinking any more of this wine,' she said, and disappeared upstairs.

The two couples ate their supper while Rita fussed around them. Her's was a busy day and she was keen to relax and go to bed. She could see the happy faces of everyone and enjoyed using her people skills to determine who was thinking of what.

The meal ended, but there seemed to be a little reluctance as to who would be the first to retire to bed.

Nicola took the lead, 'OK guys, time to end the day. Benny, I'm sure you will want to stay the night and keep Victoria company. Malcolm, come along you've had a tiring week, tomorrow is Saturday, a day of rest.'

Benny tried to make his excuses, but couldn't find his car keys, which was not surprising as Rita had hidden them in the sideboard cutlery drawer. He tried to pretend to be a gentleman, he would sleep in a spare bedroom, but as he rose from the table, Victoria took him by the arm leading him to the foot of the stairs.

'Benny, darling, what do you see if you look upwards,' she said. 'The top of the stairs. What do you see?' he asked.

'The future silly; now come along. Happiness is waiting for us,' whispered Victoria. 'Victoria,' said Nicola. 'What a wonderful sentiment, don't you think Malcolm?' 'Wonderful indeed,' he replied. 'Let us all march up the stairs together to our futures.' Nicola and I will lead the way. At the top of the stairs, we will sway to the right, and

Benny, you will sway to the left. Everything is prepared.'

The two couples started to march slowly up the stairs, but halfway the pace had picked up. As Malcolm and Nicola reached the top, they stopped, waited for a hesitant Benny to usher Victoria to her future.

Victoria took Benny by the hand and led a willing victim to the second master bedroom. As they entered, they both stood to stare at the delicate and sensuous lighting system, a mixture of discrete LED pin lights, changing in a swirl of different colours, and an exceptionally soft light bathing the wall behind the huge double bed. Scented candles slowly burned on glass shelves over his and hers dressing tables.

'Wonderful, eh! Darling, how romantic, how restful. How could we ever leave?' Benny held Victoria around the waist, gave her a huge kiss and a hug.

'You do the bathroom thing, and I will try to undo my blasted shoelaces,' said Benny, as Victoria rapidly disappeared into the spacious and elegantly equipped bathroom.

In no time, she had showered, changed, slipped into a dressing gown, emerged, and headed straight for the nearest side of the double bed and sat on its side.

Benny waited for her to get into bed, but Victoria sat still and shooed him into the bathroom. When he emerged, showered, and wearing only his boxer shorts, he found Victoria in bed, the dressing gown on the floor, the top of the Egyptian cotton sheet drawn up tightly under her chin, her arms crossed in front of her.

Benny slowly made his way to her, standing still for a moment. She looked up at him and said, 'What a fine figure of a man you are Benny. Come to bed.'

Benny lifted up the cotton sheet, to find Victoria wearing a nothing of a baby doll nightdress. Her knickers had two small bows on either side, so one tug would release them from their duty.

'Wow,' said Benny, 'Just wow. Vicky, you are so beautiful. Like the emergency release on the knickers.'

Victoria held his hand as she pulled him into bed and whispered, 'These are my American knickers. One Yank and they're off.'

'You are a temptress, the wicked witch of the north,' he muttered, as he climbed in beside her.

'No, I'm not Benny Jets. I come from the posh part of Surrey, where all the Arab Sheiks live, so there.'

Benny burst out laughing. This girl was different. He found himself madly in love with her cranky ways. But she was as intelligent as she was sexy. Benny rolled on top of her, kissing her madly as she wriggled under him. Hands started to wander into the usual places. Both were consumed by their passion for each other.

Victoria called time and rolled Benny on to his back. 'Now lay still for a moment lover,' she said, as she slowly and seductively straddled the now helpless male.

'Enjoying the view, Darling,' she cooed. 'Absolutely,' replied Benny.

'The top of my nightdress has a little bow, perhaps you would like to give it a little tug,' she whispered.

'Certainly,' whispered Benny. 'There this is better.'

Victoria kept still for a moment, she hesitated slightly. This would be a big moment after all she had been through. Benny looked serene and relaxed. She felt his hard manhood beneath her, time to find out how the future lay.

She placed his hands on her bottom, as he started to tease her by kissing her nipples. She wriggled some more as he arched his back. She moved his left hand to her side; he grasped the tape which would undo the bow and gave it a playful tug.

They kissed some more, and more, as Victoria leant forward and used her hand to assist his manhood into her. Slowly, but oh so gently, she sat up as he entered her. It hurt at first, but not too much. She should have used the tube of gel someone had left under the pillow.

She sat up, holding on to his hands. His hands were strong but gentle. She held his hands at the side of her body, then moved them behind her. The sensation of pleasure started to grow within her as he fondled her bottom. The Benny moved his hands to her breasts and the sensation of pleasure rose even stronger.

Slowly but surely their movement increased, Victoria tried to make the moment last, but Benny was coming on stronger and stronger. Their passion climaxed at the same moment in time, with both taking deep breaths to recover.

Victoria began kissing Benny more passionately than before, she rested, the side of her face next to his. She lay there, starting to sob; then the tears flowed. She startled herself.

'What is wrong Darling? That was wonderful. Why are you crying,' whispered Benny? 'Let me dry your tears.'

Victoria sobbed more tears. She couldn't understand her emotion. Benny used the corner of her baby doll nightdress to dry her eyes. She lay on top of him, gathering herself, then she realised.

'Benny darling, it's OK,' she whispered. 'It's just because I'm so happy. It's never happened before.'

'That's OK, I understand,' replied Benny. 'Just take your time. You'll be OK in a minute, drink some of this special wine.'

'Oh no,' Victoria replied. 'The wine is for you. I have some cool water here.'

Victoria emptied her glass of water, leaving Benny to wonder what was so special about this wine. Getting laid with an expensive wine, was very well, but it occurred he had enjoyed almost two bottles. It had an effect, but for the life of him he couldn't fathom out what it was.

Victoria lay down beside him as Benny refreshed himself with the last of the wine. He drank a little water to chase it down. He rested, lying beside this wonderful woman, who had come through so much, and now she was his.

Or was it the other way around. Hum, he thought, a new experience for sure.

After he rested a while, his erection came back stronger than ever. He saw her lying there, waiting, with a deep smile within her.

'Seconds?' he whispered.

'Oh goody,' she replied, and lay still on her back, her arms above her head. 'Come on tiger, your turn.'

Benny needed no second invitation, and their second love making excelled. It was as meaningful as the first. Benny felt happy and fulfilled. He had waited a long time for the right lady to come into his life.

It had been a long wait. His previous attempts at love making had been marred by caution, always seeking that which he found today. No more being pestered by star struck females interested more in his worldly goods than his worldly manhood.

A few women he had not treated so kindly but having sex whilst the female was practising her mental arithmetic was not the goal he wished. Yet, here he was in less than twenty-four hours thinking this was the girl for him.

Damn, this wine was good. He wondered why he kept thinking about the wine. Was there a secret?

He fancied so, but how to find out. These two English ladies were smart as well as cute. He found himself looking forward to improving his mental agility.

He looked down at his wife to be. She was fast asleep, her face a picture of contentment. Was that a smile of triumph on her face? If it was, she deserved it. He had been conquered, but his time would come.

She said she wanted children and this would make his life complete.

NICKY HAD TOLD Benny Victoria was a hundred percent. The doctors she mentioned were two of the very best. One of them, Nicola's uncle, would soon marry his Lady Pamela. He wondered what she looked like. Another smart-arse Brit with nice tits, what else.

The two of them slept until dawn. As Benny got up, he ran into Victoria as she was coming out of the bathroom. She had showered, with her wonderful hair up in a bun to protect it from the task of getting it dry.

'Hello, lover, fancy meeting you here. Want me to wash your back?' she cooed.

And with that, she found herself back in the shower. This love making was not slated to last long, and it didn't.

'Gosh, you are strong this morning Benny. Finish off; I'll be back in a jiffy.'

Victoria returned wearing her baby doll night dress, her knickers hanging on by just one side, and wearing her high heel ankle strap shoes. She was carrying what looked suspiciously like a waterproof camera. She switched on all the lights in the bathroom, stood at the sliding door into the shower cubicle, in an interesting pose, one arm above her head holding onto the glass side of the entrance. Her other hand parked on her hip.

'Now take the shot, I have to see what this comes out like.'

A clean Benny wrapped a large bath towel around his waist, wondering what the hell was going on. But this was fun, time to find out. He took a series of photographs and handed the camera back to Victoria. She went and sat on the side of the bed, examining the photographs.

As she scrolled through the photographs, she stopped at the last but one photograph. It was wonderful, for sure.

'And now for the magic moment,' Victoria said, 'Mirror, mirror on the wall, who is the fairest of them all,' as she scrolled to the first photograph in the camera's memory chip.

'Not bad,' she said. 'Almost, but not quite. But she hadn't been angry or pretending to be as angry, as the lady in the first photograph.

Victoria showed him the first photograph. He whistled a 'wow', what a lady, dressed like his bride to be. He looked at her, waiting for an explanation.

'This Darling, is the Lady Pamela, who had just had her passionate love making disturbed by her loving daughter.

The daughter thought it a clever idea to bug her mother's bedroom whilst she cemented her relationship with Nicola's Uncle Adam, just hours after he had proposed to her. She was spitting mad, but it soon subsided when she felt Adam's eyes burning into her behind.'

Benny could just see a male face lying in bed at the back of a large colonial bedroom, with a look of anticipation all over his face, drinking a glass of red wine from a similar ornate handcrafted bottle. Now he understood about the wine.

They got back into bed, as Victoria delighted in telling Benny the whole story from the time Uncle Adam, Nicola and herself boarded the ferry for the journey up the river Douro.

The story finished with the show put on by one 'Prince' Eugen and Mr Duke Marmaduke and the saga of the 'Pamela Collection', fast gaining traction in the classic car world.

'What classic car collection?' asked Benny.

'Oh, it's a nice collection. Her late husband turned spare cash, or spare wine, into long-term investments in cars. When we arrived, she was close to having a fire sale just to stay afloat with her horrible bank manager,' replied Victoria. 'Pass me my iPad; there is a list and a few photographs.'

Benny had started a car collection of his own. Shrewd car purchases could be very profitable. On the plus side, showing a car at the many classic car shows around America was a nice hobby and an excellent way to meet new friends.

Victoria gave her iPad to Benny, set at the first page of the file holding the information he sought. He read the two lists of cars and let out a long slow whistle. He zeroed in on the Maserati, a genuine Maserati Mille Miglia, a very rare motor car.

'Vicky, what can you tell me about the Maserati?' said Benny looking hard at the photographs.

'It's a car nobody knows about. How Pamela's late husband came by it is a mystery. It was thought it was a straight swap, wine for the car. It is the last of the last, all original, matching numbers. The factory won't talk about it, so it is reckoned to be one the brothers had made for personal use. It has the most powerful engine of any of the era, about 1956, but like I said nobody knows, which means nobody knows the price, as its never come to market.'

'You seem to know a lot about cars, Darling, pray tell,' asked Benny

'Not a lot to tell. I have a Formula Ford licence and a Formula Three licence. It lets me race other formulas, the BMW formula, for example. I couldn't keep it up. Too busy at work; not enough time and money to race properly.

I tried rally cars, but that's even more lunatic. I have an expired Group N licence, but all that happens is you end up scaring 'ten bells' out of you, and human fragility becomes more than apparent.

Then, the phone rang, Nicola's cross voice said, 'Vicky, it's for you.' Victoria took the call.

'Hello ducks, Prince here, am I disturbing you?' 'Quack,' replied Victoria.

'Very funny,' said Prince. 'Can I 'ave a word in your shell-like?'

'Prince, I am in the USA. It exists on the other side of the pond. Do the words 'time zone' mean anything to you?'

'Sorry, ducks, should have thought,' replied Prince. Quack,' replied Victoria.

'OK, ok, but now you're here, how are you doin. When can we get married?'

'I'll check your wife's diary to see when you need to attend the divorce hearing. She'll want everything you own, including your hide. If you have a question, out with it. I'm in bed with my fiancé, and he's waiting.'

'Waiting for?' replied Prince.

'You're the one with four kids. Why don't you tell me?' chided Victoria.

'Look darlin, I got a geezer 'ho wants to buy Lady Pamela's Maserati and no one can give me a price.'

'I am not in the least surprised, as there are none in the marketplace. The only true test is to auction it with no reserve at one of the posh auction houses in America or Paris and see what happens. Then, you run the risk of a 'concert party', where you will get stitched up, or an auction with a reserve price of say 'x' millions, but it won't sell because the buyer will want an after-the-hours auction deal.

So, is the buyer a 'flipper' or a genuine collector.'

'Good question Luv. Can't make 'im out. Could be either, hard to say,' replied Prince. 'And how much cash is this punter offering, just tell me. Then I can give you a better

guess.'

'Million Euros, 'ow does this sound?' asked Prince.

'The last of the two brother's pride and joy, no way sunshine,' said Victoria, 'You examined the car yourself so you should have a better idea than me.'

'Well, I must admit I don't know for certain; do you have a gut feel?'

'OK Prince put your head around this scenario. The car has very few miles, it has never been registered, and the factory will not talk about it. So, let us assume it was a factory-built car for one of the two brothers before they departed from the company.

The car has a fuel injection system which looks suspiciously German, so the factory may have been developing their own system using other's technology. It's a sixteen-valve engine, and it could be a blown engine with little difficulty, so it all adds up. For some reason, the factory didn't want to have the car out in the open, so it's never been raced, or in fact, used.

Somehow, it arrives in the hands of Pamela's ex-husband. His mechanic, Sr. Antonio, told me the car was close to priceless. Why did he say that? For sure he will not tell. The memory and trust of his dearly beloved master is very strong with this guy.

So, unless your client knows something nobody else does, then a million Euros is not a bad offer. If someone wants to take a punt on buying it, only because eventually the full providence will become known, then the price could go anywhere. Otherwise, it's just an exceptionally beautiful historic car.'

Benny sat listening to Victoria's very professional view of the subject. If desire; and not commercial considerations were the driving force, the car could be worth buying with the upside being the chance gaining of full providence. Perhaps he could find an Italian contact who could help him.

What to do? He was very tempted. He had looked through the Pamela Collection, and it occurred if he could put a package together, he might just get way ahead of the market, and get the cars he needed for his collection.

'Victoria darling, can I speak to Mr Prince?' Victoria handed the telephone over.

'Mr Eugen, this is Mr Benny Jets Vincens speaking,' started Benny. 'I understand you are very friendly with my fiancé. I have been looking at what is known as the Pamela Collection, is there a suggested price guidance for the vehicles listed?'

'Good morning Sir, nice to make your acquaintance,' replied Prince in his very best mid-Surrey accent. 'Once again sorry for the early hour.'

Victoria stifled a big giggle. Prince had defaulted to 'posh punters salesmanship' mode. 'I have heard rumours you are starting a collection, so how may I be of assistance?'

Benny thought for a moment, requesting a suggested price guide, adding he could be interested in five vehicles. The collection would be for personal use. 'Are we talking driving cars or 'trailer queens?' asked Prince.

Benny replied both, as there were car shows close to his main residence in Florida, and the more distant shows would be best by covered road transport.

'One for the lady?' asked Prince.

Benny replied he would think about it. The cars of interest were the 3.8 Litre 'E' Type, if it was truly one of the first twenty of the factory hand-built models, the Maserati, the Fiat with the Ferrari engine, and the 1931 Rolls-Royce Phantom II with the soft top.

Prince whistled to himself, some order. He would have to work hard on this one. Benny asked him a direct question, 'How much commission would he make on the sale?'

Prince replied Lady Pamela was family, and he didn't charge

commission to the family, only expenses and incidentals.

Prince asked if he wished a cash price, invoiced amount, terms, transport, and insurance costs. He added all the cars were being brought to the highest standard, and he had two of his best mechanics camped out at the vineyard these last two weeks.

Benny was impressed, this man knew his business if nothing else. Prince asked to speak to Victoria and Benny handed her the telephone.

'Thanks, Ducks, and don't say quack, just this once,' said Prince.

'Quack,' replied Victoria, she could hear Prince wince at the other end of the line.

'OK, do me a favour. Duke would like to contact Benny about importing upmarket wines; can you help me with that?'

'Of course, Prince, time to get busy, bye bye, and she rang-off.

'Impressive start to the day Darling,' said Victoria. 'Prince will look after you. He is very honest with people he likes and trusts. You managed him beautifully and now you are family.

I feel so glad for Pamela; she really came through a bad spell with flying colours. Uncle Adam is so good for her. She will become a formidable lady.'

Benny, remembering the photograph thinking she didn't have far to go.

The happy couple dressed for the day and went downstairs. At the bottom, Benny turned around and said to himself, 'Thank you stairs,' and marched towards the breakfast table.

Benny was hungry and needed to recharge himself. This coming day would bring more stairs to climb.

Chapter 23

The Seybold Jewellery Building

VICTORIA ASKED RITA as she arrived at the breakfast table with a tray laden with juices, cereals, and hot toast for breakfast.

'Any signs of the happy couple?' she asked.

'Nope, last I heard was moaning and a shriek, which was fifteen minutes ago,' she replied. 'That's OK, she won't be long,' giggled Victoria.

'Don't count on it.'

The house interphone rang. Victoria picked it up; it was the gate guard.

'Excuse me, madam, there is an elderly Scottish lady asking for a Miss Nicola or Miss Victoria. She's a bit impatient. I explained the rules on security, but . . .'

'That's OK, does the lady have luggage?' asked Victoria.

'Yah,' a large carpet handbag and an ex-military suitcase in brown leather fitted with little wheels,' replied the gate man.

'Christ, it's Great Aunt Violet. What in God's name is she doing here? Please bring her over and make sure you carry her bags if she will let you.'

Victoria put the phone down, panic stations. A voice drifted down from the top of the stairs, 'Malcolm wants to know who the hell that was,' croaked Nicola.

'Nobody important, just Great Aunt Violet,' shouted back Victoria.

The words 'for Christ's sake,' were the only words that filtered down from the top of the stairs. The doorbell rang, two seconds before it became assaulted by the curved end of someone's stout wooden walking stick.

Rita rushed to open the door and ushered in Great Aunt Violet, her long but comfortable flight had been ruined by the lack of her previously ordered taxi.

'Good morning Victoria, how are you?' she demanded.

'Just about to have breakfast, your timing is perfect,' consoled Victoria, as she gave Great Aunt Violet a big hug.

'Huh,' came the reply, 'And this would-be Mr Benjamin Vincens?'

'Yes Ma'am,' he replied.

'A fine-looking lad. You going to make an honest woman of my Victoria,' asked Great Aunt Violet.

'We got engaged last night Aunty,' Victoria hastened to add.

'He can speak, can't he? Answer the question young man,' ordered Great Aunt Violet. 'Yes Ma'am. I believe this will be my pleasure in the future,' replied Benny.

'Like the brass ring on your finger Victoria. Is that his Roller outside?' asked Great Aunt Violet.

'What Roller? I haven't been outside since yesterday morning before the open day started,' replied Victoria.

'Where's my layabout niece,' demanded Great Aunt Violet. 'Hello Great Aunt Violet, what a delightful surprise.'

The voice of Nicola came from the top of the stairs, in a slightly stronger tone than her first attempt of communication that morning.

Nicola started to descend, only to be told to stop. Nicola looked puzzled as Great Aunt Violet stared at her.

'Hold on to the safety rail child,' commanded Great Aunt Violet. 'A girl in your condition should know better.'

'What condition would this be Great Aunt Violet? I didn't drink that much last night,' came the lame reply.

'Is this another brass ring on your finger, the other hand girl, the left one,' asked Great Aunt Violet

'Yes, Great Aunt Violet, I became engaged to Malcolm last night too,' said Nicola.

'Just in time. Don't want any children without dotting fathers in my family,' said Great Aunt Violet.

Nicola blushed. Deep coloured suntan or no deep coloured suntan, she went bright red. She started to descend the stairs holding on to the safety rail.

Victoria looked shocked, 'You mean she is pregnant Aunty?'

'Two to three weeks at least. Bout' time too, keeping an old lady like me waiting all this time,' said Great Aunt Violet smiling.

Nicola came to Great Aunt Violet to give her a big hug.

'You wonderful girl Nicola,' said Great Aunt Violet with just one tear in her eye, 'You two look so beautiful, the sea voyage did you the world of good. The bad past behind you?'

'What bad past, we only have wonderful futures here in this house.'

Malcolm made an appearance, fortunately, dressed for the day. He normally didn't bother, forever wandering the house alone in his underwear, not considered by any observers as modern.

'What's all the fuss, there's too much noise for my liking,' he mumbled.

Malcolm looked tired, as well he might. It had been a long hard week, and an even longer night.

'Darling,' started Nicola, 'A great surprise. This is my Great Aunt Violet, just arrived from God knows where.'

'God's country Malcolm. I have come from Gods' country,' stated Great Aunt Violet forcefully.

'I thought you lived in Scotland,' mumbled Malcolm.

'Same thing Malcolm. How do you like being a father?' demanded Great Aunt Violet. 'That's news to me,' he said sleepily, 'Nicola?'

'Nothing definite, I'm a week late in my usual, that's all. I might get a test next week, I doubt if it's anything to worry about,' she said.

'Twins, a boy and girl. Never been wrong in sixty year, and I am not about to start now. Nicola has made me very happy, so wake up the joy of fatherhood,' stated Great Aunt Violet.

Malcolm started at all around him muttering, 'I either need a hair of the dog or my breakfast or both. Rita! Two eggs easy over, bacon, sausage, hash browns, fried tomato, and mushrooms. Come on everyone, breakfast. Time to start the new day.'

Rita arrived at the breakfast table with a large tray laden with a genuine cooked breakfast.

Victoria rushed to be first. She filled two plates to full, sat Benny down next to her, and plonked the two plates down. Nicola served Great Aunt Violet her usual of eggs on toast, with a grilled tomato.

Malcolm sat down, apparently in shock. Fatherhood: just where had this come from?

Nicola finished serving her great aunt, filled a plate for Malcolm, gave him a big kiss on the forehead and told him to eat up.

'Great Aunt Violet, and how many weeks do you think this wonderful news has been with us?' asked Benny.

'Three weeks, must have been at sea?' said Great Aunt Violet.

'Great Aunt Violet, just eat your breakfast. Malcolm looks like he's in shock,' said Nicola. 'You don't look surprised young lady. Now that is a fact,' said Great Aunt Violet.

Victoria thought, 'You witch. Always the killer blow.'

Nicola's sea time 'bouncy castle' routine had produced a result she wasn't expecting. If Nicola had recovered so soon, Christ, after last night, she could be next.

Both Uncle Adam and Professor Samuelson had cautioned their

systems would bounce back as soon as they were well. Both specialists had pronounced twins could be the probable result for either of them in the case of conception. Hell's teeth, after last night?

Victoria found Great Aunt Violet staring at her. 'And did we celebrate our engagement last night Victoria?' she asked.

'Just a little,' came the tentative reply. Great Aunt Violet gaze switched instantly to Benny. After a short pause she said, 'Benjamin, we must play poker one evening.'

Benny smiled. Yes, he did play poker and was particularly good at it. Being a successful businessman had helped hone his senses and ability to calculate the odds.

The interview continued, 'Now Benjamin, did my favourite Victoria ask you any questions last night, the eight questions, and what did we answer?'

Benny answered with a straight face, 'No, No, Yes, No, Yes, No-I think, Yes, and Yes.' Victoria cringed.

Great Aunt Violet beamed, 'So, twins for you too. Fantastic,' she said.

'Great Aunt Violet, have you been interrogating our medical advisors, on certain matters that are supposed to be confidential,' said Nicola.

'It's my job, no my craft, my trade to discover confidential secrets,' stated Great Aunt Violet, 'From the willing and the not so willing.'

Nicola knew what this meant but hoped the others didn't. Benny poker face said it all.

As breakfast came to a close, Nicola asked about a plan for the rest of the day. Nobody said a word. Benny and Malcolm were still thinking about last night, realising there were still more stairs to be climbed.

Victoria was in heaven, and Nicola had to contend with Great Aunt Violet's announcement about the condition she was supposed to have. On the basis Great Aunt Violet had never been wrong, and her usual had not arrived in time, and her bust had started to swell, it all suggested a re-examination of the realities of life.

After what could only be described as a pregnant pause, Benny commenced by suggesting the following programme, despite doubts crawling their way over his inner tranquillity.

'Can I suggest,' he started calmly enough, 'That when we are ready, we complete the programme started last night, this is to say, the choosing of the engagement rings.

By then, lunch will become of interest. I have a reservation at my club to confirm. Great Aunt Violet can come with us to the jewellers. Or she can rest-up to recover, I will send a driver to pick her up to bring her to our rendezvous for lunch, say two in the afternoon?'

The group sat and thought about it. The staircase looked pretty steep to Victoria. She held her council. Eventually, after being nudged in the ribs by Nicola, Malcolm put his hand up and said, 'Splendid idea,' as Nicola held his other hand up to match her hand similarly deployed Victoria smiled at Benny and raised both hands. Benny returned the smile pronouncing a done deal.

BENNY WENT OUTSIDE to move his 1964 Rolls-Royce Silver Cloud III, a two-door coupe with a soft top, his absolute pride and joy, from the rising sun and back it under the porch connecting the extensive double garages to the side of the house. He took a change of clothing from his automobile and collected Victoria on the way back to the master suite to rest, relax and prepare for the next event.

'You are kind of quiet Victoria,' he said as he closed the bedroom door behind him, 'Everything OK?'

Victoria looked at him answering, 'This is a wild ride, and I'm trying not to fall off.

Otherwise, yes, I'm just fine. Help me. Stay by my side and just hold me, nothing more.'

Benny could see Victoria looking overwhelmed. She was a brave girl, trying to be brave in a strange country. Well, America anyway. But she didn't look weak, a bit tired perhaps, but then they did have a wonderful night together. Time to pace things a bit slower.

Benny made up the bed and laid Victoria on the eiderdown, putting a fresh pillow under her head. She looked serene and beautiful. Her beauty began to chase away his doubts. Still, today would show the way ahead. He thought it best to relax and lay down beside her. He lay there, her head on his shoulder, holding her left hand, stroked the back of it, toying with the brass ring on her ring finger.

He wondered what she would choose. He knew what many women would choose, but he suspected he was going to be either surprised or impressed. It suddenly occurred to him Victoria had never enquired about his obvious wealth.

He was almost a billionaire, but he never mentioned it. Wealth was not his driving force. Doing good works in the community made him feel good, but keeping people employed in his businesses drove him the most.

An hour later, they rose to prepare themselves. Benny opened the bedroom door. There appeared to be activity below, then Malcolm shouted out Nicola and he were ready.

'The brave bastard,' he thought. 'In for a penny, in for a pound.'

He woke Victoria and hurried her along. She didn't take long, and he found her at the top of the staircase waiting for him.

'If this goes wrong,' he thought, 'Time to buy a bungalow.'

They descended arm in arm, to the clapping of Malcolm, his bride to be, and her redoubtable great aunt. They went outside to Benny's waiting limousine.

Benny bid Malcolm sit in the plush back seat of the Rolls-Royce with his wife-elect and mother to be, Miss Nicola Stranraer.

Next, he guided Victoria to sit in what he called the navigator's seat.

He felt at home in his Rolls-Royce. It had served him well for many years and despite frequent calls from the Florida Rolls-Royce agent to upgrade to the latest offering he had resisted. The Rolls-Royce set off on a voyage of hope. A hope the day would go well.

The Rolls-Royce headed to downtown Miami, to the Seybold Jewellery Building, Florida's premiere jewellery centre, and the second largest jewellery building in the US.

In this building, Benny had access to his own jeweller, a very discrete business with an exclusive clientele. There was no name on this door. One had to be invited and many were the rich and famous waiting for their invitation.

As they arrived at the Seybold Building, Benny handed the car keys to the valet parking concierge and proceeded inside. Nicola was hugging Malcolm, who looked a little wan. Victoria gilded with grace alongside her intended husband. They reached the entrance of the premises with no name. The door opened before the call button could be pressed.

A manager politely showed them to a reception area; to await the owner and his co-partner. Blue mountain coffee, ice-cold water and Greek sweetmeats arrived on a silver tray served by a well-dressed Chinese lady, the owner's wife. The connections with Hong Kong were everywhere in the room, from the rare and beautiful dark green jade statues to delicate Chinese ornaments.

The owner and his partner arrived and after a little small talk, the two couples were separated and shown into separate rooms.

Benny muttered a low level, 'Best of luck,' to Malcolm.

The owner looked at Victoria to see if he could guess her tastes in jewellery but came to no conclusion. Victoria politely declined all rings with a high setting stone.

Victoria described the ring she wished as a three stone ring with equal settings, three centre settings with deep green stones, about one carat each, and small settings on either side consisting of single diamonds about a quarter of a carat each, all set in the body of the ring.

'An unusual request,' thought the owner, who imagined something more extravagant would have been requested. He was not to know here, in this plush room, would be another of Benny's little tests.

No matter, Victoria admired Lady Pamela's engagement ring the most.

After a little while, the owner called the supervisor of his workshop to discuss a suitable design, only to be told the other lady had requested something similar. He presented a computer-generated sketch to show what was wanted.

Victoria saw Nicola had chosen rubies and white diamonds.

The supervisor produced the second sketch, showing exactly what Victoria wanted. She turned to Benny and said, 'Thank you very much, Darling. This is my wish.'

Even Benny could see he was about to be let off lightly, at least by his standards anyway. He thought for a moment, two girls had chosen the same design of the ring. There must a common denominator. He remembered the stunning late-night photo of the Lady Pamela. How could he forget?

She was wearing a three stone engagement ring with inlaid stones. Benny enquired from the owner if this would be a bespoke ring starting from square one, only to be told the supervisor had jumped the gun. He had seen this design of ring coming on to the market and had two examples that would fill the desires of these two classy English ladies.

The workshop supervisor accompanied by his most skilled technician returned with the basic ring and a collection of stones that would fall neatly into their settings. Victoria choose wisely, but Benny insisted the stones should be slightly more prominent to better display their colour. Victoria withdrew from any discussion; she knew she had passed her little test and Benny was looking at her with increased admiration.

Arm in arm Benny and Victoria returned to the reception area, where they found Malcolm and Nicola enjoying each other's company. Benny could see these two were permanently joined at the hip, which apart from any other configuration would explain Nicola's supposed condition. Either she was, or she wasn't. Anyway, it wouldn't take long before she definitely was.

The owner arrived to make sure his guests were comfortable, asked if forty minutes could be assigned to the completion of the two rings, and could he serve them anything else from his vast range of stock.

Benny had the urge to impress and the owner knew his client well. It had been a long time since he had graced this establishment. If this was his bride to be, he was going to be an incredibly lucky man. Both ladies had class, and something else, an inner strength, probably gained the hard way. It would not be easy to smother them in jewels.

The owner signalled his partner to bring the velvet lined tray of new watches, just arrived from Europe. The latest styles did not impress. Nicola requested something which could be considered more timeless.

The partner knew exactly what she meant and returned with another tray filled with watches by Jaeger-LeCoultre Reverso. Technically, they could be considered old stock, fashion had passed them by, but Benny was more than capable of restarting a trend.

Nicola tried one on and delighted herself in the classic move of the fingers to turn a blank face of the gold watch into its classic watch face. Victoria chose a classic Reverso with the bracelet in rose gold; it complemented the colour of her suntan. She hesitated, far too expensive, but one look at Benny's face showed he would not be denied. He was going to feel good about himself and splash the cash.

Benny indicated Nicola must choose. She almost declined but saw Malcolm being shown something he always wanted, as he chose the same gold watch with the plain black leather strap.

Nicola eventually chose a similar design to Victoria, but in yellow gold.

The four of them were left on their own for a few moments. Nicola saw her chance, came over to Benny, thanked him from the bottom her heart, and told him from now on he would always be happy. Malcolm smiled, he knew his girl, and he couldn't stop her even if he wanted to.

Fresh coffee arrived. Nicola returned to Malcolm's lap, flashing her long legs. The attendant serving the coffee had seen it all before; never wavering for a moment.

Malcolm wholeheartedly thanked Benny for his gift, only to be told it should be he thanking him for safely bringing these two wonderful girls up from English Harbour.

Malcolm knew it was the other way about. He had been ruthlessly seduced by a foam-covered woman with an appetite for passion and love.

The time passed, the rings delivered, fitted, and double checked for comfort. Despite his misgivings on their design, Benny could see they were classy, not at all showy, but at the same time conveyed the right impression.

The mission, having been successful, the four lovers returned to the comfort of the Rolls-Royce. As the valet parking attendants opened the doors of the car, Benny ushered Malcolm and Nicola into the rear seats and then jumped into the front passenger seat.

Victoria looked at him strangely. Benny indicated with his hand she should enjoy his pride and joy. Victoria had never driven a vehicle this big or expensive. It was another one of Benny's little tests. She had told him about her racing licences, now he wished to see her drive his car.

She didn't mind. Their relationship had gone too far, too fast, and the poor soul needed reassurance. She smiled at him, kissed her new ring, and asked if he wanted to know the time. 'Lunch awaits Darling,' he said.

Victoria climbed up into the driver's seat and slipped the massive door closed. She looked at the expansive dashboard, now just where was everything? As she looked, she waited for guidance from Benny and was not surprised it did not arrive.

'OK, sunshine, we can do this,' she thought.

She put out her left hand, admired her new ring, again, and counted to five on her fingers.

Seat forward, seat height, seat rake, centre mirror, both door mirrors, all adjusted in turn.

Check column mounted automatic gear shift in park, inserted the car key, where was the start button, ah there it was. She pressed the button, the engine didn't roar into life, but the rev counter moved to the correct position. Ready to go.

'Darling,' she said, smiling, 'What is this black round thing in front of me.'

'I believe it's called the steering wheel,' replied Benny, 'Could come in useful.' 'Did your first car have tiller steering, Darling?' she cooed.

Nicola started giggling in the rear of the car.

'Malcolm, stop assaulting Nicola in the back of the car. You must not distract the driver when it is motion,' cautioned Victoria.

'Are we going to be in motion anytime soon,' asked Malcolm, at which point Victoria checked the entry onto the highway, selected drive, and planted her foot almost to the floor.

The Rolls-Royce shot forward with a squeal of tyres.

'Victoria, did you see the eighteen-wheeler coming up on you far too fast?' asked Benny, calmly.

'Of course, he wasn't going that fast, and this car is good for it,' she replied.

Victoria found the button for the power hood, which neatly folded into the allotted space behind the rear seats. The Rolls-Royce cruised along the highway in great style, with Victoria's long hair streaming out behind her. She kept in mind the speed limit, as the eighteen-wheeler tried to pass. Victoria wasn't having any of that. She could see the driver of the eighteen-wheeler getting impatient.

A mile down the road, the two vehicles passed a well-hidden 'smoky bear' just where she expected it to be. She waved at Mr Policeman and accelerated as she came to the end of the speed limit. The driver of the eighteen-wheeler flashed his headlights in recognition the blonde driver of the Rolls-Royce had saved him yet another speeding ticket.

As she reached the speed limit sign, Victoria planted her foot on the floor and the Rolls-Royce hurtled into the distance. After a few miles she slowed down, Benny was looking nervous.

'Oh Darling,' Victoria said, 'I think your nice motor car needs a long hard run, the engine feels a bit coked up.'

As the Rolls-Royce headed north out of downtown along the south beach road to Benny's exclusive club, Malcolm, found himself sitting with a very happy Nicola. He fiddled around with the drinks cabinet which popped open to find a bottle of chilled Spanish Cava, with a label clearly degraded by its voyage across the Atlantic, and fresh canapés from his kitchen.

Malcolm informed Benny, who quickly checked just where they were, then used his hand to get Victoria to slow down, and then directed her to a beachside parking spot, the large sign pronouncing it as 'lovers corner' in large letters.

Victoria parked the car close to the fence, with an extensive view of the beach. The Atlantic rollers rode high up the beach, an impressive sight, with the surfers out in full force. Benny turned around to Malcolm, telling him time to be 'mum,' as he was sure he knew how to serve chilled Spanish Cava.

There could be no more a romantic interlude, than sitting in a Rolls-Royce, arms around each other, drinking an excellent beverage, snacking on fresh canapés. A little while later, the bottle of Cava almost drained, Benny asked Victoria for the time. At last, she thought, but Nicola beat her to it. Lunch time had arrived. Great Aunt Violet would be sitting in Benny's club all alone, or more likely causing panic. It could go either way.

Victoria was about to get underway again when a motorcycle cop sneaked up on the Rolls-Royce to ask if drinking and driving was about to take place.

Nicola called the police officer to her and showed him the bottle. 'It's only a bottle of Cava; it's like a fizzy soda, only with better taste.'

The police officer looked at the degraded label. The section of the label indicating the strength of the beverage appeared to be missing. The police officer had never heard of Cava, must be a new product from Coca-Cola. He then recognised Benny, made his excuses, bid them to 'have a nice day', and roared off on his motorcycle.

As he vanished, Nicola started roaring with an infectious laughter that spread instantly to everyone. Laughing their heads off, Victoria carefully reversed the Rolls-Royce, slipped onto the main road, and carefully drove to Benny's club. Without any hesitation, she drew up to the main entrance. A handsome young parking attendant opened the door and Victoria stepped out as if she owned the place.

As the others alighted, she opened her petite handbag, handing the handsome young parking attendant a twenty and the keys to the Rolls-Royce.

'Thank you very much, Miss,' he said.

'Good afternoon Wesley,' said Benny. 'This is my fiancé, Miss Victoria. We have just become engaged, so please take good care of her for me.'

Victoria almost giggled; this young man did look a bit on the yummy side until Nicola whispered in her ear this young man did more than just looking after ladies.

Wesley uttered his congratulations, knowing full well he had been catalogued by the beautiful brunette with the long legs. The two couples were ushered into the exclusive beach club by the duty manager. Benny advised him of their good news but wished to keep the occasion a private event so as not to overtax the two ladies who looked overawed at their surroundings.

Benny asked if an elderly lady guest from Scotland had arrived. The duty manager replied in the affirmative, looking relieved help was at hand.

'I trust she has been well looked after,' asked Benny.

'Yes sir. She arrived forty minutes ago. I showed her to your special table in the alcove overlooking the beach,' he replied with some tension.

'Problems?' asked Benny.

'She is a spritely old lady. She has taken over part of the club and is holding court. She asked to see the French restaurant dinner menu; then demanded to see the master chef. They have been in conference this last half hour, while she instructs him on how to improve the dishes he has been preparing for next week's special anniversary dinner,' advised the duty manager. 'The master chef has his under-chefs running backwards and forwards as they alter their recipes to her commands, recipes approved by the council only last week.'

Nicola asked, 'But do the alterations to the recipes bring an enhancement to the dishes.' 'Yes,' said the exasperated duty manager, 'But the main restaurant is now running twenty minutes behind schedule due to the chaos she is causing, and members are complaining.'

The Club's President arrived, 'Good afternoon Benny, I trust you can help us to get your guest settled down. She is an elderly lady. We have treated her very kindly but I am afraid she is also somewhat out of control.'

Benny introduced Nicola and Victoria to the club's president. Benny started to explain the old lady was Nicola's great aunt, perhaps she should be allowed to help settle matters.

Nicola and Victoria rushed to Benny's special table, 'Hello again Great Aunt Violet. Just what are you up to in this very exclusive club?' said Nicola quite crossly.

'My dear, thank goodness you have come. This restaurant has the most delightful masterchef. But he does need a little guidance, otherwise no true 'haute cuisine'. I do miss my France so. I must return one day to be at peace with the world.'

'Or for the world to be at peace with my wonderful great aunt,' said Nicola soothingly. 'Flattery will not get you anywhere dear. Don't you dare gaslight me Nicola Stranraer,' replied Great Aunt Violet testily.

Victoria sat down next to Great Aunt Violet and asked Benny to sit close to her side. She stared at Nicola to do the same. It was lunch time, and it was going to be a happy time.

'Dear Great Aunt Violet,' Victoria started. 'Let me show you my wonderful ring. Almost a bespoke design. The jeweller was very special, great service too.'

Mollified, Great Aunt Violet settled down and took interest in the important matters of the day. She looked at Benny and thanked him for following through on yesterday's eventful events.

'You must have been quite nervous this morning, Mr Vincens,' she said.

Benny smiled. Yes, he had been in two minds, no denying, although he did hope it hadn't showed.

Great Aunt Violet turned to Nicola and asked to see her engagement ring, remarking on its beauty and style.

The Maitre d' arrived at the table, with handwritten suggestions as to the recommended dishes of the day and handed it to Benny. As they perused what was, by anybody's reckoning, an exceptional menu, the wine waiter arrived with a bottle of champagne from California, simply labelled 'The President's Choice,' with the compliments of the Club President.

The champagne was served and the mood at the table lightened. Malcolm started chatting with Great Aunt Violet. Victoria decided to practice being silent and looking serene.

Benny passed the menu around the table, the men chose the four courses with the beef wellington as the main course, whilst the ladies universally chose the fish of the day in a white wine sauce.

Benny made a small speech welcoming everyone to his club. He stressed the importance of the day, which had Malcolm nodding his head enthusiastically. He especially welcomed Great Aunt Violet and hoped her visit to Florida would be a pleasant one.

He rose to his feet to toast Victoria, to praise her for accepting his proposal. Benny then nodded to Malcolm, who then performed the same duty. Duty done, the Maitre d' signalled the start of lunch and presented an exceptional bottle of Californian white wine.

Nicola noted the wine served in the club all had club labels. Benny confided the Club President was the ultimate specialist in wines and chose them on behalf of the club cellars.

Quite often Benny had tried to determine what grape and what vineyard in California had produced the many different varieties. The club ran a competition if at the end of a five-course meal the diners could correctly identify the wine they had been drinking, the wine did not appear on the meal chit. To date, only two members had managed to guess correctly.

The lunch flowed at a steady pace, the food excellent, the sauces delightful, and the final course, the sweet course was a masterpiece, which Great Aunt Violet seemed to have a hand in.

As coffees were taken, the three ladies disappeared to the ladies' room. It occurred to Malcolm they seemed to be taking their time. Benny relaxed; he was both full and content. Victoria had conducted herself with grace and poise, charming all who came in contact with her.

The three ladies returned to the table; Nicola seemed to be holding to a small thin plastic box. She sweetly sat next to Malcolm and presented it to him with a big kiss.

Malcolm seemed to be confused. The container appeared to hold a multi-coloured strip and it slowly dawned on him as to what this might be. Nicola's beaming face said it all.

Great Aunt Violet's face had 'told you so' all over it. Victoria stood there trying hard not to giggle.

'Hello Daddy,' said Nicola. 'Congratulations' and sat down.

Malcolm feigned going into shock. Benny called the Maitre d' for the oxygen bottle and face mask. It was too late in the day to order more drinks, so Victoria ordered green teas all-around and sat next to Benny holding his hand.

'Well, now that was an interesting lunch. What next?' thought Benny.

Nicola, Malcolm, and Great Aunt Violet had arranged to split out. Great Aunt Violet wanted to visit an old friend who was quite ill, today being the only chance to visit. This would leave Benny alone with Victoria. He was more than aware the 'last staircase' they had to climb would be taking this wonderful lady to his private sanctuary.

He had never taken any female to the private world in his mansion. Despite all his feelings for Victoria, doubt still nagged him. He knew full well his temperament. Ten percent of doubt today could be double tomorrow and double the following day.

He didn't feel scared; or did he? These were all new feelings and he didn't know how to deal with the devil inside himself. Yesterday he had proposed marriage, more in the fun of the moment, with a light-hearted 'let's see where this goes to' attitude.

The parking attendant brought the Rolls-Royce to them. Victoria made to sit in the front passenger seat. She looked radiant and composed, but how did she feel inside?

She had become quiet and thoughtful and one thing Benny knew about women was when they started thinking, god only knows what would happen next.

BENNY COLLECTED THE car keys in exchange for the usual tip, started the Rolls-Royce and headed for home. The traffic was light for a Saturday afternoon. He drove smoothly and with care, not wishing to attract the attention of the police. He turned off the main highway and took the back road to his estate, a road used many times.

Victoria sat quietly, looking at the passing scenery, and occasionally looking at her new engagement ring. She seemed happy and content.

'Did you enjoy your lunch Darling,' he asked. 'The others seemed to.'

'It was wonderful Darling, nice club, good food and great company. You were marvellous, thank you.'

'Penny for your thoughts,' he asked

'Nothing worth a whole penny Darling,' Victoria replied. Now this was a fib and quite a big fib too.

Benny had tested his bride to be all day, and she had passed with flying colours. The manner in which she drove his Rolls-Royce was skilful and classy.

Now he felt she was going to test him. Would she shake out his last remaining doubts? He pondered on this moment; it was the only thing he could think of. She had survived a truly dreadful occurrence; god only knows what it was or how bad.

Then, she had sailed the Atlantic Ocean and from what little he knew she was not fully fit when the voyage had commenced.

Both Victoria and Nicola had arrived in the USA to succeed at something, an engineer with two doctorates and a full-blown Professor from Oxford University. Failure would not be in their thinking.

By chance they had met Malcolm at English Harbour in the Governor-General's house and had been 'babied' out of the country ten minutes before a major revolution had erupted.

Between them, they had turned Malcolm's world around, made a project with doubts into a project which would succeed, even with a lot of hard work, and now he was the happiest man alive and about to become a father. Not bad going.

So, what were his doubts? Well, the speed of events unnerved him. However, in the past, he had moved at speed on a good deal, and all had been successful.

But Victoria wasn't a deal but a heaven-sent opportunity, so what was the problem?

When Victoria had first pointed up the staircase in Malcolm's show house and said, 'Up there is the future', she struck a deep chord within him.

He was learning her true beauty was inside, a kind sensitive and intelligent lady with class. Now he was taking her to the staircase to his private world and he didn't know what would happen next.

Victoria looked at him. He could hear the wheels going around in her head and that spelt trouble? The distance to his home was reducing quickly; he had better get his act together and fast.

The Rolls-Royce swept through the automatic entrance gates to his property and a half mile later came to a halt outside of the main entrance. Benny left the Rolls-Royce, went to open the door for Victoria. She stepped out, looking up at Benny with wide opened eyes.

'Thank you, Darling. Shall we go in?' she said.

Benny took her hand guiding her through the solid oak doors into a large hall. He described the hall as the ballroom and showed her the corridors leading to the west wing and east wing. This part of the property, the west and east wings, were single story and housed many rooms and bedrooms with ensuite bathrooms, one housed a gymnasium, one housed a private cinema, and another open reception rooms.

At the far end of the great hall stood a magnificent staircase to the private upstairs chambers. At either side of the staircase were doors leading to the dining rooms and kitchen areas.

Victoria looked around the great hall, admired the quality of its workmanship, but this old style of classic Habsburg era decoration did little for her.

A quick peek into a few of the rooms in the west wing, showed a more modern approach to interior decoration. She wandered through the great hall to eventually stand at the bottom of the great hall staircase.

The moment had come. 'Well Benny, will you escort me to your private world?' said Victoria sweetly to her lover.

The remark was a request, not an instruction. Benny hesitated and replied, 'Of course Darling.'

'Will you carry me up the stairs, over your threshold, to our future?' 'That's a big ask Victoria, it's a long way up there,' he replied. 'True. How about the first three and the last three steps.'

Benny took her into his arms and carried her up the first three steps. She was lighter than he expected, but still, seven and a half stone, whatever they were, would be more than he could manage. They walked slowly up the remainder of the stairs, stopped at the third from the top step, as Victoria opened her arms to be carried the last three steps.

They arrived on the large landing opposite the master bedroom door. Victoria gave Benny a huge passionate kiss and whispered for him to continue into the bedroom. Benny did as he was bid, his heart pounding.

He carried her into his private world, the world where he had never taken another woman. He lowered Vicky onto her feet, as she looked around. The bedroom was huge, old fashioned, very tranquil in its dark colours and velvet drapes. At the end of the elevated double bed, she saw two beautiful pieces of antique French furniture.

For the life of her she could not remember their name. Each one consisted of two half-backed love sofas, positioned back-to-back, so a couple could sit facing each other on either side with a vestige of a barrier in between.

Victoria guided Benny over to the love sofa on the far side as she sat on the side nearest to her using an outstretched hand bring him close to her.

Victoria appeared relaxed, but Benny looked nervous.

'What's up Benny. A penny for your thoughts?' she whispered. 'I'm OK, what are your thoughts?'

'My thoughts are I love you very much and I am the luckiest lady in the world if you marry me.'

Benny answered, 'I thought we had just became engaged?'

'And so we did Darling,' she replied, 'And it was wonderful. But you still have doubts. It's like a cancer which can grow very fast. I know what you are thinking; this romance has been too quick. You keep examining it. Checking to see the options, am I the girl for you forever more?'

She paused, then continued, 'Benny, 'Love at first sight' is a powerful once in a lifetime experience. But delay will bring doubt, and the whole sorry cycle will start again. We do not have time to waste. I do not wish to drift apart only to find ourselves again at some time in the future.

Life is too short. If you want a loving wife and children, now is the moment. Otherwise, you will drift, hide behind your busy work schedule getting empty inside. That would be a great shame as you are a wonderful person, so I am going to offer you the moment to reflect and then to choose. I will accept your choice, no regrets, no remorse.'

Benny was overwhelmed by her words. What came next almost made him panic.

Victoria slowly removed her engagement ring from her finger, held it in the palm of her left hand and presented it to him. Benny was flummoxed; he knew not what to do. She sat there patiently, her face with little expression.

'Are you offering me the option?' he asked. 'The yes forever, or the tearful rejection of the moment.'

Victoria remained silent and patient. She was taking a huge risk, her heart pounding within her, but she had to know either way. She had not come to the America to waste her time. She had Nicola, and Malcolm and his project to bring to success. She wanted a happy solid marriage. She did not want to go through a relationship with either one of them looking over their shoulder for the better deal.

Benny found himself reading her thoughts. This lady had matured so far in less than two days or was it her maturity had overcome her 'little girl lost' routine, her default self-defence position. He believed her. She did not want his money or status. She wanted him and him alone. She could make her own money. She would be a loving wife and mother, but she would keep the independence that was the bedrock of her very soul.

He looked intently into her eyes, into her face. He was looking for emotion, but she had mastered her emotions. He thought for another long ten minutes as he thought what to do.

Yes, he had proposed marriage, in the jest of a happy light-hearted moment. He thought he had been sincere, but he now recognised that moment had not taken into account his doubts. Just what was he going to do? He did not want to lose her, but how to overcome the moment, the impasse.

Benny looked at the ring in the palm of her hand. It was a lovely ring. Victoria started to fidget. She thought her gamble was about to go wrong. He could see she had the strength to accept his decision, no matter which way it went. Benny came to the decision and he needed his best poker face.

He held her left hand with the ring, by the wrist. With his other hand, he removed the ring from her palm, looking at her square on all the time. He turned her left hand over and used his other hand to lift her ring finger in the air as he went to replace the ring in its rightful place.

She looked at him hard, let her arms go loose, whispering to him, 'And first Benny the words, please say the words. Not in jest, not in the fun of the moment, not because of the wine, but now, just you and me.'

Benny took a deep breath and simply said, 'Victoria you are the most wonderful girl anyone would wish to have as a wife. Will you be mine?'

'Of course,' she said, as she moved her hand and her ring finger disappeared into the centre of the ring she adored so much.

The couple leant over the partition and kissed.

'You were very brave,' said Benny in a low meaningful voice.

'And so were you Darling,' whispered Victoria. 'So, now we start our new life. What fun we are going to have. Now, show me the rest of your eire, your eagle's nest.'

They left the bedroom, arm in arm, as Victoria started to look at the other rooms and spaces on his upper floor.

'Looking for anything, in particular, Vicky?' asked Benny.

'Just seeing what is what,' she replied. 'This floor will become the family floor, had you thought of that?'

'Nope, I haven't got this far. Is there any rush?' replied Benny.

Victoria turned and fluttered her eyelids, 'Well, lover boy. Given your performance in the horizontal tango last night, one could suggest a timeline,' she said.

'Gosh,' thought Benny. 'This girl has me on a hook and I'm being reeled in. It's just plain fantastic.'

'Anyway Darling, I need a shower, and I've nothing fresh to change into. Do you have a long plain tee shirt and a shower cap?' asked Victoria.

'Follow me. We go past our bed through the closet into the bathroom. I'm sure I can find something,' he said.

They passed through into the spacious bathroom of white marble tiles and green marble decoration. It had everything anyone could wish for, including a double shower cubicle with twin shower heads and vertical spray bars.

Benny raked around in a cupboard and found a large tee shirt, a big bath towel, a swimming cap to cover her hair and told her everything else was in the shower cubicle.

Victoria took these items, sat at the dressing table on one side, disrobed, covered her hair, and disappeared into the shower. Benny enjoyed the view, ruined only by the amount of steam filling the bathroom.

'Just going downstairs Darling,' he said. 'A few things to do and I need to update Alfonse, the butler. He will want to know the changes in the household.'

Benny floated down the stairs. He would remember the stairs for evermore. He even did a twirl in the middle of the main hallway.

Alfonse took the news with stoic interest. A lady in the house would ruin his perfect running of his master's property. Still, the day had come, unexpectedly, which he considered good. None of the frantic toeing and froing of lovers trying to get their sorry act together whilst they came to one conclusion or another.

He had heard the word 'children' mentioned and shuddered. Better work out where the barricades would be needed. Still, children generally arrived in baby format, which would also certainly mean, if he had anything to do with it, the hiring of a nanny, and a maid and possibly other female staff to rule over.

The disruption to his carefully planned routine may just bring unexpected bonuses. Best make friends with the lady, get her onside to present a united front to the master of the house. He hoped to hell, the master of the house and the lady would not be one and the same person. There was the risk.

BENNY RELAXED IN the downstairs drawing room nursing a cold refreshing drink of homemade lemonade. A bucket full of ice kept a second helping cool for the new lady in his life. The doorbell chimed. Alfonse answered the door. He was about to announce the arrival of new guests when the famous three fell into his hallway full of joy and extra helpings of a rum punch Great Aunt Violet had found in the home of the dear friend she had recently visited.

Their taxi sped away, grateful not only for the generous tip from Great Aunt Violet but the return of peace and tranquillity in his cab.

'Shall I serve tea, coffee, or another alcohol dilutant?' intoned Alfonse.

Benny smiled, asked it to be so, marshalling the famous three into his drawing room. Nicola looked high, Malcolm was obviously the worst for wear and Great Aunt Violet was just exactly where she wanted to be, in the middle of so much happiness.

Benny rang his little bell and requested Alfonse to bring a jug of ice-cold green coconut milk to bring a measure of restoration to the proceedings. At that, Victoria floated into the happy throng, wearing the tee shirt that came just two inches below her modesty, a towel around her head, and oversized slippers she had quickly foraged for.

Victoria was happy, very happy in fact. As she spun around like a little elf, it became obvious to Benny she had washed her knickers, dried them in a towel and put them back on to let time do its work. The damp material caused the tee shirt to stick to her delightful bottom, and if this had an effect on Benny, it had a greater effect on Malcolm, a fact Nicola noticed immediately.

Nicola stood in front of Malcolm who moved his head to the right. Nicola moved to her left, Malcolm moved his head in the opposite direction to continue the observation of a heavenly star. This continued for two more oscillations of Malcolm's head until Nicola draped Victoria's towel over his head.

Victoria laughed, came behind Malcolm and covered his eyes with her hands. Malcolm feigned sleep. Victoria said she would sit on his lap, but Nicola assumed the intended position. Malcolm's hands went to positions not normally associated with politeness in public. Nicola removed the towel and said, 'Hi, it's me.'

Great Aunt Violet concentrated on the coconut milk drink, aware of its restorative properties, directing a nonplussed Alfonse to feed Malcolm a large glass of the same. Vicky went and sat on Benny's lap and took tea with a chocolate cookie, for tomorrow she would diet, or maybe the day after?

'Nicola, darling,' began Victoria, 'And what do we owe for the pleasure of this visit.' 'Well Darling, due to the lack of any smoke signals, I thought we should come and see who needed rescuing. Also, I brought a change of clothes and a toothbrush. I see you have a change of clothes, hardly winter wear.'

'As you can see, we are not in need of rescuing, quite the opposite in fact,' said Victoria. Nicola rose and went over in front of the happy couple and examined them closely. 'Benny,' she started. 'What have you done with my Victoria; she looks different.'

Great Aunt Violet put her drink down and said, 'Nicola, she has become content, in fact very content.'

'Is it spreading Great Aunt Violet?' Nicola asked.

'Well, Benny looks just as content, so the answer must be yes.' 'Have you two been having words?' demanded Nicola.

'Guilty as charged,' replied Benny, who proceeded to give a heartfelt recall of the late afternoon's events.

'You did what Victoria Stanwick?' asked Nicola in a raised voice.

'It is as Benny says, I had to know. He made the most beautiful proposal of marriage and every lasting love, so now we are content.'

'Malcolm are you listening to all this,' demanded Nicola.

'Yes dear, I did tell you, but you were nattering to Great Aunt Violet.' Malcolm rose, like a phoenix, and went over to Benny and Victoria.

'Benny,' he said, with a fair degree of stability. 'You are one lucky son of a gun, congratulations. Glad you killed the doubt bug. Victoria, you too are blessed, can I kiss the bride?'

'On my wedding day,' Victoria replied. 'Just one little practice run, please.'

Victoria stood up, gave Malcolm a big kiss, pushing him into the arms of Nicola. 'Quiet night tonight then Nicola,' cautioned Victoria.

'We can live in hope. Time for us to go. Glad it all turned out wonderfully. See you bright on early on Monday morning, we have work to do. Benny, can your butler drive us all back home?'

Alfonse was pleased to give the fantastic three a ride home. Benny relaxed and sat down in his comfortable armchair with Victoria on his lap.

'Now where were we,' he asked?

'Well lover, we have enjoyed our spell of celibate behaviour. Now Alfonse is out of the way for a little while. I will make a snack of 'Welsh rarebit', then we can retire upstairs and see what we can do about question number eight.'

'What exactly is this Welsh rarebit,' asked Benny.

'Toast with melted cheese on top preferably with a thin slice of tomato in the middle. 'Sounds good, bring the feast on a tray upstairs with a fresh pot of tea. Question Eight here we come.'

Chapter 24

Lovely day for a Sunday Outing

THE NEXT morning, Benny and Victoria rose to start their first new day together. Benny suggested a day out and Victoria agreed. Both dressed in slacks, coloured shirts, and sports shoes. Now it was time for Benny's Rolls-Royce to get an outing too. The pair of them fought over the car keys, which had the effect of delaying departure until Benny feigned surrender and grabbed the morning papers as he headed for the 'navigators' seat.'

Victoria sat in the driver's seat and was about to do the five checks on seat position and mirrors when Benny leant over to nibble her ear and show her a memory switch he had set to the second position. 'Now push the button and wait twenty seconds.'

Victoria squealed in delight as the Rolls-Royce reset everything to the positions she had determined the day before.

The Rolls-Royce set off and joined the Florida Turnpike. Victoria asked if Benny had any preference on destination. He replied Fort Pierce was a nice run, then across the causeway over to the state park to visit a fresh style of diner he wanted to check out.

Victoria drove smoothly and not too slowly either. Benny discovered, as yesterday, Victoria was good at spotting those sneaky places 'smoky bear' liked to hide behind. Victoria left the retractable hood up but opened all the windows to let the wind blow through her long, lovely hair.

Benny was content. He tried to read his Sunday papers, but the world's news was boring. He much preferred to watch the girl soon to be his bride and mother of his children. Victoria was content and frankly astonished at her luck as she confidently drove in the silence of the Rolls-Royce wondering what darling Benny was thinking as he calmly sat by her side enjoying the ride.

Benny was musing about the last two days. The sudden change in his life had come at an opportune moment. His days had become all work and no play. He had many friends, of course, most married with families. The only eligible ladies he was introduced to were either unmarried and too young by far or divorced with someone else's children and generally looking for another mark.

Now he had met the right girl and wasn't she a piece of work. What was it she couldn't do?

'Benny darling, what are you thinking?' asked Victoria. 'Oh, nothing much,' he replied.

'Darling, I can hear the wheels going round from here. Just relax and be at peace.' 'Good advice,' he thought.

Now he would come home at night to someone special. No doubt she would drive him crazy at times, but she had undoubtedly had many wonderful facets to discover.

'What nice thoughts you are having, Benny?' 'Are you psychic?' asked Benny.

'Oh yes,' she replied. 'Surely you must know this. How do you think love at first sight happens? When two lights illuminate at the same moment, there is no way back.'

Benny relaxed. Yes, he was content. He would share his life with this lady, pity he didn't meet her long ago. Ah, the mysteries of love, the chance meeting.

TWO AND A half hours later the Rolls-Royce left the highway and purred its way across the causeway to the barrier island, heading north along the coast past frequent road signs proclaiming the opening of a new range of diner in the Creole style.

As the Rolls-Royce approached the diner, Victoria saw an adjacent service station and took the opportunity to refuel the car. The service station looked a trifle run down but it did have full service, becoming rarer each day as service station owners looked to reduce their costs.

The owner, a rather scruffy 'red neck' was pleasant enough; took her order and began filling the car. Victoria left the car to stretch her legs to keep one eye on the refuelling, well aware Benny would not be pleased if any marks were left on impeccable bodywork of the Rolls-Royce.

A tall Negro youth wandered by rather unsteadily, and as he passed Victoria he waved a plastic toy 'Sinbad the Sailor' sword, demanding money. Victoria opened her day purse and her 'little gun' fell to hand. In a flash she held her arm out straight, quietly telling him to back off and go away. The youth fell to the ground in abject despair, sobbing and holding his head. Victoria quickly put her gun away as people started to take notice and rush to her aid.

Benny was flicking through his Sunday newspaper when his attention diverted to his fiancé. He grabbed his semi-automatic from the glove box and rushed to her aid. He found the owner of the service station holding the youth up by the collar of his shirt.

Victoria recovered quickly from the shock and looked at the youth. She immediately saw he was quite emaciated. He had a kindly intelligent face racked by despair. She asked the owner to take him inside the service station and sit him in a chair. As Benny stood beside Victoria, they wondered what next. A police patrol officer appeared from nowhere. Victoria could see the whole event turning into a federal case. This she did not need.

The youth was desperately hungry, it was plain to see. Victoria felt sorry for him, a young man, no future, no nothing. Dreadful.

Victoria pulled the owner out of the way and started to question the youth. She quickly found out he was just nineteen years old, homeless, poorly dressed, badly needing a wash and an orphan, living, if you could call that, in a semi-derelict caravan at the back of the service station on a piece of waste ground.

The police patrol officer barged in looking for trouble with his nightstick in one hand and a revolver in the other. This did not look good. Victoria wasn't about to have her Sunday ruined, and for whatever reason, she decided helping this young man would be the right thing to do.

Victoria moved forward to intercept the patrol officer and told him straight there was no problem. The young man was delirious from hunger and she would put matters to rights. The police patrol officer looked disappointed but then it was Sunday and filling out paperwork on a destitute African-American was hardly going to get him promoted.

The small crowd around Victoria thinned out as matters settled down. Victoria sent Benny to park the Rolls-Royce. She turned around to the owner and asked if he was OK. He nodded, somewhat confused, muttering an affirmative.

'OK,' she said, 'Let's do this. Give this young man a drink of milk and stop using the 'N' word. With a bottle of shampoo, take him around the back and get him thoroughly washed. I see white overalls on the shelf, so get him dressed in a new pair. Better give him some new socks and a new pair of those sports sneakers.'

Victoria paused and looked around the store and saw the hot snacks next to the coffee machine looked like leftovers from the previous day.

'My fiancé, Mr Benny Vincens and I are going for lunch. I will send a meal for this boy. When we have finished our meal we will return to settle-up and give you a good tip for your services. Otherwise, you didn't see anything.'

Victoria was on top form, although the owner of the service station didn't look so happy. The return of a quiet Sunday afternoon would be welcomed, and the chance of a decent tip would be doubly welcomed. Business was not good by any stretch of the imagination.

Victoria left the service station and walked across the forecourt to intercept Benny and guide him towards the diner.

'How did you get on Darling? All fixed up,' he asked.

'Yes dear, the cop has gone away, and the young man is being fed and cleaned up. I would like to take him home with us,' said Victoria.

'What on earth for?' asked a surprised Benny.

'The young man has potential. I have seen a starving man before and I just have to do something.'

Benny knew Victoria was more than kind-hearted, but this seemed a step too far. 'Anyway,' said Victoria, 'You know I am looking after the planning for Malcolm and all

construction work is controlled by 'work-packs'. The vendors have agreed to supply materials by work-packs on a just-in-time basis. This means the warehouse needs more staff than Malcolm wants to employ. So, my plan is to use this young man as an apprentice.'

'You mean cheap labour,' said Benny.

Victoria smiled, 'It's traditional and an economic solution to the problem. Saves having a stand-up row with my CEO.'

'That's my girl, always ahead of the curve,' thought Benny.

'OK Darling, this works for me. By the way, can I look in your purse?' said Benny,

Victoria stopped for a moment. Benny looked at her and said, 'I don't think I saw anything, did I? And I do not want to not see anything again. If the police had turned you over it would be bad for me and even worse for you.'

Victoria knew he was more than correct and said, 'OK Darling, but next time you take that automatic out of its den, pull the slide back and load a fresh round into the chamber otherwise it won't fire.'

She smiled sweetly as Benny let the matter drop.

Benny and Victoria went to lunch and ordered the introductory three-course menu. Benny chose different dishes for them both to enjoy the different flavours.

Lunch finished, the happy couple made their way back to the service station, collected a cleaned-up young man, paid the bill with a large tip, and set off for home. Victoria let Benny drive back. She sat comfortably, turned to her side to admire her future husband to be.

She spoke to the young man sitting in the back of the Rolls-Royce, who was looking a little scared. Victoria decided to call him 'William 'B', simply because she liked the name.

Benny drove quickly. He couldn't remember the last time he had enjoyed such a hectic weekend. He had only accepted Malcolm's invitation to his 'open day' at the last moment, with little else to do that day.

He had been facing a weekend of playing catch-up with office paperwork. Now he was seriously behind but surprised himself by not caring; paperwork could take care of itself. He looked forward to arriving in his office on a Monday morning, but was his staff about to enjoy the new era?

During the drive home, Benny started to ask Victoria about certain matters. Where would she like to be married, and when would be of interest to his secretary who ran his somewhat overcrowded diary. Victoria replied with a special giggle. She felt part of her Sunday had become too serious. In reality, she was determined to keep Benny on the hook, in a nice kind of way. She did love this man dearly, and in truth, she was as amazed as he was, Friday had become their Friday, a special day to remember.

As they neared home, Victoria called Nicola on her mobile to give her an update on the day's proceedings. They agreed the young man should stay at the show house under the care and guidance of Rita, a decision Benny had absolutely no problem with whatsoever.

Benny and Victoria arrived back at his mansion and took a late tea. With matters now settled between them, the happy couple took the chance of a less robust evening and enjoy each other's company. Early to bed, early to rise became the order of the night. Benny had a busy week ahead, and something told Victoria she would not be far behind.

Chapter 25

The Girls Back on their Travels

MONDAY MORNING, Victoria returned to spend weekdays at the show house with great regret, but it was the sensible thing to do. After the Monday morning meeting, Great Aunt Violet called her two girls together to tell them they would travel to London later in the week. Monday's bonus was in the morning mail. Documents from the US Immigration Service arrived to confirm their interviews for their US business visas at the US London Consulate had been set for late Thursday morning. Great Aunt Violet had booked three tickets for Wednesday evening so as to arrive in London on time .

Monday afternoon became frantic, as Malcolm and his legal advisors rushed to complete the necessary documents for a contract with Nicola and Victoria's nascent company.

'Nicola, when and where are you thinking to get married?' asked Great Aunt Violet.

'Good question. There is the Harry Hatchet saga to come first and no one has told us where we are with this. Are we even safe even to go to the UK?' replied Nicola.

'Well Nicola,' Great Aunt Violet replied. 'The saga is coming to a close. I have my feelers out and expect results soon. Jus is providing discrete security when we land in London, so please not to worry.'

'Huh, it's going to be a rushed in-out visit for sure. How long is the waiting time before we get our passports returned?' replied Nicola.

Great Aunt Violet paused merely mentioning a fast turn round was more than possible.

Monday became Tuesday evening. Benny arrived just after dinner to see Victoria. He was due out of town on the 'red eye' next morning and couldn't stay long.

Victoria understood but she did miss him so. She had become rather quiet since the weekend, which Nicola put down to reflection. Still, Victoria seemed content. She had no problems with her sleep patterns and she started eating more than usual. Nicola asked if she wanted any ice cream sandwiches with pickled onions and black pepper, only to be told to bugger off.

Wednesday arrived in a flood of emotions and expectations. Victoria asked when they were visiting the US Consulate should they enquire about marriage entry visas, a subject Nicola had on her list of things to do.

The girls agreed to travel light, taking only their cabin bags. Great Aunt Violet, on the other hand, spent Tuesday afternoon in some serious retail therapy, which was considered odd, as Great Aunt Violet did not normally spend her time shopping.

Benny took time out and organised a bon voyage dinner which became, much to the girl's surprise, quite a jolly affair. The show house was fully booked that night, but the morning awoke to the grim reality both husbands-elect had remarkably busy work schedules.

It seemed no time at all Great Aunt Violet and her two girls were heading for Miami's International Airport, that vast and confusing meeting place with many cultures. Great Aunt Violet managed the checking-in ceremony with style and Nicky and Vicky ended up holding boarding passes with seat numbers 1A and 1B.

'Phew' exclaimed Victoria, 'I like it, first class. Does the airline still give you those sexy 'pyjams' to wear during the night?'

'Darling, they are the opposite of see-through. Keep them for when you're sixty-five years old, and you need to keep warm,' replied Nicola.

They found the VIP lounge full of tired and overworked businesspeople. There seemed little point drinking and eating too much when the long flight to London would provide plenty of interesting refreshments.

Victoria noticed Nicky had started to err towards being teetotal. Did motherhood bring on being teetotal? This she had not considered, as she had never smoked or over-indulged in alcohol.

Great Aunt Violet and her two girls were escorted to the waiting aircraft and made comfortable. First class travel may be expensive, but the cabin crew made them more than welcomed. The usual silver service took place shortly after take-off, and the threesome settled down for a comfortable flight.

Just as Nicola and Victoria were settling down for a good night's rest, a visitor arrived in the shape of Commander Bernard Collingwood from the UK's illustrious Special Branch.

'Good evening Ladies. Mind if I have a word?' he asked. Great Aunt Violet looked as though she was expecting him. Nicola told him to bugger off and leave her in peace.

'Nicola dear,' said Great Aunt Violet 'Be nice to Bernard. He has come to help you.' 'I thought I did greet him politely, didn't I Victoria,' opinioned Nicola.

'Considering the last time you spoke, yes. Very polite indeed,' said Victoria.

'OK you two,' said Great Aunt Violet quite sharply. 'The Commander has something important to tell you so pay attention.'

'Do you know what it is he is going to tell us, Violet?' asked Victoria. 'Yes dear, of course,' she replied.

'Nicola and Victoria,' started the Commander, 'You will not be surprised to learn Mr Hackett is not pleased with you two. He knows you are living in Florida and it will not be long before he finds out where and with whom. We in Special Branch fear the worst. Hackett's day is coming and soon. This journey of yours is an opportunity we must take. So, I am guaranteeing your safety if you agree to the following.'

'Victoria, do you hear that, we are being set-up,' said Nicola. 'Can you believe after all we have been through?'

'Hackett has sent three teams of assassins to the USA to kill you both. We are trying to track them, but it is difficult. Hackett's reach is exceptionally long. If he finds either of you in the UK, God knows what will happen. The man is a physco, totally evil.

Anyway, I have arranged the following. When the aircraft lands at Heathrow, it will park on the apron to transfer passengers to the terminal by bus. You will be taken separately to a VIP lounge the other side of the airport.

When you have refreshed yourselves, you will visit the US Consulate. There you will receive fast track service from US Consul himself. After a short break you will receive your UK passports with your new US visas. You will also be issued with US marriage visas. When you are ready to enter the USA for marriage make a quick visit to the Bahama's.

When you have collected your passports you will be taken to an RAF station for lunch in the officers mess, followed by a flight to Glasgow to take the overnight journey to Boston.

On arrival in Boston, check-in at the five-star hotel at the Marina, where you should rest for a couple of days. Then, you will be free to make your way back to Florida. With any luck, other events should have taken place to ensure your continual safety. Any questions?'

Nicola looked at Victoria nonplussed. What was there to say?

'Thank you, Bernard,' said Nicola, 'We understand and many thanks.'

Business finished Great Aunt Violet and the Commander left the two girls to get some rest. Clearly Great Aunt Violet had pulled many strings; the best that could be done had been done.

'What will be, will be,' thought Nicola.

She ordered a nightcap and then slept fitfully until morning. The following day's events went as planned. The US Consul was very polite, quite charming in fact. The RAF lunch was pleasant, as was the flight to Glasgow. The onward flight to Boston, USA, was comfortable in the front row of Business First and Nicola and Victoria slept reasonably well.

They arrived at the swanky five-star 'Boston Marina Hotel' to find there were no rooms until the checkout time of midday. The room booked for them the night before had been released in error to a VIP customer. Nicola made it known to the General Manager she was not pleased in no uncertain terms.

This conversation had not gone well until Victoria accidentally on purpose dropped Benny's business card on the floor and asked the manager if he would be so kind to pick it up for her. She thanked the manager, and after a brief name-dropping session, a change in tack was neatly executed by the manager. Victoria did admire how hotel managers could switch to professional grovelling with such ease.

The manager guided them into the breakfast lounge and bid the waiter look after his 'special' guests. Following breakfast, Nicola decided she would like to go for a walk and get enjoy the fresh air. Immediately opposite the hotel stood the main entrance to the mooring piers forming the marina.

Nicola loved to walk around marinas just to see the moored yachts, especially any classic wooden craft from yester-year. Half-way along the centre pier they came across a seventy-foot cutter, painted in royal blue with a striking gold line along the hull just below the cap rail.

They almost passed it by until something twigged and she returned to look at it again. 'Well, well, well,' said Nicola, 'Just look what we have found. Recognise this yacht,

Vicky?'

'No, I don't think so. But there again, there is something familiar.' 'It's our yacht, the yacht. Well, I never,' said Nicola.

A crew member came on deck, stepped ashore, almost passed the two girls and stopped dead in his tracks.

'Good morning Hank,' said Nicola.

'Do I know you two?' said the crew member. 'Cullen Skink for lunch is it Hank?' said Victoria.

'I don't believe,' said Hank. 'It's the terrible twins from Scotland. What brings you to Boston?'

'Oh, we're on the run from the fuzz,' said Victoria. 'But it's not been reported on TV yet.'

Nicola smiled a big smile at Victoria and told Hank the Boston Marina Hotel had given their room to someone else despite having paid for it. Now they had to wait until check-out to get their assigned room and they were at a loose end.

Hank invited them to come aboard and rest after their long overnight flight. He served coffee and cookies and asked how they were and what was their news. Nicola gave Hank the abridged version, which he struggled to believe.

'So, Nicky,' he said, 'Let me get this straight. You are pregnant and will marry the father, a real estate magnet, and Vicky is going to marry Benny Jets. Well, I don't know.'

Mr Douglas Chester Fairfield Jr. returned to his yacht, to find Captain Hank entertaining two extremely attractive, well-dressed ladies.

'Can anyone join in Hank. Any coffee left?

He introduced himself to the two ladies, 'Hi my name is Mr Douglas Chester Fairfield Jr, at your service, and you are?'

Victoria started to giggle, while Nicola just looked at this remarkably handsome man. Chester paused and looked again.

Then he said, 'I recognise that giggle. Now, where the hell was it?'

'Scotland, boss,' said Hank. 'It's the dynamic duo. Well, this is what you called them at the time.'

Chester started to ask questions but Hank butted in with his version of their events to date.

Chester sat stunned. This giggly lady was going to marry his rival Benny Jets. 'God help us all,' he thought.

'They have just flown in from Scotland, Chester. The hotel messed up with their hotel booking. They have nowhere to rest except the hotel lobby and that's not an option,' said Hank.

'There is a big medical conference at the hotel this weekend,' said Chester. 'I have just come from there and it's chaos. Why not stay on board my yacht, there is plenty of room.'

Pennies were still dropping in the head of Douglas Chester Fairfield Jr. Then he finally realised who these two were.

'You are the two ladies who sold me my father's yacht, right?' he said.

Nicola smiled, replying, 'We are the two ladies who rescued your father's yacht from some truly bad people, refurbished it at great cost and disguised it so you could escape from the UK and sail to safety. Yes. We did like the colour. What a wonderful yellow it was. Why did you have it painted royal blue?'

Chester smiled, told them yellow was not a club colour, and having managed to return to the USA unannounced he had thought it best not to advertise his presence.

'Hank,' said Chester. 'Please can you go to the hotel with my compliments and have the ladies luggage sent here. They will stay with me for the weekend.'

Nicola tried to dissuade him, but it looked as though he would be on his own and pleasant company would be well, pleasant.

The three of them spent the morning chatting, swapping stories and getting to know each other. Chester told them about his voyage across the Atlantic. Despite his objections, Hank stuck religiously to Great Aunt Violet instructions and boy didn't they pay off. The first time the yacht was buzzed by patrolling aircraft was on the third day out, by which time they were well on their way.

Chester knew the authorities were looking for a black yacht with a female crew and he was sailing on a bright yellow yacht with an all-male crew. Brilliant.

Nicola told Chester about their voyage to Gibraltar and had the luck to pick-up the daughter of the famous gynaecologist who had saved Victoria's life. She omitted the fuss at Las Palmas to concentrate on the story about the voyage across the Atlantic and the profound change it had made to everyone.

Chester was particularly interested in their arrival in the USA and how they had become involved with Malcolm Richardson's grand real estate project. Nicola took the idea Mr Chester was a player in the real estate market. Nicola tried to play down the story regarding Victoria and Benny Jets, but Victoria was having none of it. She praised her future husband so much so Nicola had to calm her down with a swift kick in the shins.

'By the way ladies,' said Chester, 'The conference at the hotel this weekend is for the medical industry. Saturday afternoon's subject is gynaecology.'

He took out his smartphone to surf the internet to find the conference website. He passed his smartphone to Nicola who looked at the list of speakers and uttered a loud shriek.

'Crikey, just what has got her knickers in a twist?' thought Victoria.

Nicola handed her the smartphone and Victoria let out an even bigger shriek. Chester looked on wondering what all the noise was for. Victoria leant over Chester and showed him the guest speaker list, a Dr A Duncan, a Professor Samuelson, and Dra S. Samuelson.

'And they are?' asked Chester.

He was soon advised. Chester retrieved his smart phone and called the hotel. The two girls looked on impatiently. Chester disconnected his phone to tell them this party had booked three rooms for two couples and a single lady and they would arrive from New York this evening.

Nicola and Victoria couldn't restrain their joy. Nicola asked Chester to leave a message at the hotel for the two couples and the single lady to visit as soon after breakfast as they could manage and to give Nicola's mobile number to Dr Duncan.

To calm his two delightful guests, Chester served cocktails. It proved one thing: Mr Chester knew how to mix a particularly good cocktail.

Victoria asked about dinner, the hour was approaching the time she liked to eat. Chester offered a range of alternative restaurants nearby. Remembering Commander Collingwood's advice to maintain a low profile, Nicola asked if a Chinese takeaway would be acceptable. Chester agreed. He had enough of restaurants for one week and it had been a long time since he had eaten Chinese food.

'Special meal for three?' he asked, only to receive nodding heads of acceptance. Nicola saw the chance to change out of day clothes, to shower and change into relax mode. Victoria quickly followed suit. They reappeared wearing short sleeve open neck floral printed cotton nightdresses. They both felt relaxed ready for a low-key evening with a most charming host.

THE SPECIAL CHINESE meal for three arrived, only to find there was sufficient food for twice that number. Chester stood his turn to look after the drinks. Nicola prepared the food in the galley, as Victoria set the large table in the centre of the main saloon. She even found flowers and candles to decorate the table.

Chester turned the cabin lights down. A calm and relaxed atmosphere invaded the yacht's main saloon. Chester asked if these two wonderful ladies had enjoyed their travels on his yacht. Victoria left for the toilet as Nicola attempted to put some positive spin on their travels. She had to warn Chester they did have bad experiences, which she was not going to talk about.

Chester let it go, unwilling to darken the mood of the evening. Nicola started wondering about the man himself. He had a son, so she asked about the mother. Yes, Chester had been married. His wife suffered from a lengthy illness and died quite young, in her thirties. His son was visiting his grandparents.

Now, he was approaching the magic age of fifty and he had been unlucky in love. Nicola told him she understood. She had friends who had been unable to find a suitable partner later in life. Their conversation became more intimate as a silent Victoria sat back to listen. She would soon be getting married at the ripe old age of thirty, and heavens above, Nicola was nearly thirty-three.

After a few more glasses of wine, Chester fell into a mellow mood. He felt really comfortable with Nicky and Vicky, their husbands would be very lucky men. Chester took the liberty of telling them his thoughts. Nicola wanted to cuddle Chester. He had all the signs of a lonely person. Lonely on the inside where it hurt most, especially during the long night hours.

Chester revealed he did have a sort of fiancé; a high society lady in her late-thirties who had been left on the shelf. She came from a rich family, so the upper-class society of Boston had it in their minds Chester would step-in and do duty by them. Nicola picked-up on the situation immediately, a rich single lady wandering around in the upper circles of society looking for who knows what?

Chester showed his two guests her photograph. Wow, what a good-looking lady. No wonder the Boston social circuit was wary. A girl like that could pounce at any moment. Husbands couldn't keep their eyes off her undoubted physical beauty, so how come she hadn't been snapped up years ago. Apparently, the lady's name was Fiona.

Victoria slipped into the conversation, 'Chester would you consider this Fiona more beautiful than us two?'

Chester smiled a tearful smile, 'It's like this if you do not mind me being forward. You two wonderful ladies are beautiful on the inside as well as the outside. You look as though you know how to love, laugh, and cry with your chosen partners. An active sex life or just going to sleep in his arms, you seem to me to be happy either way, correct?'

Nicola smiled. This man was worth his weight, he had loved, he had lost, and now he had entered a wilderness from which he could not escape. Being rich and famous was not the be all and end all of life if you are lonely.

Victoria asked, 'So, Chester how would you describe this Fiona. She looks like real 'bouncy castle' material to me.'

Nicola groaned but saw Vicky had hit the mark yet again. Chester stumbled to describe the lady, everyone thought he was going to marry. Even Fiona thought he was going to marry her. It was the correct thing to do, according to society gossip.

'She has the stiffest neck of any woman this side of the Hudson River,' exclaimed Chester. 'She is hidebound by what she sees as convention. It's rumoured she even has her stools gift wrapped before flushing them down the toilet.'

Nicola smiled a huge smile. Victoria fell off the settee with laughter.

Victoria picked herself up off the floor and sat on Chester's lap. 'I bet she rides to hounds, a steeplechaser, goes to church three times a week to see who is there, blah blah bloody blah.'

'Yep,' said Chester. 'That just about covers it, but there's more.'

'OK, stop there Chester,' said Nicola. 'We get the picture. Vicky are you going to take root there, or what?'

'I think we should take pity on Chester,' replied Victoria, in her most playful of moods. 'Why not drag him into the owner's main cabin and seduce him. You know, the condemned man gets a last request.'

Nicola thought this could be a promising idea, or perhaps not. Seducing Chester Fairfield would be many a girl's dream, but hey ho, she was spoken for, and pregnant, and … but what a temptation!

She was about to address the situation before matters got out of hand when the beautiful legs of a tall lady appeared on the companionway coming down from the cockpit. Someone had let herself into Chester's yacht.

A carefully coiffured head appeared. It spoke, in harsh and demanding words. She wanted to know what the hell was going on with her fiancé. Victoria started to giggle.

'Good start, this sure is going to help,' thought Nicola. Everyone stood up so Chester could make the introductions.

'Hi, Fiona. This is Nicky and this is Vicky,' and sat down again. The look on Fiona's face was priceless; he wanted to laugh out loud. Why he didn't puzzled him.

'Well, I guess they look cheap enough. Two for the price of one I suppose?' said Fiona. Nicola moved forward; this was going to be fun.

'Good evening, I am very pleased to make your acquaintance she said, in her best plummy accent. 'May I introduce my partner Dr. Victoria Stanwick, PhD, PhD and BSc. I am Professor Nicola Stranraer, late of Oxford University. After detailed forensic examination, my partner and I have concluded the condemned man, Mr Chester here, should be given the last opportunity.'

'Last opportunity for what?' Fiona demanded harshly.

'Dr Stanwick, have you come to a scientific conclusion?' asked Nicola.

Chester looked at his two guests. This had become a show. 'Keep it going girls, this is going to be interesting,' he thought.

'Well, Fiona this is up to you said Victoria. 'Chester is a calm, quiet man who needs a loving partner. And you are not it. Period. But you could be. You need to be dominated; made to understand just who you really are. Any comments Professor Stranraer?'

'I think we should all adjourn to the consulting room, the owner's main cabin. Chester if you would be so kind as to escort Fiona to her future.'

Chester grabbed hold of Fiona's hand but met with stiff resistance. Chester proved to be stronger, and Fiona soon found herself in the luxurious main owner's cabin. She looked down at the ornate double berth with horror.

'Keep her still Chester, pin her elbows behind her back,' ordered Nicola.

'Now then Fiona, let us find out exactly what makes you tick. Victoria removed her necklace and the adornments merely advertising the price. Now I am going to stroke you all over to see what part of you is actually living and what part of you comes from Vogue magazine.'

Victoria went behind Chester and took over with the pinning of the patient's elbows. 'Now Chester you can begin,' ordered Nicola. 'Stroke her back, over her bottom, then down her legs. Feel anything?'

'Not much,' replied Chester, 'Nothing at all. Shop window mannequins have more sensation than this.'

'Remove her dress, Chester, let us see if the lady has arrived this evening dressed to be undressed,' ordered Nicola.

'This is more interesting,' thought Chester.

Fiona's dress fell to the floor revealing a lady who had dressed to impress. The exotic effect lasted only seconds as Victoria dryly observed the reason Fiona was late was she had been to an afternoon Victoria Secrets party with the usual jet set crowd and the party host had been most unkind dressing Fiona in an undergarment trousseau more fitting for a red-light shop window in that certain part of Amsterdam that attracted many of the male tourists.

Nicola smiled; she knew exactly what Victoria meant. Here was a woman with a wonderfully full figure, dressed like a thousand bucks a night tart in uptown New York, from her half cup bra, minuscule florid knickers with a Velcro tab on one side, black stockings and suspenders and the ever-fashionable high heel shoes with a fancy ankle strap in fake gold chain, with the whole ensemble covered in unnecessary bling.

Nicola thought to herself, 'Oh dear, this girl is totally naïve. Even Victoria couldn't wear this kit and get away with. Even in her most playful of 'little girl lost' moods.'

Chester looked on, not knowing what to think. The next part had him thinking even more as Nicola told him to put sleeping shades on to cover Fiona's eyes and then to start stroking her skin wherever he felt like it. Victoria let out a little giggle and found Fiona was reacting to having her elbows held behind her back. The bitch was starting to like what was going on. It would not be long before she would start to moan and demand more of the same.

Victoria thought, 'It's like launching a jet fighter from an aircraft carrier. Chester is the pilot, although he's not sure if this aircraft will actually fly once the catapult is released, Fiona is the jet fighter, and Nicky and me, well we are the flight deck crew preparing the launch.'

Chester got down to work. As he progressed Fiona became more alive. Her bra found its way to the deck of the cabin. The tab on her knickers proved a sound starting point for something more adventurous. After a few more long moments of pleasure, Victoria knew it was time to let the catapult do its work. She nodded at Nicola who knew the moment had come.

'Chester,' she called out, 'Come off your knees and stand-up straight in front of Fiona. She's all yours. Go to work tiger, for King and Country,' as Victoria shoved Fiona into the arms of an increasingly rampant lover.

Nicky and Vicky beat a hasty retreat to the main saloon.

'Phew. That was fun. Well Victoria, would you like a nice cup of tea dear?' asked Nicola. 'Good idea, what do you reckon?'

'If that doesn't work, nothing will. Did you see the look on Chester's face when you pushed Fiona into his arms? The poor man didn't know whether to fart or blush.'

Victoria fell about laughing. She hadn't heard that expression in a long time. The sounds coming from the main owner's cabin started to get louder, so much so Nicola decided she could not sit here and listen to the noise when her beloved Malcolm was so far from her arms.

'OK Stanwick, get dressed, walkies, otherwise…' ordered Nicola.

Victoria couldn't agree more, she was missing Benny just as much as Nicola was missing 'hot lips,' her new name for the ever-compliant Malcolm.

They left the yacht as it started to respond to Victoria's idea of what a 'bouncy castle' should do on any Friday evening as they made their way in the direction of the hotel.

They sauntered into the hotel lobby to find a cast of thousands all trying to check-in at once. Why couldn't conference goers arrive a few days early and enjoy the city.

'Look who's here,' said Nicola. 'Quick, sit down here with our backs to them.'

They sat down in the comfortable lobby armchairs. Nicola took out her smartphone and texted Adam, 'about turn and walk eight paces in front.'

Adam took the call and did as requested. Adam bumped into the armchair Victoria was sitting in.

'Bleedin' hell Guv,' said Victoria in her best Eliza Doolittle voice, 'Look at where you are a goin' to.'

'Good evening to the terrible twins,' said Adam dryly. The other members in his party turned to pay attention, wondering what was going on.

Adam turned to his party and said, 'It's all right folks, it's just Nicky and Vicky touting for business. Samantha caught sight of Victoria, let out a shriek of delight, nearly falling over the back of the armchair Victoria was sitting in.

Nicola rose to greet her uncle in the more traditional manner and gave him a big hug. Pamela smiled and joined in the family hug fest as Professor Samuel looked on with his arm around Sylvia. Eventually, with hugs and kisses out of the way came the long wait to check-in.

Nicola caught the eye of the general manager, who, in the interests of self-preservation, was minded to become her best friend. He walked briskly to her side and asked how could he of service?

Nicola told him these guests were waiting to check-in but had been invited to visit with Mr Chester Fairfield Jr. as soon as possible. The general manager, seeing a chance for redemption, whistled up two porters who were trying to look busy, as he consulted his iPad asking for names. Within seconds he confirmed the double room for Dr. Adam Duncan and guest, and a family room for Professor Samuelson, daughter, and guest.

Nicola assured the general manager the Professor had booked two rooms, only to receive the response the hotel had advised and assumed no reply was an acceptance.

'Miss Nicola,' said the general manager. 'The hotel is swamped, so there is little I can do. I can offer a substantial discount on the family room if this will assist in the matter.'

Samantha stood next to Victoria asking if she could sleep on the yacht? Victoria whispered it was possible, but to keep stum so her father could get the offered discount.

Sylvia slid next to Nicola to ask the same question. Having a referee in the same bedroom as the new man in her life was not what she had in mind.

The matter became resolved very quickly; the two porters took their luggage up to the correct rooms as the general manager supplied the required door keys. Nicola suggested they scoot before anything else happened. On the walk back to the yacht, it occurred to Nicola to phone Chester.

'Incoming Chester,' she advised. 'A 'pax' of seven persons. Is the coast clear?'

Vicky suggested if the coast was not clear, could a viewing area be set-up for the comfort of all. Nicola replied, 'Victoria, you should Keep Calm and Carry On.'

Chester told her to come on down. He looked forward to meeting her family and friends. He asked if Nicola had any spare clothes as Fiona had brought nothing to change into. Nicola told him she had a spare nightdress she could use. Chester thought of Fiona wearing something ordinary from your local store.

'Should do her the world of good,' he mused.

The visitors boarded the yacht, making themselves comfortable in the main saloon. Fiona showed she was a capable host, serving drinks, coffee, and a cocoa for the Professor. The mood soon relaxed after Nicola completed the introductions.

Samuel fiddled with the straps of the carry bag he had brought with him, removed a small electronic device and a probe. He asked Nicola to come and sit with him, asking if he could take a small blood sample to assess his latest creation.

Nicola asked what task this new instrument would perform.

'We doctor's get pestered by patients always demanding ever earlier and more certain confirmation of pregnancy. The subject was well covered by existing test kits, but he had thought of a way to use more modern electronics to bring an improvement to the testing scene.'

Samuel said tests of his new system had provided promising results and it was able to determine, with accuracy, the actual day the fertilised egg attached itself to the wall of the uterus.

With care, other parameters could be measured, and with a skilful examination of the results produce an opinion whether the expectant mother would have multiple births. He stressed his new instrument would not change the way the world rotated around the sun, but in certain situations, the data could help in other investigations.

'Go on then,' said Nicola. 'Are you going to prick my finger? Victoria don't say anything.' Samuel performed the simple test and gave Nicola a date, adding that twins were expected. 'I know,' said Nicola. 'Great Aunt Violet has already pronounced her view of this result as a fact.'

Nicola whispered to Adam to drag Victoria over to receive the next test. Victoria resisted but Adam was having none of it. Victoria reluctantly offered her thumb, as Samuel repeated the test. He asked for the most likely day of conception, only to be told just over one whole week to this very day.

Samuel smiled and informed the audience Benny's little tadpoles must be swimming the fast crawl because he had a preliminary result suggesting the positive.

'When does Benny arrive, is it Sunday?' asked Samuel.

Victoria nodded in shock. 'Well, that's OK, by Sunday morning the result will be a hundred percent positive, and Daddy will be pleased.'

Nicola saw Fiona hanging back from the crowd looking pensive and unsure of herself. Dressed in one of her nightdresses Fiona looked well but in need of reassurance. Chester stood behind her holding her waist. It seemed to provide comfort.

'Fiona, come and meet my family and friends. They will be delighted to meet you,' said Nicola. From the other side of the saloon, Victoria could see what was going on and went to Chester's side persuading him to start circulating in the opposite direction.

Chester was impressed with Adam and even more impressed with the Lady Pamela. Chester could see this couple were a team, relying on each other, helping each other, and plainly deep in love. They knew nothing about the constraints of social life in Boston and his not so happy social circle.

Pamela's vineyard was soon to become famous. She started to talk about the other love of her life, classic cars. Her late husband's collection was slowly being sold to good owners who would cherish their cars, spending time and money showing them off.

On the other side of the saloon, Fiona had become engrossed with Samantha, who saw a bright young lady with the goal of ruthlessly succeeding in whatever direction she wanted to achieve. Pretty girl too. Her proud father was engrossed in conversation with his lady love.

Chester stood back to watch with Nicola by his side. 'What am I looking at here Nicky,' he asked.

Nicola replied Fiona was about to meet a couple who had only recently found the space to be together in public. She explained the daughter thing. Samantha had truly blossomed on the journey across the Atlantic on Moody Blue her wonderful 44ft yacht now lying unattended in Miami.

Chester, between serving refreshments to his guests, waited for Fiona to complete her circling of the saloon, and come to his side. He asked how she was feeling.

'These are just wonderful ordinary people,' she said, 'So easy to talk too, easy to like and easy to make friends.'

Nicola smiled.

'Nicola, what was the smile for?' asked Fiona.

'Well Fiona, I am so glad you feel comfortable with them. But look around, they are the best but hardly ordinary. Adam is one of the best doctors in his field and an absolute wiz at micro-surgery. He is now building an extraordinarily successful operation in Europe.

Pamela is rebuilding her life and is on the cusp of bringing to market a fabulous new wine. Professor Samuelson will soon become a partner with Adam, who has the same expertise but he also specialises in pre-natal and anti-natal medicine. His lady love Sylvia is the best hospital administrator I know, and Samantha is a chip off the old block and some.'

'But don't worry,' she continued, 'With Chester you can become whatever you want to be. Victoria is quite correct. You can be naïve and you are a blank canvas. Vicky is particularly good at understanding other people. Sometimes she is too direct, but for her, the truth is the truth. Today your life changed; at least I hope it did. Your secrets of today will never be known except for us four of that you can be certain.'

Fiona reeled at the onslaught of the truth. She held her council realising only good friends would be so direct purely for her benefit. She began to feel grateful, and a smile slowly broke across her face as Chester held tightly on to her.

'What's up Fiona? Nicola telling you what you need to know' he said. 'Yes, Darling, and now it's your turn,' Fiona replied.

Chester looked at Nicola, 'OK Nicky, I'm ready,' he said.

'Well, Chester. There is not much to say. It is up to you to make this lady into a wonderful wife and develop her talents. Keep her close, keep her safe, give her passion, but for god's sake let her have her independence too. You know what I mean?' she said.

Chester replied, 'You two girls get down range pretty fast don't you. I should be upset with your directness, but no. I am incredibly grateful. We have found ourselves and need to keep building and understanding.'

'So, you will become engaged?' asked Nicola.

'Yes, I guess I should make a proposal of marriage,' said Chester 'Can't do that without a ring,' replied Nicola.

'I was looking at yours,' said Chester. 'Classy; quite classic in a way. I see Victoria has the same style.'

'We copied the style from Pamela. Here look at mine,' offered Nicola. From across the saloon, Pamela could see what was going on. 'Chester, can I look at Nicola's ring after you?'

'If you show me yours, I'll show you Nicola's,' said Chester. 'Now, that's an offer you don't get everyday Nicky,' said Pamela. 'I was thinking the same,' smiled Nicola.

'Is that all you English ladies think about, sex,' butted in Fiona.

'It's what matters most dear. It is the weapon of choice,' laughed Pamela. 'Vicky, come here please.'

Victoria sashayed across to what looked to be a more interesting conversation, 'Are we talking about my favourite subject?' she asked.

'Sex,' said Fiona.

'I thought so,' said Victoria. 'Fiona, Vicky can lip read, so be on your guard,' said Nicola. 'No darling we are discussing engagement rings.'

Victoria switched to full outrageous mode. She flashed the original brass ring on her finger; the ring that had started her future with Benny, saying, 'If a girl can get wonderfully laid with this brass ring, just think what will happen with this real one.'

Smiling, Victoria replaced her formal engagement ring next to the brass one.

Chester almost choked on his drink. Was there no end to these two English ladies having fun; and now they had called up reinforcements. He looked more closely at Pamela and saw she did indeed exceed all he had been told about her.

Pamela took charge of the conversation about rings before they all ended up doing something embarrassing.

'Fiona, this is my ring from Adam. It has blue stones to go with the white diamonds. Vicky has the same style, only with emeralds, and Nicky has rubies.'

'I like your ring Pamela with the London Blue topaz,' said Fiona.

'Err, they're not topaz,' said Nicola. 'They are aquamarine and the colour is exceedingly rare. These stones are about two carats each and were part of a much larger stone Adam inherited from his Father. The main stone had a flaw. Adam found a specialist who could cut it into a flawless sixteen carat stone with these stones left over. That ring still in the bank vaults Pamela?'

'Of course, Adam had it valued. I couldn't believe the numbers they came up with.'

'So, where did Nicola and Victoria get their rings from?' asked Chester. 'Can I guess a certain specialist in downtown Miami, the shop with no name at the Seybold Jewellery Building? It is where people like Benny like to shop.'

Nicola smiled an affirmative and nodded to Chester perhaps Fiona should miss the next part of the conversation. Chester asked Fiona to look after their guests and he would like a small top-up of his Kentucky Bourbon with more ice.

'Pamela, what would you recommend for Fiona? I like the simple style you three are wearing. Any chance Benny could get a ring made up in time for him to bring to him tomorrow?

Having watched Fiona look at the three rings he had no doubt she liked them.

Pamela suggested the style would be most suitable. She continued, 'Chester, three stones all diamonds. One yellow in between two red ones with deep colour. It will depend on what stones they have in stock, but you can always ask.'

Nicola saw Fiona was still busy serving drinks, took out her smart phone to call Benny. It was a little late. Benny was still working. He wasn't unpleasant but he had to clear his desk if he was going to fly to Boston on Sunday.

'Benny, we are guests aboard Chester Fairfield's yacht. He would like you to obtain on his behalf an engagement ring similar to mine or Vicky's. Would it be possible for you to work your magic?'

Benny thought for a moment. One of the drivers for flying to Boston was the chance to meet Chester Fairfield, not that he would tell anybody. He had a sweet deal on the horizon needing finance and Chester would be the man most likely to help.

'Tell me what is requested. I can but ask,' replied Benny.

'Same style as mine, and the same size,' said Nicola. 'Three stones at one carat each, diamonds, two red and one yellow.'

'That's clear enough, I will call the owner. His name is Owen, but I never told you that. I will get him to call this number, anything else.'

'Victoria says she loves you and could have good news on Sunday,' concluded Nicola. 'She's not pregnant, is she? Probably too soon for news like that. Here's hoping. Tell her I miss her madly and look forward to Sunday lunch. By the way, send me a text as to how to get to where you are. Love to all,' then Benny rang off.

'That was efficient?' said Chester.

'You should get a phone call anytime soon,' said Nicola. 'It's kind of late surely,' said Chester.

Fiona brought Chester a cup of coffee, 'Everything OK Darling?' she said. At that, Nicola's mobile phone rang.

'Excuse me, Fiona, I must take this call. Thanks for the coffee. Just check on everyone else, please,' said Chester.

Chester took the call, 'Fairfield speaking,' said Chester.

'Mr Vincens asked me to call,' said the voice. 'Are we free to talk?'

'Yes indeed,' said Chester. 'I wish to purchase a ring similar in style and design as the one purchased for Miss Nicola Stranraer, who is betrothed to Mr Richardson, but with a different set of stones. I wish, if possible, for Mr Vincens to bring to Boston, I believe he will fly first thing Sunday morning.

'Yes, it is possible, depending on the choice of stones and their availability,' said the voice. 'Splendid, Miss Nicola is suggesting two red diamonds, one yellow diamond. The size of

the main stones to be one carat each, with the peripheral white diamonds of a suitable size.' 'This is for an engagement?' asked the voice.

'Correct,' confirmed Chester.

'Please hold,' said the voice at the other end of the line.

The voice returned, 'Sir, it is possible. A wonderful combination, I have the stones before me.'

Chester asked Nicola who nodded her head vigorously. 'Yes, this would be most acceptable,' said Chester.

'Thank you for your order,' said the voice. 'I will have it gift wrapped and delivered to Mr Vincens's residence late Saturday afternoon. Can I take your credit card number and can I ask if you are you price sensitive?'

Chester answered, 'I do not think there will be a problem. I will send my credit card number after this call, divided between two texts.'

'Thank you, sir,' said the voice. 'You are most kind and your order is guaranteed. Can I take the liberty of sending you an invitation to be included on our client's list? Mr Vincens gave you a splendid recommendation. We are always pleased to serve discerning clients.'

'A most acceptable offer. Perhaps Mr Vincens would be kind enough to bring your communication along with the order,' said Chester.

'It will be done and once again thank you for your order, Mr Fairfield.'

'Wow,' said Chester, giving Nicola a big hug. 'That was a surprise. An invitation to be included on their client's list. Is there anything you can't arrange?'

'Peace in the Middle East, heat without humidity, and getting a woman in the White House,' smiled Nicola.

Pamela smiled and congratulated both Nicola and Chester.

'Samantha, are you slumming it on board the yacht tonight?' asked Pamela and saw a head nodding in acceptance. 'OK gang, time for bed, it's been a long day.'

This was good news for Silvia, who started to prize Samuel away from his third glass of malt whisky, to propel him towards the exit up to the cockpit and hence to shore.

Adam had a bit more life in him, said good night, thanking Chester and Fiona for their hospitality, and they were looking forward to the gathering on Sunday. Nicola would confirm all arrangements.

The night passed peacefully aboard the yacht. Nicola bagged a spare cabin for herself, leaving Victoria and Samantha to share the forward master cabin. Chester and Fiona had a settled night together after their rumbustious afternoon.

SATURDAY MORNING DAWNED clear, cool, and rather windy. The programme for the day revolved around the fact going sailing would require everyone to enjoy getting cold and wet when there were much better things to do.

Like getting one's hair washed and attending to one's nails, Victoria. Bringing her extensive wardrobe onboard, Fiona. Catching up on unfinished paperwork and organising lunch aboard the yacht on Sunday, Chester. Taking time out to rest after two days flying, Nicola.

Samantha was long gone just after breakfast as she had to change for the conference formal lunch and prepare for her afternoon presentation.

After lunch, the three girls enjoyed a retail therapy cruise downtown, leaving Chester to his own devices, something he did enjoy. The evening programme included a vigorous discussion on where to dine, followed by accepting one should have booked ahead with the big conference in town.

They ducked into Chester favourite Thai restaurant, which always had a table for him. Following a delicious meal of East Asian cuisine, Chester suggested ten pin bowling which turned out to be great fun. It did wonders for Fiona because nobody in the bowling alley had the slightest idea of who she was, so she didn't need to go posing. Just being with friends, having fun and not worrying about being on parade became an experience she would wish to try much more often.

The group returned to Chester's yacht. As they prepared for bed, Nicola received a message on her smart phone. Seeing Fiona had disappeared into the main owner's cabin, Nicola called Chester to her side and said, 'Hello sailor, I have a photograph for you to view.' Chester looked at the screen and saw a most beautiful engagement ring with a strong yellow diamond in between two red diamonds. He gave her a big hug and said thank you. 'Do you think Fiona will like it?' asked Chester.

'She will be over the moon, Chester. Don't worry about a thing. We had three hours girl talk when shopping this afternoon, remember,' said Nicola.

The night aboard Chester's comfortable yacht was quiet. Samantha did not return until some ungodly hour.

Sunday arrived with little fanfare for what would prove to be an interesting day and who gave a damn about the weather.

The caterers arrived at nine-thirty a.m. to prepare the grand lunch only to find themselves with added duties concerning breakfast. The bonus of the morning was a parade of scantily dressed females wandering between the breakfast table in the main saloon and whichever shower facility had momentarily become free.

Ten a.m. on the dot, saw the arrival of the two doctors and their smartly dressed ladies, looking forward to a genuine English roast beef lunch with all the trimmings. Pamela wondered how such an expansive meal for so many people could be cooked on a galley range in what was arguably quite a large yacht.

She saw the catering staff hard at work but realised the meal had been prepared earlier then delivered to the yacht to be brought to perfection before serving.

Adam and Samuel took their medical equipment to the forward guest cabin. Nicola was ready to receive her first pre-natal examination. Samuel took the time to give her a pre-natal massage and a list of do's and don'ts. Given her unhappy history she was advised to receive continuing care from a specialist centre in Miami.

'Nicola,' said Samuel, 'Remember, anything at all just call Adam and one of us will come immediately. Best get copies of any results. Just send the details direct to the convent hospital. I'll connect with your pre-natal doctor during any on-going examinations. Otherwise, you are just one very healthy mother-to-be.'

Nicola felt thrilled at the news.

Victoria was next. She was nervous and asked Samantha to help her father. It took a little longer to go through the issues, after all, she had suffered the most. At the end of the examination, Samuel prepared his experimental instrument and asked for an erect finger.

Victoria waited anxiously to know the result, only to see Samuel frowning. She stiffened, expecting unwelcome news. Samuel looked down at her and said, 'Do you know, I can't tell if its twins or triplets Victoria.'

Victoria swore under her breath, taking advantage of a poor girl like that. Samantha was smiling, gave her a kiss and whispered Daddy was just having fun and she should expect twins at the most.

Victoria kept her peace, planning revenge. But this was the doctor who had saved her life with only minutes to spare, and it was reassuring to know if there was any concern either he or Adam would be on the first available flight.

Examination time successfully completed, Nicola served coffees and the tasty snacks she had pinched from the caterer's van parked on the pier.

The sounds of a taxi crawling along the pier looking for Berth 31 were heard. Nicola shouted out to Victoria in a joyous mood.

Victoria, on the other hand, had the 'collywobbles' on just how she was going to tell Benny the good news.

Nicola rushed up on deck to meet Malcolm with what was later described as 'the greeting of the year'. Benny brushed past the loving couple as it would take time to split these two into their component parts.

Victoria met Benny at the bottom of the companionway from the cockpit, with big kisses and hugs. Benny told her he was anxious for the good news she had mentioned on the telephone.

'Come this way Darling,' she said guiding him into the guest cabin where a waiting Professor Samuel was sitting patiently. The couple both sat down as Victoria produced the required finger. Professor Samuel repeated his earlier test, smiled at Victoria, and told her the result was the same as ten minutes ago.

'You mean,' stuttered Benny, 'she is   ?'

'Indeed she is Benny. What a wonderful way to meet someone with such happy news.

Congratulations,' exclaimed Professor Samuel.

Benny gave Victoria the biggest kiss he could muster, his heart raced he was so happy. 'Err, Benny, best tell Vicky how happy you are,' said Samuel. 'She has been like a cat on a

hot tin roof these last two days.'

'You've known for two days?' demanded Benny.

'The first test, late on Friday, was not proof positive. The advance in progress these last few days has been exceptional. Today I have no doubt.

Vicky had her first pre-natal exam this morning and she is just a fantastically one hundred percent fit person. She needs to be careful during term, but we are just a flight across the Atlantic away.'

Adam came into the cabin, propelled by Nicola. 'Benny, this is my wonderful Uncle Adam, I'm so happy you two could at last meet.'

Benny smiled and said, 'I need a drink.'

Nicola took him by the hand and led him into the main saloon to find a waiter carrying a large tray full of champagne glasses.

Benny and Malcolm were introduced to the four ladies. 'A good start,' they thought.

The two friends did the rounds of kisses and handshakes. As Benny passed Chester, the handshake lasted a little longer as Benny slipped a small box into Chester's pocket.

'Best of luck dear boy. Hope it goes well.'

With everyone gathered in the main saloon, Chester took the floor to welcome everybody and to wish them god speed when the time came to depart.

'A couple of announcements, today we have the wonderful news both Nicola and Victoria will be mothers in a few month's time. Dr Adam and Professor Samuel tells me the fathers-to-be are as well as they can. Please raise your glasses; the toast is many happy nights of disturbed sleep for the fathers.'

Benny pushed Malcolm forward to make the reply, which he managed very well.

Chester looked over at Victoria and Nicola, standing either side of Fiona. The three of them looking identical, brimming with health and purpose, wearing chic designer day slippers, dressed in coloured slacks, flowery silks blouses, hair up, and sporting the haul of accessories from yesterday's shopping spree. Nicola and Victoria, the 'dynamic duo' someone had christened them, standing there like the Praetorian Guard.

In just forty-eight hours they had descended on his staid existence, turning his world upside down. The girl he was about to propose marriage too, had been adopted, reformed, re-energised, reformatted, revised, rehabilitated, and converted to new. He would have to follow Nicola's advice, give her a new life and a new purpose. God help him.

Chester took a deep breath, 'And now for my final announcement, it gives me immense pleasure to ask my darling Fiona to accept my sincere proposal of marriage and to accept this ring as a token of my love.'

Victoria felt Fiona go weak at the knees. She would have collapsed but found herself supported by her two new friends. Fiona recovered as Nicola whispered in her ear, 'Remember what we told you yesterday. Just say 'Yes' to any question. It's quite simple.'

In a daze, Fiona moved closer to Chester, her left arm elevated with the assistance of Nicola, her long fingers outstretched, as Chester showed her the ring, then slipped it onto her ring finger. She flung her arms around him to give him a big kiss.

When the big kiss ended Fiona looked at her engagement ring in disbelief. She was no expert but these looked like real diamonds. The two red ones had a fabulous colour and the settings were simply perfect.

Standing the back of the crowd, Samuel whispered to Adam he didn't know love could be this expensive. Adam smiled whispering, 'And this is only the down payment.'

The ladies all gathered around to marvel at Fiona's engagement ring.

The men drank their champagne looking for a refill. Chester moved to stand next to Benny and Malcolm.

'I am pleased to meet with you Vincens and Mr Richardson I believe,' said Chester.

Benny returned the compliment on behalf of them both. It was a long time since Benny had been addressed by his surname, a politeness rarely practised in this day and age. Latin men were more apt to do so with people they knew and trusted, especially in business circles.

The women folk were still making a fuss over the good news. Fiona's ring generated most of the attention, but the way Fiona was looking across at Chester there was a fair chance it would give value for money.

Fortunately, the gong went for lunch. Chester rounded up everybody and directed them to the dining table in the large and spacious coach roof with its extensive views across the marina. The assembled guests found their names on embossed place cards, laid out in a gentleman, lady, gentleman formation, the idea being the men would move one place after each course.

The meal started with a cocktail of fresh Boston prawns, followed by a sorbet or clear soup, before the main course of thick cut roast beef, cooked to perfection, with crisp Yorkshire puddings, homemade grain mustard and the usual vegetables.

The guest layout promoted strong social intercourse between them all, as opposed to the normal format of women at one end of the table and the men at the other end of the table.

By common consensus, everybody learnt much from each other, none more so than Fiona, who enjoyed the experience of talking naturally to all who were around her. There were a few hands-on other knees, all taken in good fun.

At the end of the meal, the men gathered under the cockpit awning to enjoy a range of cigars and liqueurs. The ladies returned to the comfort of the main saloon and girl gossip.

Chester invited Benny to discuss his ideas, knowing Benny would have something of interest.

Benny recalled since the arrival of the lovely Miss Stanwick, he had managed to get the finances of his different businesses into a better balance.

Recently, an opportunity had come to purchase a mid-sized medical centre sitting on a prime development site. Malcolm told him he could build a large multi-story development on this site with a high net rate of return.

However, the medical centre was close to Malcolm's 'Villages Leigh' development and the medical centre would enhance the drive to sell his properties.

Nicola and Victoria would fund the 'Village Shops' development, and keeping the medical centre would be good business, and enhance his reputation with the expanding local community.

Benny had checked out the site and his take-over team had run the numbers. The owner of the medical centre wished to retire but did want to see his life's work bulldozed for yet another high-rise development, of which Miami had a great sufficiency.

SO, BENNY WAS close to a very discrete deal with the owner, but the question remained how to finance the purchase of the medical facilities, plus its eventual transformation into a private hospital.

Benny looked to Dr Adam and Professor Samuel who would know the ins and outs of such a venture. He had heard good things about their operations. Health care would always be a rising market and a mix of high-level high-profit operations could co-exist side by side with meeting the demands of the general market.

Time for the basics.

'OK, Benny let's talk money,' said Chester. 'How much to buy the business including assets and debts, how much to refurbish, and to increase specialist staff.'

Benny handed him a spreadsheet stating the owner's bottom line was to be free of all encumbrances with five million in his pocket net of tax. Chester saw the first two categories had sound numbers, but the recruitment of medical specialists had, to his mind, an exceptionally small number.

He invited Adam to give his view. Adam said the way his operation worked in Portugal revolved around the set-up where he rented his facilities from the Mother Superior, but he also sold his services to the Mother Superior.

He said Samuel would join as a partner in the New Year bringing his private patients with him. Soon, they would need a base in the USA for his patients unable to travel or afraid to go to any country that did not speak American.

Adam knew an up-and-coming young gynaecologist looking for a base in the USA to start a service similar to the way he ran his Oporto operation. The medical centre could rent space to like-minded medical specialists who could purchase support facilities from the main facilities.

Chester asked for numbers, and told a flat ten million, subject to negotiation and five million for upgrades, additional facilities and working capital. Benny turned to Adam and asked, 'Fancy a quick trip to Miami so you two superstars could check-it-out.'

Adam spoke with Samuel and quickly agreed. Benny called his pilot and posed the problem of flying eleven pax to Miami, in the next ninety minutes.

'Call you back,' said his pilot.

Ten minutes later the pilot called, 'Boss, your aircraft does not have the capacity, and a straight charter is going to cost. However, I have the chance of an evening charter to the mid-west. A friend of mine has an empty charter back to Fort Lauderdale. He's offering a good deal and happy to provide a service.'

'Deal,' said Benny. 'I will text the passenger list right away. I would like to depart in ninety minutes.'

'That was efficient,' said Adam. 'Accommodation?'

Benny smiled, 'I live in a mansion. East wing or the west wing? West wing is best, it has the snooker room.

Chester said, 'Guess we better tell the ladies and pack the camels. OK boys, to work.'

Ninety minutes later, the party found themselves in an old but well-appointed executive-jet, climbing rapidly to twenty thousand feet. As the aircraft levelled out, Pamela came to Benny to ask what the hell was going on. She found herself kidnapped from a promising examination of Boston's fair city.

Benny ordered refreshments and smiled at Pamela. 'It's business darling, what else. You will enjoy.'

Pamela returned to her seat muttering about men and when would they ever change. She quizzed Adam, who just smiled and said, 'Miami is very nice this time of year. We are going to stay at Benny's mansion. You could even work on your suntan.'

Benny did the rounds to explain what was going on. Pamela asked if this project had real upside. Malcolm said it provided self-preservation for his housing project, the danger being one of the big contractors could build a multi-story condo on the site close to his.

Then, the captain of the aircraft announced, 'Fifteen minutes to landing.' 'Quick flight,' thought Benny.

The aircraft executed a good landing, and the passengers disembarked into a waiting mini-bus to take them to Benny's mansion. Malcolm and Nicola disembarked at the show house with the three

Samuelson's. Benny and Victoria, arm in arm, arrived 'back at the ranch' with everybody else, at the end of what had turned out to be a remarkably good day.

Chapter 26

New Business

MONDAY MORNING and Benny's party stayed late in bed. Victoria departed early to attend Malcolm's Monday morning meeting, leaving a note to say they would meet for lunch and then visit the medical centre.

Benny and Nicola attempted to get up early but needed a lie in. Chester and Fiona suffered the same fate. The matter was settled at 10 a.m. as Alfonse rang the breakfast gong.

Breakfast turned out to be a leisurely affair. Chester said he was impressed with Benny's home. Fiona said little. Her father's mansion was bigger, pity he did not make more use of it.

Adam thought it too big and Pamela would always prefer her Quinta.

Team Benny set off to collect Samantha on their way to the medical centre. The medical centre occupied an interesting site close to the interstate highway. The centre looked clean enough, the car park only half full. The owner told them the Monday morning rush had tailed-off and the next wave of the sick and the ailing would commence sometime after three in the afternoon.

Inside, Adam and Samuel saw the simple things to improve patient comfort. They engaged with the owner and discovered his vast accumulated experience over the many years. It was just a pity he had not kept up-to-date with the advances in medical practice.

They retired for lunch to meet up with Team Malcolm. Over a simple meal of fried chicken and salad, Adam and Samuel gave their opinion of the existing set-up. All in all, the opportunity looked to be closely aligned with Benny's original thoughts.

The afternoon visit gave the advantage of being able to spend time with the owner, just to get a feel for the general run of things.

At the end of the visit Chester assured the owner they were impressed with the business and intended to pursue the matter further but asked for total confidentiality.

On the return to Benny's corporate offices. Benny suggested a meeting in his board room and let his PA Beth take notes .

On their arrival at Benny's offices the car park had started to empty. The executive lift whisked them to the top floor. Chester looked impressed.

The offices were almost deserted until they entered the board room to be confronted by a happy crowd of managers and staff. A large ornate sign with the words 'Congratulations' hung across the face of a huge television screen.

Benny's long-term associate, Mr Brad Shaw, had organised an impromptu party to introduce his lucky lady to the company.

Benny discovered Brad did not actually know the name of his fiancé, and here he was surrounded by four beautiful ladies who had recently accepted proposals of marriage. He figured this moment would provide good entertainment, how right he was going to be. Benny motioned for the four ladies to stand next to each other.

'OK Brad, which one of these lovely ladies are going to introduce as the lucky lady,' said Benny.

Brad took a chair from the nearest table to sat in down in front of the four ladies. He looked at Benny and said, 'Sit down, Boss.' Benny sat down, looking at Pamela next to Nicola, then Fiona, and on the left, and an interested Victoria.

'OK ladies,' said Brad. 'I'm sure we would all like to see the engagements rings. The four girls held out their left hand, to the sound of 'Oohs' and 'Ahs.'

Brad started to walk the line to ask each bride to be a question asking, 'And your name is?' 'Pamela,' came the smiling reply.

'Ah,' said Brad. 'A lovely English lady. Very classy. Could be a top contender folks.' Next came Nicola. 'Ah another lovely English lady. Fabulous. This is getting tough folks.'

Then, Brad came to Fiona and stopped dead in his tracks, 'Wow,' he said, 'An all-American lady. Phew, this is getting real tough. Sure you ain't a goin' to marry all four, Boss?'

Benny smiled thinking, 'Did he have space in his diary or his bank balance?'

Last, but by no means least, he came to Victoria. Brad asked her name and Victoria uttered the biggest giggle of the year. Even Nicola was impressed.

Benny was laughing, and it was catching around the room. Victoria leant over to Brad and whispered her name.

'Well folks, we have a Victoria from the UK. Golly gee another beauty.'

Brad sat down next to his boss and said, 'Benny, it's got me beat, never happened before.' 'Anyone in the room a goin' to help me?' asked Brad.

He received no takers. Brad stared hard at the four lovely ladies, slapped his knee and said,

'Hey boss, I know the one. A hundred bucks says I got me the right one.' 'Go on old timer, I'll play the game,' conceded Benny.

Brad walked up to Pamela, saying 'Huh, very classy but no.' Continuing to his right, he passed Nicola with a 'nice try sister,' and Fiona, 'Ooh, you are my favourite,' came to Victoria, and gently put his hands on her waist and propelled Victoria into the arms of Benny. 'So, Brad, just how could you tell with such certainty?' asked Benny as he handed over a crisp one-hundred-dollar bill.

'Well boss, I just looked at their eyes. Three of them were glancing at their future husbands. Victoria just stared at you with all the passion a woman can give.'

Benny was impressed. Brad, his sidekick for many a year, always providing sound advice.

The party ended as the long distant commuters made for the exit.

The end of a long day required a suitable conclusion. Benny led his guests the short distance to the local Tex-Mex where the fajitas were especially delicious with ice cold beer to wash down the feast. At the end of the meal, Benny asked who would be returning where and when.

Adam and his party chose to go to the International Airport Hotel in Miami ready for a redeye to Portugal the next morning.

Saying goodbyes to Nicola and Victoria took a while but they were sad they had spent so little time in Florida and its marvellous winter weather.

Fiona and Chester chose to stay another night in the comfort of the mansion. Benny invited Chester and Malcolm to a game of snooker, with a few beers added for a very convivial evening. The ladies slipped into the depths of the kitchen to discuss the important affairs of the female world.

The next day was business as usual. Benny took Chester and Fiona to the airport in his Rolls-Royce.

Wednesday was sailing along as usual in the busy world of Malcolm Richardson and his housing project when Nicola took an international call on her smartphone. Malcolm was trying to catch with his paperwork, paying little attention to Nicola until he heard the words 'Yes Great Aunt Violet,' and 'No Great Aunt Violet.'

When the call finished a happy Nicola had become a pensive Nicola, 'And?' he asked.

Nicola asked for a few minutes. Malcolm offered her a coffee; readily accepted. Nicola drank the coffee asking for a refill. Malcolm remained patient, knowing instinctively something was up. Best to wait until Nicola became settled.

The moment came, 'That was Great Aunt Violet,' she said, double checking they were alone. The final phase of the Harry Hackett saga is underway. I needed to print this file. It is very secret.

Moody Blue is being prepared for the short voyage to the Bahamas. Vicky and I will sail with two crew supplied by Jus . We will hole up on New Providence Island, protected by the UK Military, and use our US marriage visas on the return journey by air. The big event in the UK will take place over the weekend. By Monday, it should all be over except for one problem.'

'Which is?' asked Malcolm.

Nicola continued, 'When we went to London, Hackett had three hit teams travelling to Florida. The FBI caught up with the one in Texas and one gun fight later that hit team was no more. By all accounts, it was a diversion for the two more professional hit teams to get into Florida unseen.

A second hit team was discovered near Chicago by a combined FBI and Special Branch team and dealt with, but the third team, led by Hackett's top man known as 'Target One' was never detected. It is believed he stayed in the Canada to await developments. It's all very cloak and dagger, so if you're confused, so are we.

So, we will leave early Thursday morning to join Moody Blue at the Immigration Terminal in Miami and sail immediately. During Thursday morning, two specialists will arrive at the show house to install a range of clever electronics in the master bedroom Victoria and I share. This will interfere with viewing appointments so please can you help keep their work unseen.

On Monday when we will return, Vicky and I will work during the day and continue living in the show house during non-working hours. 'Target One' is expected to come to the show house at night, where everything will be prepared, I hope,' said Nicola with a slight tremble in her voice.

'In the meantime, Jus has mobilising his team to the site taking up duties as gardeners. If they catch 'Target One' before he gets to us, all well and good. If nothing else they will catch 'Target One's two companions because he always leaves them in the lurch when he makes his getaway. Any questions?'

'About two thousand,' said Malcolm, 'What else?'

'What I am told, Darling,' continued Nicola, 'is 'Target One' is a specialist who delights in the 'clean kill.' He does not smoke, drink, or engage any vices. The UK Special Branch have contacted two of his former SBS comrades for more information. So now we have an edge we can use.'

Malcolm became upset about the whole escapade and said so. He demanded he and Benny would protect their two brides-to-be no matter what. Nicola could see Malcolm wanted to do something, and would put him at risk, which would never do.

Nicola forced break from the conversation to let Malcolm readjust his thoughts. Nicola returned to her fiancé's side.

'Malcolm, Darling,' she began, 'This is a terrible shock to you and Benny. But now is the chance to end this disgraceful situation. A number of very clever people have put together a scenario that will end it all. I cannot have you put your life at risk and neither will Victoria.

So, Victoria and I will go with the programme. You and Benny will be protected . You will not be harmed. Victoria and I will prevail. We prevailed before and we will prevail again, for all our sakes.'

Malcolm was impressed with Nicola. Her voice was firm and sure. To be fair, he had no plan to counter a truly experienced assassin.

'So, what really happened on the yacht?' He asked.

Nicola told him up front. 'You must never tell anybody,' she said. Malcolm nodded his head in agreement. She retold the sorry tale, hopefully for the last time.

'So, we are going to end this very soon, and you will forget anything I told you,' finished Nicola.

Malcolm sat still, not in shock, but something close to it. He could not believe how strong his future wife could be. He realised he just had to trust her and get Benny on board with the programme.

WEDNESDAY EVENING, THE four dined together. Nicola explained the plan. Benny attempted to interject, but Malcolm headed him off. Benny asked to bring his own men on site. Nicola said she preferred not, but if they did come, they should make their peace with Jus first.

Benny found great difficulty taking a back seat. Malcolm was about to calm the waters when a man arrived in the dining room from behind the French windows drapes.

Before Benny could take any action, Nicola told him to stop, it was only Jus but then she remembered Benny had never met Jus. Malcolm stood up to greet the man who would be the lynchpin for whatever would happen next and keep his fiancé safe.

'Bonsoir Mesdames et Messieurs, so sorry for the intrusion. I hope I did not disturb.' said Jus.

'Benny darling,' said Victoria. 'This is Jus. The lifelong companion of Great Aunt Violet.

He is here to guide us and keep us safe.'

'And just how did he get past my security men,' asked Benny rather testily.

Jus replied, 'Your men were quite good. Necessary it was to use my higher level of skill. I think a good practice for the coming days.'

Benny was not happy and said so. Nicola explained, 'Jus is the expert. He is a L'homme qui passe à travers les murs, a man who passes through walls. He is a ghost; he is the man to keep us safe.'

'Messieurs', Jus said, 'Today commences the end of the disgrace that is this Hackett person. This weekend he will not prevail, I can say no more. The man known as 'Target One' will come Monday maybe Tuesday next week. He will not prevail either.'

Malcolm said, 'Nicola and Victoria will return Monday morning. Explain.'

'Oui Monsieur, it is necessary for them to do so. Your show house will have been prepared for his visit. He will be surprised,' informed Jus.

'How?' demanded Benny forcibly.

'Astuces électroniques, Monsieur,' said Jus, 'Ruse très intelligente, very clever trickery. The art of projecting things that are not there. During WW2, the British created many illusions for the German air force to bomb. This will be similar, but more effective.

'Les dames' will be in no real danger. Tonight, I will sleep in one of your wings, and collect them at three of the morning. Bonne nuit et fait de beaux rêves,' and with that Jus vanished, almost into thin air.

Early next morning, the escape from Miami was assisted by some truly dreadful weather, namely a Gulf Stream tropical storm. Jus took the two girls to the Miami immigration dock where they were quickly babied through the system.

Nicola and Victoria boarded Moody Blue shown into the aft master cabin and asked to remain below.

Moody Blue sailed immediately into the back of the tropical storm, fortunately moving swiftly north. The voyage to the Bahamas was rough at first. Both girls were happy to recover their sea legs the easy way, lying down in a comfortable berth.

Three hours out to sea, the weather began to calm down, and they were able to come on deck to enjoy their first love, sailing Moody Blue.

They reached the naval harbour early that evening and enjoyed a tasty French dinner onboard, cooked by one of the crew. They spent the remainder of their time in seclusion wondering what events were happening at Mr Hackett's castle.

Chapter 27

The End of the Hackett Saga

NICOLA AND VICTORIA returned to Miami on the morning red-eye. The immigration officer at the airport welcomed them to the United States of America and wishing them happiness when they became married.

'A good start to the day Miss Stanwick,' said Nicola. Victoria replied, 'Mrs Vincens to you. I can't wait.'

'Just one more minor event to go through; then we are done,' said Nicola. 'I'm not too keen on the word, done,' replied Victoria.

'Yes, I see what you mean, sorry,' said Nicola.

'So, we need to see off this 'Target One,' then two quick private weddings on Saturday. Then, we let the men organise an extravagant event when it suits them, subject to our input of course, which will be final,' smiled Victoria.

The two friends left the airport terminal to be met by Jus.

'Hi Jus,' said Victoria. 'How did the Hackett removal event go?'

Jus smiled and said, 'It went very well. Better than expected . HMG now have quite a few vacancies to fill, or not, as the case may be.'

'Is my friend Commander Collingwood a happy bunny?' asked Nicola.

'Well, Monsieur Collingwood is reported to be calm, tranquil and unavailable,' smiled Jus.

He has done something quite unusual, taken some leave.'

'Bugger Mr Policeman,' said Victoria, testily. 'What about this week's final event?'

Jus paused before he continued, 'What has become understood is your demise should have occurred on Sunday. Today is Monday. If your demise does not occur in the next twenty-four hours, Target One will lose his commission.

We have recently discovered a great deal about this man. He is a lone wolf. His name is 'Gerald.' We are informed of his remuneration. With

Hackett dead, his efforts cannot be rewarded. Finally, it is known he has family, wife and three children, living in great secrecy in the Caribbean. Thus, we have the upper hand.'

'So, what do we have to do?' asked Nicola.

'Mon Cherri, you will both continue as normal during the day. I will show the method by which you will prevail, so when you have refreshed yourselves, I will begin.'

It took two hours to show Nicola and Victoria the method by which the following day would be the start of the new era.

During the afternoon, they both got down to work, which pleased Malcolm no end. The commercial world of 'Villages Leigh' was hotting up and the construction programme had started to slip.

As evening approached, the building site and the show house office closed for business.

Jus asked Malcolm to disappear to Benny's place and stand together with his friend.

After dinner, Rita and William 'B' were told to make themselves scarce at Benny's mansion.

Nicola and Victoria found themselves with Jus and two females about the same age as themselves. Jus spent time making them look similar to his two charges. At bedtime, the two made-up decoys were bundled up stairs to the rear master bedroom.

Victoria asked where the hell they were supposed to sleep. Jus smiled asking them to follow him to an RV which had been on site since before their voyage to the Bahamas.

The two friends made themselves comfortable in the RV. Nicola thought this all a bit strange before noticing an array of electronics not normally associated with home entertainment systems.

Jus told them this RV was his special home from home and asked them both to please shower and prepare for bed. Then, he gave them teenage style nightdresses that highlighted their figures and expertly arranged their hair in a flirty style known as a floral crown. He added small flower buds for a whimsical touch.

Nicola and Victoria looked at each other and burst out laughing. Jus smiled and thought about his younger days.

Soon, they were ready.

'Mon Chère Nicola,' he said. 'Get into bed to sit up with the headboard at your back. Let me put these cushions for reading in bed. Now keep in the centre of your side of the bed and keep still.'

Jus went to the back of the RV to make some adjustment to a range of different lighting systems. When finished, he used a small two-way radio to converse with someone in French. He appeared satisfied with his work. All was now ready.

Nicola and Victoria went to bed early. Jus remained in the back of the RV relaxing in a comfortable chair to count the hours. Just after one a.m. he received the signal to tell him visitors had arrived. Jus gently shook Nicola to bring her to full consciousness. Victoria, on the other hand, remained fast asleep, although she did manage a sleepy 'bugger off.'

It remained quiet outside, too quiet. Jus instinctively knew the time was near. Jus activated his holographic systems, bidding Nicola to sit up in bed and pretend to read a book. At the foot of her bed, she could see on two flat screen monitors, the inside of their master bedroom in the show house. She saw herself sitting up in bed with a book and Victoria at her side fast asleep. It all looked very real.

It was not long before the door of the master bedroom silently opened. A soft dim light illuminated at the bottom of Nicola's bed.

Nicola could see the dark silent shape, illuminated by the light at the end of her bed. 'Come Gerald,' said Nicola. 'We have been waiting for you.'

'Target One' could see Nicola sitting up in a bed with a book on her lap. He raised a firearm fitted with a silencer. He hesitated. Something was wrong.

'Are you going to shoot me first or my friend, Victoria?' Nicola asked of the dark shape. 'She is sleeping you know. It will be for the best, Gerald. This is your name I believe. Breaking news Gerald. You won't get paid. Hackett is dead. His castle is no more, burnt to the ground.'

'Target One' fired two shots at the image of the sleeping form that was Victoria. Like that the image disappeared. Now 'Target One' could only see Nicola in a half a bed; he realised he'd been tricked.

'Now what?' he asked himself.

In the place where Victoria's image had been, a new image, the video of the Hackett castle being consumed by great flames.

'Where are you?' asked Target One.

'Oh, I am somewhere else,' said Nicola, 'But the two women your lookout saw come to this bedroom are right behind you. They work for Monsieur Jus William, the man who has tracked you these last few years. He admires your work. It is a great pity he cannot offer you employment. Your skills are hard to find. Oh, by the way, there are two handguns trained upon your back. The American 'Desert Eagle,' the 0.5" model. Bulletproof vest or not, these guns will knock you clear across the room.'

'So, what now,' asked Target One, 'A deal?'

'Could be, Mr Jus is here with me, he will advise, I am sure of that.'

'Bonjour monsieur Gerald,' said Jus, 'First your gun to the floor please. Then, remove all clothes to your underwear and don the orange overalls now landing at your side.'

'Who survived at the castle?' asked Target One.

'Nobody, except for the accountant and Miss Mary, Hackett's PA,' replied Jus.

'The accountant is very busy. As we speak. He is emptying Mr Hackett's many bank accounts, and I believe, your six treble zero accounts too.'

Miss Mary, armed with a bag full of pen drives and legal documents, is, as they say, helping the police with their many enquiries.'

'And me?' asked Target One.

'Ah,' said Jus, 'If you wish, you can be taken to your Caribbean Island to be with your lovely family. There you will enjoy long conversations with our specialist investigators. With luck, you should be able to provide such useful information that allows both you and your family to survive. If not, we promise to be sensitive about such matters.

There will be some financial support, and afterwards, and in time, you may be needed to serve your country again, at truly profitable rates. Your trust will be total, or else, Monsieur Gerald.'

'Deal,' said Target One. 'Now can I be taken for a good night's rest, or what is left of it?'

Two FBI agents entered the show house to remove 'Target One' for onwards transportation. The FBI then removed Target One's two companions in body bags.

Nicola shook Victoria with the news it was all over. A head appeared from under the blanket, and asked, 'Can I get rid of this ridiculous hairdo and wear something that's more me?'

'Sure, we're going to Benny's house. Here's a nice white dress for you to wear,' said Nicola.

A sleepy Victoria changed into the white dress, noticing Nicola wearing a white dress. She muttered something but Nicola paid no attention.

Jus drove them to Benny's mansion.

As they entered the ground floor ballroom, Malcolm and Benny welcomed them in formal daywear.

Victoria gave Benny a huge hug using his broad shoulder for support. The two friends took their fiancés into an adjoining room to be confronted by a small altar, a padre in full regalia, and several witnesses.

Nicola smiled, the end to a long day.

A still sleepy Victoria looked on wondering just what was going on. Nicola leant over to say, 'The gentleman in drag is going to ask you some questions. Just say 'Yes, I do,' when asked.'

It wasn't until a heavy gold band appeared on Victoria's ring finger did she cotton on. She looked with surprise at Nicola, also sporting a similar heavy gold band on her ring finger.

'What the,' muttered Victoria, still very sleepy.

Rita emerged from the back of the room carrying a large tray of ice-cold champagne, uttering congratulations to everyone.

Benny held on to his new wife, and started to dance around the room with Victoria in his arms, 'Good morning Mrs Vincens, can I offer you something to snack on with this glass of champagne?

Victoria suddenly realised what had happened.

She lay back in his arms and whispered, 'Oh Darling, there are some stairs around here somewhere, let's go.'

Chapter 28

A YEAR PASSED at speed and everything in the world remained happy. Nicola and Victoria both gave birth to twins, a boy and girl. Their fathers were overjoyed and bathed in the glory which was the hard work of fatherhood. The children grew quickly and became a delight to their doting parents.

If Malcolm and Nicola were even closer together, but the big change came in Victoria. At last, she reached the level of stability she had yearned for over the many years. She now had a loving husband and two wonderful children. She kept herself busy with Malcolm's project, bringing freshmen from the local university to bring an up to-date approach to the task of ensuring a successful project.

Then came the sad news Great Aunt Violet had died a recluse, spending time in the stone cottage she had been born in, overlooking Port St. Peter's harbour.

Frequently she had been seen sitting in her rocking chair positioned in the centre of her glass sun lounge facing out to sea. Her main residence, a magnificent Georgian property in the centre of Port St. Peter's had remained unused for some time.

One night, the cottage caught fire in the middle of a gale, the old woodwork virtually exploded and quickly burnt to the ground. Her remains were few and only her dental records and the remains of a replaced hip joint confirmed the death.

The funeral of Great Aunt Violet became the event of the year in that small original Scottish village. The village folk turned out in force.

The harbour pub and hotel organised a great celebration in accordance with Great Aunt Violet long term wishes. Strange men in dark suits swelled the throng and one or two bookmakers attended the funeral in the hope their nemesis had finally departed from the racetrack.

Nicola looked for a Mr Scott McGregor, Great Aunt Violet's lawyer for these last forty years. His organisation of the funeral arrangements proved impeccable, and where was Jus William she wanted to know? She couldn't find him. She received the message Great Aunt Violet's long-term companion had been struck down by illness and sent his apologies.

A grieving Nicol took the message at face value. It would be much later before she thought further about the matter.

Following the funeral, many hours were required for the affairs of Great Aunt Violet to be finalised. It was early autumn before Nicola was called to attend a lengthy meeting to learn of her Great Aunt Violet's final wishes and sign a mountain of documents as the main recipient of her extensive will.

Nicola and Victoria, complete with their children and nannies, flew in from Florida's oppressive late-summer heat. A European holiday had been planned, resulting in Malcolm and Benny spending long nights burning the midnight oil to clear their respective desks before boarding flights to sunny England and a much-needed holiday.

Nicola opened Great Aunt Violet's main residence, which she had rarely visited. Everything was as she remembered, although a few pieces collected over the years, seemed to be missing.

The day of the reading of the will arrived, hosted by Great Aunt Violet's solicitor, Mr Scott McGregor. The solicitor, with a voice as dry as sandpaper, droned through the details which boiled down to the basics.

Over the years Great Aunt Violet purchased many properties in the area, incorporating them into a fiscal entity called the 'Port St. Peter Trust'.

The trust's assets included the hotel on the hill overlooking the harbour, the 'Conrad', the ever-busy harbour public house and hotel, the residential properties surrounding the harbour, and a street on the outskirts of the village comprised of vacant properties due to be converted into a charitable hospice for the terminally ill.

Last, but by no means least, there was a large area of farmland surrounding the village which would remain for the tenant farmers known as the 'sons or daughters' of Port St. Peter.

It did not take Victoria long to realise the trust had been set-up with remarkable efficiency with regards to the taxman. The company who controlled the Trust had a list of shareholders of which Nicola held fifty-one per cent, Victoria fifteen percent and the other shareholders consisting of the ex-service personnel involved with the running and management of the commercial businesses, of which the harbour pub and hotel generated the most profit.

Every other property had long-term rental agreements at favourable rates in exchange for meeting the conditions of the tenancy. In other words, the village was to remain as a time capsule of a traditional Scottish village and harbour.

Outside of the meeting, Great Aunt Violet's accountant, a Mr Jock Maudlin, told the two girls their combined yearly income from the trust was a healthy five-figure sum.

Nicola asked the accountant about Great Aunt Violet's personal bank accounts. The accountant smiled advising her UK bank statements were in a folder included in the documents she had received. Nicola looked at the accountant asking about any other liquid assets she may have stashed. She saw him smile before realising further unofficial communication would become apparent over time to which her accountant could not be seen to be a part of.

Nicola knew Great Aunt Violet trusted him explicitly after his long years of service. Great Aunt Violet's foreign funds were out of the reach of the revenue, but it would be necessary to be careful.

Last, but not least, came the subject of Great Aunt Violet memoirs. The autobiography of her many wartime exploits had been banned by the British government citing national security issues. At the time of the ban, it was stated the book could only be legally published following the death of the author.

Nicola asked Scott McGregor, what exactly was the current situation? McGregor smiled a knowing smile.

'The lady has passed away,' he said. 'Publish and be damned. The French publisher is printing now as we speak and will go on sale at the beginning of next month. Advance orders are substantial.'

'Who has the rights to the book,' ask Nicola. 'Oh, you do my dear,' said McGregor.

'And Aunties wishes?' asked Nicola.

'Full steam ahead; before the UK authorities wake up to the fact she has indeed passed away. This country has never publicly recognised her achievements, whereas the President of France decorated her twice with the highest honours. The book contains acute embarrassment for certain sections of our political landscape. Publish the book and they will tremble,' stated Mr McGregor.

'Where do I sign?' smiled Nicola.

A formal looking document arrived on the desk in front of Nicola, along with Mr. McGregor's gold fountain pen, a gift from Great Aunt Violet many years ago.

As the meeting closed, refreshments were served to all attendees. An unusual sight arrived as two classic Rolls-Royces and a Rolls-Royce support vehicle parked in front of Great Aunt Violet's main residence.

The first Rolls-Royce looked to be a pre-war Phantom III in cream and burgundy, the second one looked similar in a very attractive two-tone green.

An elegant gentleman by the name of Mr T. Sinclair, Director of Rolls-Royce Scotland Ltd stepped forward to state his business.

'Madam,' Mr Sinclair began, 'I have been charged with delivering this Rolls-Royce 1938 Phantom III, the property of the late Ms Violet Stranraer. I have the documents and everything is in order. You are now the new owner. Congratulations.'

Nicola said she never knew Great Aunt Violet even had a Rolls-Royce, asking if she had ever used it?

Mr Sinclair stated Madam Violet had enjoyed the vehicle during her many years on her twice-yearly visits to the County of Caithness in the very north of Scotland to visit her lifelong companion, a lady, a former school friend.

Nicola vaguely remembered this person at the time when Great Aunt Violet had hitched a secret ride aboard Moody Blue to the Irish Republic and the friend had remained at Great Aunt Violet's home pretending to be her.

'Mr Sinclair, the other Rolls-Royce, is this for another lucky customer?' asked Nicola. 'Indeed madam,' Mr Sinclair replied. 'It is the property of a French gentleman, the Conte St. George de Guglielmu de Champsecret. He lives in a Chateau in Normandy. I do not have the address as the le Conte is a recluse. My instructions are to deliver the vehicle to a restored post house hotel in Saint Lo, Normandy and speak to the owner/manager who will arrange everything.'

Nicola asked, 'So tell me about the history of Great Aunt Violet's Rolls-Royce. It looks very grand.'

Mr Sinclair told her the car was quite special. Great Aunt Violet's father had ordered the vehicle shortly before WWII. In this era, Rolls-Royce only supplied a running chassis, and a coach builder given the task of building the bodywork.

The vehicle had spent the war years in storage. After the war it was taken to northern France where it acquired an aluminium body furnished by out of work aircraft artisans and specialist carpenters. The style followed tradition but with a French flair.

As the bodywork proved to be substantially lighter than one based on traditional materials, the chassis had been lightened also. The running chassis had been upgraded with the latest modern technology of the time.

All in all, the modified vehicle had a greatly enhanced performance.

Mr Sinclair concluded by stating the vehicle had been the subject of a ground-up restoration these last two years, including the engine, as had the green Rolls-Royce.

Mr Sinclair, now supplied with a strong coffee and a healthy glass of malt whisky, commenced a long discourse on the second Rolls-Royce, and by the time he had finished everybody in the room was a great deal wiser on the subject of pre-war Rolls-Royce's in general and the second Rolls-Royce in particular, a 1938 Rolls-Royce Wraith, a two-door coupe with removable soft top.

Victoria thought the two-tone green Rolls-Royce very sexy with the top down and rather fancied one for herself. A bit pricey, though. She might just have to revise her policy of not letting her loving husband 'splash the cash' on expensive gifts. There was the 1931 Phantom II Benny had bought from Prince Eugen, but there was little chance of getting her hands on it on a regular basis.

Nicola went outside to sit in her new automobile. The driving position was very comfortable. This was a car she would love to drive. She reached over to the glove box to find an old copy of Sporting Life, the famous UK horse racing newspaper no racecourse punter should be without.

The headline proclaimed the news about an unknown spinster who had placed a large amount of money on a five-race accumulator that had won her, and her syndicate, several millions of pounds in the early 1960s. Nicola vaguely remembered the event.

As she thumbed through the ageing newspaper, a single page, quite recent, appeared to have been inserted into the back pages. On its second side was a small article about a retired British lady living in France, who had won another three-race accumulator, netting a figure in the region of two hundred thousand pounds.

As Nicola made to fold the newspaper away and return it to the glove box, a small postcard of a French chateau fell onto the floor of the Rolls-Royce. She picked it up and turned it over to read a simple inscription. Nicola smiled a big smile and lovingly put it in her handbag.

Nicola returned to the house where she found Mr Sinclair and his support driver enjoying the sandwiches and pastries provided for the long meeting. The level in the bottle of malt whisky also appeared to have steadily sunk in step with the sinking of the Scottish sun as it headed for the distant horizon.

'Mr Sinclair,' asked Nicola, 'Are you pressed for time? I have an idea and need your help. I would like to depart Port St. Peter tomorrow morning, say 9 a.m. and accompany your convoy to London Thief Row Airport, Terminal Five.'

'We could all stay the night in the airport hotel and collect our husbands early the morning after they arrive sometime after six or seven a.m.

Then, next day, we could all depart to catch the afternoon ferry from Portsmouth to Normandy and stay in Saint Lô and visit a part of France I would love to enjoy. All expenses on my account, of course.'

Mr Sinclair agreed, it had been a long day, and his plan of an overnight stay somewhere near Birmingham held little attraction. He liked Nicola. She was a nice lady, a class act, just like her great aunt.

He smiled at the now common name for London's busiest airport, a result of the most famous attempted robbery, involving forty million in gold and forty million in cash a few years ago. The airport had suffered other high-value robberies, but Mr Sinclair had to admit, the continuing robbery of his fellow Scotsmen in the over-priced airport restaurants and snack bars took a lot of beating.

Nicola took out her smartphone to call hubby, toiling away, unknowing of the surprise she had in store. A tired Malcolm answered the phone with the usual greetings of love and missing his adored children.

'Darling,' started Nicola.

'Yes,' said a suspicious Malcolm.

'Tomorrow, I think it would be just fabulous if you finished at lunchtime, showered, to get ready and take any flight that gets you into London Heathrow Terminal Five, as early as possible, say six a.m. in the morning. We will be waiting in our suites in the airport's terminal hotel.'

'Why?' asked the tired husband.

'Well, I thought you might like to join with me and Victoria in our new Rolls-Royce and visit northern France. It's very nice this time of year, autumn colours, great seafood, and other big surprises,' invited a loving Nicola.

'Tell me about the Rolls-Royce?' requested Malcolm, who was now not so tired.

Nicola explained her good fortune and please could he bring Mr Vincens with him on the same flight.

Malcolm thought, 'The witch is up to something, better follow orders.' He bid her a fond farewell and looked forward to the holiday in Europe.

Nicola got a hold of Victoria who was busy winding up Mr Sinclair's support vehicle driver, a youngish lad from Glasgow's Gorbals area. His accent was a thick as pea soup and Victoria just loved different accents.

'Mrs Vincens,' Nicola started, 'Tomorrow we will drive in these two

Rolls-Royces to London Heathrow and stay at the airport hotel. Our darling husbands should arrive very early the next morning.'

'Then?' enquired Victoria, smiling in anticipation.

'We take the ferry from Portsmouth Harbour to Normandy and stay at a very nice coach house in Saint Lô. It's very pretty there at this time of year.'

'OK,' grinned Victoria, knowing full well Nicola was up to mischief and the coming event should be fun.

The next morning, just after the designated hour, a convoy of British motoring elegance made its uneventful way to London's favourite airport and checked-in at its Terminal Five hotel, taking two adjoining suites on the top floor and a twin room for a tired Mr Sinclair and his support driver.

The two Rolls-Royce's and the support vehicle were parked directly opposite the entrance to the hotel, where they caused a bit of a fuss from motoring fans until the silk covers shrouded them for the night. Nicola requested additional security for the Rolls-Royces which seemed to be a problem until Victoria waded in with some blatant name dropping.

EARLY NEXT MORNING, two tired American travellers were shown to their family's suites and offered breakfast. After a quick shower, a change into more expressive clothing, and catching up with their adored children, the two husbands could hardly wait to see the silk covers removed from the two Rolls-Royces, supervised by an anxious Nicola.

As the silk covers were removed, it was love at first sight. Nicola ushered the two husbands into her Rolls-Royce. Benny sat at the wheel with Nicola sitting beside him. Malcolm stretched out in the back seat saying this was the way to travel.

Benny became disappointed to learn the green Rolls-Royce belonged to a French Count. 'So, what is the big surprise,' both husbands asked. 'We know you're bursting to tell us.' Victoria leant through the open driver's window.

'Pray tell, fair maiden,' instructed an eager Victoria.

Nicola took out the newspaper she had so keenly read yesterday to show Benny the headline about the 'big win.'

'Now Benny,' asked Nicola, 'Look at the back of the newspaper and you will find a recent single sheet.'

Benny did so, looked at Nicola and said, 'And?'

Nicola replied, 'A single lady living in France won a three-race accumulator, at the beginning of last month?'

Well, the green Rolls-Royce is to be delivered to a Conte St. George de Guglielmu de Champsecret in Normandy and here is a postcard of his magnificent French chateau.'

Benny and Malcolm liked the French Chateau, but still looked confused.

Nicola continued, 'Guglielmu is Corsican for the name William. Jus is a dark swarthy Frenchman, tough as they come. Read the back of the postcard, Benny.'

'It says, 'Bring the grandchildren,' said an even more confused Benny.

'Exactly, gentlemen. It is time to visit a lady, a wonderful grand old lady.'

THE END

Printed in Great Britain
by Amazon

48228047R00198

Printed in Great Britain
by Amazon

48228047R00198